Book 4

Never Judge a Lady by Her Cover

THE ~~WITHDRAWN~~ RELS

piatkus

PIATKUS

First published in the US in 2014 by Avon Books,
An imprint of HarperCollins Publishers, New York
First published in Great Britain in 2014 by Piatkus
by arrangement with Avon

ISBN 978-0-349-40060-0

Printed and bound in Great Britain by
Clays Ltd, St Ives plc

1 3 5 7 9 10 8 6 4 2

Papers used by Piatkus are from well-managed forests
and other responsible sources.

MIX
Paper from
responsible sources
FSC® C104740

Piatkus
An imprint of
Little, Brown Book Group
100 Victoria Embankment
London EC4Y 0DY

An Hachette UK Company
www.hachette.co.uk

www.piatkus.co.uk

For Carrie Ryan, Sabrina Darby & Sophie Jordan,
who kept Chase's secrets from the start.

For Baxter,
who keeps all my secrets.

And for Lady V,
who I hope grows up to have tremendous
secrets of her own.

Chase

March 1823
Leighton Castle
Basildon, Essex

"I love you."

Three strange, small words that held so much power.

Not that Lady Georgiana Pearson—daughter of one duke and sister to another, child of honor and duty and pristine presentation, and perfectly bred female of the *ton*—had ever heard them.

Aristocrats did not love.

And if they did, they most certainly did not do something so base as to admit it.

So it was a shock, frankly, that the words spilled from her lips with such ease and comfort and truth. But Georgiana had never in her sixteen years believed anything so well, and she had never been so quickly rid of the shackles of expectation that came with her name and her past and her family. In truth, she embraced it—the risk and reward—thrilled to feel at long last. To live. To be.

Risk be damned; this was *love*.

And it had freed her.

Certainly, there would never be a moment as beautiful as this—in the arms of the man she loved, the one with whom she would spend a lifetime. Longer. The one with whom she would build a future, and hang her name and her family and her reputation.

Jonathan would protect her.

He'd said as much as he'd shielded her from the cold March wind and shepherded her here, into the stables of her family estate.

Jonathan would love her.

He'd whispered the words as his hands had unfastened and lifted, peeled and unwrapped, promising her everything as he touched and stroked.

And she'd whispered them back. Giving him everything. *Jonathan*.

She sighed her pleasure to the rafters, nestling closer to him, cushioned by lean muscle and rough straw and covered in a warm horse blanket that should have scratched and bothered, but was somehow made soft, no doubt by the emotion it had just witnessed.

Love. The stuff of sonnets and madrigals and fairy tales and novels.

Love. The elusive emotion that made men weep and sing and ache with desire and passion.

Love. The life-altering feeling that made everything bright and warm and wonderful. The emotion all the world was desperate to discover.

And she'd found it. Here. In the frigid winter, in the embrace of this magnificent boy. No. Man. He was a man, just as she was a woman, made one today in his arms, against his body.

A horse in the stables below whinnied softly, pawing at the floor of its stall, huffing its desire for food or drink or affection.

Jonathan shifted beneath her, and she curled into him, pulling the blanket tighter around them. "Not yet."

"I must. I am required."

"*I* require you," she said, putting on her best flirt.

His hand spread over her bare shoulder, warm and rough where she was smooth, sending a thrill of delight through her. How rare it was that someone touched her—first a duke's daughter, then one's sister. Pristine. Unmarked. Untouched.

Until now.

She grinned. Her mother would have a fit when she learned that her daughter had neither need nor intention of coming out. And her brother—the Duke of Disdain—the most impossible, entitled aristocrat London knew . . . he would not approve.

But Georgiana didn't care. She was going to be Mrs. Jonathan Tavish. She wouldn't even keep the "Lady" to which she was entitled. She didn't want it. She only wanted him.

It did not matter that her brother would do his best to stop the match. There was no stopping it any longer.

That particular horse had left the proverbial barn.

But Georgiana remained in the hayloft.

She giggled at the thought, made giddy by love and risk— two sides of one very rewarding coin.

He was shifting beneath her, already sliding out from the warm cocoon of their bodies, letting the cold winter air in and turning her bare skin to gooseflesh. "You should dress," he said, pulling on his trousers. "If anyone catches us—"

He didn't have to finish; he'd been saying the same thing for weeks, since the first time they'd kissed, and during all the stolen moments that had ensued. If anyone caught them, he'd be whipped, or worse.

And she'd be ruined.

But now, after today, after lying naked in this rough winter hay and letting him explore and touch and take with his work-hewn hands . . . she was ruined. And she didn't care. It didn't matter.

After this, they would run away—they would have to in order to marry. They'd go to Scotland. They'd start a new life. She had money.

It did not matter that he had nothing.

They had love, and it was enough.

The aristocracy was not to be envied. It was to be pitied. Without love, why live?

She sighed, watching Jonathan for a long moment, marveling at the grace with which he pulled on his shirt and tucked it into his breeches, the way he tugged on his boots as though he'd done it a thousand times in this low-ceilinged space. He wrapped his cravat about his neck and shrugged on his jacket, then his winter coat, the movements smooth and economical.

When he was done, he turned for the ladder that led to the stables below, all long bones and lean muscle.

She clutched the blanket to her, feeling cold with the loss of him.

"Jonathan," she called softly, not wanting anyone to hear her.

He looked to her, and she saw something in his blue gaze—something she did not immediately identify. "What is it?"

She smiled, suddenly shy. Impossibly so, considering what they had just done. What he had just seen. "I love you," she said again, marveling at the way the words slid over her lips, the way the sound wrapped her in truth and beauty and everything good.

He hesitated at the top of the ladder, hanging back, so effortlessly that he seemed to float in the air. He did not speak for a long moment—long enough for her to feel the March cold deep in her bones. Long enough for a thread of unease to curl quietly through her.

Finally, he smiled his bold, brazen smile, the one that had called to her from the beginning. Every day for a year. For longer. Until this afternoon, when he'd tempted her finally, finally up to the hayloft, kissed away her hesitation, and made his lovely promises, and taken all she'd had to offer.

But it hadn't been taking.

She'd given it. Freely.

After all, she loved him. And he loved her.

He'd said so, maybe not with words, but with touch.

Hadn't he?

Doubt curled through her, an unfamiliar emotion. Something that Lady Georgiana Pearson—daughter to a duke, sister to one—had never felt before.

Say it, she willed. _Tell me._

After an interminable moment, he spoke. "You're a sweet girl." And he dropped out of sight.

Chapter 1

Ten Years Later
Worthington House
London

When she looked back on the events of her twenty-seventh year of life, Georgiana Pearson would point to the cartoon as the thing that started it all.

The damn cartoon.

Had it been placed in *The Scandal Sheet* a year earlier, or five years earlier, or a half dozen years later, she might not have cared. But it had run in London's most famous gossip rag on March the fifteenth.

Beware the Ides, indeed.

Of course, the cartoon was the result of another date entirely. Two months to the day earlier—January the fifteenth. The day that Georgiana, utterly ruined, unwed mother, walking scandal, and sister to the Duke of Leighton, had decided to take matters in hand and return to Society.

And so she stood here, in the corner of the Worthington ballroom, on the cusp of her reentry into Society, keenly aware of the eyes of all London upon her.

Judging her.

It was not the first ball she'd attended since she was ruined, but it was the first at which she was noticed—the first at which she was not masked, either with fabric or paint. The first at which she was Georgiana Pearson, born a diamond of the first water, devolved into a scandal.

The first at which she was present for her public shaming.

To be clear, Georgiana did not mind her ruination. Indeed, she was a proponent of the state for any number of reasons, not the least of which was this: Once ruined, a lady was no longer expected to stand on ceremony.

Lady Georgiana Pearson—who barely claimed the honorific and barely deserved the descriptor—was thrilled with her ruination, and had been for years. It had, after all, made her rich and powerful, the owner of The Fallen Angel, London's most scandalous and most popular gaming hell, and the most feared person in Britain . . . the mysterious "gentleman" known only as Chase.

It was of little consequence that she was, in fact, female.

So, yes, Georgiana believed that the heavens had smiled upon her that day a decade prior when her fate had been forged. Her exile from Society, for better or worse, meant a dearth of invitations to balls, teas, picnics, and assorted events, which, in turn, eliminated the necessity for battalions of chaperones, inane conversation over tepid lemonade, and pretending to show interest in the holy trinity of aristocratic female conversation—mindless gossip, modern fashion, and marriageable gentlemen.

She had little interest in gossip, as it was rarely the truth and never the whole truth. She preferred secrets, offered by powerful men who had scandal to trade.

Similarly, she had little interest in fashion. Skirts were too often taken as a mark of feminine weakness, relegating ladies to doing little but smooth them and less refined females to doing little but lift them. When on the floor of her gaming hell, she hid in plain sight inside the brightly colored silks that costumed London's most skilled prostitutes, but in all other places, she preferred the freedom of trousers.

And she had no interest in gentlemen, caring not a bit if

they were handsome, clever, or titled as long as they had money to lose. For years, she had laughed at the eligible gentlemen who had been marked for marriage by the women of London, their names listed in the betting book at The Fallen Angel—their future wives speculated upon, their wedding dates predicted, their progeny forecasted. She'd watched London's bachelors from the owners' suite at her casino—each more rich, handsome, and well-bred than the last—as they were felled, shackled, and married.

And she'd thanked her maker that she hadn't been forced into the silly charade, forced to care, forced to marry.

No, Georgiana ruined at the tender age of sixteen—now a decade-old warning for all jewels of the *ton* who had followed her—had learned her lesson about men early, and blessedly escaped any expectation of the parson's noose.

Until now.

Fans fluttered to cover whispers, to hide smirks and snickers. Eyes grazed by, pretending not to see, even as they settled on her, damning her for her past. For her presence. No doubt, for her gall. For sullying their pristine world with her scandal.

Those eyes hunted her, and if they could, they would slay her.

They know why she was here. Despised her for it.

Christ. This was torture.

It had begun with the dress. The corset was slowly killing her. And the layers of underskirts were constricting her movement. If she was required to flee, she'd no doubt be tripped by them, land on her face, and be swallowed up by a cackling horde of lace-trimmed aristocratic ladies.

The image flashed, unexpected, and she nearly smiled. Nearly. The honest possibility of such an end kept the expression from making an appearance.

She'd never felt the urge to fidget so much in her entire life. But she would not give them the pleasure of playing prey. She had to keep her mind on the task at hand.

A husband.

Her target was Lord Fitzwilliam Langley—decent, titled,

in need of funds, and in need of protection. A man with virtually no secrets save one—one that, if it were ever discovered, would not only ruin him, but send him to prison.

The perfect husband for a lady who required the trappings of marriage and not the marriage itself.

If only the damn man would turn up.

"A wise woman once told me that corners of rooms were for cowards."

She resisted the urge to groan, refusing to turn toward the familiar voice of the Duke of Lamont. "I thought you did not care for Society."

"Nonsense. I quite like Society, and even if I didn't, I wouldn't have missed Lady Georgiana's first ball." She scowled, and he added, "Careful, or the rest of London will question your decision to dismiss a duke."

The duke, widely known as Temple, was her business partner, co-owner of The Fallen Angel, and immensely irritating when he wished to be. She finally turned to face him, pasting a bright smile on her face. "Are you here to gloat?"

"I believe you meant to finish that question with 'Your Grace,'" he prompted.

She narrowed her gaze. "I assure you, I meant no such thing."

"If you're going to land yourself an aristocratic match, you had better practice your titular acumen."

"I would rather practice my acumen in other areas." Her cheeks were beginning to ache from the expression.

His dark brows rose. "For example?"

"Exacting revenge on supercilious aristocrats who take pleasure in my pain."

He nodded, all seriousness. "Not a skill that is precisely feminine."

"I'm out of practice with femininity."

"Surely not." A smile flashed, white teeth against his olive skin, and she resisted the urge to wipe it from his face. She muttered an invective under her breath, and he snickered. "Neither is *that* very feminine."

"When we get back to the club—"

He cut her off. "Your transformation is remarkable, I will say. I barely recognized you."

"That was the idea."

"How did you do it?"

"Less paint." Georgiana's public persona was most often in disguise as Anna, the madam of The Fallen Angel. Anna did not spare the maquillage, the extravagant wigs, or the heaving bosom. "Men see what they wish to see."

"Mmm," he said, clearly disliking the words. "What in hell are you wearing?"

Her fingers itched, begging to smooth skirts. "A dress."

The gown was pristine and white and designed for someone far more innocent than she. Far less scandalous. And that was before one knew what she had made of her life.

"I've seen you in a dress. This is . . ." Temple paused, taking in the ensemble. He coughed a laugh. "Not like any dress I've ever seen you wear." He paused, considering her further. "You've feathers exploding from your hair."

Georgiana gritted her teeth. "I'm told it's the height of fashion."

"You look ridiculous."

As though she didn't know it. As though she didn't *feel* it. "Your charm knows no bounds."

He grinned. "I wouldn't like you to get too full of yourself."

There was no chance of that. Not here, surrounded by the enemy. "Don't you have a wife to entertain?"

His dark gaze flickered past her to settle on a gleaming auburn head at the center of the ballroom. "Your brother is dancing with her. As he is lending his reputation to her, I thought I might do the same for his sister."

She turned to him in disbelief. "*Your* reputation."

Mere months earlier, Temple had been known as the Killer Duke, thought to have murdered his future stepmother in a fit of passion on the eve of her wedding. Society had welcomed him back into the fold only once the accusation had been proven false and he'd married the woman he was to have killed—a scandal in her own right. But he remained as much a scandal as a duke could be, as he'd spent years first on the streets and then in the ring at The Fallen Angel as a bare-knuckle boxer.

While Temple might carry the title of duke, his reputation was tarnished at best—the opposite of her brother's. Simon had been perfectly bred for this world; his dancing with the Duchess of Lamont would go miles toward restoring her name and, indeed, the name of Temple's dukedom.

"Your reputation might do more damage to me than good."

"Nonsense. Everyone loves a duke. There aren't enough of us to go around, so beggars can't really be choosers." He smirked and offered a hand. "Would you care to dance, Lady Georgiana?"

She froze. "You jest."

The smirk turned into a full-blown grin, his black eyes sparkling with humor. "I wouldn't dream of jesting about your redemption."

She narrowed her gaze on him. "I have ways of retaliating, you know."

He leaned in. "Women like you don't turn down dukes, Anna."

"Don't call me that."

"A woman?"

She slapped her hand into his, irritation flaring. "I should have let you die in the ring."

For years, he had been a near-nightly attraction at The Fallen Angel. Those in debt to the club had one way of winning back their fortunes—beating the unbeatable Temple in the ring. An injury and a wife had retired him from boxing.

"You don't mean it." Temple tugged her into the light. "Smile."

She did as she was told, feeling like an imbecile. "I do mean it."

He collected her in his arms. "You don't, but as you are terrified of this world and what you are about to do, I shan't press you on the subject."

She stiffened. "I am not terrified."

He cut her a look. "Of course you are. You think I don't understand it? You think Bourne doesn't? And Cross?" he added, referring to the two other owners of the gaming hell. "We've all had to crawl out of the muck and back into the light. We've all had to clamor for acceptance from this world."

"It's different for men." The words were out of her mouth before she could stop them. Surprise crossed his face and she realized that she had accepted his premise. "Damn."

He lowered his voice. "You will have to control your language if you want them to believe you're a tragic case mislabeled a scandal."

"I was doing perfectly well before you arrived."

"You were hiding in the corner."

"It was not hiding."

"What was it then?"

"Waiting."

"For those assembled to issue you a formal apology?"

"I was rather hoping for them to drop dead of plague," she grumbled.

He chuckled. "If wishing made it so." He spun her across the floor, the candles lit around the room leaving trails of light across her field of vision. "Langley has arrived."

The viscount had entered not five minutes earlier. She'd noticed immediately. "I saw."

"You don't expect a real marriage from him," Temple said.

"I don't."

"Then why not do what you do best?"

Her gaze flickered to the handsome man on the other side of the room. Her choice for husband. "You think blackmail is the best way to go about securing a husband?"

He smiled. "I was blackmailed in advance of finding a wife."

"Yes, well, I am told that most men are not such masochists, Temple. You've been saying I should marry. You and Bourne and Cross," she added, ticking off her partners in The Fallen Angel. "Not to mention my brother."

"Ah, yes, I've heard that the Duke of Leighton has placed

a heavy dowry on your head. It's remarkable you are able to stand upright. But what of love?"

"Love?" It was difficult to voice the word without the disdain.

"You've heard of it, no doubt. Sonnets and poems and happy-ever-after?"

"I've heard of it," she said. "As we are discussing marriage at best for convenience and at worst for debt relief, I hardly think a lack of love is of issue," she said. "And besides, it is a fool's errand."

He watched her for a long moment. "Then you are surrounded by fools."

She cut him a look. "Every one of you. Besotted beyond reason. And look at what has happened because of it."

He raised his dark brows. "What? Marriage? Children? Happiness?"

She sighed. They'd had the conversation a hundred times. A thousand. Her partners were so idyllically matched that they could not help but foist it on everyone around them. What they did not know was that idyll was not for Georgiana. She pushed the thought away. "I am happy," she lied.

"No. You are rich. And you are powerful. But you are not happy."

"Happiness is too highly prized," she said with a shrug, as he turned her across the room. "It's worth nothing."

"It's worth everything." They danced in silence for a long moment. "Which you see, as you wouldn't be doing this if not for happiness."

"Not mine. Caroline's."

Her daughter. Growing older by the second. Nine years old, soon ten, soon twenty. And the reason Georgiana was here. She looked up at her hulking partner, this man who had saved her as many times as she had saved him. Told him the truth. "I thought I could keep her from it," she said quietly. "I steered clear of her."

For years. To the detriment of them both.

"I know," he said quietly, and she was grateful for the

dance that kept her from having to meet his gaze too often. She didn't know that she could.

"I tried to keep her safe," she repeated. But a mother could keep a child safe for only so long. "But it wasn't enough. She'll need more if she's to climb out of our swill."

Georgiana had done her best, sending Caroline to live at her brother's home, doing her best to never sully her with the circumstances of her birth.

And it had worked, until it hadn't.

Until last month.

"You can't be talking about the cartoon," he said.

"Of course I'm talking about the cartoon."

"No one gives a damn about scandal sheets."

She cut Temple a look. "That isn't true and you of all people know it."

The rumors had abounded—that her brother had told her she could not have a season, that she'd begged him. That he'd insisted that, as an unwed mother, she remain indoors. That she'd pleaded with him. That neighbors had heard screaming. Wailing. Cursing. That the duke had exiled her and she'd returned without his permission.

The gossip pages had gone wild, each trying to outdo the other with tales of the return of Georgiana Pearson, Lady Disrepute.

The most popular of the rags, *The Scandal Sheet*, had run the legendary cartoon—scandalizing and somewhat blasphemous, Georgiana high atop a horse, wrapped only her hair, holding a swaddled baby with the face of a girl. Part Lady Godiva, part Virgin Mary, with the disdainful Duke of Leighton standing by, watching, horrified.

She'd ignored the cartoon, as one did, until one week prior, when an uncommonly warm day had tempted half of London into Hyde Park. Caroline had begged for a ride, and Georgiana had reluctantly left her work to join her. It had not been the first time they'd appeared in public, but it had been the first time since the cartoon, and Caroline had noticed the stares.

They'd dismounted on a rise leading down to the Serpentine, grey and muddy with late winter, and led the horses down toward the lake where a group of girls barely older than Caroline stood the way girls did—in a cluster of whispers and barbs. Georgiana had seen it enough times to know that no group of girls like this one would bring any good.

But Caroline's hope had shone on her bright young face, and Georgiana hadn't had the heart to pull her away. Even as she was desperate to do just that.

Caroline had moved closer to the girls, all while attempting to look as though her movement was unintentional. Unplanned. How was it that all girls everywhere knew this movement? The quiet sidle that hinted of simultaneous optimism and fear? The silent request for notice?

It was a miracle of courage born of youth and folly.

The girls noticed Georgiana first, recognizing her, no doubt from bearing witness to the wide eyes and wagging tongues of their mothers, and they surmised Caroline's identity within seconds, heads lifting and craning while whispers increased. Georgiana hung back, resisting the urge to step between the bears and their bait. Perhaps she was wrong. Perhaps there would be kindness. Greeting. Acceptance.

And then the leader of the group saw her.

She and Caroline were rarely identified as mother and daughter. She was young enough for them to be mislabeled as sisters, and Georgiana, while she did not hide from Society, rarely entered it.

But the moment the pretty blond girl's eyes went wide with recognition—curse all gossiping mothers—Georgiana knew that Caroline done for. She wanted desperately to stop her. To end it before it could begin.

She took a step forward, toward them.

Too late.

"The park is not what it used to be," said the girl, with knowledge and scorn beyond her years. "They allow anyone simply to wander here. With no regard to *pedigree*."

Caroline froze, reins of her beloved horse forgotten in her hand as she pretended not to hear. As she tried not to hear.

"Or *parentage*," another girl said with cruel glee.

And there it was, hovering in the air. The unspoken word. *Bastard*.

Georgiana wanted to slap their faces.

The gaggle tittered, gloved hands flying to lips, ostensibly hiding smiles even as teeth flashed. Caroline turned toward her, green eyes liquid.

Don't cry, Georgiana willed. *Don't let them see that they've struck true.*

She wasn't sure if the words were for herself or her daughter.

Caroline did not cry, though her cheeks blazed with color. Embarrassed of her birth. Of her mother. Of a dozen things she could not change.

She returned to Georgiana's side then, moving idly, stroking the neck of her mount, fairly wandering—bless her—as though to prove that she would not be chased away.

When she returned, Georgiana had been so proud, she'd had difficulty speaking past the knot in her throat. She hadn't had to speak. Caroline had spoken first, loud enough to be heard. "Or *politesse*."

Georgiana had laughed her shock, even as Caroline had mounted her horse and looked down at her. "I shall race you to the Grosvenor Gate."

They'd raced. And Caroline had won. Twice in one morning.

But how often would she lose?

The question returned her to the present. To the ballroom, to the dance, in the arms of the Duke of Lamont, surrounded by the aristocracy. "She has no future," Georgiana said quietly. "I destroyed it."

Temple sighed.

She continued. "I thought I could buy her entrance to wherever she liked. I told myself that Chase could open any door into which she desired entry."

Her words were quiet, and the dance kept anyone from hearing the conversation. "Not without people asking questions about why the owner of a gaming hell is so concerned about the bastard daughter of a lady."

Her teeth clenched tight. She'd made so many promises in her life—promises to teach Society a well-deserved lesson. Promises never to bow to them.

Promises never to let them touch her daughter.

But some vows, no matter how firm, could not be kept.

"I wield such power, and still, not enough to save a little girl." She paused. "If I don't do this, what will happen to her?"

"I'll keep her safe," the duke vowed. "As will you. And the others." An earl. A marquess. Her business partners, each wealthy and titled and powerful. "Your brother."

And yet . . .

"And when we're gone? What then? When we are gone, she'll have a legacy, filled with sin and vice. She'll have a life of darkness."

Caroline deserved better. Caroline deserved everything.

"She deserves light," she said, to herself as much as to Temple.

And Georgiana would give it to her.

Caroline would want a life of her own. Children. More.

To ensure she could have those things, Georgiana had only one choice. She must marry. The thought brought her back to the moment, her gaze falling to the man across the room, whom she had chosen as her future husband. "The viscount's title will help."

"And the title is all you require?"

"It is," she replied. "A title worthy of her. Something that will win her the life she wants. She might never be respected, but a title secures her future."

"There are other ways," he said.

"What other ways?" she asked. "Consider my sister-in-law. Consider your wife. They are barely accepted here, untitled, scandalous." His eyes narrowed at the words, but she pressed on. "The title saves them. Hell, you supposedly murdered a woman and weren't fully cast out because you were a duke first, a possible killer second—you could have married if you'd chosen to. The title is what reigns. And it always will.

"There will always be women after titles and men after dowries. God knows Caroline's dowry will be as big as it needs to be, but it won't be enough. She'll always be my daughter. She'll always carry my mark. As it stands, even if she found love—even if she wanted it—no decent man could marry her. But if I marry Langley? Then she has the possibility of a future devoid of my sin."

He was quiet for a long minute, and she was grateful for it. When he finally spoke, it was to ask, "Then why not involve Chase? You need the name, Langley needs a wife, and we are the only people in London who know why. It is a mutually beneficial arrangement."

Under the guise of Chase, founder of London's most desired men's club, Georgiana had manipulated dozens of members of Society. Hundreds of them. Chase had destroyed men and elevated them. Chase had made matches and ruined lives. She could easily manipulate Langley into marriage by invoking Chase's name and the information he had on the viscount.

But need was not want, and perhaps it was her keen understanding of that balance—of the fact that the viscount needed marriage as much as she did, but wanted it just as little—that made her hesitate. "I am hoping that the viscount will agree that the arrangement is mutually beneficial without Chase's interference."

Temple was quiet for a long moment. "Chase's interference would speed up this process."

True, but it would also make for a terrible marriage. If she could win Langley without blackmail, all the better. "I've a plan," she said.

"And if it goes to waste?"

She thought of Langley's file. Slim, but damning. A list of names, all male. She ignored the sour taste in her mouth. "I have blackmailed bigger men."

He shook his head. "Every time I am reminded that you

are a woman, you say something like that . . . and Chase is returned."

"He is not easily hidden."

"Not even when you are so . . ." He made a show of looking at her feathered coif. "Ladylike is, I suppose, the word for this ensemble?"

She was saved from having to either spar with Temple or further discuss the lengths to which she was willing to go for her daughter's future by the orchestra's completion of the set. She pulled away and curtsied, as was expected. "Thank you, *Your Grace.*" She emphasized the title as she stood once more. "I believe I shall take some air."

"Alone?" he asked, an edge in his tone.

Frustration flared. "You think I cannot care for myself?" She was the founder of London's most infamous gaming hell. She'd destroyed more men than she could count.

"I think you should take care of your reputation," Temple replied.

"I assure you that if a gentleman attempts liberties, I shall slap his hand." She smiled a wide, false smile and dipped her head, coyly. "Go to your wife, Your Grace. And thank you for the dance."

He held her hand tightly for a moment, until she met his gaze again, and he cautioned softly, "You cannot beat them. You know that, don't you? No matter how hard you try— Society will always win."

The words made her suddenly, unpredictably furious. She tamped down the emotion and replied, "You are wrong. And I intend to prove it."

Chapter 2

The conversation had unsettled her.

The *evening* had unsettled her.

And Georgiana did not care for being unsettled, which was why she had so long resisted this moment—her return to Society and its prying, judging gaze. She'd hated it from the start, a decade earlier. Hated the way it followed her every time she dressed for Mayfair's streets instead of the floor of her casino. Hated the way it mocked her inside modistes' shops and haberdasheries, in bookshops and on the steps of her brother's home. Hated the way it sealed her daughter's fate—the way it had done so long before Caroline had drawn breath.

She'd exacted her revenge for the judgment, building a temple to sin at the center of Society, collecting the secrets of its members day after day for six years. The men who gamed at The Fallen Angel did not know that every card they turned, every die they cast, was the purview of a woman their wives shunned at every possible moment.

Nor did they know that their secrets had been collected with care, cataloged and made ready for use when Chase needed them most.

But for some reason, this place, these people, their untouchable world was already changing her, making her hesitate where she would never before have hesitated. Before, she might have lay Viscount Langley's future out before him in terms black and plain—marry her or suffer the consequences.

But now, she knew too well what those consequences were, and she did not care for throwing another to the wolves of scandal.

Not that she wouldn't if it came to that.

But she hoped there was another way.

She stepped onto the balcony of the Worthington House ballroom and took a deep breath, desperate for the way the fresh air tricked her into believing that she was free of this night and these obligations.

The April night was crisp and full of promise, and she moved from the ballroom into the darkness, where she felt more comfortable. Once there, she released her breath and leaned against the marble balustrade.

Three minutes. Five at the most. And then she'd return. She was here for a reason, after all. There was a prize at the end of this game, one that, if won well, would mean safety and security and a life for Caroline that Georgiana could never give her.

Anger flared at the thought. She had power beyond imagination. With the stroke of a pen, with a signal to the floor of her hell, she could destroy a man. She held the secrets of Britain's most influential men, and their wives. She knew more about the aristocracy than they knew about themselves.

But she could not protect her daughter. She could not give her the life she deserved.

Not without them.

Not without their approval.

And so she was here, in white, feathers protruding from her head, wanting nothing more than to walk into the dark gardens and keep going until she reached the wall, scaled it, and found her way home to her club. To the life she had built. The one she had chosen.

She'd have to remove the gown to scale the wall, she supposed.

The residents of Mayfair might take issue with that.

The thought was punctuated by a passel of young women spilling out of the ballroom, giggling and whispering at a pitch the neighbors could no doubt hear. "I'm not surprised he offered to dance with her," one was crowing. "No doubt he's hoping she'll marry a gambler who will spend all that money at his hell."

"Either way," another replied, "she shan't benefit from dancing with the Killer Duke."

Of course they were discussing her. She was no doubt the talk of the *ton*.

"He is still a duke," another offered. "Silly, false nickname or no." That one was halfway intelligent. She'd never survive among her friends.

"You don't understand, Sophie. He isn't *really* a duke."

Sophie disagreed. "He holds the title, doesn't he?"

"Yes," said the first, irritation in her tone. "But he was a fighter for so long, and he married so far *beneath* him, it's not the same at all."

"But the laws of primogeniture—"

Poor Sophie, using fact and logic to win the day. The others were having none of it. "It's not important, Sophie. You never understand. The point is, she's horrid. And enormous dowry or no, she'll never land a husband of quality."

Georgiana rather thought it was the leader of this pack who was horrid, but was clearly in the minority, as the woman's minions nodded and cooed agreeably.

She moved closer, searching for a better vantage point. "It's clear she's after a title," opined the leader, who was small and incredibly thin, and whose hair appeared to have been shot through with a collection of arrows.

Georgiana realized that she was in no condition to cast the first stone on coiffures, what with the fact that she had half an egret's plumage in her own hair, but arrows did seem a bit much.

"She'll never land a gentleman, even. An aristocrat is *impossible*. Not even a baronet."

"Technically, that's not an aristocratic title," Sophie pointed out.

Georgiana could no longer hold her tongue. "Oh, Sophie, will you never learn? No one is interested in the truth."

The words cut through the darkness and the girls, six in all, turned en masse to face her, varying expressions of surprise on their faces. She probably should not have called attention to herself, but this was definitely a case of in for a penny, in for a pound.

She stepped forward, into the light, and two of the women gasped. Sophie blinked. And the little Napoleon of a leader stared quite perfectly down her nose at Georgiana, who stood an easy eight inches above her. "You were not included in the conversation."

"But I should be, don't you think? As its subject?"

She'd give the other girls credit; they all had the decency to look chagrined. Not so their leader. "I do not wish to be seen conversing with you," she said cruelly, "I would be afraid your scandal would stain me."

Georgiana smiled. "I wouldn't let that worry you. My scandal has always sought out . . ." She paused. " . . . higher ground."

Sophie's eyes went wide.

Georgiana pressed on. "Do you have a name?"

Eyes narrowed. "*Lady* Mary Ashehollow."

Of course she was an Ashehollow. Her father was one of the most disgusting men in London—a womanizer and a drunk who had no doubt brought the pox home to his wife. But he was Earl of Holborn, and thus accepted by this silly world. She thought back on the file The Fallen Angel had on the earl and his family—his countess a wicked gossip who would no doubt happily drown kittens if she thought it would help her move up in the social structure. Two children, a boy at school and a girl, two seasons out.

A girl no better than her parents, evidently.

Indeed, lady or no, the girl deserved a thorough dressing-down. "Tell me. Are you betrothed?"

Mary stilled. "It's only my second season."

Georgiana advanced, enjoying herself. "One more and you're on the shelf, aren't you?"

A hit. The girl's gaze flitted away and back so quickly that another might have missed it. Another who was not Chase. "I have a number of suitors."

"Mmm." Georgiana thought back to Holborn's file. "Burlington and Montlake, I understand—they've got enough debt to overlook your faults for access to your dowry—"

"You're one to talk about faults. And dowries." Mary chortled.

The poor girl didn't know that Georgiana had five years of life and fifty years of experience on her. Experience dealing with creatures far worse than a little girl with a sharp tongue. "Ah, but I do not pretend that my dowry is unnecessary, Mary. Lord Russell does perplex, however. What's a decent man like him doing sniffing around someone like you?"

Mary's mouth went wide. "Someone like me?"

Georgiana leaned back. "With your appalling lack of social grace, I mean."

The barb hit true. Mary pulled back as though she'd been physically struck. Her friends covered their gaping mouths, holding back laughter that they could not help. Georgiana raised a brow. "Cruelty lacks pleasure when it's directed at you, doesn't it?"

Mary's anger came sharp and unpleasant. And expected. "I don't care how large your dowry is. No one will have you. Not knowing what you really are."

"And what is that?" Georgiana asked, laying her trap. Willing the girl into it.

"Cheap. A trollop," Mary said, cruelly. "Mother to a bastard who will likely grow into a trollop."

Georgiana had expected the first, but not the last. Her blood ran hot. She stepped into the golden light spilling from the ballroom, her words quiet. "What did you say?"

There was silence on the balcony. The other girls heard the warning in the words. Murmured their concern. Mary took a step back, but was too proud to retreat. "You heard me."

Georgiana advanced, pressing the girl from the light. Into darkness. Where she reigned. "Say it again."

"I—"

"Say it again," Georgiana repeated.

Mary closed her eyes tightly. Whispered the words. "You're cheap."

"And you're a coward," Georgiana hissed. "Like your father and his father before him."

The girl's eyes shot open. "I did not mean . . ."

"You did," Georgiana said quietly. "And I might have forgiven you for what you called me. But then you brought my daughter into it."

"I apologize."

Too late. Georgiana shook her head. Leaned in. Whispered her promise. "When your entire world comes crashing down around you, it will be because of this moment."

"I am sorry!" Mary cried, hearing the truth in the words. As well she should. Chase did not make promises she did not keep.

Except she was not Chase tonight. She was Georgiana.

Christ.

Georgiana had to back away from the moment. Mask her anger before she revealed too much. She stepped away from Mary and laughed, loud and light, a sound she'd perfected on the floor of her club. "You lack the courage of your convictions, Lady Mary. So easily frightened!"

The other girls laughed, and poor Mary came unhinged, disliking the way she'd been so thoroughly toppled from her position. "You'll never be worthy of us! You're a whore!"

Her friends gasped collectively, and silence fell on the balcony. "Mary!" one of them whispered after a long moment, voicing their mutual shock and disapproval at the words.

Mary was wild-eyed, desperate to resume her place at the top of the social pyramid. "She started it!"

There was a long pause before Sophie said, "Actually, we started it."

"Oh, be *quiet*, Sophie!" Mary cried before turning and running into the ballroom. Alone.

Georgiana should have been happy with the scene. Mary

had gone too far and learned the most important lesson of Society—that friends would stay with you only as long as they weren't marred by your tarnish.

But Georgiana wasn't happy.

As Chase, she prided herself on her control. On her still-ness. On her thoughtful action.

Where the hell was Chase tonight?

How was it that these people held such sway over her—over her emotions—even now? Even as she wielded such deft power over them in another parallel life?

You're a whore.

The words lingered in the darkness, reminding her of the past. Of Caroline's future if Georgiana did not make this world accept her.

The girls held sway because she allowed it. Because she had no choice but to allow it. It was their field, and the game was to make her feel small and insignificant.

She hated them for playing so well.

She turned on the remaining women. "Surely you all have someone waiting for the next dance?"

They dispersed without hesitation—all but one. Georgiana narrowed her gaze on the girl. "What's your name?"

She did not look away, and Georgiana was impressed. "Sophie."

"I know that bit."

"Sophie Talbot."

She did not use the "Lady" she was due. "Your father is the Earl of Wight?"

The girl nodded. "Yes."

It was virtually a purchased title—Wight was exceedingly wealthy after making a number of impressive investments in the Orient, and the former King had offered him a title that few believed was warranted. Sophie had an older sister who was a newly minted duchess, which was no doubt why she'd been accepted into this little coven.

"You go, as well, Sophie, before I decide that you're not the one I like, after all."

Sophie's mouth opened, and then closed when she decided not to speak. Instead, she spun on her heel and returned to the ball. Smart girl.

Georgiana let out a long breath when she was once again alone, hating its tremor, the way it sounded of regret. Of sorrow.

Of weakness.

She gave silent thanks that she was alone, with no one to witness the moment.

Except she wasn't alone.

"That won't have helped your cause."

The words came dark and quiet from the shadows, and Georgiana whirled around to face the man who had spoken them. Tension threaded through her as she peered into the darkness.

Before she could ask him to show himself, he stepped forward, his hair gleaming silver in the moonlight. The shadows underscored the sharp angles of his face—jaw, cheek, brow, long straight nose. She inhaled sharply as frustration gave way to recognition . . . then relief, and more excitement than she'd like to admit.

Duncan West. Handsome and perfectly turned out in a black topcoat and trousers with a crisp linen cravat that gleamed white against his skin, the simplicity of the formal attire making him somehow more compelling than usual.

And Duncan West was not a man who needed to be more compelling than usual. He was brilliant and powerful and handsome as sin, but with intelligence and influence and beauty came danger. Didn't she know that better than anyone?

Hadn't she built a life upon it?

West was the owner of five of London's most-read publications: one daily, meticulously ironed by butlers across the city; two weeklies, delivered by post to homes throughout Britain; a ladies' magazine; and a gossip rag that was the joy of the untitled and the secret, shameful subscription of the aristocracy.

And, besides all that, he was also the nearly fifth partner

in The Fallen Angel—the journalist who built a name and a fortune on the scandal, secrets, and information he received from Chase.

Of course, he did not know that Chase stood before him now—not the terrifying, mysterious gentleman all of London believed him to be, but a woman. Young, scandalous, and with more power than any woman had the right to claim.

That ignorance was why, no doubt, West had allowed his gossip pages to run the horrendous cartoon, painting Georgiana both Godiva and Mary, virgin and whore, sin and salvation, all in service to the newspaperman's bankroll.

His papers—he—had forced her hand. He was the reason she stood here tonight, feathered and preened and perfect, in search of her social second chance. And she did not care for that—no matter how handsome he was.

Perhaps she cared for it less *because* of how handsome he was. "Sir," she said, affecting her best admonition. "We have not been introduced. And you should not be lurking in the dark."

"Nonsense," he said, and she heard the teasing in his voice. Was tempted by it. "The dark is the very best place to lurk."

"Not if you care for your reputation," she said, unable to resist the wry words.

"My reputation is not in danger."

"Oh, neither is mine," she replied.

His brows rose in surprise. "No?"

"No. The only thing that can possibly happen to my reputation is that it become better. You heard what Lady Mary called me."

"I think half of London heard what she called you," he said, coming closer. "She's improper."

She tilted her head. "But not incorrect?"

Surprise flared in his eyes, and she found she liked it. He was not a man who was easily surprised. "Incorrect is a given."

She liked the words, too. Their certainty sent a little thread of excitement through her. And she could not afford excitement. She returned the conversation to safety. "No doubt our contretemps will be in the papers tomorrow," she said, letting accusation into the words.

"I see my reputation precedes me."

"Should mine be the only one?"

He shifted uncomfortably, and she took a modicum of pleasure in the movement. He should be uncomfortable with her. As far as he knew, she was a girl. Ruined young, yes, but did not youthful scandal somehow make for the most innocent of girls?

It did not matter that she was no kind of innocent, or that they had known each other for years. Worked together. Exchanged missives, she under the guise of all-powerful Chase, flirted with each other, she under the guise of Anna, the queen of London's lightskirts.

But Duncan West was not acquainted with the part she played tonight. He did not know Georgiana, even though it was he who had flushed her out into society. He, and his cartoon.

"Of course I know the man who ran the cartoon that made me infamous."

She recognized guilt in his gaze. "I am sorry."

She raised a brow. "Do you apologize to all the recipients of your particular brand of humor? Or only to those whom you cannot avoid?"

"I deserved that."

"And more," she said, knowing that she was on the edge of going too far.

He nodded. "And more. But you did not deserve the cartoon."

"And you've only tonight had a change of heart?"

He shook his head. "I've regretted it since it ran. It was in poor taste."

"No need to explain. Business is business." She knew that well. Had lived by the words for years. It was part of why Chase and West worked so well together. Neither asked questions of the other as long as information flowed smoothly between them.

But it did not mean she forgave him for what he'd done. For requiring her to be present this night, to find marriage, to be accepted. Without him . . . she might have had more time.

Not much time.

She ignored the thought.

"Children are not business," he said. "She shouldn't have been a part of it."

She did not like the turn in the conversation, the way he referred to Caroline, gently, as though he cared. She did not like the idea that he cared. She looked away.

He sensed the shift in her. Changed the topic. "How did you know me?"

"When we arrived, my brother pointed out the lions in the room." The lie came easily.

He tilted his head. "Those who are regal and important?"

"Those who are lazy and dangerous."

He laughed low and deep, the sound rippling through her. She did not like that, either, the way he seemed to catch her off guard even as she was at her most guarded. "I may be dangerous, Lady Georgiana, but I have never in my life been lazy."

And then she wasn't off guard at all, but rather exceedingly comfortable. Tempted. He could not have meant the words to be so tempting, but damned if they weren't . . . damned if they didn't make her want to flirt shamelessly with him and ask him to prove just how hard he would work for a reward. Damned if he didn't have the same effect on her that he did in her club, when she was disguised and he was diverting.

Damned if he didn't make her wonder what it might be like to meet him in the darkness, another woman at another time in another place. To give in to temptation.

For the first time. Since the last time.

Since the only time.

She stiffened at the thought. He was a very dangerous man, and she was not Chase tonight. This was not her club. She had no power here.

He did, however.

She looked toward the glittering ballroom. "I should return to the festivities. And my chaperones."

"Which are legion, no doubt."

"I've a sister-in-law with sisters-in-law. There is nothing a gaggle of women enjoys more than adorning the unmarried."

He smiled at the word. "Adorned is right." His gaze flickered to the feathers protruding from her coif. She resisted the urge to rip them out. She'd agreed to the damn things as a trade—she wore them, and in return was allowed to arrive at and leave the ball in her own conveyance.

She scowled. "Don't look at them." He returned his attention to her eyes, and she recognized the humor dancing in his brown gaze. "And don't laugh. You try dressing for a ball with three ladies and their maids fawning about."

His lips twitched. "I take it you do not enjoy fashion."

She swatted at an errant feather that had fallen into her field of vision, as though she'd summoned it with her vitriol. "Whatever gave you such an idea?"

He laughed then, and she enjoyed the sound, almost forgetting why they were here.

He reminded her. "A duchess and a marchioness will help you change minds."

"I don't know what you mean." He was no fool. He knew precisely what she was doing.

He rocked back on his heels. "Let's not play games. You're angling for Society to welcome you back. You've trotted out your brother, his wife, her family—" He looked over her shoulder toward the ballroom. "Hell, you've even danced with the Duke of Lamont."

"For someone who does not know me, you seem to be rather focused on my evening."

"I am a newsman. I notice things that are out of the ordinary."

"I'm perfectly ordinary," she said.

He laughed. "Of course you are."

She looked away, suddenly uncomfortable—not knowing how she should behave—not knowing who she should pretend to be for this man who seemed to see everything. Finally, she said, "It seems an impossible feat, changing their minds."

Something flashed across his face, there, then gone. Irritation flared. "That was not a demand for pity."

"It was not pity."

"Good," she said. *What, then?*

"You can hold your ground with them, you know." She could do more than that. His thoughts appeared to go in a similar direction. "How did you know who Lady Mary's suitors are?"

"Everyone knows that."

He did not waver. "Everyone who has paid attention to the season for the last year."

She shrugged. "Just because I do not attend parties doesn't mean I am ignorant of the workings of the *ton*."

"You know a great deal about the *ton*, I think."

If he only knew. "It would be stupid for me to attempt to return to Society without basic reconnaissance."

"That is a term usually reserved for military conflict."

She raised a brow. "It is London in season. You think I am not at war?"

He smiled at that and inclined his head, but did not allow the conversation to lighten. Instead, he played the reporter. "You knew that the girls would turn on her if you pushed her."

She looked away, thinking of Lady Mary. "When given the opportunity, Society will happily cannibalize itself."

He bit back a laugh.

She narrowed her gaze on him. "You find that amusing?"

"I find it remarkable that someone so desperate to rejoin its ranks sees the truth of Society so clearly."

"Who said I was desperate to rejoin its ranks?"

He was paying close attention now. "You're not?"

Suspicion whispered through her. "You are very good at your job."

He did not hesitate. "I am the best there is."

She should not like his arrogance, but she did. "I nearly gave you your story."

"I already have my story."

She did not care for the statement. "And what is that?"

He did not reply, watching her carefully. "You seemed to enjoy your time with the Duke of Lamont."

She did not want him thinking of her time with Temple. Did not want him considering how it was that she and the duke who owned a gaming hell knew each other. "Why are you interested in me?"

He leaned back against the stone balustrade. "The aristocracy's prodigal daughter is returned. Why would I not be interested in you?"

She gave a little huff of laughter. "Fatted calf and all that?"

"Fresh out of plump calves this season. Would you settle for canapés and a cup of tepid lemonade?"

It was her turn to smile. "I'm not returned for the aristocracy."

He leaned in at that, coming closer, wrapping her in the heat of him. He was a devastatingly handsome man, and in another time, as another person, with another life, she might have welcomed his approach. Might have met it head-on. Might have given herself up to the temptation of him.

It seemed unfair that Georgiana had never had such a chance. Or was it a desire? Lady Mary's insult echoed. *Whore.* The word she could not escape, no matter how false it was.

She'd thought it was love.

She'd thought he was her future.

Learned quickly that love and betrayal came together.

And now . . . *whore*.

It was a strange thing to have one's reputation so thoroughly destroyed with such a flagrant lie. To have a false identity heaped upon one's shoulders.

Oddly, it made one want to live it, just to have a taste of truth.

But to live it, she was required to trust, and that would never happen again.

"I know you're not returned for them," he said softly, the tone tempting. "You're returned for Caroline."

She snapped back from him. "Don't speak her name."

There was a beat as the cold warning in the words wrapped around them. He watched her carefully, and she tried her best to look young. Innocent. Weak. Finally, he said, "She is not my concern."

"But she is mine." Caroline was everything.

"I know. I saw you nearly topple poor Lady Mary for mentioning her."

"Lady Mary is in no way poor."

"And she should know better than to insult a child."

"Just as you should have?" The words were out before she could stop them.

He inclined his head. "As I should have."

She shook her head. "Your apology is rather late, sir."

"Your daughter is the only thing that could have brought you back to this. You don't need it for yourself."

Warning flared. What did he know? "I don't understand."

"I only mean that with this many years between you and scandal, an attempt at redemption would only draw long dead attention to you."

He understood what others seemed to miss. The years away had been tremendously freeing once she'd accepted the idea that she'd never have the life for which she'd been so well prepared. It wasn't just the corset and skirts that constricted now. It was the knowledge that mere feet away, there were hundreds of prying eyes watching, judging, waiting for her to make a mistake.

Hundreds of people, with no purpose, desperate to see her fall. *But this time, she was more powerful than any of them.*

He spoke again. "No doubt, your love for her is what will make you the heroine of our play."

"There is no play."

He smiled, all knowing. "As a matter of fact, my lady, there is."

How long had it been since someone had used the honorific with her? How long since they'd done it without insult or judgment or artifice?

Had it ever happened?

"Even if there were a play," she allowed, "it is in no way *ours*."

He watched her for a long moment before he said, "I think it might be ours, you know. You see, I find myself quite fascinated."

She ignored the heat that came with the words. Shifted, straightening her shoulders. "I can't imagine why."

He came closer. His voice dropped even lower. "Can't you?"

Her gaze snapped to his, the words echoing through her. He was her answer. He, the man who told Society what to think, and when, and about whom. He could tempt Langley for her. He could tempt anyone he liked for her.

Lord knew he was a very tempting man.

She resisted the errant thought. Returned to the matter at hand.

Duncan West could secure her a title and a name.

He could secure Caroline a future. Georgiana had allowed herself to watch this man for years, in the world where they stood on equal footing. But now, in the darkness, faced with him, he seemed at once threat and savior.

"No one's ever done what you're about to do," he said, finally.

"What's that?"

He returned to his relaxed position against the marble balustrade. "Returned from the dead. If you succeed, you shall sell a great deal of newspapers."

"How very mercenary of you."

"It doesn't mean I don't wish you to succeed." After a long moment, he added, sounding surprised, "In fact, I believe I want just that."

"You do?" she asked, even as she told herself not to.

"I do."

He could help her win.

He studied her for a long while, and she resisted the urge to fidget beneath his gaze. Finally, he said, "Have we met before?"

Damn.

She looked nothing like Anna tonight. Anna was primped and painted, stuffed and padded, all tight corset and spilling bosom, pale powder, red lips, and blond hair so bold it gleamed nearly platinum. Georgiana was the opposite, tall, yes, and blond, but without the extravagance. She had breasts of a normal size. Her hair was a natural hue. Skin, too. And lips.

He was a man, and men saw only that for which they were looking. And still he seemed to see into her.

"I do not think so," she replied, resisting the thought. She turned to head into the ballroom. "Will you dance?"

He shook his head. "I've business to attend to."

"Here?" The question was out, filled with curiosity, before she realized that simple Georgiana Pearson would not care enough to ask.

His gaze narrowed slightly on her, no doubt as he considered the question. "Here. And then elsewhere." With the barest pause, he added, "You are certain we have not met?"

She shook her head. "I have not been in these circles for many years."

"I am not always in these circles myself." He paused, then added, as much to himself as to her, "I would remember you."

There was an honesty in his words that had her catching her breath. Her gaze widened. "Are you flirting with me?"

He shook his head. "No need for flirting. It's the truth."

She allowed one side of her mouth to lift in a smile. "Now I know you are flirting. And with aplomb."

He dipped his head. "My lady does me great compliment."

She laughed. "Cease, sir. I've a plan, and it does not include handsome newspapermen."

White teeth flashed. "I'm handsome now, am I?"

It was her turn to raise a brow. "I am certain you own a mirror."

He laughed. "You are not what I would have expected."

If he only knew.

"I may not be very good at selling your newspapers, after all."

"You let me worry about selling newspapers." He paused. "You worry about your plan—every debutante's plan since the beginning of time."

She gave a little huff of laughter. "I am no debutante."

He watched her for a moment. "I think you are more of one

than you would like to admit. Don't you wish a breathless waltz under the stars with a suitor or two?"

"Breathless waltzes have only ever led girls into trouble."

"You want a title."

There, he was right. She let her silence be her agreement.

One corner of his mouth lifted. "Let's dispense with the artifice. You're not looking for just any unmarried gentleman. You have a mark. Or at least a list of requirements"

She cut him a look. "A list would be mercenary."

"It would be intelligent."

"Admitting it would be crass."

"Admitting it would be honest."

Why did he have to be so clever? So quick? So . . . *well matched*. No. She resisted the descriptor. He was a means to an end. Nothing more.

He broke the silence. "Obviously someone who needs money."

"It's the point of a dowry, correct?"

"And one who has a title."

"And one who has a title," she conceded.

"What else does Lady Georgiana Pearson wish?"

Someone decent.

He seemed to read her mind. "Someone who would be good to Caroline."

"I thought we agreed that you would not speak her name?"

"She's the bit that makes it difficult."

Georgiana had pored over the files in her office at the Angel. She'd eliminated a dozen unmarried men. Whittled her options down to a single viable candidate—a man about whom she knew enough to know he would make a fine husband.

A man she could blackmail into marrying her if need be.

"There isn't a list," he said finally, watching her carefully. "You have him selected."

He was very good at his job.

"I do," she admitted.

She should end this conversation now. She'd been away from the ballroom long enough to be noticed, and there was no one else on the balcony but this man. If they were discovered . . .

Her heart pounded. If they were discovered, it would add to her reputation. The risk tempted, as was always the case with risk. She knew that well. But it was the first time in a very long time that the risk came with a handsome face.

The first time in ten years.

"Who?"

She did not answer.

"I'll discover it soon enough."

"Probably," she said. "It is your profession, is it not?"

"So it is," he said, and fell silent for a long moment before asking the question around which he'd been dancing. "There are other dowries, Lady Georgiana," he said. "Why yours?"

She stilled. Answered, perhaps too truthfully. "There are none as large as mine. And none that come with such freedom."

One golden brow rose. "Freedom?"

A thread of discomfort curled through her. "I do not have expectations for the marriage."

"No dreams of a marriage of convenience turning into to a love match?"

She laughed. "None."

"You're awfully young to be so cynical."

"I am six and twenty. And it's not cynicism. It's intelligence. Love is for poets and imbeciles. I am neither. The marriage comes with freedom. The purest, basest, best kind."

"It comes with a daughter, as well." The words weren't meant to sting, but they did, and Georgiana stiffened. He had the grace to look apologetic. "I am sorry."

She shook her head. "It is the truth, is it not? You know that better than anyone."

The cartoon again.

"You should be pleased," she offered. "My brother has been trying to bring me back to Society for years—if he'd only known that a ridiculous cartoon would be so motivating."

He smiled, and there was a boyish charm in the expression. "You suggest I do not know my own strength."

She matched his expression. "On the contrary, I think you know it all too well. It is only unfortunate that I do not have another newspaper on hand to reverse the spell your *Scandal Sheet* has cast."

He met her gaze. "I have another." Her heart began to race, and though she was desperate to speak, she kept silent, knowing that if she let him talk, she might get what it was she wanted.

And he might think it was his idea.

"I've four others, and I know what men search for."

"Besides a massive dowry?"

"Besides that." He stepped closer. "More than that."

"I don't have much else." Not anything she could admit to, at least.

He lifted one hand, and her breath caught. He was going to touch her. He was going to touch her, and she was going to like it.

Except he didn't. Instead, she felt a little tug at her coif, and his hand came away, a snowy white egret feather in his grasp. He ran it between his fingers. "I think you have more than you can imagine."

Somehow, the cold March night became hot as the sun. "It sounds as though you are offering me an alliance."

"Perhaps I am," he said.

She narrowed her gaze. "Why?"

"Guilt, probably."

She laughed. "I cannot imagine that is it."

"Perhaps not." He reached for her hand and she stretched her arm out to him as though she were a puppet on strings. As though she did not have control over herself. "Why worry about the reason?"

The feather painted its way over the soft skin above her glove and below her sleeve, at the inside her elbow. She caught her breath at the delicate, wonderful touch. Duncan West was a dangerous man.

She snatched her hand back. "Why trust you when you've just admitted you're in this to sell newspapers?"

That handsome mouth curved in wicked temptation. "Wouldn't you rather know precisely with whom you are dealing?"

She smiled at that. "Surely this is the best fortune a girl on a dark balcony has ever had."

"Fortune has nothing to do with it." He paused, then added, "There's little love lost between me and Society."

"They adore you," she said.

"They adore the way I keep them entertained."

There was a long moment as Georgiana considered his offer. "And me?"

That smile flashed again, sending a thread of excitement pooling in her stomach. "The entertainment in question."

"And how do I benefit?"

"The husband you wish. The father you desire for your daughter."

"You will tell them I am reformed."

"I've seen no evidence that you are not."

"You saw me goad a girl into insulting me. You saw me threaten her family. Force her friends to desert her." She looked into the darkness. "I am not certain what I have is desirable."

His lips curved in a knowing smile. "I saw you protect yourself. Your child. I saw a lioness."

She did not miss the fact that he'd been a lion mere minutes earlier. "Every tale has two tellers."

He opened his coat and inserted the feather in the inside pocket, before buttoning the coat once more. She could no longer see the plume, but she felt it there nonetheless, trapped against his warmth, against the place where his heart beat in strong, sure rhythm. Trapped against him.

He was a very dangerous man.

He grinned, all wolf, this powerful man who owned London's most-read papers. The man who could raise or ruin with the ink of his printing press. The man she needed to believe her lies. To perpetuate them.

"There you are wrong," he said, the words threading through her like sin. "Every tale worth telling has only one teller."

"And who is that?"

"Me."

Chapter 3

*H*e should not have flirted with the girl.

West stood on the edge of the Worthington ballroom, watching Lady Georgiana dance across the room on the arm of the Marquess of Ralston. The man was rarely seen in the company of any but his wife, but there was no doubt that the Duke of Leighton had called in all of his chips—including his brother-in-law—that evening, in the hopes that the combined wealth and power of the Ralston and Leighton clans would blind Society into forgetting the lady's past.

It wasn't working.

She was all anyone in the room talked about, and it was neither her powerful champions nor her beauty that fueled the whispers.

And she was beautiful, all length and grace, smooth skin and silken hair, and a mouth—Christ. She had a mouth made for sin. It was no wonder she'd been ruined at such a young age. He imagined she'd had every boy for twenty miles salivating over her.

Idly, he wondered if she'd cared for the man who had taken advantage of her, and found he did not like the idea that she had. He had little patience for boys who could not keep their hands to themselves, and the idea of Lady Georgiana on the receiving end of those hands grated more than usual. Perhaps it was the child. No child deserved to be born into scandal.

He knew that better than most.

Or perhaps it was Georgiana, who looked every inch the perfect, pristine aristocrat, born and bred into this world that should be at her feet, and instead waited to eat her alive.

The orchestra stopped, and Georgiana had only a few brief seconds before she was in the arms of Viscount Langley—an excellent choice for husband.

West watched them with the eye of a newspaperman, considering their match from all angles. Langley was a big fish, no doubt—he'd recently assumed a venerable title that came complete with several massive estates, but he suffered from the great bane of the aristocratic existence—inheritances could be prohibitively expensive. Each of his properties had fallen into disrepair, and it was his responsibility to restore them.

A dowry the size of the one attached to Lady Georgiana would restore the earldom to its former glory, and leave him with enough money to double its size.

West did not know why the idea was so unsettling and unpleasant for him. She was neither the first nor would she be the last to buy a husband.

Nor to be sold to one.

For the price of a long-standing, irrelevant title. One valued only for its place in the hierarchy. Yes, it might buy her daughter silent judgment instead of vocal insult. And yes, it might buy that same young woman marriage to a respectable gentleman. Not titled, but respectable. Possibly landed.

But it would buy her mother nothing but snide barbs and hushed whispers. No additional respect, no additional care. Few of the aristocracy into which she was born would ever consider her worthy of their civility, let alone their forgiveness.

Hypocrisy was the bedrock of the peerage.

Georgiana knew it—he'd seen it in her gaze and heard it in her voice as she'd talked to him, far more fascinating than he would have ever imagined. She was willing to wager everything for her daughter, and there was tremendous nobility in that.

She was like no woman he'd ever known.

He wondered, vaguely, what it might be like to grow with the love of a parent willing to sacrifice all happiness for one's sake. He'd had the love, but it had been fleeting.

And then he'd become the caretaker.

He resisted the memory and returned his attention to the dance.

Langley was a good choice. Handsome and intelligent and charming, and a skilled dancer, gliding the lady across the ballroom floor, underscoring her grace with his own. West watched her ivory skirts caress the viscount's trouser leg as he turned her. Something about the way silk clung to wool briefly before giving in to gravity's pull irritated him. Something about the way they moved, all grace and skill, grated.

He shouldn't care. He was here for something else entirely.

So what had he been doing on a balcony making silly promises of social redemption to a girl he didn't know?

Guilt was a powerful motivator.

The damn cartoon. He'd dragged her through the muck, as surely as her peers had done so a decade earlier. He'd been irate when it had run—hated the way it teased and mocked an unwed mother, a child who'd had no choice in the matter. He didn't read *The Scandal Sheet* the way he read the rest of his papers, as he had little taste for gossip. He'd missed the cartoon, inserted at the last minute, before the pages went to print.

He'd sacked the editor in charge the moment he'd seen it. But it had been too late.

And he'd helped to further scandalize the girl.

She smiled up at Langley, and something tugged at West's memory. He did not remember meeting the lady before, but he could not shake the idea that he had at some point. That they'd spoken. That she'd smiled at him in just the same way.

Lady Disrepute, they called her, in no small part because of him. It did not matter that she was everything they adored—young, aristocratic, and more beautiful than one woman should be.

Perhaps her beauty mattered most of all. Society hated the

most beautiful among it nearly as much as it hated the least. It was beauty that made scandal so compelling—after all, if only Eve had not been so beautiful, perhaps the serpent would have left her alone.

But it was Eve who was vilified, never the serpent. Just as it was the lady who was ruined, never the man.

He wondered about the man in her case, again. Had she loved him?

The thought left a foul taste.

Yes, he would redeem the girl. He would make her the star of the season. It would be easy enough—Society adored its gossip pages, and easily believed the things it read in them. A few well-placed columns, and Lady Georgiana would marry her viscount and leave West's conscience appeased and his focus on other, more important matters.

Matters that would ensure his freedom.

"You are not dancing."

He'd expected the meeting—had attended the ball for it—but went cold at the words nevertheless, spoken with false cordiality at his elbow. "I do not dance."

The Earl of Tremley chuckled. "Of course you don't."

West was mere days older than Tremley; he'd known the earl for his entire life, and hated him for nearly that long. But now Tremley was one of King William's most trusted advisors, with tens of thousands of acres of the lushest land in Suffolk that earned him close to fifty thousand pounds a year. He was rich as a fictional king and had the ear of a real one.

West deliberately kept his focus on Georgiana, something about her helping to keep him calm. "What do you want?"

Tremley feigned shock. "So cold. You should show more respect to your betters."

"You should be grateful that I resist pummeling you in public," West said, taking his gaze from Georgiana, not liking the idea that his unwelcome companion might discover his interest.

"Big words. As though you would take such a risk."

West grew more irritated, loathing the fear that whispered

through him at Tremley's words. Hating it. "I'll ask again. Why are you here?"

"I noticed your column last week."

He stilled. "I write a great deal of columns."

"This one was in favor of abolition of the death penalty for theft. A brazen choice, for someone so . . . close to the situation."

West did not reply. There was nothing to say here, in this room filled with people who did not worry about their futures. Who were not terrified of their pasts.

Who did not wait, every day, to be discovered. Punished. *Hanged.*

Lady Georgiana spun away on the arm of her future husband, lost in the crowd as Tremley sighed. "It is so tiresome, having to threaten you. If only you would accept that this is our arrangement—I command, you act—it would make our conversations much more palatable."

West looked to his enemy. "I own five of the most successful newspapers on the globe. You grow ever closer to destruction at the stroke of my pen."

Tremley's tone went cold and direct. "You own them thanks to my benevolence. That pen stroke would be your last, and you know it. Even if you got your law passed."

As though he would ever forget that Tremley held such power.

As though he would forget that the earl was the only person in the world who knew his secrets, and could punish him for them.

Tremley had secrets of his own, however—dark secrets that would see him dancing on the end of a rope if West was correct. But until he had proof . . . he had no weapon against this man who held his life in his hands.

"I'll ask again," he said, finally. "What do you want?"

"There is a war on in Greece."

"This is the modern world. There's always a war on somewhere," West said.

"This one is nearly over. I want the *News of London* to come out against the peace."

A vision flashed, Tremley's file in his office, filled with nervous speculation from men who were terrified of their names being published. Speculation about this war. About others. "You want me to oppose Greek independence." When Tremley did not reply, he added, "We had soldiers on the ground there. They fought and died for this democracy."

"And here you are," Tremley said, the words snide and unpleasant, "alive and well. And free."

West did not miss the earl's point. At any moment, with a word from this man, West could be destroyed. Sent to prison for a lifetime.

Worse.

"I won't write it," West said.

"You don't have a choice," Tremley said. "You are my lapdog. And you had best remember it."

The truth of the statement made it infinitely more infuriating.

But it would not be true for long, if he found what he was looking for.

West's fist clenched at his side. He was desperate to use it, to pummel this man as hard as he'd wanted to when they were children, and he'd spent his days being taunted and teased. Hurt. Nearly killed.

He'd escaped, come to London, built a goddamn empire. And still, when with Tremley, he was the boy he'd once been.

A memory flashed, tearing through the darkness on a horse worth triple his life. Five times it. His sister bundled in his lap. The promise of the future. The promise of safety. Of a life worth living for both of them.

He was tired of living in fear of that memory.

He turned away from the conversation, feeling trapped, as he always did. Owned. Desperate for something that would destroy this man now, before he was forced to do his bidding another time.

"Why?" he asked, "Why sway public opinion away from peace?"

"That's not your concern."

West was willing to wager that Tremley was breaking any

number of laws of king and country, and that was his concern. And the concern of his readers. And the concern of his king.

But most importantly, proof of it was enough to keep his secrets safe. Forever.

Alas, proof was not easily come by in this world of gossip and lies.

It had to be found. Bought, if possible.

Bargained, if necessary.

And there was only one man who had enough power to get what West himself had not been able to find.

"You shall do it," the earl insisted.

He did not speak, refusing to voice his agreement to whatever it was Tremley asked. He had done the earl's bidding before, but never anything that would so clearly derail the crown. Never anything that would so clearly risk English lives.

"You shall do it." Tremley repeated, firmer this time. Angrier.

As the words were not a question, it was easy for West not to answer. Instead, he exited the ballroom, hesitating at its edge as the orchestra finished its set, looking back over the crowd, watching the throngs of aristocrats revel in their money and power and idyll.

They did not understand what fortune smiled upon them.

He collected his coat and hat and headed for the exit, already at his club in his mind, calling for Chase's messenger, calling in—for the first time—a favor.

If anyone could access Tremley' secrets, it was Chase, but the owner of The Fallen Angel would want payment, and West would have to offer something massive for what he desired.

He waited on the steps of Worthington House for his carriage to emerge from the crush of conveyances waiting to be summoned by their masters and mistresses, eager to get to his club and begin negotiations with its owner.

"And here we are again."

He recognized her voice immediately, as though he'd

known it his whole life. Lady Georgiana stood behind him, with her clear eyes and her voice that somehow brought light with it—as though years away from this world, this place, had made her more than she could have ever been had she stayed.

He met her gaze, inclined his head. "My lady," he let the words fall between them, enjoying the honorific, one he had never considered so possessive before now. Enjoying, too, the way her eyes widened at it. He repeated her words. "And here we are again."

She smiled, soft and secret, and the expression sent a thread of pleasure through him. He stopped it before he could enjoy it. She was not for pleasure.

She came to stand next to him at the top of the Worthington House steps, looking down over the carriages assembled below.

It was early enough in the evening that they were alone, accompanied only by her maid and a collection of liveried footmen, all of whom were paid handsomely to disappear into the background.

"I realized after we parted that I should not have spoken to you," she said, her gaze not wavering from where a footman scurried into the neighboring mews to locate her conveyance. She elaborated. "We have not been introduced."

He looked to the crush of black vehicles. "You are correct."

"And you are an unmarried, untitled man."

He smiled. "Untitled?"

She matched the smile. "If you were titled, I would worry less."

"You think the title would make you safe?"

"No," she said, serious. "But as we established, a title would make you an excellent husband."

He laughed at her boldness. "I would make a terrible husband, my lady. That, I can assure you."

Her gaze turned curious. "Why?"

"Because I have worse traits than being unmarried and untitled." That much was true.

"Ah. You mean because you have a trade."

No, because I haven't a future.

He let his silence be his reply.

"Well, it's silly that we are taught to look down our noses at hard work."

"Silly, but true."

They stood for a long moment, each seeming to wish the other to speak first. "And yet it seems I need you."

He cut her a look. He shouldn't like those words. He shouldn't want to be needed. Want to help her.

Shouldn't find this woman so very compelling.

Shouldn't need to remind himself that he did not think about her.

"It's early," he said, eager to change the subject. "And you are for home already?"

She wrapped her heavy silk cloak around her, blocking the chill from the night air. "Believe it or not," she said dryly, "I have had something of a time tonight. I find myself quite exhausted."

He smirked. "I noticed you found the energy to dance with Langley."

She hesitated. "Would you believe he was forced into it?"

Not in the wide world. "I'm sure it was not a trial."

"I am not so certain," she said, her gaze clear and direct, "But he could do worse than my dowry."

West hadn't been thinking of her dowry. He'd been thinking of her—all long and lithe and lovely. He could have done without the ridiculous headpiece, but even with the feathers protruding from her coif, she was a beautiful woman.

Too beautiful.

He did not correct her misinterpretation of his words. "Much worse."

For a long moment, there was silence but for the sound of approaching hoofbeats and carriage wheels. Her coach arrived, and she made to leave him. He didn't want it. He thought of the feather from her hair, now in the pocket of his coat, and for a wild moment, he wondered what she would feel like there, against him. He resisted the thought. "No chaperone?"

She looked back to the little, unassuming maid standing several feet away. "I'm for home, sir. This conversation shall be the most scandalous thing I do all night."

He could think of any number of scandalous things he might be willing to do with her, but blessedly, his curricle arrived and saved him from madness. She lifted a brow at him. "A curricle? At night?"

"I have to get through London streets quickly when there is news to be had," he said as his groom leapt down from the conveyance. "A curricle works well."

"And for escaping balls?"

He inclined his head. "And for that."

"Perhaps I should acquire one."

He smiled. "I'm not sure the ladies of Society would like it."

She sighed. "I don't suppose it's proper for me to say, 'Hang the ladies of Society.' "

She meant the words to amuse—spoke them with the perfect combination of ennui and wit to make a lesser man chuckle. A man who did not notice the underlying tone.

Sadness. Loss. Frustration.

"You don't want it, do you?"

Her gaze turned surprised, but she did not pretend to misunderstand. He liked that about her. Her forthrightness. "This is my bed, Mr. West. In it, I shall lie."

She did not want to return. She did not want this life. That much was clear. "Lady Georgiana," he began, not entirely knowing what to say next.

"Good night, Mr. West." She was already moving, trailed by an unassuming maid. Already down the steps headed for her carriage, which would take her away from this place, from this night.

From him.

She would regroup. Heal. And repeat the performance tomorrow.

And he would do his best to keep her safe from the horde.

He rarely took an interest in society, and even more rarely

in its women, who were in large part more trouble than they were worth—all idle drama. But there was something in Lady Georgiana that seemed familiar, oddly. Something that echoed through him. Resignation, perhaps. Discontent. Desire—for what he did not know, but it was enough to intrigue him.

He watched her for a long moment, the way she moved, certain of her destination. Sure of herself. He found himself fascinated by the way her pale skirts seemed to chase after her, as though they might be left behind if they weren't careful. The way one long arm reached out to keep her balanced as she lifted those skirts and entered her carriage.

He caught a glimpse of turned ankle in a gleaming silver slipper. For a moment, he was transfixed by that foot, slim and shadowed, until the door snapped closed and she was gone, her outrider—a massive man who had no doubt been hired by her wealthy brother to keep her safe—storing the stepping block away at the back of the carriage before climbing onto his perch and indicating to the driver that they should move on.

He imagined what he might write about her.

Lady G— is more than her reputation promises, more than scandal and past sins. She is something that we all wish we could have been—separate from our world. Somehow, ironically, despite her past, purer than all of us. Untouched by us. Which is perhaps her greatest value.

The words came easily. But then again, the truth always did write well.

Unfortunately, the truth did not sell papers.

He ascended the stairs to his curricle, pulling himself up into the seat and taking the reins, dismissing his groom for the night. He liked to drive himself; found solace in the rhythm of hoofbeats and the circling of wheels.

He followed behind the lady's coach as it trundled at a snail's pace, attempting to leave the Worthington property, and had no choice but to think of her, inside that carriage, with her thoughts. He imagined her staring out the window at the lanterns that hung on the carriages that remained along the street. Imagined her wondering how her carriage might have been with the others—might have been one of the last to leave that evening, after she had danced again and again and again, with a myriad of gentlemen until her feet were sore and her muscles straining from exhaustion. Imagined her thinking about the way she might have left the ball—not to escape Society, but as a queen of it.

If only she hadn't been ruined.

He imagined her pretty eyes filled with regret, for all the things she might have been. All the things she might have done. All the life she might have led.

If things had been different.

He was so lost in thinking of the lady that he did not realize that she had missed her turn—the one to her brother's home—and instead, she was headed through Mayfair, oddly, in his same direction.

He certainly wasn't following her intentionally.

The carriage wheels clattered along the cobblestoned streets of Mayfair, turning down Bond—where the shops had closed for the evening—and then onto Piccadilly toward St. James.

It was then that he began to question where she was headed.

He allowed his curricle to fall back, for no reason at all, he told himself. He allowed a few carriages to come between them, barely able to make out the lanterns on her conveyance as it made the turn onto Duke Street, then cut into the labyrinth of streets and alleyways behind the men's clubs of St. James. He sat up in his seat.

She was behind The Fallen Angel.

Duncan West was arguably the greatest newspaperman in London, but it did not take an investigative mind such as his own to recognize the truth.

Lady Georgiana Pearson, sister of the Duke of Leighton, with a dowry big enough to buy Buckingham Palace, and supposedly desperate for a restored reputation—one he had offered to secure for her—was headed straight for Britain's most celebrated men's club.

Which just so happened to be *his* club.

He stopped his curricle before making the final turn to the rear entrance of the club, leaping down and heading the rest of the way on foot, not wanting to draw attention to his presence. If she were seen here, her reputation would be destroyed forever. No man would have her, and her daughter would have no future.

It was a risk of outrageous proportions.

So what in hell was she doing?

West remained in the shadows, leaning against the alley wall, watching the great black carriage that had stopped, its occupant still inside. He realized that the carriage boasted no markings; there was nothing about it that would draw attention. Nothing but the enormous outrider, who climbed down from his perch, moving to bang on the heavy steel door that marked the back entrance to the club. A small slot opened, then closed when the servant spoke. The door opened, revealing a great black chasm—the dark rear entry to the club.

Still the doors to the carriage remained firmly shut.

Good. Perhaps she was reconsidering whatever idiocy this was.

Perhaps she would not exit.

Except she would. No doubt, she had before. No doubt, that was why she had such easy access to this club, run by London's darkest men, any one of whom could destroy her without hesitation.

He should stop her. He moved to, coming off the wall, ready to cross the wide mews, tear open the door to the carriage, and give her what for.

But the outrider was closer than he, opening the door and setting the step on the ground below.

West hesitated, waiting for her, for her white skirts, and

that innocent silver slipper that had been his last, lingering glimpse of her.

Except the slipper that emerged was in no way innocent.

It was sinful.

High-heeled and dark—too dark to tell the color in the spare light from the carriage—showcasing a long, slender foot that arched with perfection. He came off the wall where he'd been leaning, gaze focused as the foot gave way to ankle and then a sea of silk the color of midnight, the mass of fabric ending at the point of a corseted bodice, threaded and tightened to showcase a glorious bosom designed to make a man salivate.

He swallowed.

And then she stepped into the light, painted lips, kohled eyes, and blond hair gleaming platinum.

Blond *wig* gleaming platinum.

Recognition flared, and he swore in the darkness.

Shock soon gave way to the acute pleasure that came with uncovering a remarkable story.

Lady Georgiana Pearson was no innocent. She was London's finest whore.

And she was his answer.

Chapter 4

... Lady G— may not be thought much a lady, but she comported herself with grace and aplomb at the W— Ball, and attracted the attention of at least one duke and a half-dozen aristocratic gentlemen in search of wives ...

... it seems that Lady M— and her compatriots are in rare form this Season, eager to dress down any who dare come near. Gentlemen of the *ton* should take care ... the daughter of the Earl of H— appears to lack the grace of some of her lessers ...

The Scandal Sheet, April 20, 1833

The following night, Georgiana entered her apartments high above the club, startling Asriel, one of the Angel's security detail, who sat quietly, reading.

He came to his feet in a single, fluid motion, all six and a half feet of him, wide as a barn, with fists at the ready.

She waved him back. " 'Tis only me."

He narrowed his dark gaze on her. "What is it?"

She looked to the closed door he guarded. "She is well?"

"Hasn't made a sound since she retired."

Relief pressed the air from her lungs.

Christ.

Of course Caroline was well. She was guarded by half a dozen locked doors and as many men in the corridors beyond, and Asriel, who had been with Georgiana for longer than anyone else.

It did not matter. When Caroline was in London, she was at risk. Georgiana preferred the girl in Yorkshire, where she was safe from prying eyes and whispered gossip and hateful insults, where she could play in the sun like a normal child. And when she was in the city, Georgiana preferred the girl at her uncle's home, far from the Angel.

Far from her mother's sins. From her father's.

The thought rankled. Fathers' sins never seemed to stick. It was the mother who bore the heavy weight of ruin in these situations. The mother who passed it on to the child, as though there were not two involved in the act.

Of course, Georgiana had never spoken his name after he'd left.

She'd never wanted anyone to know the identity of the man who had played havoc with her future and ruined her name. Her brother had asked a thousand times. Had vowed to avenge her. To destroy the man who had left her with child and never looked back. But Georgiana had refused to name him.

He had not been the instrument of her ruin, after all. She'd lain in the hayloft with him under her own power, with her full faculties. It had not been Jonathan who had destroyed her.

It had been Society.

She had broken their rules, and they'd rejected her.

There had been no season, no chance to prove herself worthy. She'd never had hope of that proof—they had played judge and jury. Her scandal had been their entertainment and their cautionary tale.

All because she'd fallen victim to a different tale, pretty and fictional.

Love.

Society hadn't cared about that bit. No one had—not her family, not her friends. She'd been exiled by all save her brother, the duke who married a scandal of his own and, in doing so, lost the respect of their mother. Of the *ton.*

And so she'd vowed to make Society beholden to her. She'd collected information on the most powerful among them and, if they owed money they could not pay, she rarely hesitated to use it to wreck them. This whole world—the club, the money, the power—it was all for one thing. To hold court over the world that had shunned her all those years ago. That had turned its back on her, and left her with nothing.

Not nothing.

Caroline.

Everything.

"I hate it when she is here," she said, to herself more than to Asriel. He knew her well enough not to reply. And yet Georgiana could not help but bring Caroline to London every few months. She told herself that it was because she wanted her daughter to know her uncle. Her cousins. But it wasn't true.

Georgiana brought Caroline here because she could not bear the emptiness she felt when the girl was far. Because she was never in her life so satisfied as when she placed her hand on her sleeping daughter's back and felt the rise and fall of her breath, filled with dreams and promise.

Filled with everything Georgiana did not have, and everything that she had promised to give her child.

No dreams of a marriage of convenience turning into a love match?

The words from the prior evening came quick and unwanted, as though Duncan West were with her again, tall and handsome, blond hair falling over his brow begging to be brushed back, to be touched. The man was handsome to a dangerous degree, in large part because he was so intelligent—his mind understanding more than was said, his eyes seeing more than was revealed. And his voice, the darkness of it, the way it traced the peaks and valleys of language, the way it cradled her name, the way it whispered the honorific she so rarely used.

The way it made her want to listen to him for hours.

She resisted the thought. She did not have time to listen to Duncan West. He'd made a generous offer of help, which was all she needed. Nothing else.

She wanted nothing else.

Liar.

The word whispered through her. She ignored it. Returned her attention to her daughter. To the promise she'd made to give her a life. A future.

It had been ten years since Caroline was conceived and Georgiana had run from the world for which she had been bred. Ten years since that world had damned them both. And in the years since, Georgiana had built this empire on Society's greatest truth—that none of its members was far from ruin. That none of those sneering, insulting, horrible people would survive if their secrets were revealed.

She had partnered with three fallen aristocrats, each stronger and more intelligent than the rest of Society, each ruined without question. Each desperate to hide from the *ton* even as he ruled it.

And together, they did rule it. Bourne, Cross, Temple, and Chase held London's most powerful men and women in their thrall. Discovered their darkest truths. Their deepest secrets. But it was Chase alone who reigned, in part because it was Georgiana alone who would never fully be able to return to Society.

Every mistake, every scandal, every humiliation faced by the men of the aristocracy could be wiped away. Titles bought respectability, even for those who had fallen from grace.

Had she not proven it?

She'd chosen her partners for the mistakes they'd made when they were young and stupid. Bourne had lost his entire fortune, Cross had chosen a life of gaming and whoring over a life of responsibility, Temple had landed himself in bed with his father's fiancée. Not one of them had deserved the punishment Society had meted out.

And each of them had been restored to his place, richer, stronger, more powerful.

In love.

She resisted the thought.

Love had been secondary. Her partners had been restored to their places because Georgiana gave them the avenue for their restoration. She was lucky enough to have—despite her failings—a brother who was willing to do anything she asked. Secure any invitation. Provide any cover. He owed her.

With her scandal, she'd given him the freedom to marry the woman of his choosing, and he'd given her something much much more valuable . . . a future.

She might never again be accepted by Society, but now she held the power to destroy it.

For years, she'd planned and plotted her revenge—the moment she showed them all the truth—that they were nothing without her—the ruined girl they'd thrown away.

Except, she couldn't.

As much as she loathed it, she needed them.

Not just them.

She needed him.

West's handsome face flashed again—all easy power and lazy smiles. The man was far too arrogant for his own good. And that arrogance tempted more than it should.

But he was everything she did not desire. Everything she did not require. He was untitled, not even a gentleman—come from nowhere, accepted in polite company because of his sickening wealth more than anything else. For God's sake, the man had a career. It was a miracle he was allowed this side of Regent Street.

She required his assistance for one thing and one thing only.

Securing Caroline's future.

The door behind Asriel snapped open, revealing her

daughter, lit from behind by a collection of blazing candles. "I thought I heard you."

"Why are you still awake?"

Caroline waved a red leather book. "I cannot sleep. This poor woman! Her husband forces her to drink wine from her own father's skull!"

Asriel's eyes went wide.

Caroline turned to him. "I feel the same way. It's no wonder she haunts the place. Though, to be honest, if it were me, I'd want as far away from it as possible."

Georgiana plucked the book from Caroline's grasp. "I think we could find something more appropriate for bedtime reading than"—she read from the book's cover—"*The Ghosts of Castel Teodorico*, don't you?"

"What would you suggest?"

"Surely there's a book of children's poetry lying about?"

Caroline rolled her eyes. "I am not a child."

"Of course not." Georgiana knew better than to argue. "A novel? Including a noble steed, a shining castle, and a happy-ever-after?"

Rolling eyes turned forthright. "I shan't know if this one has a happy-ever-after unless I finish it. But there is a romance."

Georgiana's brow raised. "The husband in question does not strike me as a viable hero."

Caroline waved a hand. "Oh, of course not him. He's a proper monster. Another ghost. From two hundred years earlier, and they are in love."

"The two ghosts?" Asriel asked, his gaze falling to the book.

Caroline nodded. "Through time."

"How inconvenient," Georgiana said.

"Thoroughly. They only appear together one night a year."

"And what do they do together?" Asriel asked. Georgiana turned surprised eyes on him, big as a house and silent as the grave—unless romantic novels were in discussion, apparently.

Caroline shook her head. "It's unclear. But apparently it's quite scandalous, so I assume it's some kind of physical manifestation of their passion. Though considering they are ghosts . . . I'm not sure how it works."

Asriel choked.

Georgiana raised a brow. "Caroline."

Caroline grinned. "It's just so easy to shock him."

"You are what is referred to as 'precocious.'" She handed the book to Asriel. "And so you must be reminded that I am older, wiser, and more powerful. Go to bed."

The girl's eyes sparkled. "What of my book?"

Georgiana bit back a smile. "You may have it in the morning. Asriel will take excellent care of it in the meantime."

Caroline whispered to Asriel, "Chapter fifteen. We shall discuss it tomorrow."

Asriel grunted in feigned disinterest, but did not protest his receipt of the book.

Georgiana pointed to Caroline's bedchamber. "In."

The girl turned at the order, and Georgiana followed behind, watching as she climbed into bed, then perching on the edge of the bed, smoothing the linen coverlet over Caroline's shoulders. "You realize that when you are invited to Society events—"

Caroline groaned.

"*When you are invited to Society events* . . . you cannot discuss physical manifestations of anything." She paused. "And it's best to avoid discussion of drinking of blood from skulls."

"It was *wine*."

"Let's settle on no skull drinking of any kind."

Caroline signed. "Society events sound terribly boring."

"They're not, you know."

Caroline turned surprise eyes on her mother. "They're not?"

Georgiana shook her head. "They're not. They're really quite entertaining if you're . . ." she hesitated. *If you're welcome to them* didn't seem to be the appropriate finish to the sentence. Particularly since Caroline was fairly ruined. "If you're interested in that sort of thing."

"Are you?" Caroline asked softly. "Interested in Society events?"

Georgiana hesitated. She had been. She'd adored the few country dances to which she'd been invited. She could still remember the dress she'd worn to that first ball—the way the skirts had weighed heavy and lush around her. The way she'd played demure, lowering her gaze and smiling carefully every time a boy asked her to dance.

Caroline deserved that memory. The dress. The dances. The attention. She deserved the breathlessness that came from a wild reel, the pride that came from a compliment on her coif. The increase in her heart rate when she met the beautiful blue gaze that proved to be her ruination.

Dread pooled in Georgiana's stomach.

Caroline knew her past—knew she had no father. Knew that Georgiana was unmarried. And Georgiana assumed that Caroline knew the consequences of those things—that her reputation was blackened by association and had been since her birth. That she needed more than a mother and a motley collection of aristocrats with questionable reputations to save her. To garner Society's approval.

And yet, Caroline had never once acknowledged those truths. She had never—even in the frustrated moments a girl had with her mother—said a word to indicate that she resented the circumstances of her birth. That she wished for another life.

But it did not mean she did not want it. And it did not mean Georgiana would not do everything she could to give it to her.

"Mother?" Caroline prompted, bringing Georgiana back to the present. "Are you interested in Society?"

"No," she said, leaning down and kissing Caroline's forehead. "Only in its secrets."

There was a long moment as Caroline considered the words before she finally said, all conviction, "Neither am I."

It was a lie. Georgiana had been a girl once, too, full of hope and ideas. She knew what Caroline dreamed of in quiet moments. In the dark of night. She knew, because she'd dreamed of the same things. Of marriage. Of a life filled with happiness and kindness and partnership.

Filled with love.

Love.

The thought of the word came on a wave of bitterness.

It was not that she did not believe in the emotion. She was not a fool, after all. She knew it was real. She'd felt it any number of times. She loved her partners. She loved her brother. She loved the women who had taken her in all those years ago, who had protected her even as she'd risked their safety—a duke's sister, escaped and on the run. She loved Caroline more than she'd ever thought possible.

And there had been a time when she'd thought she'd loved another. When she'd believed that the remarkable way he made her feel had made her invincible. When she'd thought she could conquer the world with the way she felt.

That they could conquer the world together.

She'd trusted it, that feeling. Just as she'd trusted the boy who had made her feel that way.

And she'd been left broken.

Alone.

So, yes, she believed in love. It was impossible not to every time she looked into her daughter's face. But she also knew the truth of it—that It destroyed. It consumed. It was the source of pain and fear, and it could turn infinite power into powerlessness. Could reduce a woman to a simpering girl on a balcony, taking the brunt of insult and shame in the infinitesimal hope that her pain might save someone she loved.

Love was bollocks.

"Good night, Mother." Caroline's words shook Georgiana from her reverie.

She looked down at her daughter, blankets pulled up to her chin, somehow looking both young and far too old at the same time.

Georgiana leaned down and pressed a kiss to her daughter's forehead. "Good night, sweet girl."

She left the room, closing the door quietly behind her before turning to face Temple, now standing with Asriel in the hallway beyond. "What is it?"

"Two things," the duke said, all business. "First, Galworth is here."

The Viscount Galworth, in debt to his eyeballs to the Angel. She took the file Temple offered, looked inside. "Is he ready to pay?"

"He says he has little to offer."

She raised a brow, paging through the file. "He has a town house, and acreage in Northumberland that earns him two thousand a year. Not so little."

Temple's brows rose. "I didn't know about the land."

"No one knows about the land," she said, but it was Chase's job to know more than the rest of the world about the members of The Fallen Angel.

"He's offered something else."

She looked up. "Don't tell me. The daughter."

"Offered with pleasure, to Chase."

It was not the first time. Too often, the aristocracy had a disrespect for its daughters and a willingness to deliver them into the arms of unknown men with dangerous reputations. In Chase's case, that particular package was never well received. "Tell him Chase is not interested in his daughter."

"I'd like to tell him to throw himself off a goddamn bridge," the former bare-knuckle boxer said.

"Feel free. But get the land first."

"And if he doesn't agree?"

She met his eyes. "Then he owes us seven thousand pounds. And Bruno should feel free to collect however he likes." The hulking security guard enjoyed punishing men who deserved it. And most of the members of the Angel deserved it.

Most of the members of the aristocracy deserved it.

"It is also worth reminding him that if we find he's planning to do anything but marry the girl off to a decent man, we'll release the information on his throwing horse races. Tell him that, too."

Temple's black brows rose. "It never fails to surprise me just how ruthless you can be."

She smiled her sweetest smile at him. "Never trust a woman."

He laughed. "Not you, at least."

"If he did not wish the information found out, he should not have used it to gain entrance to the club." She moved to leave the room, but turned back. "You said two things."

He nodded. "You've a visitor."

"I'm not interested. Go yourself." It would not be the first or the last time one of the other owners of the casino took a meeting meant for Chase.

Temple shook his head. "Not Chase. He insists on Anna."

Neither would it be the first or last time that a man on the floor of the hell drank too much and called for Anna. "Who?"

"Duncan West."

She caught her breath, hating the way the name rioted through her, as though she were a green girl. "What is he doing here?"

"He says he is here for you," he said, and she heard the curiosity in his tone.

Matched it with hers. "Why?"

"He did not say," the duke said, as though she were dim. "He simply asked for you."

Perhaps it was the result of the melancholy she'd felt in Caroline's room. Or perhaps it was because Duncan West had seen her at her weakest the prior evening and agreed to help her return to Society nonetheless. Or perhaps it was because she was so drawn to him—despite knowing better.

Whatever the reason, Georgiana surprised herself. "Tell him I shall be with him presently."

She waited a quarter of an hour, taking a moment to make certain that her maquillage was perfectly applied. Satisfied with her outward appearance, Georgiana made her way through the web of passageways that connected her rooms to the main floor of the club, unlocking and relocking several doors carefully to ensure that no one could accidentally gain access to Caroline.

When she opened the final door and was delivered onto the floor of the club, she released a long breath. There was something terribly freeing about playing the lightskirt, though playing wasn't precisely the verb Georgiana would use to describe her masquerade as Anna. After all, when one had worn the silks and satins of a celebrated prostitute for years, one tended to embrace the role.

Or, most of the role. Everything but the most obvious piece of it.

She hadn't planned to avoid that bit—after all, the horse was rather out of the barn when a woman had birthed a child. Neither was it a lack of opportunity—half of London's male population had approached her at one point or another.

It had simply never happened.

Which served Georgiana well. With no men on the floor of the club able to recount their time with her, her legend had grown. She was known now as a skilled madam, protected by the owners of the club and more expensive than any mere member of The Fallen Angel could afford.

And that legend had offered its own protection, giving her the freedom to move about the floor, to interact with members, and to play her part without fear of threat. No member of the club was willing to risk his membership for a taste of Anna.

She stood at the center of the casino floor, loving the massive room filled with gamers and tables, cards and dice, wins and losses. Every inch of the place was hers, every corner in her dominion.

It was a heady pleasure, this place of sin and vice and secrets—the throngs before her swayed in excitement, vibrating with desire and nerves and greed. London's wealthiest and most powerful sat here night after night, money in their pockets and women in their laps, and played at chance, never knowing—or perhaps never acknowledging—that they would never beat the Angel. They would never win enough to reign here.

The Fallen Angel had its monarch.

It was the greed that kept them here—desperation for money, for luxury, for the win. Whatever club members wanted was theirs for the taking, often before they recognized the desire that ran hot within. And because of that, the club was marked the greatest in London's history.

As White's and Brooks's and Boodle's were for public schoolboys, the Angel was for men. And to gain entrance to the club, they would reveal all their secrets.

Such was the draw of sin.

And it was a pretty, pretty draw.

Her gaze landed on a collection of tables at the center of the casino floor, where roulette wheels spun in a blur of red and black, wagers strewn across green baize. It was her favorite place in the hell, in the middle of everything, where she could survey all she owned from its heart. She adored the sound of ivory balls on mahogany wheels, the clatter of the spin, the collective breath holding of the gamers at the table.

Roulette was like life; its utter unpredictability made it immensely rewarding when it delivered a win.

She turned slowly, searching the crowd for West, resisting the pounding of her heart, the excitement of the hunt for the man who held near-equal power in this room. She resisted, too, the way he made her feel, as though she'd met her match.

She knew she should be nervous at his summons . . . but she could not resist the temptation he represented.

Georgiana was bound by propriety around him.

Anna, however . . . Anna could flirt. And she found she was looking forward to seeing the man again.

The thought had barely come when she was captured from behind, heavy steel arms wrapping around her waist and lifting her clear off the floor. She resisted the urge to scream in surprise as a hot, drunken voice breathed at her ear, "Now, here's a treat."

She was trapped against the man, on show for the entire floor of the club—a score of members, who lacked either the courage or the stupidity required to approach her, stood, mouths agape, watching. Not one came to her defense. She watched a croupier at a nearby hazard field reach beneath the table, to no doubt pull a cord that would ring a corresponding bell in any number of rooms abovestairs.

Security summoned, Georgiana turned her head, craning to identify the large man who held her in his grasp. "Baron Pottle," she said calmly, letting her weight fall dead in his arms. "I suggest you restore me to the earth before one of us is hurt."

He lifted her into his arms, feet in the air, skirts tumbling back to reveal ankles which received a collective leer before he said, "Hurting is not what I have in mind, darling."

She leaned away from his alcohol-laden breath. "Nevertheless, you shall be hurt if you don't put me down."

"And who'll do that?" he slurred. "Chase?"

"Anything is possible."

Pottle laughed. "Chase hasn't shown his face on the floor in six years, love. I doubt he'll do it for you." Prediction made, he leaned in. "And besides, you'll like what I have in store for you."

"I highly doubt that." She squirmed in his arms, but he was stronger than he looked, dammit. And the idiot drunken aristocrat was going to kiss her. He licked his lips and came closer even as she craned backward—but there was only so far a woman could escape when held in a man's arms. "Baron Pottle," she said, "this shan't end well. For either of us."

The assembled crowd snickered, but no one came to her aid.

"Come now, Anna. We're both adults. And you're a professional," Pottle said, lips closer, a hairsbreadth from her. "I'd like a ride. It's not as though I won't pay you, and handsomely. And who's going to stop me?"

It was only then that Georgiana realized that, were she not who she was, with the protection of The Fallen Angel and all of its power behind her, no one would stop him. Women with her reputation, with her past, were not worth fighting for.

And shockingly, it was that thought, and not the physical experience, that wreaked havoc. Security would come, she thought, trying to keep the thought alive as she fought the anger and frustration and humiliation of the moment.

Pottle's lips were on hers now. Two dozen so-called gentlemen watched, and not one willing to help.

Cowards. Every one of them.

"Release the lady."

Chapter 5

... That said, fortune hunters might have cause to worry, as Lady G—'s charm and grace threaten to result in the *ton* forgetting her past and instead promising her a bright future ...

... We are told a certain Baron P— is sleeping off his drink and regretting a night at his club. We recommend averting one's gaze from his right eye, as the shine of it threatens to blind the unsuspecting ...

The gossip pages of *The Weekly Britannia*,
April 22, 1833

She hated the relief that came with the words, with the certainty in them.

Her gaze flew over her captor's shoulder to meet Duncan West's furious brown gaze, and the relief diminished. Was he the only man in creation?

On the heels of that thought came another. He could see her ankles. So could the rest of Christendom, honestly, but it seemed only to matter that *he* could.

Who in hell cared?

Or, rather, why did *she* care?

He interrupted her thoughts. "Do not make me repeat myself, Pottle. Release the lady."

The drunken baron sighed. "You are no fun, West," he slurred. "And besides, Anna's not a lady, is she? So what's the harm?"

West looked away for a moment. "Remarkably, I was prepared to let you go." He turned back, eyes flashing furious and focused.

Georgiana was smart enough to get out of the way before the punch landed with a wicked crunch, hard and fast and more powerful than she'd expected. Pottle dropped to the ground with a howl, hands flying to his nose. "Christ, West! What in hell is wrong with you?"

West leaned over his opponent and took hold of his cravat, lifting Pottle's head to meet his gaze. "Did the *lady*"—he paused for emphasis on the word—"ask to be touched?"

"Look at the way she dresses!" Pottle fairly shrieked, blood escaping from his nose. "If that's not a request for touching, what is?"

"Wrong answer." The next punch was as fierce as the first, snapping Pottle's head back on his neck. "Try again."

"West." One of Pottle's cronies spoke from the sidelines, apologetic. "He's soused. He'd never have done it if not for the drink."

An age-old excuse. Georgiana resisted the urge to roll her eyes.

West had no interest in eye rolling. He lifted the man from the ground and replied, "Then he should drink less. *Try again*." The demand was cold and unsettling, even to her.

Pottle winced. "She did not ask."

"And so?"

"And so what?" Pottle replied, confused.

West lifted his fist again.

"No!" Pottle cried, lifting his hands to block his face. "Stop!"

"And so?" West prompted. His voice was low and dark and menacing, the opposite of his usual calm.

"And so I should not have touched her."

"Or kissed her," West added, his gaze moving to her.

There was something there, alongside the anger, gone before she could place it. West had seen Pottle kiss her. Georgiana's cheeks began to burn, and she was grateful for the pale face powder that covered the wash of heat.

"Or kissed her."

"He's repeating whatever you say at this point," she said, trying for more boldness than she felt. "Ask him to speak a child's nursery rhyme."

West ignored her and the laughter she elicited from the circle of men around them. He spoke to his foe. "Are you sobering?"

Pottle pressed fingertips to his temple, as though he could not remember where he was, and swore roundly. "I am."

"Apologize to the lady."

"I am sorry," the baron grumbled.

"Look at her." West's words rolled like approaching thunder, threatening and unavoidable. "And mean it."

Pottle looked at her, gaze pleading. "Anna, I am sorry. I did not mean to offend."

It was her turn to speak, and for a moment she forgot her role, too enthralled by the act playing out in front of her. Finally, she offered the baron her savviest smile. "Less whiskey next time, Oliver," she said, deliberately using the baron's given name, "and you might have had a chance." She looked to West, taking in his irate gaze. "With both Mr. West and me."

West released Pottle, letting him collapse in a heap to the casino floor. "Get out. Don't come back until your faculties have been restored."

Pottle scurried backward like a crab escaping a wave, finally turning to his hands and knees and pushing himself up and away from the scene he had caused.

West turned his attention to her. She was used to men's eyes upon her. Had experienced it hundreds of times. Thousands. Capitalized on it. And still, this man—his quiet assessment—unsettled her. She resisted the urge to fidget, instead placing her hands on her hips to still their slight tremor and speaking, the honest words injected with false sarcasm. "My hero."

One blond brow rose. "Anna."

And there, in the simple name, the diminutive she had selected for this small, secret, false piece of herself, she heard something she'd never heard from him before.

Desire.

She went cold. Then blazing hot.

He knew.

He had to. They'd spoken a hundred times. A thousand. She'd been Chase's emissary, ferrying messages back and forth between West and the fabricated owner of The Fallen Angel for years. And he'd never once looked at her with anything more than vague interest.

Certainly never desire.

He knew.

The cool assessment had returned to his eyes, and she suddenly wondered if she was going mad. Perhaps he didn't know.

Perhaps she only wished he did.

Nonsense.

She was misreading the situation. He'd done battle for her. And men who defended ladies' honor were often left in dire need of attention. It was as simple as that, she told herself. Violence and sex were two sides of the same coin, were they not?

"I suppose you require some token of my thanks."

His gaze narrowed. "Stop."

The word threaded through her, making her more nervous than she had been when caught up in the Baron Pottle's arms. She did not know what to say. How to respond.

Reaching for her hand, he took control of the moment. As he had since he'd appeared only minutes earlier. She looked at the extended arm for a long moment, deliberately canting one hip and biting a red lip for their audience.

But Duncan West cared not a bit about their audience. He grasped her hand and pulled her away, into a curtained-off alcove, made for darkness and promise. Inside, he turned her to face into the light of the single candle mounted on the wall and then released her. The candles were designed to keep the space dim and seductive. To force any couple who found themselves inside to approach each other and have a closer look.

Right now, Georgiana hated that candle. It felt bright as the sun with its threat of revelation.

What if he saw the truth?

She resisted the thought. She'd lived as Georgiana, sister of a duke, daughter to one, exiled but periodically in town for years, shopping on Bond Street, walking in Hyde Park, visiting the London Museum. No one had ever noticed that she was the same woman who reigned over The Fallen Angel.

The aristocracy saw what they wished to see.

Everyone saw what he wished to see.

And cleverest newspaperman in Britain or no, Duncan West was no different.

She gave him her most wicked smile. "Now you have me here. What will you do with me?"

He shook his head, refusing the game. "You should not have been alone on the floor."

Her brow furrowed. "I am alone on the floor every night."

"You should not be," he repeated. "And that Chase allows it does not speak well of him."

She did not care for the anger in the tone. The censure. The emotion. Something had changed, and she could not divine precisely what. She met his gaze. "Had I not been summoned, sir, I would have had no reason to be accosted on the casino floor."

Now the anger in his words was in his eyes. "It is my fault?"

She did not answer, instead saying, "Why call for me?"

He paused, and for a long moment, she thought he might not reply. Finally, he said, "I've a request for Chase."

She hated the disappointment that flooded through her at the words. It wasn't as though she should have expected him to ask for Anna for any other reason—but after their interaction the day before, she rather wished he had.

She wished he'd come with a request for her.

Which was ridiculous . . . in large part, because she *was* Chase, and therefore he had, technically, come with a request for her. But in slightly smaller part, because she had no skill whatsoever in answering men's requests.

Unfortunately.

She did not like Chase's name on his lips. He was a man who saw too much already. "Of course," she said, feigning affability. "What would you like?"

"Tremley," he said.

"What about him?"

"I want his secrets."

Georgiana's brow furrowed at the strange request. "Tremley is not a member. You know that."

The Earl of Tremley was not a fool. He would never get into bed with The Fallen Angel—no matter how tempting the tables might be. He knew the price was too high.

The founders of the Angel had worked for years to establish the invitation to join the club as the most coveted offer in Britain—perhaps in Europe. Unlike other men's clubs, there were no membership dues, and there was no allowance for vouching for friends or cohorts—members rarely knew why they were invited to the club, and they were encouraged not to discuss their membership. Few did, in part because of the high price of entry to the casino floor.

They were not willing to risk their secrets becoming public.

For years, Bourne, Cross, Temple, and Georgiana—masked as Anna and Chase—had been amassing secrets on London's most powerful men and women, each piece of privileged, clandestine information given freely in exchange for membership in London's darkest, most promising, most sinful gaming hell. There was nothing that the Angel could not give her members, and few requests that the owners of the casino would not accommodate.

That kind of luxury was worth unfathomable information, and information was the currency of power.

But the Earl of Tremley was too well connected to the

crown to risk a connection to The Fallen Angel. "Try the clubs across the street," she said, injecting her words with teasing. "White's is more to the earl's liking."

He inclined his head. "That may be true, but I need Chase for what I'm asking."

She was immediately intrigued. "What do *you* have on him?"

He raised a brow. "Does Chase have anything?"

The Angel had tried to hook the earl any number of times since King William ascended to the throne with Tremley at his right hand, but few were willing to talk about a man with so much political power. Was there something they'd missed?

If West was asking, there was. Without doubt. "There is no file on Tremley," she said. It was the truth.

He did not believe her. She could see it in his eyes even here, in the dim light. "There will be when Chase invites the earl's wife to the ladies' side."

She stilled at the words. "I don't know what you are referring to."

For as many years as there had been a Fallen Angel, the coveted public men's club and casino run by four fallen aristocrats, each richer than the next, there had been a secret, unspoken second club that operated beneath the gentlemen's noses and utterly beyond their notice. A ladies' club, with no name and no public face.

It was never discussed.

And she wasn't about to acknowledge its existence.

West did not seem to care; he took a step closer and the small, dark space became smaller. Darker. More dangerous. "Chase is not the only one who knows things, love."

The words were low and graveled, and she hesitated, the pleasure of their sound unfamiliar and unsettling. Finally, she remembered herself. "We do not take ladies."

His lips curved and she was reminded of the lion they'd discussed the previous evening. "Come now, you can lie to the rest of London, but don't think to lie to me. You will offer the lady membership. She will trade proof of her husband's deeds for it. And you'll get me my information."

She collected herself. "Chase will not be happy."

He leaned in, whispered low at her ear, sending a thrill through her. "Tell Chase I do not care where his women play." He pulled back, meeting her eyes. "I want the information the lady provides."

She resisted him, curious. Why the earl? Why now? "What do you know?"

He leaned in. "I know he steals from the exchequer."

She met his gaze. "He, and every councilor to every monarch since William the Conqueror."

"Not to aid the Ottoman Empire in their war."

Her gaze went wide. She lowered her voice. "Treason?"

"We'll see."

"Why do I think you already do see?"

His gaze snapped to hers. "Because I see a great deal."

And suddenly, it seemed that they were having a different conversation altogether. "Who is to say the lady will offer the proof?"

"She'll offer," he said. "He's a beast of a husband. She'll want to share what she knows."

"And you do nothing to help her?"

"This will help her," he said.

"What makes you think she knows anything?"

He inclined his head. "Therein lies the wager I make."

"You think luck is on your side?"

He smiled, all wolf. "Luck has been on my side for eleven years; I have no reason to believe it has changed."

"That is a very specific number."

A shadow crossed his face, there, then gone. "I shall pay handsomely for his information."

He, too, had secrets. The thought comforted her. She resisted the urge to ask about them, instead forcing a smile. "How handsomely?" She brazened on. "Tit for tat, Mr. West."

He watched her for a moment, and the air in the little space seemed to shift. "What would you like, Anna?"

Had she imagined the strange emphasis on the false name? She ignored it. "It is not me you must pay," she said, putting on her best flirt, leaning back against the wall of the alcove, pressing her breasts up and looking up at him through her darkened lashes. "You've already given me so much. Saving me from Pottle." She offered her best moue. "What a lucky girl am I."

His gaze moved to her lips, as expected, and then dropped several inches to the line of her dress. "What is on the chain?"

She did not reach for the silver pendant that lay beneath the edge of the dress, heavy between her breasts, hiding the key that opened the doors to Chase's rooms and the passage to the upper floors of the club, where Caroline slept. Instead, she smiled. "My secrets."

One side of his mouth lifted at the words. "Legion, no doubt."

She reached for him then, letting her fingers trail along his coat sleeve. "How can I thank you, Mr. West? For being such a tremendous champion?"

He leaned in, and she thought of that feather, the one he'd stolen from her hair. She wondered if it was there, in that interior pocket. Wondered what he would do if she reached into his jacket and slid her hand along his warm chest, searching for it.

He interrupted her thoughts. "I met a woman last night."

Her breath caught, and she sent up a little prayer hoping that he had not noticed. "Should I be jealous?" she teased.

"Perhaps," he said. "Georgiana Pearson seems quite the innocent. All white silk and fear."

"Georgiana Pearson?" She feigned surprise at the name, straightening off the wall as he nodded. "I assure you, the girl is not afraid."

He stepped toward her, pushing her back. Closing her in. "You're wrong. She's terrified."

She forced a laugh. "The girl is sister to a duke with a dowry large enough to purchase a small country. Of what is she afraid?"

"Of everything," he said, all casualness. "Of Society. Of its judgment. Of her future."

"She may not care for those things, but she is certainly not afraid of them. You've misjudged her."

"And how do you know anything about her?"

She was caught. He was too nimble with words, with questions. And too distracting with his long, lean form and his beautiful broad shoulders that blocked out the light, making her nervous and eager all at once. "I don't. Only what I read in the papers." She paused. "There was a telling cartoon a month or so back."

The barb hit true. She heard it in the way his breath caught. Felt it in the way he stiffened, nearly imperceptibly, before he lifted a hand, set it to the wall beside her head. Leaned in. "I did misjudge her. There's no doubt of that," he said. "She is not the simpering girl I expected her to be."

He leaned closer, his lips by her ear, the nearness of him setting her off balance. Making her want to push him away and grab hold of him all at once. "I offered the girl my help."

Relief flooded through her. "I don't know why you think I'm interested in what you do with the girl."

The moment the words were out, she cursed herself, images of precisely what he might do with her flooding her thoughts.

He laughed, low and dark. "I assure you, what I do with the girl will be well worth watching." He met her gaze, and she resisted the urge to back away. Anna did not back away from men, even when she wished to. But for some reason, few men made her as uncomfortable as this one, with his beautiful, knowing gaze that seemed to see right into her.

She was taller than most women, and wearing heeled slippers that added several inches to her height, but still she was forced to look up at him, to take in his strong, square jaw, his equine nose, the fall of blond locks across his brow.

He had to be the handsomest man in Britain. And the cleverest.

Which made him incredibly dangerous.

He shifted, and she wondered if he was as uncomfortable as she was.

"You should not be alone with me."

"It is not the first time we have been alone." They'd been alone the night before. On that balcony. When he'd tempted her just the same.

One of his brows rose. "Yes, it is."

Damn. She'd been Georgiana on the balcony. Another woman. Another time. She quickly recovered from the mistake, pouting and pretending to think. She let her lips curve seductively. "Perhaps I am merely dreaming it."

His gaze narrowed. "Perhaps," he said, the word dark and liquid. "It's a wonder that Chase allows it."

"I do not belong to Chase."

"Of course you do." He paused. "We all do, in a sense."

"Not you," she said. He was the only person who was not beholden to her. This man, whose secrets were as well kept as her own.

"Chase and I need each other to survive," he said, "just as it seems you need him."

She inclined her head. "We are all in this boat together."

He narrowed his gaze on her. "You and I are in the boat," he said. "Chase may have built it and set it on its course. But it is our boat." The words were punctuated by the sound of his wool coat sleeve shifting. He lifted his hand and brushed a curl back from her neck, sending a thrill through her. "Perhaps we should sail away. How do you think he would like that?"

She caught her breath. In all the time that they had worked together—in all the time they'd spent passing messages back and forth from the mysterious, nonexistent Chase—he'd never touched her in any way that could be considered remotely sexual. But that was about to change.

She shouldn't allow it. She'd never allowed it before. Not with anyone.

Not since—

But she'd wondered about it. She'd wanted it.

And if she admitted it, she'd wanted it from this man, handsome as sin and twice as brilliant.

This man, who was offering it to her.

"He wouldn't like it," she whispered.

"No, he wouldn't." His fingertips a lick of heat following their path as they stroked along her jaw, down the edge of her neck to where her shoulder gave way to the hollow of her throat. "How did I fail to see it before?"

The words echoed the caress, soft and tempting, and her breath caught there, beneath his fingers, as they retraced their path up the column of her neck and tilted her face to his. She watched his beautiful mouth as he spoke. "How did I not notice it? The scent of you? The curve of your lips? The line of your neck?" He paused, and leaned in close, his mouth a hairsbreadth from hers. "How many years have I watched you?"

Good Lord, he was going to kiss her.

She wanted him to kiss her.

"If I were him," he whispered, so close, so quiet that she fairly ached in anticipation, "I would not be happy at all."

If he were whom? The question formed and dissipated in an instant, like opium smoke, taking thought with it. He was drugging her with words and looks and touch.

This was why she stayed clear of men.

But just once, just this time, she wanted it.

"If I were him," he continued, his thumb stroking high across her cheek as he cupped her head and brought her to him. "I wouldn't let you go. I would keep you. My lady."

She froze at the words, fear and panic threading through her. She looked up at him, finding his clear, intelligent gaze. "You know."

"I know," he said. "But what I do not understand is why?"

He did not know everything. He did not understand the life that she had chosen was not Anna, but Chase. Not the lightskirt, but the king.

She told the truth. "Power."

His gaze narrowed. "Over whom?"

"Over everyone," she said, simply. "I own my life. Not them. They think me a whore, why not play one?"

"Under their noses."

She smiled. "They see only what they wish to. It's a beautiful thing."

"I saw you."

She shook her head. "Not for years. You thought I was Anna, too."

"You could own your life beyond these walls," he argued. "You do not have to play this part."

"But I like this part. Here, I am free. It is Georgiana who must scrape and bow and beg for acceptance. Here, I take what I want. Here, I am beholden to none."

"None but your master."

Except she was the master. She did not reply.

He misread the silence. "That's why you seek a husband. What happened?" he asked. "Has Chase tossed you aside?"

She pulled away from him, needing the distance between them to return her sanity. To take her next steps. To craft her careful lies. "He hasn't tossed me aside."

His brows snapped together. "He cannot expect your husband to share you."

The words stung, even as they should not. She'd lived all of this life in the shadows of The Fallen Angel masquerading as a whore. She'd convinced hundreds of London's aristocrats that she was an expert in pleasure. That she'd sold herself to their most powerful leader. She dressed the part, with heaving bosom and painted face. She'd taught herself to move, to act, to be the part.

And somehow, when this man acknowledged the reputation she had worked so hard to cultivate, the façade she had built with care and conviction, she hated it. Perhaps it was because he knew more of her truth than most, and still, he believed the lies.

Or perhaps it was because he made her wish she did not have the lies to tell.

No. She was falling victim to the hero in him, to the way he'd leapt to her aid only minutes earlier.

She caught her breath at the thought.

Only once he knew the truth. Her other identity. Her other life.

Anger flared alongside disappointment and something akin to shame. "You wouldn't have saved me."

It took him a moment to follow the change in topic. "I—"

"Don't lie to me," she said, one hand flying up as if to stop the words on his lips. "Don't insult me."

"I came after Pottle," he said, raising his own hand, brandishing knuckles that would be sore in the morning. "I did save you."

"Because you knew the truth of my birth. If I'd been Anna alone . . . just a woman with a centuries-old profession. Just a painted whore—"

He stopped her. "Don't speak like that."

"Oh," she scoffed. "Do I offend?"

He ran his bruised hand through blond locks. "Christ, Georgiana."

"Don't call me that."

He laughed, the sound humorless. "What should I call you? Anna? A false name to go with your false hair and your false face and your false . . ." He trailed off, one hand indicating her bodice, padded and cinched to make her ordinary bosom look extraordinary.

"I am not certain that you should call me anything at this point," she said, and she meant it.

"It is too late for that. We are together in this. Bound by word and greed."

"I think you mean deed."

"I know precisely what I mean."

They faced each other in the dim light, and Georgiana could sense his anger and frustration, matched by her own. How strange was this moment? Born of his protection of one half of her because of the existence of the other?

It was mad. A wicked web that could not be unwoven.

At least, not without ruining everything for which she'd worked.

He seemed to understand her thoughts. "I would have stepped in," he insisted. "I would have done the same."

She shook her head. "I wish I could believe you."

He took her shoulders. Met her gaze, serious in the dim light. "You should. I would have stepped in."

Her heart pounded. "Why?"

He could have said a dozen things. But she did not expect: "Because I need you."

There was a little twinge of sadness at the words, so cool and collected. He needed her, but not in the way men needed women—impassioned and desperate. Not that she should care.

"Need me for what?"

"I want Lady Tremley to receive invitation to the ladies' side of the club. I want the information she offers for entry. And for that information, you get your payment."

She should have been grateful for the change of topic. For the movement to safer ground. She wasn't. She heard the frustration in her words when she said, "You mean Chase gets his payment."

He smiled. "No, I mean you."

Her eyes went wide. "Me."

"I get my information, you get Viscount Langley. My papers, at your disposal. Or, at Georgiana's disposal, at least."

Tit for tat.

Understanding flooded through her—understanding and respect for this man who so easily manipulated every situation to suit himself. Her match in power and prestige.

"Or what?"

He raised a brow. "Don't make me say it."

She lifted her chin. "I think I shall."

He did not waver. "Or I shall tell the world your secrets."

She narrowed her gaze on him. "Chase may not care."

"Then you shall have to make him care." He started to push past her and she hated the movement. Hated that he was leaving her. She wished he would stay, this man who seemed to see so much. "You need my power," he said quietly. "Your daughter needs it."

She winced at the reference to Caroline here, in this place, in this conversation, as he continued, "You think they won't see it?" he asked. "You think they won't notice the way I did? That your two masks bear a striking resemblance to each other?"

"They haven't before."

"You weren't news before."

She met his gaze and told him the only thing she knew was certain. "People see what they wish to see."

He did not disagree. "Why risk it?"

"I wish I did not have to." Truth.

"Why now?" The questions came fast.

"One cannot live a lifetime in my profession." Either of them.

He didn't like that. She could see it in his eyes. "So, how will it work? Instead of giving you a house in the country and enough money to last a lifetime, Chase has given you a dowry? It's not your brother's money, is it?" he asked, the words full of understanding.

Ironic, that, as he did not understand at all.

I give it to myself.

He laughed, and the sound lacked humor. "He cannot give you what I can give you, though. He would never reveal himself with such public deeds. You need me to give you the reputation. You need me to land you Langley."

"Something for which you appear to be charging a handsome fee," she said.

"I would have done it for free, you know." There was disappointment in his words.

"If only I'd been the little lost girl you thought I was hours ago?"

"I never thought you lost. I thought you strong as steel."

"And now?"

He lifted a shoulder. Dropped it. "Now, I see you are a businesswoman. I will help you for payment. And you are lucky for that, or else I'd be done with the lot of you. I do not typically get into bed with liars."

She gave him her most coquettish smile, desperate to shield the way his words stung. "No one's invited you into bed."

She did not expect the air to shift, nor did she expect him to return to her, pressing her back against the wall, hunting her. She'd never in her life felt as she did now, her power stripped from her along with her lies. Most of her lies.

All but the biggest one.

His hands pressed against the mahogany on either side of her head, his arms caging her. "You've invited me into your bed every time you've looked at me for years."

She hesitated, not knowing what to say. How to proceed with this man who was so different than he'd ever been. "You're wrong."

"No," he said. "I'm right. And to be honest, I've wanted to accept. Every . . . single . . . time."

He was so close, so warm, so devastatingly powerful that for the first time in her life, she understood why women swooned in men's arms. "What has changed?" she said, hearing the breathlessness in her tone, brazening through. "A taste for innocents?"

"We both know better."

She ignored the sting of the reply. The way they made her wish she did not masquerade as a whore. The way they made her wish he knew the truth. Instead, she soldiered on. "Then nothing has changed."

"Of course it has."

Now she was Georgiana.

"You like the idea of a ruined aristocrat," she said, blood pounding in her ears. "What did you call me? Terrified? What is it . . . you think you can save me every day? Every night?"

He hesitated. "I think you want saving."

"I can save myself."

He smiled then, all wolf. "Not from everything. That's why you need me."

She had more power than he could ever imagine. More power than he could ever know. When she lifted her chin and spoke, it was to prove it. "I don't need you."

He found her gaze, close and hot. "Who will save you from them then? Who will save you from Chase?"

She did not look away. Did not wish to. "I am in no danger from Chase."

His hand was on her again, cupping her jaw, tilting her head back. "Tell me the truth," he commanded, refusing to let her hide. "Can you leave him? Will he allow you to walk away? To start a new life?"

If only the truth were that simple.

He saw the hesitation. Closed the distance between them and hovered a breath away from her. "Tell me."

How would it feel to lean into him? To let him help? To bring him into her inner sanctum and tell him everything?

"You can help by getting me married."

"You don't want marriage. Not to Langley, at least."

"I don't want marriage at all, but that's irrelevant. I need it."

He considered her words, and she thought that he might fight her. Might refuse. Not that he should care. Not that any of it should matter.

After a long moment, he closed in on her, one hand moving from the wall to the side of her face, caressing her jaw, lifting her chin. His brown eyes searched hers, and when he spoke, it was in a low, dark whisper, demanding honesty. "Do you belong to him?"

She should say yes. It would be safer. It would keep West at arm's length if he thought for one moment that Chase might fight him for her. He needed Chase and all the information garnered and protected by The Fallen Angel.

She should say yes. But in this moment, with this man, she wanted to tell the truth. Just once. Just to know what it was like to do so. And so she did. "No," she whispered. "I belong to myself."

And then his lips were on hers, and everything changed.

Chapter 6

... And yet, there is a mystery to our Lady G—. One that forces even the staunchest of aristocrats to raise her lorgnette and consider the girl across the room. Is it possible that we have heaped her with false disdain all these years? Only the Season will tell ...

... Young ladies of London, heed our call! By all accounts, Lord L— is on the hunt for a wife. His list of desired attributes no doubt includes beauty, good humor, and proficiency with a string instrument. Alas, those who are not exceedingly wealthy need not apply ...

Pearls & Pelisses Ladies Magazine, April 1833

He didn't care that she was lying.

Didn't care that she had been protected for years by the most powerful, secretive man in London. Didn't care that a man with that kind of money would not take kindly to anyone touching that which was his.

He didn't care that she was nothing she seemed—that she was somehow neither whore, nor ruined aristocrat, nor innocent.

All he cared was that she was pressed against him in this empty space, all long limbs and soft skin, and, for a fleeting moment, she was his.

The kiss was sin and innocence, like the lady herself—at once all experience and none at all. Her hand came to the nape of his neck, fingers threading into his hair with remarkable purpose while she gasped against his lips as though she'd never been kissed.

Christ.

It was no wonder she was London's most coveted companion. She was red silk and white lace. Two tempting, unbearable sides of one coin. And for this moment, she belonged to him.

But first . . .

He pulled away barely, giving her a scant inch to breathe as he whispered, "I would have stepped in. Either way."

He hadn't liked her implication that he'd only pummeled Pottle because she was from an aristocratic family. It had grated to think that she would imagine that he'd have left any woman to be mistreated so roundly. But more importantly, it sickened him to think that she believed he'd have left *her* if circumstances had been different.

He didn't know why it was important to him that she believe him. That she believe he was the kind of man who would fight for a woman. Any woman. *Her.* But it was important. "I would have stepped in," he repeated.

Her fingers danced at the nape of his neck, playing with the curls there and making him want her with their innocent, teasing promise. "I know," she whispered.

He captured the words with his mouth, stealing her open lips and taking the kiss deeper. Longer. More.

Information or no, arrangement or no, double identity or no, this woman was irresistible. He would never betray her secrets. Not now that he knew she was so much more than she seemed.

He wanted her without quarter.

He caught her by the waist, pulling her closer, pressing one leg into hers, tangling in her skirts, in her scent, in her seduction. And she seduced him just as he did her. He'd never felt so well matched in his life.

She leaned into the kiss, taking as he took, reveling as he reveled. And the sounds she made—the little sighs and gasps and pants—she was glorious.

He lifted her in his arms and turned her, walking her to the opposite wall of the alcove as his lips trailed across her cheek and captured the lobe of one ear. "You've wanted this for years," he whispered, teeth worrying the soft flesh as her fingers spread across his shoulders.

"No," she said. And in the lie, he heard such truth.

He grinned against the skin of her neck, running his teeth down the glorious column. "You think I haven't seen you? Haven't felt you watching?"

She pulled back from his caress. "If you've noticed, why haven't you come for me?"

He watched her for a long moment, staring into those eyes the color of liquid gold. "I'm coming for you now," he said as he leaned in and bit her lower lip, pulling her toward him, reveling in the low, lush laugh that erupted from her.

He chased the sound down the column of her neck to the place where it vibrated in her throat, worrying the spot with his teeth. She sighed at the sensation and he wanted to roar his satisfaction. His pleasure. Her lips curved, and he ached for them. Reached for them.

She pulled back. "You didn't want me until now. Until you discovered I'm her, too."

He stilled at the words. "Her."

"Georgiana."

The way she spoke of herself in the third person called to him. He turned her to the light, to see her. "Georgiana is other?" She closed her eyes briefly, considering her answer, and he changed the question. "You must think on the answer?"

"Mustn't we all?" she asked, the words soft and thoughtful. "Aren't we all two people? Three? A dozen? Different with family and friends and lovers and strangers and children? Different with men? With women?"

"It's not the same," he insisted. "I don't play at being two people."

"It is not play," she replied. "I do not revel in the game of it."

"Of course you do," he said, and she was again struck by how well he saw what few others did. "You adore it. I've seen you here, holding court over the floor of the club, as though you own it. Beautiful. Perfectly turned out . . ." He let his fingers trail over the edge of her gown, loving the way her breasts swelled as she inhaled at the touch. " . . . and that laugh, rich and welcome.

"I've seen you entertain and entice, hang on the arm of the Angel's wealthiest patrons while somehow giving those down on their luck the idea that they might one day bask in the glow of your attention."

She lifted her chin, acting out his words. "You have my attention now, sir."

"Don't. Not with me. Why do it, if not for the pleasure of the masque?"

Something flashed in her gaze at the question, there, then gone. "Survival."

Duncan had lied enough in his life to recognize the truth in another. It was what made him such a tremendous newspaperman. "What are you afraid of?"

She laughed at that, but the sound lacked humor. "Spoken like a man with no fear of ruin."

If she only knew the fear he had in the dead of night. The way he woke every morning, afraid that today would be the day of his ruin. He pushed the thoughts aside. "Then why do it?" he asked, "Why assume the role of Anna? Why not simply live life as Georgiana? Isn't Anna the role that threatens to destroy you thoroughly?"

She shook her head. "You don't understand."

"I don't. You worry that you cannot marry a high enough title to render your daughter's reputation clean, and still you don your wicked silks and paint your face and run the light-skirt brigade at London's most renowned casino."

"You think it idiocy."

"I think it reckless."

"You think I am selfish."

"No." He was not a fool.

"What then?"

He did not hesitate. "I think there is no profession in the wide world that a woman would be less likely to choose than yours."

She smiled at that, and he was surprised at the honesty in the expression, as though she knew something that he did not know. And perhaps she did. "There, Mr. West," she said, all feminine wile, "you are wrong."

"So what is it?" he asked, now desperate for the answer. "Why do it? Is it his power? You like being the exclusive property of the elusive Chase, who strikes fear into the hearts of men Britain-wide?"

"Chase is part of it, certainly."

He hated the truth in the words. Couldn't stop himself from saying, "He is that good of a lover, is he?"

She was quiet for a moment, and he cursed himself for the question. Even more so when she said, "What if I told you that my relationship with Chase had nothing to do with sex?"

Sex. The word curved over her tongue and lips, wrapping around them in the dark alcove, all temptation and promise. God, he wanted to believe her—he hated the image of foreign hands on her, of lips stroking over her most private, precious of places. And for some reason he hated the thought even more without a clear image of the man who claimed her.

"I wouldn't believe you."

"Why not?"

"Because any man who has exclusive access to you would not be able to go a day without touching you."

He shocked her. He saw the expression pass, there, then gone so quickly that another, lesser man would not have noticed. Because another man would have been so enthralled with the expression that replaced it—her beautiful mouth curving in utter satisfaction—that he wouldn't have cared to notice the first.

But it was the combination of the two—evidence of somehow innocence and vice—that threaded straight to West's core, spreading desire through him.

He worked to steady his breath when she took a step closer. "Are you saying you would like exclusive access to me?" It was Anna who spoke, the skilled prostitute, all wickedness and vice.

And so he returned it in kind. "I'm a man, am I not?"

Her hands came to his shoulders, running smoothly down the lapels of his coat and inside, over his linen shirt. "Does Chase strike fear into your heart?" she asked quietly, her hand settling over the organ in question. "Is that quaking I feel?"

His heart pounded for this maddening, mysterious creature. He'd never wanted anyone like he wanted her. Even as he knew she was a terrible wager, worse than all the ones he had made on the floor of the casino beyond. Out there, he risked only money.

Here, he risked something much more serious.

"Don't tempt me," he whispered in the darkness, pulling her hands from him.

"Or what?" The question was a lick of fire.

"Or you shall get that for which you ask."

He felt the curve of her smile at his cheek. " 'Tis a lovely promise."

He turned his head and caught her lips once more, lifting her against him, adoring the way her arms came around his neck and she pressed herself to him, giving in to him. Allowing him the lead.

He pressed her to the wall, fitting himself between her thighs, cursing her diaphanous silk skirts. He wanted her closer. Open. Hot. Wet.

His.

She signaled her pleasure with a little, lovely sound, and he deepened the kiss, stroking long and soft until she followed his movements with her own. His hand came along her side in a long caress, his thumb finding the swell of her breast at the edge of her gown. Unable to resist the temptation, he slipped his fingers beneath the silk and lifted her breast from its padded confines, running the edge of his thumb over the straining tip.

He lifted his mouth from hers. "I would give anything for more light."

She arched against the caress. "Why?"

"I want to see the color of this gorgeous thing. I want to watch it strain for me." She bit her lip at the words. "Does it ache?"

There was a long moment of silence before she replied, the truth coming on a whisper. "Yes."

He heard something there, in the single, stunning word. Something like embarrassment. There was no room for that here. "Don't be ashamed of what you like." He punctuated the words with a gentle pinch.

"I like that," she said, the words forced from her.

"As do I," he said, his lips coming to the high swell of her breast. "As do I," he repeated just before he let his tongue slide around the straining tip.

She tasted as good as she smelled.

"Anna?"

They both froze, remembering where they were.

He lifted his head. Met her wide eyes.

"Shit." She whispered, and he did not have time to be surprised by the curse. After all, she'd taken the words right from his lips. "It's Temple."

Regret flared. And irritation. He let her down, setting her feet on the ground.

"Don't come in!" Georgiana cried, Anna disappeared.

"A moment, Temple," he said at the same time, unable to tear his gaze from the pretty pale globe of her breast.

"Too late," Temple said, closer than before.

Duncan turned to protect her from view, facing the Duke of

Lamont with a calm he did not feel. Later, he would wonder at the squeak that escaped Georgiana's lips, as though she'd never been found in such a situation before. Perhaps it was Temple who caused her embarrassment, but whatever it was, she was furious. "Get out!"

"There was some concern that you'd been manhandled," Temple said calmly. "I see it was not without merit."

"I'm fine," she said. "As you can see."

Temple met his gaze. "West," he said, "You certainly have made yourself comfortable."

Duncan lifted one shoulder. Let it drop. "It's my club."

"Not your woman, though." Duncan had no doubt that Chase would hear of this before the night was through.

"Not yours, either," Georgiana retorted.

Temple looked to her, and Duncan moved to block the other man's view. "Give the lady some privacy."

The Duke of Lamont's eyes widened for a moment. "Shall I turn around?"

"That would suit me well, as I wouldn't like to have to call you out."

"Afraid you'd lose?" The duke was London's winningest bare-knuckle boxer.

"Afraid I'd win," Duncan said. "I'd like to continue to call you a friend when this unfortunate event is through."

Temple nodded once and turned his back on them. "Put away your—bits—Anna."

She exhaled in pure exasperation. "You know, you could take your leave if you are embarrassed, Temple."

"No chance," the duke said, "I'm offering my protection."

"She doesn't need it." And damn it, if she did need it, Duncan could give it to her.

Not that he wanted to.

Liar.

Temple turned just enough to meet Duncan's gaze. "No?"

"No," he said.

"No," she said at the same time, yanking up her bodice,

sending a thread of disappointment through Duncan. "You may turn around."

"I'm not offering it to you," the duke said, turning and lifting his chin in Duncan's direction. "I'm offering it to him."

West didn't care for the words. "I am well able to protect myself in this situation."

"You haven't the faintest idea what this situation is," the duke said. Duncan did not like the ominous tone in the words.

"Get out!" Georgiana fairly yelled.

Surprisingly, Temple did as he was bid.

They stood in silence for a long moment, Duncan trying to convince himself that he was grateful for Temple's interruption. Grateful for the fact that the evening had not gone any further.

The woman was too tempting and altogether too dangerous, and it would be best if he stayed away from her. He turned to bid her farewell. "My lady."

"Don't call me that here," she said.

"I shall call you that wherever I like. It is your due, is it not?"

"That's not why you use it."

It wasn't. But he did not admit it. Instead, he said, "Do we have an agreement?"

It took her a moment to follow, and he resisted the pleasure that came at the knowledge that he unsettled her as much as she did him.

"I shall take it to Chase." Her beautiful amber eyes met his. "This can never happen again."

He raised a brow. "There's one way to ensure it doesn't." Her gaze turned questioning. "Get me my information. And I'll get you married."

He turned and left the room. And the club.

Vowing to resist the woman.

Chapter 7

. . . Lady G— once more, dear readers! Beautifully
turned out at the opera in robin's egg blue. And there
has never been a more beautiful chick to emerge from
such a casing. The aristocracy is no doubt thrilled by
the lady's return and very eager to witness her rise . . .

. . . With the three owners' impressive marriages in the
last twelve months, we recommend that women on the
hunt limit their search to members of a certain casino.
We are coming to believe that there is something remarkable in its water supply . . .

The gossip pages of *The News of London*,
April 24, 1833

"Chase is halfway to sleeping with Duncan West," Bourne
said, taking his seat at the owners' table, tumbler of scotch
dangling from his fingers.

She'd done her best to avoid her partners since the embar-
rassing incident involving West and Temple two days earlier.
In fact, she'd almost skipped the faro game that stood for the

owners of the Angel every Saturday evening. She'd almost taken to her rooms in frustration and embarrassment.

But she was not a coward, and her partners would have happily called her one if she'd missed the card game.

Nevertheless, it did not mean that she was required to tolerate their questioning.

She pretended Bourne had not spoken, and leaned forward to collect her cards from the table, used only for this game. She, Temple, and Cross played while Bourne occupied the fourth chair with his scotch. The Marquess of Bourne had lost everything in a game of cards on the day he'd turned eighteen, and had not played since.

Unfortunately, he attended the games nonetheless, complete with his foolish grin. He did not seem to care that she had not replied to his initial overture. Instead, he continued, "Though it sounds to me that there would not have been much sleeping involved."

"I should never have saved your asses all those years ago," she said.

Six years earlier, Temple and Bourne had been running dice games on the edge of Seven Dials, and they'd made more than a few enemies. On the night Georgiana had decided to offer them the chance to enter into partnership with her, she'd saved them, quite luckily, from a group of ruffians who would have taken their money and left them for dead.

"Probably," he said happily as he leaned back in his chair and crossed his arms over his chest. "But lucky for all of us, you didn't."

She scowled at him. "It is not too late to have you handled."

"As you are occupied with handling West, I cannot imagine you would have the time for Bourne," Cross said as he took the round.

She tossed her cards to the table, turning wide eyes on him. "You, as well?"

He smiled, there, then gone. "I'm afraid so."

"Traitor." She looked to Temple. "And you? Do you have insults to add to the pile?"

Temple shook his head as he shuffled the cards, the waxed paper flying through his fingers before he dealt the cards expertly around the table. "I want nothing to do with this. In fact, if my memory of the event were wiped clean, I would not be unhappy about it." He closed his eyes. "Like seeing one's sister in the nude."

"I was not nude!" she protested.

"It was close enough."

"Was it?" Bourne asked, his curiosity piqued.

"It was nowhere near close enough," she insisted.

"But you would have liked for it to have been?"

Yes. No. *Perhaps.* Georgiana pushed the unwelcome response aside. "Don't be ridiculous."

Bourne turned to Temple. "Do you think we should tell her that she didn't answer the question?"

She looked down at her cards, cheeks hot. "I hate you."

"Which one of us?" Temple asked, playing a card.

"All of you."

"It's a pity, as we are your only friends," Bourne said.

It was true. "And asses every one of you."

"They say you can tell a man by his friends," he replied.

"It is a good thing I am a woman," she said, discarding.

"Which Temple can now confirm." Bourne paused. "Why do you think none of us have ever had cause to see for ourselves before now?"

Death was too kind for Bourne. He deserved some kind of torture. She glared at him, considering any number of medieval devices. Temple laughed. "We've already established that she's more sister than seductress. None of us would consider it."

"I considered it," Bourne said, refilling his drink. "Once or twice."

The entire table looked to him.

"You did?" Cross asked, voicing all their shock.

"We can't all be as saintly as you are, Cross," Bourne replied. "I thought better of it."

She raised a blond brow. "By 'thought better of it,' I assume you mean that you realized I wouldn't have had you if you were the last man in London?"

"You wound me." He placed a hand over his heart. "Truly."

In the six years since the owners of The Fallen Angel had come together with the singular purpose of proving themselves more powerful than the aristocracy, there had been little time and even less interest for anything that detracted from such a goal. Truly, it had only been in the last year, once the club was everything they had planned it to be, that Bourne, Cross, and Temple had made time for love.

Or, rather, that love had ensnared them.

She played another card. "God protect Lady Bourne, as she surely has her work cut out for her. I feel I should apologize to her for my hand in your match."

Georgiana had been instrumental in matching each of her partners with their wives—none more so than Bourne's. Lady Penelope Marbury had once been betrothed to Georgiana's brother, but the match was imperfect, and Georgiana had used her own scandal to extract the Duke of Leighton from his impending marriage, leaving Lady Penelope a spinster for nearly a decade . . . until Bourne desired her for himself.

Georgiana had been only too happy to repay her debt to the lady.

Temple laughed. "You don't regret a moment of your meddling."

She'd played a similar hand in Temple's match to Miss Mara Lowe, now Duchess of Lamont. And in Cross's match to Lady Penelope's sister, Lady Philippa, now Countess Harlow.

Bourne grinned, all wolf. "Nor should she regret it. I ensure my lady is quite happy with her match."

She groaned. "Please. Say no more."

"Here is something," Cross interjected, and Georgiana was grateful for the impending change of topic.

There were a dozen things he could have said. A hundred. The four present ran a casino. They traded in secrets of the richest and most powerful people in Britain. The building they were in boasted a remarkable collection of art. Cross's wife cultivated beautiful roses. And yet, he did not speak of any of those things. Instead, he said, "West is not a bad choice."

She turned surprised eyes on him. "Not a bad choice for what?"

"Not what," he corrected. "Whom. For you."

She wished there was a window somewhere nearby. Something through which she could leap. She wondered if she could ignore the statement. She looked to Bourne and Temple, hoping they might find the statement as preposterous as she did.

They didn't.

"You know, he's not wrong," Bourne said.

Temple spread his massive legs wide. "There's no one else who matches her in power."

"Except us," Bourne said.

"Well, of course," Temple said. "But we're spoken for."

"He hasn't a title," she said.

Temple's brows rose. "That's the only reason you don't consider him a reasonable choice?"

Dammit. That's not what she'd meant at all. "No," she said. "But it would help if the rest of you remembered that I'm in need of a title. And I've selected it. Langley will not meddle in my affairs."

Cross laughed. "You sound like a villain in a romantic novel."

She rather felt like one with the direction in which this conversation was moving.

As though she had not spoken, Bourne added, "West is talented, rich and Penelope seems to think he's handsome. Not that I have any idea why." He grumbled the last.

"Pippa feels the same way," Cross said. "She says it is an empirical fact. Thought I myself have never trusted grown men with hair that color."

"You realize you haven't a leg to stand on when it comes to hair color," Temple said.

Cross ran a self-conscious hand through his ginger locks. "Irrelevant. It's not me Chase thinks is handsome."

"I am sitting right here, you know," she said.

They did not seem to care.

"He's a brilliant businessman and rich as a king," Bourne added. "And if I were a betting man, I'd lay money on him eventually holding a seat in the House of Commons."

"You are not a betting man, though," Georgiana pointed out. As though it would stop him.

"He doesn't have to be. I'll put money on it," Cross said, "I'll happily mark it in the book."

The betting book. The Fallen Angel's betting book was legendary—an enormous leather-bound volume which held the catalogue of all wagers made on the main floor of the club. Members could record any wager—no matter how trivial—in the book, and the Angel bore witness, taking a percentage of the bets to make certain the parties were held to whatever bizarre stakes were established.

"You don't wager in the book," Georgiana said.

He met her gaze. "I shall make an exception."

"For West running for Minister of Parliament?" Temple asked.

"I don't care about that at all," Cross said, throwing a card down. "I've one hundred pounds that says that West is the man who breaks Chase of her curse."

She narrowed her gaze on the ginger-haired genius, recognizing the words. She'd made the same wager an age ago. She'd won.

"You shan't have my luck," she said.

He smirked. "Care to wager on it?"

She shrugged one shoulder. "I shall happily take your money."

"Mistake," Bourne said. "He's clearly after you. It's a good bet."

"Well, he's after Anna, at least," Temple corrected.

"It's only a matter of time before he puts two and two together and discovers that Anna *is* Georgiana. Especially now that he's . . ." Bourne waved a hand in her direction. "Sampled the wares, so to speak."

She'd had enough. "First of all, there was no *sampling* of *anything*. It was a kiss. And second of all, he already knows that Anna and Georgiana are one and the same."

The other three went silent.

She added, "Well. Miracle of miracles, I've rendered the three of you silent. The rest of London would be shocked beyond reason to discover that the owners of The Fallen Angel were nothing more than chattering magpies."

"He knows?" Cross was the first to talk.

"He does," she said.

"Christ," Bourne said. "How?"

"Does it matter?"

"It does if others know, too."

"No one else knows," she said. "No one else has looked too long at Anna's face. They're too interested in her other assets."

"But West has looked at her face. And Georgiana's. And realized the truth." This, from Temple.

"Yes." The word made her feel guilty. As though she could have changed the situation. And perhaps she could have.

"You should never have brought him into this," Bourne said. "He's too quick. Of course he discovered you are both women. He was bound to. He likely knew the moment he agreed to help you land Langley."

She did not reply.

"But he doesn't know about Chase?" Cross asked.

She stood from the table, moving to the stained glass window that covered a full wall of the room, massive and menacing, depicting the fall of Lucifer. Hundreds of pieces of colored glass meticulously assembled to reveal the enormous angel—four times the size of the average man—as he tumbled from Heaven. From the casino floor, far below, it appeared that he was cast from light into darkness, from perfection into sin.

Destroyed and, in destruction, renewed. A king in his own right, with power unrivaled by all but one. Georgiana sighed, suddenly keenly aware of how powerless second-most-powerful could be.

"No," she said. "And he won't know who Chase is."

That, she could promise.

"Even if he did," Temple said. "He's to be trusted."

Georgiana had spent years working with the worst of humanity—learning them, judging them. She knew good men and bad. A day ago, she would have said that Temple was right. That West was to be trusted.

But that was before he'd kissed her.

Before she'd been drawn to him as she'd been drawn to another, long ago. One whom she'd trusted with her heart. With her hope. With her future.

One who had betrayed her without hesitation, and taken everything she'd given, ensuring that she would never be able to give it to another.

Ensuring that she would never want to.

Now, she did not trust her instincts around West. Which meant she had to rely on a different set of skills. "How do we know that?" she asked Temple, setting her cards on the table, no longer interested in the game. "That he is to be trusted?"

Temple shrugged one massive shoulder. "We've trusted him for years. He's never betrayed us. You're paying him handsomely with Tremley's file . . . there's no reason to believe that he'll do anything but help. As always."

"Unless he discovers Chase," Cross said. "Now that she's under his skin, he'll be livid if he feels he's been duped."

Bourne nodded. "There's no 'feels' about it. He *has* been duped."

"I don't owe him anything," she said. The three men cut her identical looks. "What is it?"

"He knows you're not simply Anna," Cross said.

"And he's not able to keep his hands off you," Temple said. "If he finds that you're also Chase . . ."

She did not like the words, or the implication that West was more connected to her life than she imagined. Nor did she like the way that implication made her feel—as though she couldn't quite take a deep breath. She'd felt this way before, and she did not fancy feeling it again.

She channeled Chase, remembering the shadow that had crossed his face as he'd discussed the Earl of Tremley. *Eleven years.* Remembering the threat he'd voiced—the hint that if she did not provide him with information on Tremley, he would release her secrets. He was a smart man—one who knew what he wanted. "What do we know about him?"

Bourne's brows rose. "West?"

She nodded. "What's in his file?"

"Nothing," Cross said absently, collecting the cards and shuffling once more. "There's a sister." *Cynthia West.* A pretty girl, welcome in Society despite her lack of breeding. West's money had purchased her support. "Unmarried."

Georgiana nodded, knowing better than anyone what was inside the slim file in her safe. "And nothing else."

"Nothing at all?"

She'd looked a few times in the early years, but she'd stopped as West had become ally in her battle with Society. "Not much," Bourne replied. "His initial funding came from an anonymous donor for the gossip rag, which came to pay for the other papers. I've looked for evidence of the donor for years, but no one seems to know anything about it, except that there was a fair amount of money involved."

"Nonsense," Cross said. "There's always a trail when it comes to money."

"Not this money," Bourne replied.

"Family money?"

"He's not landed. There appears to be no one but the sister," she said.

"So, he had a mysterious benefactor," Temple said. "So did we at the beginning." The Duke of Leighton had bankrolled his sister's whim, with the understanding that no one ever know his identity—a condition to which Georgiana had been only too happy to agree.

She met the Duke of Lamont's black gaze. "You're saying he's a man with no secrets."

"I'm saying that he's a man with no interesting secrets."

She shook her head. "Everyone has an interesting secret. West is man enough to have more than one. So tell me, why don't we know them?"

Temple's gaze narrowed on her. "You can't mean to search for them."

She did not like the condemnation in his tone. "You've never stopped me before. When we founded this casino, it was with the understanding that you were in charge of the ring, Bourne the tables, Cross the books. And I was in charge of the information we needed to ensure that the venture succeeded."

Cross spoke up. "If you do this, you play with fire. He has a great deal of power."

"As do I."

"But his power grows as Chase's is diminished. Your secrets will destroy you."

"West won't discover the truth."

Cross did not look so certain. "They always learn the truth."

"Who?"

He did not answer the question, which suited her fine, as she did not like the hint of what he might have said. "Do not tempt the lion, Anna. Not this one. Not one who is so much a friend."

She thought of the kiss earlier in the evening. There was nothing about it that was friendly. Indeed, it had pleasured and tempted and teased and devastated, but it had not been friendly. It had done nothing but make her want him, and she knew that wanting a man was not the same as trusting him. She'd learned that the last time she'd been kissed. The first time she'd been kissed.

She needed protection from him.

Not him. The thought whispered through her.

Perhaps it was right. Perhaps she did not need protection from him. Perhaps she needed protection from herself. From how he made her feel.

But either way, one thing was certain.

"Friend or foe, he knows my secrets." She looked to her partners. "I need to know his."

She was saved from having to face their questions by a knock at the door. Cross called for the newcomer to enter—only a handful of people knew the owners' suite existed, each person trusted without question.

Justin Day, the casino's pit boss, entered, finding her instantly, and crossing the room to her.

"Is it done?" she asked.

The majordomo nodded once. "Burlington, Montlake, and Russell, each happy to end their suit."

Bourne turned curious. "Suit of whom?"

Temple replied, "Aren't they all after the Earl of Holborn's girl?"

Four heads turned in the duke's direction. Georgiana voiced their collective disdain. "Your newfound interest in Society is terribly unsettling."

Temple shrugged one enormous shoulder. "They are after her, though, aren't they?"

Not since Lady Mary Ashehollow called Caroline a whore, they weren't.

She did not reply, and neither did Justin. "There is more," he said.

She turned to a nearby clock, noted the time, and knew without asking what news he brought. "Lady Tremley."

Justin nodded. "At the ladies' entrance."

Bourne's brows rose. "How did you know that?"

"What is she doing here?" Cross asked.

"She was invited," she said, drawing a dark look from her partners.

"We did not discuss inviting her," Temple said.

No, they hadn't. She had sent the invitation within the hour of West's leaving, several days earlier.

She did not tell them the whole truth, afraid that they might reject West's request. Afraid they would not realize how much she needed West. The fear made her angry. She did not like feeling out of control. "I made a decision for all of us."

"She's dangerous. Tremley is dangerous," Bourne warned. "If she offers his information—if he finds out—"

"I am not a child," she reminded him. "I can connect the spots. What of the lady?"

Justin said, "Bruno says she's a black eye."

"Ah. Vengeance, thy name is woman."

"If her husband is such a coward that he must resort to beating his wife, I'll personally help her exact it," Bourne said.

Justin replied. "She asks for Chase."

"She shall have Anna instead." She turned and smoothed her skirts.

Bourne met her gaze. "Be careful. I don't like you dressed like a whore when none of us are there to protect you."

"This isn't a dark alley in the East End."

"Chase," he said, using the name he'd given her a half decade earlier, reminding them all of their history. "This is much more dangerous."

She smiled, warm with the knowledge that they worried about her, this motley band of rogues she'd amassed. "Yes, but it is danger of my own design. I'm native to it."

Bourne looked to the stained glass, his gaze lingering on Lucifer's wings, useless as he fell. "It does not mean that there won't come a day when it will swallow you up."

"Possibly," she allowed. "But it won't be today." She followed his gaze to the window, where the beautiful blond angel tumbled into Hell. "Today, I reign."

In minutes, she was belowstairs, at the ladies' entrance to the club, where Bruno, one of the Angel's main security detail, stood watch in the dim light. Next to him was Lady Tremley, a beautiful woman in her twenties who sported one of the worst shiners Georgiana had ever seen, despite the Angel being known for its nightly bare-knuckle fights.

With a nod to Bruno, she opened the door to a small antechamber off the dark entryway. "My lady," she said quietly, startling the other woman. "Will you join me?"

Lady Tremley looked skeptical, but followed Georgiana into the room, taking in the sitting room, appointed as though it were prepared for ladies of the *ton* to take their afternoon tea instead of gambling and gossiping and playing at life as their husbands did.

Georgiana indicated a settee, upholstered in blue velvet. "Please."

The lady sat. "I asked to see Mr. Chase."

And Chase she saw.

Georgiana sat across from Lady Tremley. "Chase is indisposed, my lady. He sends his regards, and hopes you will consider speaking to me instead."

The marchioness took in the low neckline of Georgiana's dress, the height of her pale blond wig, the dark kohl around her eyes, and saw what everyone saw when they looked at her. A skilled prostitute. "I don't think—"

A rap came on the door, and Georgiana opened it to receive a package from Bruno, who was long-skilled in the art of knowing what the founders of The Fallen Angel required without being asked. Closing the door, she approached the lady, extending the linen parcel, filled with ice. "For the eye."

The marchioness took it. "Thank you."

"We know about bruises here." Georgiana sat. "All sorts."

They remained unspeaking as Lady Tremley held the compress over her eye. Georgiana had had this precise meeting too many times to count, and she recognized the lady. A woman eager for something more than that which life had offered her. Eager for something that would entertain and enrich and engage. Something that would change her in some small, private way, allowing her to suffer through her long days of propriety. And if the black eye were to be considered, something that would see her through long days of marriage, as well.

The key was to let the lady speak first. Always.

After long minutes, Lady Tremley lowered the ice and unlocked herself. "Thank you."

Georgiana nodded. "Of course."

"I am sorry."

It always began this way. With apology. As though the lady had some hand in the cards she had been dealt. As though she weren't simply made female and, therefore, less than.

"There is no need to be." It was the truth.

"Surely you have something else . . ." The lady trailed off.

Georgiana waved a hand dismissively. "Nothing of import."

Lady Tremley nodded once, looking down to confess to her skirts, "I judged you harshly when you appeared."

Georgiana laughed. "You think you are the first?" She leaned back in her chair. "I am Anna."

The marchioness's eyes went wide. Georgiana was used to shock from proper ladies when she treated them as equals. It was the first test; the one that proved their mettle. "Imogen."

The lady passed.

"Welcome to The Fallen Angel, Imogen. You may trust that whatever is said between us is shared only with Chase."

"I have heard of you. You're his . . ." She stopped, rethinking the word *doxy*, choosing a rhyming one instead. "His proxy."

"Among other things."

The lady hesitated, fiddling with the gold satin. Georgiana thought it was not a common action for the wife of one of the King's closest councilors. "I received an invitation from Mr. Chase. I am told there is a woman's club."

Georgiana smiled. "No sewing circles or reading societies to be found, I am afraid."

Lady Tremley's gaze turned shrewd. "I am not as simpering as you might imagine."

Georgiana let her attention fall to the bruise on the lady's face. "I don't imagine that you are simpering at all."

Lady Tremley flushed, but Georgiana didn't imagine that it was embarrassment that caused it. No doubt, if the woman were here, she'd long passed embarrassment at her husband's actions. She was well into anger. "I understand that to gain acceptance, I must provide information."

Georgiana was still for a long moment. "I don't know where you would have heard such a thing."

Imogen's gaze narrowed. "I am not a fool."

"Who is to say that Chase does not already have this information? As you must have heard, we've a file thick as his thumb on every important man in London."

"He does not have this," the lady said, lowering her voice and looking to the door. "No one has this."

Georgiana did not believe that for a moment. "Not even the King?"

The lady shook her head. "It would ruin Tremley. Forever." There was something in the words, eagerness. Excitement. The heady triumph that comes with revenge.

Georgiana leaned back. "We are aware that your husband steals from the exchequer."

Lady Tremley's eyes went wide. "How do you know that?"

It was true.

How had West known it, dammit?

How had West known it and she hadn't?

She collected herself, took a second run. "And we know that he pays it to fund the arming of our enemies."

The lady looked as though the wind had been taken from her sails, even as years of practice kept Georgiana from leaning forward in her seat and asking, *Truly?* Because she hadn't entirely believed it when West had said it. If it were true, after all, the earl was guilty of treason. And he would hang for it if it were ever let out.

It was the kind of information that a man would kill to keep secret. And from the look of his wife's face, he was not a man to hesitate when it came to violence.

Georgiana spoke again. "I am afraid, my lady, that the price of your entry to The Fallen Angel will be proof of these things that we know. However, before we continue, you must be very certain that you are willing to offer this proof freely to Chase. To the Angel." She paused. "You should understand that once it is ours, given in exchange for membership, we reserve the right to use it. At any time."

"I understand." The marchioness's gaze was full of eager triumph.

Georgiana leaned forward. "You understand that you speak of treason."

"I do."

"That he would hang if he were discovered."

Triumph turned dark. Cold. "Let him hang."

One of Georgiana's blond brows rose at the unfeeling words. That Tremley was a bastard was of little surprise. That his wife was a Boadicea was entirely the opposite. "Fair enough. Do you have proof?"

The marchioness reached into her bodice and extracted several pieces of torn paper, singed around the edges. She thrust them in Georgiana's direction. "Show him these."

Georgiana opened the slips of paper, piecing them together on the red silk of her skirts. She scanned the incriminating text on them. Looked up at the wife. "How did you—"

"My husband is less intelligent than the King gives him credit for. He tosses his correspondence into the fire, but he does not wait to ensure that it is incinerated."

"Then—" Georgiana began.

Imogen finished the sentence. "There are dozens more."

Georgiana was silent for a long moment, considering the implications of this woman. Of her stolen letters. Of the way they might help her this very night.

They would win her Duncan West's help and, by extension, they would secure her future and that of her daughter.

New information always gave her a heady thrill, but this—it was a good day.

"I am certain I speak for Chase when I say, 'Welcome to The Other Side.'"

Lady Tremley smiled then, and the expression opened her, removed the weathered lines of her face. Returned her youth.

"You are welcome to stay," Georgiana said.

"I should like to explore a bit. Thank you."

The lady did not understand. "Longer than an evening, my lady. The Other Side is not simply a place to game. If you wish sanctuary, we can provide it."

The smile disappeared. "I don't require it."

Georgiana cursed the world into which they were born—where women had little choice but to accept the danger in their everyday lives. The great irony of ruin was this—once survived, it brought freedom with it. Not so for women of propriety, of good standing. Of good marriage.

Bad marriage, more like.

Georgiana nodded, standing and smoothing her skirts. She had witnessed this particular circumstance enough times that she knew better than to force the issue. "If you ever do . . ." She trailed off, letting the rest of the sentence hang between them.

Lady Tremley did not speak, but she did stand.

Georgiana opened the door, and gestured into the lush hallway beyond. "The club is yours, my lady."

Chapter 8

. . . The Fashionable Hour grows ever more fashionable, however, with Lady G— in attendance this week
along with her charming Miss P—. The two will soon
make the sloping hills of Hyde Park the only place to
be seen, this author has no doubt . . .

. . . How the mighty have fallen! The Duke of L— has
been seen pushing a pram through Mayfair! For a man
so known for doing other, more violent things with his
hands, these authors wish there were an artist present
for this particular event, as we would like to have seen
it commemorated in oil . . .

The gossip pages of the *Weekly Courant*,
April 26, 1833

There was nothing worse than gossip pages. It did not
matter that they made him a fortune.

Duncan West sat in his office on Fleet Street, considering
the next issue of *The Scandal Sheet*.

The paper was his first business endeavor, started years

earlier when he'd first landed in London. He'd designed it to capitalize on Society's ridiculous interests in clothing and courtship, scandal and scoundrel. And to capitalize on the commoners' universal interest in Society.

It had worked; the first paper made him scads of money— everything necessary to begin his second, infinitely more worthwhile paper, the *News of London*. It never failed to surprise and discourage him, however, that scandal had always and would always sell better than news and entertain more than art.

He knew he was the worst kind of hypocrite, after all, it was the paper he had to thank for his entire empire, but it did not make him loathe the business any less. Most days, he paid no attention to the contents of the rag, allowing his second in command to handle its business and content. But today the item that dominated the pages reserved for "Scandal of the Season," was written and placed by West alone. It was a shot over the bow in the battle for Lady Georgiana Pearson's marriage match.

He scanned the text, checking for misprints or unfortunate word choices. *Unlike most who succumb to her fate, this lady has survived with cleverness, intelligence, and temerity.*

No. None of those three words would work. While they suited Georgiana to a T, they would not call to the *ton*. Indeed, Society did not hold in high regard any of the traits that made the lady in question so captivating.

And damned if she wasn't tremendously captivating.

He wished he could say that it was because of the kiss. Which he should not have pursued, and he certainly should not have allowed to continue beyond what was chaste.

Except there was nothing about the woman that made a man think of chastity. And it was not even the mask of Anna that tempted the most. It was the other—Georgiana, the freshness of her face, the brightness of her eyes. When he'd had the woman in his arms on the floor of the casino, he'd wanted to tear the ridiculous wig from her head and loose her blond waves and make love to the real woman beneath all the pomp and padding.

Not that she required padding.

She was rather perfectly padded as she was.

He shifted in his chair at the thought, returning his attention to the paper in his hand. Which did not help to put the lady out of his mind, as she was the subject of the damn paper.

A few strokes of red ink and *cleverness* became *charm*, *intelligence* became *elegance* and *temerity* became *grace*. Not incorrect as descriptors of Lady Georgiana, but certainly not as accurate as his former choices.

As others: beautiful, fascinating, unbearably tempting.

More than she seemed.

He set the draft on his desk and leaned back, closing his eyes and pressing finger and thumb to the bridge of his nose. She was dangerous. Altogether too dangerous. He should put someone else on the story and vow never to see her again.

"Sir."

He looked up to find Marcus Baker, his secretary and general man of service, in the doorway. He waved him in. "Enter."

The man set a stack of newsprint on the desk, topped with a collection of envelopes. "Tomorrow's news and today's mail," Baker said before adding, "And word is that Viscount Galworth owes thousands to The Fallen Angel."

West shook his head. "It's not news."

"He is trying to marry his daughter off to a wealthy American."

He met his secretary's gaze. "And?"

Baker nodded to a large envelope on the desk. "Chase sends proof that the viscount has been throwing horse races."

"That could be news," West said, opening the letter and turning his attention to the stack of papers inside.

It was remarkable what Chase knew.

West tutted his disapproval. "Galworth has made Chase very angry."

"The Angel does not like its debts to go unpaid."

"Which is why I have always taken great care not to go into

debt at the Angel," West said, idly, setting aside the information and turning to a note at the top of the pile that caught his attention. He slipped it free of the rest of the mail and reached for a letter opener, an unpleasant knot forming deep in him as he broke the seal and read the simple message.

> *I understand you've made a new friend.*
> *Where is my article? I grow impatient.*

It was unsigned, as messages in the Earl of Tremley's hand always were. He folded the page and held it in a nearby candle flame, letting the frustration and anger that always came with these missives—filled with entitled demands that he could not help but accommodate—ebb as the fire licked up the edges of the note. He could put off writing the piece on the war for a few days, perhaps a week but he needed Chase's proof, and soon.

He tossed the burning letter into the metal wastebasket at his feet, watching the flames consume the message before he turned back to Baker, who had yet to take his leave. "What else?"

"Your sister, sir."

"What about her?"

"She is here."

He gave Baker a blank stare. "Why?"

"Because you promised to take me for a ride," his younger sister announced from the doorway.

Cynthia West was intelligent and bold and thoroughly unruly when she wanted to be. It was no doubt his fault, as he'd spoiled her for the last thirteen years, since he'd had the funds to do so. Cynthia believed, in the remarkable way that young women could, that the world was and should be at her feet.

And that world included her brother.

"Damn," he said. "I forgot."

She entered, removing her cloak, and seated herself in a small chair on the other side of his desk. "I assumed you would, which is why I am here and not at home, waiting to be collected."

"I've three newspapers that print tonight."

"Then it does seem like poor planning that you have promised me a ride today."

He narrowed his gaze on her. "Cynthia."

She turned to Baker. "Is he always so irritable?"

Baker knew better than to answer the question, instead taking his leave of the whole situation with a quick bow. "Smart man," West said.

When the door closed behind the secretary, his sister said, "You know, I don't think he likes me."

"Probably not," he said, rifling through the papers Baker had brought. "Cynthia, I can't—"

"No," she said. "You've canceled these particular plans three times, now." She stood. "It is the fashionable hour. I wish to be fashionable. For once. Come, Duncan. Humor your poor, unmarried, spinster sister."

"Unmarried spinster is redundant," he said, enjoying her look of exasperation.

"Would you accept bored spinster sister instead?"

He shook his head. "Entertaining you is not my job. I'm required to entertain the rest of Britain first."

She moved to the window of the office. "As though you haven't a hundred underlings who can check spelling or whatever it is you do all day."

He raised a brow. "It's a bit more than that."

She waved a hand dismissively. "Yes, I know. You run a veritable empire from behind that desk."

He didn't like to brag. "I do, rather."

"There are Society pages in every one of your papers, and one of the things is entirely comprised of scandal. A ride in Hyde Park during the season is practically business."

"It's nowhere near business," he clarified.

"Shouldn't you allow me to be seen? Are you not concerned about my marriage prospects? I'm twenty-three, for heaven's sake. On the shelf!"

"By all means, find a husband. I've scores of eligible bachelors working here. Choose one of them. Any one you please. Choose Baker. He's a good worker."

She pressed a hand to her breast. "A good worker. My heart. I can hardly bear its pounding."

"He's all his teeth, and a brain in his head."

"High praise, indeed."

"I don't know what women want." Georgiana Pearson seemed to be interested in nothing but a title.

Not that he cared what the woman wanted.

What had he been saying? Ah. Yes. Cynthia.

He waved a hand at the door. "Choose any man in the building. Just don't make me go riding today."

"I've half a mind to take you up on that, just to see you change your mind." She swung her cloak around her shoulders. "You promised, Duncan."

And there, for a moment, she was the five-year-old he'd scooped onto that horse twenty years ago, promising her that they'd go somewhere safe—somewhere their life would be better. Where they would be strong.

He'd made good on those promises.

And so he would make good on this one.

Within the hour, they were in Hyde Park, barely moving in the crush of the afternoon ride. Rotten Row—aptly named, in West's estimation—was filled with the throngs of aristocrats and landed gentry who had returned to London for the season, dissatisfied with their pallid, whiled-away winters in the far reaches of Britain, and desperate for color—a blush of gossip.

West nodded to the Earl of Stanhope, who came alongside the carriage on a stunning black horse. "My lord."

"West. I saw your editorial in the *News* in favor of the Factory Act. Well put. Children shouldn't work more than we do."

"Children shouldn't work at all," West replied. "Though I shall take the act's passage as a sound first start—if word of our combined voices does not frighten away those who might otherwise be inclined toward our views." The earl was known for his impassioned speeches on the floor of the House of Lords.

Stanhope laughed. "Think of the damage we could do if you'd run for a seat in the House of Commons."

A wind whipped through the park, as though the universe knew the truth—that West could never run for a seat in the Lower House. That he would not be allowed to converse with earls if his truths were known, and that at some point, at any point, his secrets could become public. For a secret was only a secret until two people knew it.

And in his case, two people knew it. "Too much damage, my lord."

The earl seemed to sense the shift in the conversation, and he tipped his hat in their direction before heading off down the path.

West and his sister rode in silence for long minutes, until another wind blew, and Cynthia decided to lighten the mood in the curricle. Holding on to her enormous hat, she smiled wide at a passing group of doyennes of the *ton*. She spoke with a bright, happy voice. "It's a beautiful day for a ride."

"It's grey and threatening to rain."

She smiled. "It's London in March, Duncan. That's practically blue sky."

He narrowed his gaze on her. "How is it that we are siblings and yet you are so damn impractical?"

"You say impractical, I say cheerful." He did not reply, and so she offered, "I suppose the gods were smiling down upon you when they delivered you a baby sister."

The gods were doing no such thing at the time of her arrival. But he still remembered that day, covered in tar, blisters on his young hands, sent into the laundry where his mother lay hidden in a corner on a makeshift pallet of old blankets, holding a tiny baby.

The memory came without warning. *Go on, Jamie, hold your sister.*

He had, taking the little mewling bundle. She'd been

wrapped in the master's shirt, one in need of mending. He'd barely seen the baby for that shirt. *He'll be angry that you've ruined his shirt.*

There'd been sadness in his mother's eyes when she'd replied, *You let me worry about him.*

He'd unwrapped the shirt then, to get a good look at this little creature that had been identified as his sister, with a headful of brown hair and the bluest eyes he'd ever seen.

He extinguished the memory before it went too far. "You looked like a goblin."

She turned shocked eyes on him. "I did not!"

"Maybe not. Perhaps it was more like an old man—all red and blotchy, as though you'd been in the sun or in your cups for too long."

She laughed. "That's a horrible thing to say."

"You grew out of it." He shrugged one shoulder and added, so no one nearby could hear him, "And the first time I held you, you pissed on me."

"I've no doubt you deserved it!" she said, indignant.

He smiled. "You grew out of that, too, thank goodness."

"I'm beginning to think that I should not have invited you for this ride," she said. "It's not nearly so rewarding as I thought it would be."

"Then I have achieved my goal."

She scowled at him before her attention turned to two ladies riding ahead of them, heads bent in the telltale sign of gossip. "Now shush. Those two look like they have something to say."

"You realize that your brother has the line on all the significant gossip of the *ton*? You receive at least three gossip rags to the house a week."

She waved away his words. "It's no fun reading it with the rest of the world. Get closer. And pretend as though we are conversing."

"We *are* conversing."

"Yes, but if *you're* talking I can't hear *them*. So *pretend*."

The dirt path was packed with aristocrats and gentry, all

here for the same reason Cynthia was here, and so the whole damn group was moving at a snail's pace, which made it perfectly easy to eavesdrop. The gossip shared on Rotten Row was never very valuable, in part because everyone on Rotten Row had heard it already. Nevertheless, he slowed to a creep so his sister could listen to the ladies, now next to them, despite lacking any semblance of interest in their conversation.

"I heard that she's got her eye on Langley," one said.

"He'd be a tremendous catch for her, but I don't think he'd marry into such a family," the other opined.

"'Such a family,'" came the unconvinced reply. "She's the Duke of Leighton for a brother, and Ralston through the duke."

Suddenly, West was very interested in the conversation.

"They're speaking of Lady Geo—"

He raised a hand and Cynthia stopped speaking. For once.

"They may have titles, but they shouldn't matter when you consider the rest of the story—Leighton's duchess has been a scandal from the start."

"She's received everywhere," the first pointed out.

"Of course she is. She's a duchess. And a rich one at that. But it doesn't mean people wish her presence. Italian. *Catholic.* And a bastard."

"What a horrible woman," Cynthia whispered, leaning closer.

It was only years of practice that kept West from doing the same. The woman in question was Lady Holborn, a wicked gossip and a terrible person if talk was to be believed. The other was Lady Davis, not the most prized guest at a gathering, but in comparison, a veritable saint, it seemed.

It was important that he hear what they were saying about Georgiana, of course. After all, he had promised to get her married, hadn't he? Any reconnaissance he could do as far as societal opinion of her would help get his part in the play done.

That was the only reason that he cared about what the ladies were saying.

Still, when the Countess Holborn said, "The point is, the girl is ruined. Name or no, she's loose. What man could be assured his heir is his? And the fact that she parades the *daughter* around Hyde Park as though she weren't a bastard and just as cheap as her stock is . . . offensive. Just look at them . . ."

She was here.

"What a *horrible* woman," Cynthia repeated.

The ladies' conversation trailed off as they picked up speed. West no longer cared, as he was too busy searching for the subject of their conversation. They'd said she was here. With her daughter.

And suddenly, West wanted very much to make the girl's acquaintance.

He did not see them on the path, but the throngs of people made it difficult to find anyone, he supposed, even as he resisted the thought. Even as he told himself that he would notice her. That if she were here, in either of her costumes, he would know her.

He kept looking, turning to see if she was behind. That was when a flash of deep, sapphire blue caught his eye, away from the throngs of people. He released the breath he had not known he'd been holding. Of course she wasn't here with the rest of the *ton*. She didn't wish to be a part of their world.

She stood on a slow rise beyond the trees, a young girl at her side, two horses trailing behind them, and the Serpentine their backdrop. They were deep in conversation, and he watched for a long moment, until the girl said something and Georgiana laughed. Bright. Bold. As though she were in private and not in full view of half of London.

The half of London that she required for her acceptable marriage.

West found himself wondering what had been so amusing.

And then wondering what it would take to amuse her himself.

He did not take his gaze from her as he pulled the curricle

to the edge of the path and dismounted, speaking to his sister. "Would you like to meet the subject of their gossip?"

From high atop the conveyance, Cynthia's surprise was clear. "You know her?"

"I do," he said, wrapping the reins around a hitching post and stepping off the dirt path and onto the grass. He moved up the slope toward where Georgiana walked. He willed her to stay, to keep off those beautiful horses and remain in the grass a little while longer. Until he could reach her.

Cynthia was with him, having rushed to keep up. "I see."

He cut her a look at the words. "What do you see?"

She smiled. "She's very pretty."

She was more than that. "I hadn't noticed."

"You hadn't."

"No." There had been a time when he'd been able to lie much more effortlessly. A week ago.

"You hadn't noticed that Lady Georgiana Pearson, blond and lithe and lovely up on the hill, to whom you are rushing—"

He slowed. "I am not rushing."

"To whom you *were* rushing," she clarified. "You had not noticed that she was pretty."

"No." He deliberately did not look at her then, because he did not wish to see the understanding and the surprise and the interest he heard in her reply.

"I see."

Lord deliver him from sisters.

Chapter 9

... in case of fire, this paper cautions you to resist relying upon the Viscount Galworth's horses for escape. They never run as fast as one would wager ...

... Meanwhile, Lady G— continues to edge away from her dreadful and utterly unsuitable moniker. There's been not a scandal in sight this season, though, in truth, this author is somewhat disappointed ...

The Scandal Sheet, April 27, 1833

"Tell me again why we are walking here and not down there with all the others?"

Georgiana looked to Caroline, surprised by the question. They'd been wandering the edge of the Serpentine for the afternoon—something they'd done a dozen times before, whenever Caroline was in town.

But they'd never done it while Georgiana was out and on the marriage mart. And in all the times that they'd done it, Caroline had never asked that question—why here, and not Rotten Row.

Georgiana supposed that she should have been prepared for it. After all, Caroline was nine, and girls eventually learned that the world did not solely exist for their pleasure. Eventually, they learned that the world existed solely for the pleasure of the aristocracy. And so, this close to throngs of aristocrats, Caroline was bound to ask.

"Do you wish to walk down there with the others?" Georgiana asked, evading her daughter's original, pointed question. Willing her to answer in the negative. She didn't think she could face the stares if they took their afternoon ride with the rest of London. She didn't think she could stand the way they whispered about her. The way they whispered about her daughter.

Being within sight of them made things bad enough.

"No," Caroline said, turning to peruse the crush below. "I was just wondering why *you* didn't wish to be there."

Because I should rather spend an afternoon being ritually stung by bees, Georgiana thought. She supposed she couldn't quite tell her daughter that. She settled on, "Because I would rather be here. With you."

Caroline cut her a disbelieving look, and Georgiana was struck by the honesty in her pretty, open face—by the way her wide eyes filled with knowledge far beyond her years. "Mother."

She supposed she was responsible for that, for the knowledge. For the fact that Caroline had never in her life acted her age—she'd always known more than a child should. It came with being a scandal. "You don't believe me?"

"I believe you wish to spend the afternoon with me, but I don't believe that is the reason we are not down there. The two are not mutually exclusive."

There was a pause, after which Georgiana said, "You are too intelligent for your own good."

"No," Caroline said thoughtfully. "I am too intelligent for *your* own good."

"That is *definitely* true. Would you believe me if I promised to take you to Rotten Row the next time we come to the park?"

"I would," Caroline allowed, "but I did notice that the promise is contingent upon us returning to the park, full stop."

Georgiana laughed. "Foiled again."

Caroline smiled, and they walked together for a few quiet minutes before she said, "Why are you planning to marry?"

Georgiana nearly choked on her surprise. "I—"

"It was in this morning's newspaper."

"You shouldn't be reading the newspaper."

Caroline gave her a dry look. "You've been telling me to read the newspaper since before I could read. 'Ladies worth their salt read newspapers,' do they not?"

Caught. "Well, you shouldn't be reading anything about me." Georgiana paused. "In fact, how did you know it was about me?"

"Please. The gossip pages are designed to be obvious. Lady G—? Sister to Duke L—? With a daughter, Miss P—? In actuality, I was reading about *me*."

"Well," said Georgiana, casting about for something to say that was appropriately parental. "You shouldn't be doing that, either."

Caroline looked at her, those brilliant green eyes, at once so knowing and curious. "You didn't answer the question."

"What was the question?"

Caroline sighed. "Why are you looking to marry? And why now?"

She stopped walking and turned to face her daughter, not knowing quite what to say, but knowing that she must say something. She'd never lied to her daughter, and she did not think it right to begin now, with the most difficult question she'd ever asked. She thought she'd simply open her mouth and let the words come out. It might not be articulate, but it would give Caroline an answer.

But by the grace of God, she did not have to find words. Because behind Caroline's horse, Duncan West came up the rise.

Her savior.

Once more.

Her breath caught in her throat as she watched him approach, all golden, as though the sun shone upon him even on this grey day. He was perfectly turned out in grey trousers, crisp white shirt and cravat, and navy topcoat. His greatcoat swung around him, making him seem larger than life.

But, it occurred to her, he would seem larger than life anyway. Something about the way he moved, with such sureness, as though he had never in his life made a misstep. As though the world simply bent to his whim.

She'd been born the daughter and sister to the most powerful dukes in Britain, and this man, not an aristocrat—not even a gentleman—seemed equal to them in power. More so.

Which was the reason she was so drawn to him, surely.

Not that power should be of interest to her. She had plenty of it herself.

And still, her heart pounded. To cover the noise, which she was certain all assembled could hear, she said brightly, "Mr. West!"

Caroline gave her a strange look. Perhaps she'd spoken too brightly.

She ignored her daughter, instead looking to the woman at West's elbow. Miss Cynthia West, his sister, younger by ten years, and widely believed to be a charming eccentric, spoiled by her brother.

"Lady Georgiana," West said, executing an impressive bow in Caroline's direction. "And Miss Pearson, I presume?"

Caroline giggled. "You presume correctly, sir."

He winked at the girl and righted himself. "May I present my sister? Miss West."

Miss West dropped into a curtsy. "My lady."

"Please," Georgiana said, "there's no need to stand on ceremony."

"But you are the daughter of a duke, no?"

"I am," Georgiana replied, "but—"

"She rarely uses the privilege," Caroline interjected.

Georgiana looked to the Wests. "One should always travel with a nine-year-old to complete one's thoughts."

Cynthia replied, all seriousness, "I so agree. In fact, I was thinking of finding one for myself."

"I'm certain my mother would happily lease me." Caroline's jest drew laughter from the group, and Georgiana was supremely grateful for the girl's quick wit, as she did not know quite what to say to Duncan West, considering their last interaction ended with her bodice around her waist.

The thought made her blush, and she pressed gloved fingers to her cheek as the heat rushed up her face. She looked to West, hoping that he hadn't noticed.

His warm brown gaze lingered where she touched her cheek.

She pulled her fingers away. "To what do we owe the pleasure of your visit?" The words came out harsher than she expected. More shrill. His sister's eyes widened, as did Caroline's.

He ignored the tone, instead saying, "We were riding and saw you here. I thought that was a much better idea than creeping along Rotten Row for another hour."

"I would have thought that you liked creeping along Rotten Row. Does it not provide food for your work?"

"Ha!" Cynthia interjected. "As though Duncan cares a bit for gossip."

"You don't?" Caroline asked pointedly. "Then why publish it?"

"Caroline," Georgiana said, maternal scolding in her tone. "How did you even know that Mr. West is a newspaper publisher?"

Caroline beamed. "Ladies worth their salt read the newspaper. I always assume that included the bit where they list the staff." She looked at West. "You are Duncan West."

"I am."

She considered him for a long moment. "You're not as old as I would have imagined."

"Caroline!" Georgiana interjected. "That's inappropriate."

"Why?"

"It's not at all inappropriate." He smiled at her daughter,

and Georgiana did not like the way it made her feel. In fact, it made her feel somewhat queasy. "I shall take it as a compliment."

"Oh, you should," Caroline said. "I would have thought you quite old. Considering you've so many different papers. How did you manage that? Did you have a brother who is titled?"

Warning bells rang, as Caroline knew that part of the reason why The Fallen Angel existed at all was because of her uncle Simon. There was no need for West to grow curious about the reason for her questioning. "Caroline, that's quite enough."

Cynthia interjected, "If only we had a brother who was titled. Everything would have been much easier."

Don't be so certain, Georgiana wanted to say, but she bit her tongue.

"Well, if I can't ask him that, then can I at least ask why he publishes gossip if he doesn't care for it?"

"No," Georgiana said. "We do not ask probing questions."

"Well, he does, doesn't he? He's a reporter."

Lord deliver her from nine-year-old girls wise beyond their years.

"She has a point, Lady Georgiana, I am a reporter," West said.

And from thirty-three-year-old men too handsome for their own good.

"There, you see?" Caroline said.

"He's being polite," Georgiana replied.

"I wasn't, really," he interjected.

"You were being polite," Georgiana insisted firmly, wishing she'd stayed inside today. She turned to her daughter. "Which you might try sometime. What did we discuss relating to Society events?"

"This is not exactly an *event*," Caroline argued.

"It's close enough. What did we say?"

Caroline's brow furrowed. "Not to bring up skull drinking?"

Shocked silence fell, broken almost instantly by West's and Cynthia's laughter. Finally, the lady said, "Oh, Miss Pearson. You are great fun!"

Caroline beamed. "Thank you."

"Now tell me about these beautiful horses, will you? You must be a very fine horsewoman."

And with that, Caroline had been deftly extricated from any situation that might end in her being either scolded or murdered by her mother. Georgiana's head spun as she was overcome by the distinct feeling that she and West had been left alone on purpose. She was not used to losing so roundly.

She missed her club.

She turned back to West, who was still smiling. "Skull drinking?" he asked.

She waved away the words. "Do not ask."

He nodded. "Fair enough."

"You see now why I need a husband. She's too precocious for her own good."

"I don't see it at all, honestly. She's charming."

She smirked. "You are obviously not good *ton.*" He went serious, and she suddenly felt as though she'd misspoken. She added. "And you do not have to live with her."

"You forget, I have a sister who is similarly eccentric."

It was a perfect word for Caroline. "Tell me, are most gentlemen seeking eccentricity in their wives?"

"As I am not a gentleman, I would not know."

Something flared inside her, unfamiliar and yet thoroughly recognizable. *Guilt.* "I didn't mean—" she said.

"I know," he replied. "But you were not wrong. I am not born a gentleman, Georgiana. And you would do best to remember it."

"You play the part well," she said. And he did, looking every inch the gentleman now, and each night on the floor of her club. He'd played it well when he'd rescued her from Pottle's slithering, disgusting grasp. And in the years leading up to that moment, during which he'd never propositioned her. Not once.

"You think so?" he asked casually, as they trailed behind Caroline and Cynthia, whose conversation grew more animated by the minute. "You think I played it well when I manhandled you on the floor of a casino? When I nearly stripped you bare?"

They were in public—in the middle of Hyde Park. And to an unsuspecting observer, they were all propriety. No one would ever know that his words sent heat coursing through her, warming her straight through, as though they were in that shadowed alcove in her casino once more.

She did not look at him, afraid he would see what he had done to her.

"When I wanted to do much more than that?" he added, the words soft and full of promise.

She'd wanted it, too. She cleared her throat. "Perhaps you are not such a gentleman after all."

"I promise you, there is no perhaps about it."

She was certain that anyone who watched them would know what he said. How she enjoyed it. How shameless they both were. She looked to the Serpentine, trying to pretend they discussed something else. Anything else. "What are you, then?"

He did not answer for a while, and she finally turned to look at him, finding him watching her carefully. She met his gaze, finally. He held it for a heartbeat. Two. Ten. "I would have thought you'd recognized it the moment we met. I'm an utter scoundrel."

And in that moment, he was. And she didn't care.

Indeed, she wanted him more for it.

They walked farther, trailing his sister and her daughter as they edged around the curve of the Serpentine lake. After long moments of silence, she could not bear it any longer, the wondering what he was thinking. The hoping he'd give voice to thought. The hoping he wouldn't.

So she spoke first. "My brother's wife nearly drowned in this lake once."

He did not hesitate. "I remember that. Your brother saved her."

It had been the beginning of a love for the ages. One that did not end in tragedy, but in happiness. "I suppose you wrote about it."

"Probably," he said. "At the time, if I recall, *The Scandal Sheet* was the only paper I had."

"I just had a conversation with Caroline that leads me to believe that it still holds a fair amount of influence."

He turned to look at the girls. "Oh?"

"Yes. As you may have divined, she reads the gossip pages."

He smiled. "She and every other girl in London."

"Yes, well, most girls of her age aren't reading about their mother's search for a husband."

He slowed his pace. "Ah."

"Well put."

"What did she say about it?"

"She asked why I wish to marry. And why now."

The girls now quite a distance away, and she and West were both public and private. As with everything in Georgiana's life these days. The situation was by design, yes, but it did not mean she enjoyed it.

Although, if she were fully in private with Duncan West, there was no telling what might happen.

They walked a little farther in silence before he said, "And how did you answer?"

She turned to him, shocked. "You too?" He lifted a shoulder in an expression she was coming to recognize in him. "You know, you do that when you want someone to think that you aren't interested in what they are about to say."

"Perhaps I'm not interested. Perhaps I'm simply being polite."

"Since when does politeness include prying, personal questions?" she asked. "Did you not receive the lesson I just delivered to my daughter?"

"Something about skull drinking." She laughed, taken by surprise, and he smiled briefly, the expression there, then gone, leaving only a pool of warmth in her stomach as he added, "Well, as your daughter pointed out, I am a reporter."

"You're a newspaper magnate," she corrected.

He smiled. "A reporter at heart."

She couldn't help her matching smile. "Ah. Desperate for a story."

"Not for all stories. But for your story? Quite."

The words dropped between them, and they both seemed surprised by them. She was taken aback. Did he really mean it? Did he really care about her story? Or was he simply in it for the information she promised? For the payment she always rendered when he did the Angel a favor?

And why did the answers matter so much?

He saved her from the questions swirling through her mind. "But today, I will settle for an answer to Caroline's question."

Why did she wish to marry.

She shook her head. "There are a dozen reasons why I should marry."

"Should is not wish."

"That's semantics."

"It is not at all. I *should* not have kissed you yesterday. But I very much *wished* to. There's nothing at all the same about the two."

She stopped, the words sending surprise and something richer through her. Desire. She met his gaze, registering the heat in his brown eyes. "You just . . ." She hesitated. "You cannot simply announce things like that. As though we are not here, in a public place. In Hyde Park. At the fashionable hour."

"That must be the most idiotic description for four o'clock in the afternoon that ever there was," he said, and the conversation had changed. As though he hadn't just said the word *kiss* in full view of London's aristocracy.

Perhaps she'd dreamed it.

"So, tell me, Georgiana." Her name was a caress even as they walked, a yard between them, in a perfectly innocuous portrait. "Why do you wish to marry?"

The question was quiet and liquid, and made her want

nothing more than to answer it, even as she knew it was none of his business. She started with the obvious. "You know already. I require a title."

"For Caroline."

"Yes. She needs the protection of a decent title. With your help, she'll receive it, and with it, hopefully, a future."

"And you expect Langley to be a decent father."

The words came so easily, with such a lightness, that she almost didn't notice the way they probed, searching for the answer to the question she'd been asked her whole adult life. "If she's lucky, yes."

He nodded, and they walked farther. "Fair enough. But that is all for Caroline. What of you?"

"Me?"

"The meat of it is right there in the question, Georgiana, why do *you* wish to marry?"

The wind blew once more, and it carried the scent of him to her—sandalwood and something else, something clean and entirely masculine. Later, she would tell herself that it was the scent that made her tell the truth. "Because I haven't any other choice."

The truth of the words shocked her, and she wished she could take them back. She wished she'd said something else, something bolder and more brazen. But she hadn't. Instead, he'd asked his questions and stripped her bare. Exposed her vulnerabilities. Even as she was the most powerful man in Britain, one who ruled the night, here, in the day, she was still just a woman, with a woman's rights. And a woman's insignificant power.

By day, as a mother with a daughter, she needed help.

He didn't know all of that, of course. He knew she was ruined, but not the extent to which she could be destroyed. And even as he heard the truth in her words, he did not fully understand them. He did not press the issue, however, instead asking, "And why now?"

He'd asked her the question before. The night they'd met on the balcony at the Worthington Ball. The night he'd met

Georgiana. She hadn't answered then. But now, she spoke without hesitation, her gaze finding Caroline ahead. "She needs more than I can give her."

He raised a brow. "She lives with your brother. I imagine she does not want for much."

She watched her daughter for a long moment, a memory coming thick and nearly overwhelming. "Not like that. She deserves a family of her own."

"Tell me," he said, the words soft and warm and tempting, making her wish they were somewhere else, where she could curl into his heat and do precisely as he asked.

She answered. "Just after the New Year, I visited her on my brother's estate." Those assembled had barely given her a look, each more interested in the rare warm winter's day than in their eccentric aunt, who often turned up at strange times wearing breeches and boots.

But Caroline had noticed.

"She was surprised to see me."

"You don't see her often?"

Georgiana hesitated, guilt flooding through her. "The estate . . . it is far from Mayfair."

"The opposite end of the world from where you live." Precisely. She simultaneously adored and hated the understanding in the words. "What happened?"

She tried to explain, realizing that the story might seem simple. Unimportant. "Nothing of particular note."

He didn't accept the answer. "What happened?"

She lifted a shoulder. Let it drop, hoping the movement would cover her shame at the memory. "I thought she would be happy to see me. But instead, she was confused. Instead of smiling and rushing to me, she blinked up at me and asked, 'What are you doing here?' "

He exhaled, and she thought she heard understanding in the sound, but she didn't dare look at him. Didn't dare ask. "I was so shocked by the question. After all, I am her mother. Shouldn't I be there? Isn't that my place? With her?" She shook her head. "I was furious. Not with her, but with myself." She stopped, lost in the memory, in the way Caroline had smiled, as though Georgiana were a welcome stranger.

And that was what she had been. Not a mother. Not in the way a woman should be. She'd been so concerned with sullying her daughter with her reputation that she'd become a secondary player in Caroline's life.

No more.

Not if she could help it.

"I never—" she started. Stopped. He did not speak, infinitely patient. No doubt it was that patience that made him such a remarkable reporter. She filled his silence. "I never feel quite as though I belong there."

Because she did not belong there.

They walked for a bit longer. "But that does not mean that you cannot belong there."

"First I have to wish to belong there."

He understood. "The devastating battle between what one wants, and what one should want."

"She deserves a family," she said. "A respectable one. With a home. And a—" She stopped, considering the rest of the sentence. "I don't know." She cast about for something that would provide normalcy, finally settled on: "A cat. Or whatever normal girls have."

As though that did not sound positively idiotic.

He did not seem to think so. "She is not a normal girl."

"But she could be." *If not for me.* She left the last unsaid.

"And you think Langley's title will make her so."

The title was a means to an end. Couldn't he see that? "I do," she said.

"Because Chase won't have you." The words were a shock, unexpected and unpleasant. Filled with anger, she realized, on her behalf.

"Even if Chase did want me."

He raised a hand, and she sensed the irritation in the gesture. "You cannot tell me he is not an aristocrat. A wealthy and powerful one at that. Why else keep his identity such a secret?"

She did not speak. Could not risk revealing anything.

"He could give you everything you seek, but even now, as he hangs you in the wind, as he offers you as prey to Society's wolves, you protect him."

"It is not like that," she said.

"So you love him. But do not for one moment believe that it is not his fault that your hands are tied. He should marry you himself. Throw his mighty weight behind you."

"If he could . . ." She let the words trail off, hoping he would not hear their implicit deceit.

"Is he married?"

She did not answer. How could she?

"Of course, you won't tell me that." He smiled, but the expression lacked humor. "If he is, he's an ass. And if he's not . . ." He trailed off.

"What?" she prodded.

He looked away, out at the lake, still and silver in the March light. For a moment, she thought he would not answer. And then he said, "If he's not, he's a fool." She caught her breath at the words, as he turned back toward her and met her gaze. "I find I tolerate him less and less these days."

"Even if he were unmarried, I do not want him," she said, hating the words. Hating the lie she perpetuated with them. That Chase was other. That Chase was some mysterious, powerful man to whom they were both beholden.

"No, you want Langley," he said.

I want you. She bit back the words. Where had they come from? "He's a good choice. Kind. Decent." *Safe.*

"Titled," he said.

"And that," she agreed.

They walked for a long moment, and he said, "It's not a choice if there's only one man on the list, you know." When she did not reply, he added, "You should have a choice."

She should.

But she didn't.

By the end of the season, she would be married. Whether Langley agreed to it on his own or with prodding, he would marry her. He'd been selected for his qualities. And his secret, which she wouldn't hesitate to use if necessary.

It did not matter that somehow, something had upset the balance of Chase-Anna-Georgiana, and that, in this situation, blackmail made her squeamish. It was the only way.

Choice was a farce.

But here, in this moment, she had one. West wanted her. And she wanted him. And here, now, she had a choice.

She could have what she should have for a lifetime . . . or have what she wished for a moment.

Or perhaps she could have both.

Why not take a moment with West? He was the perfect partner—he knew her secrets—but not her whole truth. He knew she was Anna and Georgiana, knew why she was searching for a husband, was instrumental in the search. There was something tremendously freeing in the idea that he might be her choice. Now. Before she had no choice but to choose another.

It was tremendously clear all of a sudden.

"Do you have a mistress?"

She blurted out the question with a lack of finesse that appalled her. What had happened to Anna? Where was London's greatest lightskirt? More importantly, where was all-powerful and ever-certain Chase?

She wanted to toss herself into the Serpentine.

Why did this man have such a horrifying effect on her?

His brows rose at her question, but he somehow, blessedly, resisted the no doubt overwhelming urge to mock her delivery. "I do not."

She nodded once, and continued to walk along the edge of the lake. "I only ask because I would not wish to . . . overstep."

Why were the words so difficult?

Because he was watching her. She could see him out of the corner of her eye. He would be watching her a great deal more if she got the damn words out.

The thought did not help.

"By all means, Lady Georgiana, I encourage you to overstep. As much as you'd like."

She took a breath. Now or never. Forward, or forever here. "I propose an arrangement. Not a long-term arrangement. That would be silly. And disrespectful."

And foolish, as anything long-term with Duncan West would surely end in her wishing it more than she should.

Those words again.

He did not respond except to say, "Go on."

She stopped. Turned to him. Attempted to behave as though she ran one of London's finest men's clubs. "You said you wished to kiss me."

"Was my desire unclear?"

She ignored the flood of heat that came at the words. "It was not. And you wished to do other things as well."

His gaze turned dark. "A great number of other things."

The words did strange things to her insides.

She nodded. "Then I propose we do those things."

One of his golden brows rose. "Do you?"

Embarrassment flared, but she brazened it through. "I do. You haven't a mistress. And neither have I."

That did shock him. "I should hope not."

She tilted her head to one side and spoke as Anna, feeling altogether more powerful now that the proposition had been made. "I see no reason why I shouldn't until I've landed Langley. Discreetly, of course."

"Of course."

"I think you'll do."

"As mistress."

"You cannot imagine I would choose the word *master*."

His shock compounded. Obviously. She enjoyed the moment. Particularly when he said, "I feel certain I should be insulted."

She laughed, feeling suddenly freed by the conversation. "Come now, Mr. West, I am no delicate flower. Aren't you the one who said I should have a choice?"

He narrowed his gaze on her. "I meant in your long-term future."

"I have chosen my long-term future. And now I am choosing my immediate future," she said, stepping closer, bringing a yard to a foot. She lowered her voice to a whisper. "I choose you."

He moved at the words, and she thought for a fleeting moment that he would capture her and pull her close. She would not have resisted. But he stopped himself, likely realizing that they were in public. It did not make the moment less exciting. She'd never been near a man who wanted her so much and was still so willing to resist her.

She smiled. "I take it you accept."

"On one condition," he said, crossing his arms, turning his back to the wind as it blew across the lake. Protecting her from the cold.

"Name it."

"While you are in my bed, you are not in his."

Chase.

It was an easy condition to accept. "Done."

He seemed to hesitate at her easy acceptance of his term, and she wondered if she'd given too much away. But then she saw the emotion cross his face. Disbelief.

He thought she was Chase's woman.

It should not have frustrated her as it did. It should not have angered her that he did not trust her. That he did not believe her. After all, she was lying even as she told him the truth.

But it did frustrate. Because she wanted this, above all else, to be something that was true. She began again, prepared to convince him. "We are not—"

He cut her off. "I accept."

Relief coursed through her.

Then he said, "We begin tomorrow night."

And relief turned to desire.

"I—" she started, but he stopped her again.

"I am in control."

The words sent a little thrill through her, even as she told herself she had no intention of allowing him to be in charge. "It was my idea."

He laughed at that, the sound low and graveled. "I assure you, I had this idea long before you did."

He called ahead to his sister, who immediately turned to acknowledge him. He indicated the curricle, and she passed the reins of Georgiana's horse to Caroline to head in the direction of the conveyance. Once that was done, he returned his attention to Georgiana and repeated himself. "I am in control."

Her brows snapped together. "I don't much care for that."

His lips twitched in a small smile. "I promise that you will."

And with that, he left, headed back down the rise.

"Mr. West." She called him back, not knowing what she would say, but knowing, nonetheless, that she wished him to turn. To look at her once more.

He did. "Considering the most recent turn of events, I think you should call me Duncan, don't you?"

Duncan. It felt far too personal. Even after she'd propositioned him. Perhaps *because* she'd propositioned him. Dear God. She'd propositioned him. In for a penny, in for a pound. "Duncan."

He smiled, slow and wolfish. "I do like the sound of that."

A blush rose in her cheeks, and she willed the color away. Failed. One side of his mouth kicked up. "And I like the *look* of that. There's nothing of Anna in that color. Nothing false."

The heat increased.

At once, he seemed to know too much of her. To see too much.

She cast about for something to rebalance their power. "Where were you? Before you came to London?"

He stilled, and understanding shot through her—something about the question had unsettled him. She knew with the keen sense of one who dealt in truths and lies that there was something there, in his past. Something that his instincts told him to lie about.

"Suffolk."

Not a lie, but neither was it the whole truth.

And he did not stay for more questions.

"Tomorrow night," he said, and the words left no room for refusal.

She nodded, a mix of anticipation and nervousness threading through her "Tomorrow night."

He turned and left her, and she watched his retreating back as his long legs dissolved the distance between him and his sister, who was already halfway to his curricle. *Tomorrow night*.

What had she done?

"Mother?" Caroline interrupted her rumination, and Georgiana looked to her daughter, poised a few yards away, both their horses in tow.

Georgiana forced a smile. "Shall we head back? Are you through?"

Caroline looked to West's retreating back—Georgiana would not think of him as Duncan, it was too personal—then to her mother. "I am through."

She would marry another man. She would give Caroline the world she deserved. The opportunity she deserved. But was it asking too much to find a moment of pleasure for herself in the meantime?

What would be the harm?

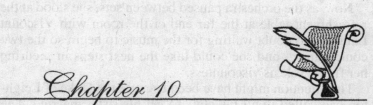

Chapter 10

> ... This paper has it on excellent authority that a cer-
> tain impoverished Lord has taken an interest in a very
> well dowered Lady. While we cannot confirm the lord-
> in-question's plans, we can confirm that they spent a
> quarter of an hour on a dark balcony several nights
> ago. We are assured that, while Lord L— was a perfect
> gentleman, he shan't need to be for much longer ...

> ... Truly, there are few couples we adore more than the
> Marquess and Marchioness of R—. It has been more than
> a decade that we've watched them make eyes at each
> other, and of such obvious adoration, this paper does not
> tire. Rumor has it that they even fence together ...

> The gossip pages of *The Weekly Britannia*,
> April 29, 1833

The columns were beginning to work.

Georgiana had danced with five potential suitors at the
Beaufetheringstone Ball, including three impoverished for-

tune hunters, an ancient marquess, and an earl of questionable breeding. And the night was only half over.

Now, as the orchestra paused between sets, she stood at the refreshment table at the far end of the room with Viscount Langley, no doubt waiting for the music to begin so the two could dance—and she could take the next steps in securing her future role as viscountess.

The attention might have been because the Duke of Leighton had called in all his chits to get his sister married. The duke and duchess were in attendance, as were the duchess's extended family including the Marquess and Marchioness of Ralston, and Lord and Lady Nicholas St. John.

Or it might have been because the owners of The Fallen Angel were also in attendance, though their support was required to be slightly less public. But they were in attendance, nonetheless, which was something of a marvel, as there were few things the Marquess of Bourne and Earl Harlow enjoyed less than Society functions. Yet they were here, posted about the room like silent sentries.

It might have been because of the wives—each a power in her own right, newly minted, a new generation of the aristocracy. Some scandal, some utter societal perfection.

It might have been any of those things, but West knew better.

It was the newspaper columns.

And West wasn't certain how he felt about their success.

He stood watch over the entire scene, observing as Lady Beaufetheringstone, the most gossip-prone doyenne of the *ton*, lifted her lorgnette and cast a discerning eye in Georgiana's direction. After a long moment, Lady B lowered the glass and nodded once before turning to the ladies in her surrounds, no doubt to discuss the new addition in her ballroom.

It was remarkable that Georgiana required West's support—what with the collection of lords and ladies in her orbit, those who had navigated the myriad pitfalls of Society themselves in their own scandalous journey to acceptance.

But there was nothing in the world more dangerous than a woman cloaked in scandal and without marriage.

So it had been when Eve had tasted the apple, when Jezebel had painted her face, when Hagar had lain with Abraham.

He watched as she lifted a glass of champagne and drank. When she lowered the glass and smiled at her companion, West imagined her lips gleaming with residual wine, imagined sipping it from them.

It might have been days since their kiss, but the taste of her lingered, and every moment he thought of her or caught a glimpse of her, he grew more desperate for this ball to end, and the night to begin. He was simply biding his time until he could touch her.

Langley placed a hand at her elbow, guided her to the ballroom floor for their dance.

He was beginning to dislike Langley.

He was beginning to dislike the viscount's easy smile and his perfectly tailored coats and his untouched cravats. He was beginning to dislike the way he moved, as though he were born for this place, for this world, and perhaps for this woman. It didn't matter that such a thought was supremely irrational, as Langley had been born for all those things.

And he was really beginning to dislike the way the viscount danced. All smooth grace and gentlemanly movements. And the way Georgiana smiled up at him as they twirled across the floor—not up at him, West edited disagreeably, as Langley was equal to her in height and no taller.

He tried his best to avoid the scowl that threatened. He didn't like how handsome a couple they made. How easy it was to see them as one.

How easy it was to realize that they would make handsome children.

Not that he cared about their children.

She met his gaze, and pleasure shot through him. She was beautiful tonight. Even at six and twenty, she was brighter than most of the women in attendance. She fairly glowed in the candlelight, the silk of her gown gleaming as Langley twirled her through the room, her golden curls brushing against the place where the long column of her neck met her shoulder. The place where she smelled of vanilla and Georgiana. The place he intended to lick the next time they were alone.

He nodded his head in her direction, and she flushed, looking away instantly. He wanted to crow his success. She wanted him. He was willing to bet nearly as much as he wanted her.

And they would both have what they wanted tonight.

He itched to touch her. He'd thought of little else since the moment she'd turned to him in the park the prior day and said, "I choose you." Christ, he'd wanted to lift her into his arms and carry her into the nearest copse of trees and lay her bare and worship every inch of her with every inch of him, damn the world into which she'd been born and the one in which she'd chosen to live.

I choose you.

It did not matter that she'd likely said the same words to a dozen other men in her life. That she likely knew their power and wielded it like an expert.

When she'd said them to him, he'd been hers. Instantly. Filled with a dozen ideas of how to make her his. His desire had been primitive at best—he'd wanted her. Fully.

And tonight, he'd have her.

"Did you receive my note?"

He stiffened at the words, turning to face the Earl of Tremley, now at his shoulder. "I did."

"You have not run the article we discussed."

The war in Greece. Tremley's support of the enemy. "I have been busy."

"Gambling and socializing are not business. I do not like being ignored. You would do well to remember that."

Everything about the words angered West, but he knew that the marquess was angling for a fight. "I am paying attention now."

"Because one word from me and every one of these people would happily turn up to see you hang."

West hated the truth in the words—the fact that, no matter the reasons for what he did, no matter the outcome of the actions, no matter the power he now wielded as a newspaper magnate, he was not one of them.

He never would be.

He ignored the thought, turning back to the ball, pretending to care, as he had for more than a decade, about this world that would never be his. "What do you want?"

He asked the question as a collection of young men passed, no doubt looking for a card game to pass the time at a ball their mothers had forced them to attend. Several of them turned to acknowledge Tremley and West, finding nothing strange about the two men deep in conversation.

They both held important positions—Tremley, as an advisor to King William, and West as a newspaperman to whom much of Society was beholden. There was only one other man who shared their influence.

The man Tremley had come to discuss. "I want Chase."

West laughed.

"I fail to see the humor in it," Tremley said.

West raised one brow. "You want Chase."

"I do."

He shook his head. "You and the rest of the known world."

Tremley smirked. "That may be, but the rest of the known world doesn't have you."

That much was true. For a decade, West had been funneling information about Society to Tremley as blackmail payment for the earl's silence about his past. About their mutual past.

And every day, every piece of information he shared and printed killed West a little more. He was desperate to get out from under this vicious man. Desperate for the information that would free him.

Years of practice kept him from revealing the fury and frustration that roiled in him whenever Tremley was here. "Why Chase?"

"Come now," Tremley said, the words low and nearly teasing. "There are only two men in London who come even close to having my power. One of them is in my pocket." West's fists clenched at the words even as Tremley continued. "The other is Chase."

"That's not enough for me to go after him."

Tremley laughed, cold and full of hate. "I like that you think you've a choice. He's shown an interest in my wife. I don't like being threatened."

Anger flared as West considered Tremley's treatment of his wife. "Chase is not the only man who might threaten you."

"Surely you don't mean yourself." When Duncan did not reply, the earl continued. "You can't ruin me, Jamie."

The whisper of the name, decades old and unused, sent a thread of unease through Duncan. It made him itch to destroy the smug earl. It made him willing to do anything for the information Lady Tremley had offered for her membership to The Fallen Angel.

He took a breath. Affected calm. "You think I have not looked for Chase before? You think I am not aware of how well that reveal would sell papers? While I'm flattered by your confidence, I assure you, not even I can gain access to Chase."

"But the whore can."

The words—the *word*—rocketed through him, and it was only the ball whirling around them that kept West from sinking his fist into the earl's smug face. "I don't know whom you mean."

"You are tiresome when you wish to be," the earl sighed, feigning interest in those dancing past. "You know exactly who I mean. Chase's woman. Now, apparently left over. To you."

West stiffened at the description, at the way she was tossed about as nothing more than an accessory. At the way he referenced her—cheap and used and unwanted.

She was the daughter of a duke, for Christ sake.

Except she wasn't to Tremley. Just as she wasn't to the rest of London.

"There's no use denying it," the earl continued. "Half the

ton saw you steal into a private room at the casino the other night. I've heard three different stories that say Lamont stumbled upon you up her skirts. Or was it she who was down your trousers?"

He wanted to roar his anger at the insult. If anyone else dared speak in such a manner, West would destroy them. They would suffer for a week at his hands. And they would suffer for years at the tip of his pen.

But Tremley was safe from West's anger, because he knew too well how it had been used in the past. What it had fought for. What it had won.

And so instead of beating him bloody, West said, "You should be careful with how you speak of the lady."

"Oho, she's a lady now? The *whore*"—he emphasized his crass wording—"must be tremendous between the sheets if you're elevating her so far." Tremley looked back at him. "I don't care what you do to her. But she's Chase's whore first and foremost. And you'll get me his identity."

One day he would destroy this man, and it would feel glorious.

The earl seemed to hear the unspoken thought. "You loathe it, don't you?" he said, watching West carefully. "You hate that I have so much power over you. That with a single breath, I could ruin you. That you are beholden to me. Forever."

Hate was too easy a word for what West felt for Tremley. "Forever is a very long time."

"Indeed, you would learn the truth of that statement if you were ever found out. I am told that forever in prison is even longer of a time."

"And if I cannot get you his identity?"

Tremley looked away and West followed his gaze, the way it flickered over the *ton*, finding his wife in the throngs of dancers. West noticed the lady's eye, yellowed around the edge. It took a moment to realize that Tremley was not in fact looking at his wife; her partner turned her, revealing the couple behind. The *woman* behind.

Cynthia.

"She's a pretty girl."

West's blood ran cold at the threat. "She stays out of it. That's always been the deal."

"It was. It still is. After all, the poor thing doesn't know the truth about her perfect brother, does she? What you did? What you took?"

The words were a cold, brilliantly crafted threat. West did not look to the earl. Could not guarantee that if he did, he would not assault the man. Instead, he took the words Tremley spoke. "It would be a pity if she were told the truth. What would she think of you then? Her unimpeachable brother?"

It was a perfect threat. Not empty in any way. It did not threaten West's future. It was enough to keep him under Tremley's thumb without being enough to force Tremley to make good on the larger, constant threat that hung between them.

He did not threaten to reveal West's secrets.

He threatened to reveal Cynthia's.

"You cannot save all the women in the world, Jamie."

Anger flared, hot and nearly unbearable. He spoke, a low, dark promise. "I will wreck you someday. I shall do it for me, yes, but for everyone else you've ever hurt."

Tremley smirked. "Such a hero. Tilting at windmills. Still the boy who cannot win." The words were designed to make Duncan feel powerless. "I don't care how much money or influence you have, Jamie, I've the protection of a king. And your freedom exists only through my benevolence."

With the words, Duncan was a child once more, furious and eager for a fight. Desperate to win. So desperate for a different life that he was willing to steal one.

He did not reply.

"That's what I thought," said the other man, taking his leave.

West watched him as he approached a young woman, a duke's daughter, just out, and asked her to dance. She smiled and accepted the offer, sinking into a deep curtsy, knowing that a turn with the Earl of Tremley, who held King William's ear, would only increase her value.

It was ironic that the aristocracy did not notice the filth among them—only its title.

He needed to know what Chase knew about Tremley. Immediately.

She'd had too much to drink.

It was unplanned. Unexpected, even. Indeed, she could drink scotch with the best of them. She *had* drunk scotch with the best of them.

But tonight, she'd had too much champagne. And champagne, as everyone who had lived since Marie Antoinette knew, was perfume going in and something altogether different once it got there.

She paused. Was it Marie Antoinette with the champagne?

It did not matter. What mattered was that she had had too much champagne, and now she was expected to dance. And later, she would be expected to do other things entirely.

Things she wanted to do. With Duncan West.

Things she'd *asked* to do.

Things she was terrified of doing incorrectly.

But all those thoughts were for a different time. Now, all she had to do was dance.

Thank heavens that Viscount Langley was an excellent dancer.

It should not have come as a surprise, as he was exceedingly well bred—charming and amusing and more than willing to keep up his end of the conversation—but Georgiana was always surprised when the viscount whirled her across the ballroom without a single misstep, ignoring the fact that she was not an exceedingly talented follower at this point in the evening.

She didn't think she'd ever danced with someone so clearly athletic.

She had enjoyed it in the past, and might have done so this evening if she hadn't had too much champagne, which she would never have done if she weren't so damn focused on another man, who was not dancing. Indeed, Duncan West had not moved from his post at one end of the ballroom since he'd arrived at Beaufetheringstone House an hour earlier. And his lack of motion was making it quite difficult for her to watch him without being caught.

Nonetheless, she met his gaze across the room, excitement and nervousness spiraling in the pit of her stomach.

Tonight was tomorrow night.

I am in control.

The thought of his words from the prior evening, of their promise, sent a wash of color across her cheeks. She tore her gaze away.

Good Lord. It was possible she'd made a terrible mistake in making such a bold, brazen suggestion. Now she was going to have to go through with it.

She'd never simultaneously wanted and been terrified of something so much.

"What has you so interested in Duncan West?"

And it was clearly, thoroughly obvious.

She turned her gaze to Lord Langley, affecting surprise. "My lord?"

Langley smiled, all affability. "I am not without powers of observation."

She shook her head. "I don't know what you mean."

His brows rose. "You only make the situation more curious with your protests." She let him twirl her across the room, taking a moment to collect her thoughts. He did not wait for her to find her words, continuing. "I suppose it is gratitude?"

"My lord?" This time she did not have to affect anything. Duncan West was making her terribly nervous simply by breathing. Why would she be grateful for that?

"He is doing excellent work in bringing your qualities to the attention of the *ton*." He smiled, self-deprecating. "I suppose that when West is done, you shan't even give me a second look."

It seemed that Langley noticed more than she'd given him credit for. "I doubt that, my lord," she said. "Indeed, it is you who condescends to be seen with me."

He smiled. "You are very good at that."

"At what?"

"At making it seem as though I am a catch."

"You are a catch," she insisted.

He smiled, and she recognized the irony that others would not see. *Chase* recognized the irony. "I am no such thing. I'm impoverished. Can barely afford the shoes on my feet."

She made a show of looking down at them. "They are exceedingly well polished, if for the holes." When he laughed, she added, "My lord, I am said to be impoverished in any number of other ways—ways that cannot be so easily rectified."

He watched her carefully. "Then I am to be grateful for the title?"

"I would be." The words were out before she could stop them. Before she could realize how many different and inappropriate ways they could be taken. "I did not mean—"

He smiled. "I know what you meant."

She shook her head. "I don't think you do. I merely meant that any number of others would happily trade places with you."

"Do you know anyone?" He smirked.

Her gaze flickered over his shoulder again, to the place in the crowd where Duncan West's golden hair gleamed, his height making him thoroughly visible. She wondered—if he could trade it, would he take the title?

If he had a title—

She did not allow herself to finish the thought. "I'm afraid I don't."

"Aha," he announced. "So you admit that titles are not all they are cracked up to be."

She smiled. "They do seem to be a great deal of requirement and obligation."

"I was not supposed to have the obligation," he said, wistfully.

"Damn distant infertile cousins," she said, her hand flying to her lips to stop the words after they'd been spoken.

He laughed loud enough to draw attention from fellow dancers. "You are more than you seem, Lady Georgiana."

She thought of the file in her office. Disliked the guilt that came with the idea that she might have to use it to win him. She smiled up at him. "As are you, my lord."

He grew quiet at that, and she wondered if he realized what she was saying. What she knew. What she was willing to use if need be.

Her gaze flickered to West, still standing sentry, this time with a companion.

Tremley.

She would have barely noticed their conversation a week earlier—but now, there was something about them, about the way Tremley smiled that smile that did not reach his eyes, and the way West stood, strangely stiff, unsettled.

She owed West the information on Tremley—the file now filled with the secrets his wife had shared. But now, watching them together, she wondered at their connection. Why was he so interested in the earl? How had he known there were such secrets to be had?

Something unsettling curled through her as she watched, and then the dance required a turn, and she exhaled her irritation at this world, where she was beholden to custom instead of her own curiosity.

They were at the edge of the room now, near to the doors that stood open onto a crowded balcony. Langley looked down at her. "Shall we take some air?"

It was possible Langley had noticed that she'd overimbibed.

And perhaps it was a good thing that he had, as outside would distract her from Duncan West, and anything that distracted her from Duncan West this evening was a good thing.

Langley guided her to the edge of the ballroom, past a lone woman standing at its edge—Lady Mary Ashehollow, alone, bereft of suitors. Georgiana experienced a slight tinge of remorse at the young woman's sad eyes.

She paused on Langley's arm. "Lady Mary," she acknowledged, willing the girl to show some remorse.

The girl scowled and turned her back on Georgiana, an undeniable, public cut direct.

Georgiana raised a brow, and returned her attention to Langley, who had been shocked by the interaction. They pushed outside onto a balcony, where half a dozen people played chaperone. He walked her to the balustrade, away from the others, and she placed her hands on the stone, drawing a deep breath of cool air, hoping it would stop her spinning head.

"Is that normal?" he asked after a moment. "The rudeness?"

"It's never been quite so obvious," she said. "But Lady Mary might have a slightly more understandable reason for it."

He nodded, then asked, "Did she deserve it?"

"Deserve what?"

"Whatever you did to make her angry."

"She did, rather," Georgiana said.

She deserved it more than you would.

She left the last unsaid.

"It's exhausting, isn't it?" Langley went on. "The playacting?"

She looked to him, registered the understanding in his gaze. He acted, as well. Every moment. She smiled. "It is, rather."

He leaned back against the balustrade and indicated the group of women at the far end of the balcony, a collection of them, now whispering. "They are discussing us."

She looked over to them. "No doubt they are wondering what I've done to win you out here into such a clandestine moment."

He leaned in. "And wondering if they might witness something scandalous."

"Poor girls," she said. "They won't."

"Poor girls?" he feigned affront. "Poor me!"

She laughed at the words, even as she knew he didn't mean them, drawing more overt glances from the young women. Perhaps it would not be so bad to marry Langley. Perhaps he would make a good companion. Charming and entertaining. Kind. Clever.

But lacking in any attraction.

Lacking in any *possibility* of attraction.

Which was what had made him so perfect. Indeed, attraction had only ever been the source of her trouble.

She was best without it, and the events of the last week proved that. Without it—without the way Duncan West made her feel—she would not be so topsy-turvy. He would not have such unnerving power over her.

She should not be *thinking of West*, dammit. On what was to come that evening. On the promises he'd made, dark and sinful and wicked. On the promises she'd made, to give in. And why not give in? Now, once. Why not allow herself the pleasure of him? The experience with him? And why not then retreat, quietly, to a life as Viscountess Langley?

She had to be asked to be Viscountess Langley, first.

And that was not going to happen tonight.

Another girl stepped onto the balcony, one whom Georgiana recognized. It was Sophie, the daughter of the Earl of Wight, her champion from the other night.

She was alone, clearly exiled by her friends, no doubt for her defense of Georgiana. And the poor thing looked lost.

Georgiana turned to Langley, wanting to end this moment. Wanting to release him from her web. "You should dance with her," she said. "She's sweet. She could use the support."

He raised a brow. "From an impoverished viscount?"

"From a handsome, kind gentleman." It was an apology, but he did not know it. An apology for the way she used him. For the way she was willing to use him. She nodded in Sophie's direction. "Dance with her. I shall be fine here. It's nice to have the fresh air."

He cut her a look, his first acknowledgment of her inebriated state. "I imagine it is."

She shook her head. "I am sorry."

"No apologies necessary. Lord knows I've needed that particular brand of courage once or twice with the *ton* myself." He bowed, reaching for her hand and pressing a kiss to her gloved knuckles. "As my lady wishes."

He left her then, moving to Sophie, who was first shocked and then obviously flattered by his favor. Georgiana watched them return to the ballroom and take immediately to the dance. They were well matched, the handsome viscount and the nervous wallflower.

It was a pity that Langley could not give Sophie that for which she no doubt wished.

Georgiana turned away from the couple and took another deep breath, looking to the darkness, searching for solid ground.

"You won't find me out there."

The words sent a thrill through her, and she tried to hide it, which was more difficult than she would have imagined. She turned to find Duncan a few feet away.

She wished he was closer.

No. She didn't.

"As it happens, sir, I was not looking for you."

He met her gaze. "No?"

He was exasperating. "No. And as you came to me, one might believe that it was *you* searching for *me*."

"Perhaps it was."

It took all of her energy to hide the satisfaction she felt. "We must stop meeting on balconies."

"I came out to tell you that it is time to leave," he said. It seemed apt that the statement came from the darkness, as it brought a deep sense of sin with it, pooling inside her in a pit of nerves and anticipation. And not a small amount of fear.

"Farewell," she said, willing her fear away. Wishing for more alcohol.

"I'm for the club," he said, moving just enough for her to see his face in the candlelight that spilled from the ballroom. "I've a message for Chase." He was all seriousness. She stilled, disappointment rocketing through her. She thought he'd come for her, but he hadn't. He'd come for Chase.

It occurred, vaguely, that they were one and the same, but she could not think too much on that.

"Chase is not there," she snapped before she'd thought about it.

His brows snapped together. "How do you know that?"

She hesitated, then said, "I don't."

He watched her for a long moment. "You do, but now is not the time to discuss how. It is time for us to leave."

"It is ten o'clock. The ball has just begun."

"The ball is half over, and we have an arrangement."

"We did not have an arrangement that involves my carrying messages to Chase." She heard the peevishness in the words. Did not particularly care. "I am not ready to leave. I am dancing."

"You've danced with six men, nine if you count Cross, Bourne, and the Marquess of Ralston."

She smiled. "You've been watching."

"Of course I've been watching." The information was pleasing indeed. As was that "of course." "And I allowed you a quarter of an hour here with Langley."

"You *allowed me*?"

"I did. And nine dances is plenty for one evening."

"It's only six. Married men don't count."

"They count for me."

She did move closer then, unable to resist the words, dark and filled with irritation. "Be careful, sir, or I shall think you're jealous."

His eyes were liquid, the color of mahogany. And tremendously compelling. "Have you forgotten? Me, and no one else?"

"No, the arrangement was you, and not Chase."

Mahogany turned black. "There's a new arrangement, then." This Duncan West was like none she'd ever seen— utterly focused, filled with power and might. And desire.

A desire that would be mutual if she allowed it to be. If he weren't so unnerving.

"You could have danced with me," she said softly, stepping closer.

He met her halfway, closing the distance between them and whispering, "No, I couldn't have."

"Good God."

Georgiana spun around at the words to find Temple standing a few feet away, his wife on his arm.

"Christ, Temple, you have terrible timing," Duncan grumbled before bowing. "Your Grace."

Mara, Duchess of Lamont, smiled, and Georgiana did not like the knowledge in the smile, as though she knew everything that had transpired between the others on the balcony. And she likely did. "Mr. West. Lady Georgiana."

"The two of you need a chaperone," Temple said.

"We're in full view of half of London," Georgiana snapped.

"You're on a dark balcony in full view of half of London," Temple replied, coming closer. "That's *why* you need a chaperone. Look at him."

She did as she was told. Not that it was a challenge. "He's very handsome."

West's brows rose.

"I . . ." Temple paused and gave her a strange look. "All right. Well. I'm not talking about that bit—though I assume a chaperone wouldn't care much for such a statement—I'm talking about the fact that he looks as though he's planning to steal you away."

"You look that way as well," she pointed out.

"Yes. But that's because I *am* planning to steal *my wife* away. As we are married, we are allowed to do the things that people do on dark balconies."

"William," the duchess said. "You'll embarrass them. And me."

He looked to his wife. "I shall make it up to you." The words were filled with dark promise, and Georgiana rolled her eyes before he continued, "Tell me he doesn't look as though he's planning to steal her away."

Mara considered them, and Georgiana resisted the urge to smooth her skirts. "He does, rather."

"As it turns out," Georgiana said, "he is planning that very thing."

"Good Lord," Temple said.

"It wasn't going to be quite so overt," Duncan said.

"Well, she's not going anywhere now," Temple replied. He turned to her and cocked his head in the direction of the dancing. "Let's go."

She blinked. "Let's go where?"

"I'm going to dance with you."

"I don't wish to dance with you." She heard the petulance in her tone and couldn't summon the energy to change it. She waved a hand at the duke and duchess. "Besides, don't you have other plans?"

"I did, and we shall discuss later how irritated I am that you are forcing me to change them."

"I don't need you to dance with me," she whispered. "West can dance with me."

"I'm not sure that will solve the issue of him looking like he'd like to steal you away," Mara said, altogether too thoughtfully.

Duncan's reply was more forthright. "No."

"No?" she asked, taken aback by his quick refusal.

"I'm not titled," he said. "You can't be seen dancing with me."

How silly. "But you're the man who is restoring my reputation."

"Among others," Temple interjected.

"You mean others like you?"

"Your Grace," Temple and Duncan prompted in unison.

Georgiana shook her head, confused. "You needn't call me that; I am not a duchess."

The trio looked at her as though she were mad. And that's when they all realized what was happening.

"Christ," said Duncan.

"Are you drunk?" asked Temple.

She put her fingers to her lips. "It's possible."

The men looked at each other, then back to her. "How in hell are you drunk?"

"I imagine it happened when I consumed too much alcohol," she said smartly.

Mara snickered.

"Why?" Temple asked.

"I enjoy champagne."

"You loathe champagne," Temple said.

She nodded. "Was it Marie Antoinette with the champagne?" These three would know.

Temple looked as though he might murder her. Duncan watched her carefully, as though she might turn into some sort of animal. "She's responsible for the champagne glass."

"Yes! The glass is the shape of her breast!" It was all coming back, if a touch too loudly.

"Christ." Temple said.

"Perhaps we should limit the use of the word *breast* in public," Duncan said, dryly. "Why don't you tell us why you felt the need to drink in excess?"

"I was nervous!" she said in her own defense, then realized what she'd admitted. She looked to Duncan, whose expression had gone from surprised to smug. *Damn.* "Not because of you."

"Of course not," he said, meaning the opposite.

Temple looked about. "I don't want to know anything about that. Stop talking."

"There's nothing to worry about, *Your Grace.*" She emphasized the title. She returned her attention to Duncan. "There are any number of men who make me nervous."

"Jesus, Anna, stop talking."

"Don't call her that," Duncan said, and the warning in his voice was enough to draw the attention of both her and Temple.

"It's her name."

"Not here, it's not. And not really, it's not." Duncan and Temple stared each other down, and something happened between them. Finally, Temple nodded.

"William," Mara said quietly. "We are making it worse. You are not supposed to be so . . ."

"Boorish with me," Georgiana said.

Mara tilted her head. "I was going to say 'familiar.'"

She was not incorrect. The Duke of Lamont was not supposed to know her well enough to scold her on a balcony.

Temple was quiet for a long moment before he acquiesced to his wife. It was something that never failed to impress Georgiana—the massive man entirely engrossed in his wife. He looked to Duncan. "You're supposed to keep her reputation intact."

"All of Society knows I have a vested interest in her. They won't be surprised in the slightest by our conversing," he said. "They shall think she's thanking me for my hand in her blossoming acceptance."

"I am standing right here," she said, supremely irritated by the way the group seemed to have forgotten that fact.

Temple thought for a long moment, and then nodded. "If you do anything to hurt her reputation—"

"I know, I shall answer to Chase."

Temple's gaze flickered from Duncan to Georgiana. "Forget Chase. You shall answer to me. You get her home."

She smirked at Duncan. "No messages for Chase tonight. You'll have to deal with me, only."

Duncan ignored her, extending his arm. "My lady?"

She warmed at the words, hating the way they brought her such keen pleasure. She set her hand on his arm, letting him guide her a few steps down the balustrade before she pulled back. "Wait." She turned back. "Your Grace." He raised his brows in question. She returned on Duncan's arm, spoke softly. "The Earl of Wight's daughter. Sophie."

"What of her?"

"She is dancing with Langley, but deserves a dance with someone tremendous." She mentally cataloged the single men in attendance. "The Marquess of Eversley." Eversley was a long-standing member of the Angel, rich as Croesus and handsome as sin—a rake to end all rakes. But he'd do as Temple asked. And Sophie would have a lovely memory of the evening.

Temple nodded. "Done." He and Mara were gone, returned to the ball, leaving no trace of their time on the balcony.

Her good work for the evening complete, she returned her attention to Duncan, who asked, "Lady Sophie?"

She lifted a shoulder in a little shrug. "She was kind to Georgiana."

Understanding lit in his eyes. "And so Anna rewards her."

She smiled. "There are times when it is useful to be two people."

"I can see how that might be true," he said.

"I don't need a caretaker, you know," she said, the words soft enough that only he could hear them.

"No, but apparently you needed someone to tell you when to stop drinking."

She cut him a look. "If you hadn't made me nervous, I wouldn't have done it."

"Ah, so it was because of me." He smiled, full of pride, and it occurred to her that to the rest of those assembled on the balcony, their conversation seemed perfectly ordinary.

"Of course it was. You and your 'I am in control.' It's unsettling."

He grew very serious. "It shouldn't be."

She took a deep breath. "Well, it is."

"Are you unsettled now?"

"Yes."

He smiled, looking down at her hands. "I am disappointed in you. I would have thought you'd have been utterly prepared for this situation."

Because of Anna. He thought her a prostitute. Experienced in all matters of the flesh. Except she wasn't. And as if their arrangement weren't nerve-wracking enough, the idea that he would discover her lie—her truth—was thoroughly disquieting.

"I am usually the one in control," she said. It was not a lie.

He looked over her shoulder to confirm that the others on the balcony were far enough away not to hear their conversation.

"And tell me, do you like it? Being in control?"

She'd made a life of it. "I do."

"Does it pleasure you?" The question was low and dark.

"It does."

His lips twitched into a smile, there, then gone. "I don't think so."

She didn't like the way he seemed to know her. The way the words rang true—more true than anyone had ever noticed. Than she had ever admitted.

She didn't like the way he took control for himself, smooth and nearly imperceptibly, until she was bound in his dark voice and his broad shoulders and his tempting gaze. She wanted him, and there was only one way she could have him now, here. "Dance with me," she whispered.

He did not move. "I told you, dancing with me will not help your cause."

She looked into his eyes. "I don't care. I am unclaimed for this dance."

He shook his head. "I don't dance."

"Ever?"

"Ever," he said.

"Why not?"

"I don't know how."

The admission revealed more than she would have expected. He did not know how to dance. Which meant he was not born a gentleman. He was born something else. Something harder. Something baser. Something that had required work to conquer. To leave behind.

Something much more interesting.

"I could teach you," she said.

He raised a brow. "I'd rather you teach me other things."

"Such as?"

"Such as where you like to be kissed."

She smiled. "Be careful, or I shall think you are trying to turn my head."

"I've already turned your head."

It was true, and she couldn't stop herself from going serious at the words. At the hint of sadness that coursed through her at them. At the feeling that he was right, and she was ruined in more ways than she was willing to admit. She hid the thoughts with her best flirt. "You're awfully sure of yourself."

He was quiet for a long moment, and she wondered what he was thinking before he said, "Langley?"

She did not misunderstand. He asked how things proceeded with the viscount. "He likes me," she said, wishing he hadn't returned them to the present. To reality.

"That will make it easier for me. The columns will speed the courtship."

If only she wanted that. She was silent.

He continued. "It's a sound title. Clean. And he's a sound man."

"He is. Clever and charming. Poor, but there is no shame in it."

"You would change that for him."

"So I would." Her lips twisted in a wry smile. "He's infinitely better than me."

"Why do you say that?" The question came like steel. Without quarter.

She took a breath. Let it out. "May I tell you the truth?" she asked, realizing that she must be in her cups to offer him the truth. She dealt too often in lies.

"I wish you would," he said, and she thought perhaps he referred to more than this moment. This place.

Guilt flared, all too familiar that evening. "I only wish her to be happy."

He knew she spoke of Caroline. "Ah. Something far more difficult than well married."

"I'm not certain it is possible, honestly, but respectability will give her the widest opportunity for happiness . . . whatever that means."

He was watching her. She could feel his dark gaze on her. Knew that he was going to ask her something more than what she was willing to share. Still, his question shocked her. "What happened? To bring you Caroline?"

To bring you Caroline.

What a lovely way of saying it. Over the years, she'd heard Caroline's existence described in a hundred ways, ranging from euphemistic to filthy. But no one had ever said it so well, and so simply. And so aptly. Caroline had been brought to her. Perfect and innocent. Unaware of the havoc that she had wreaked on a woman, a family, a world.

Of course this man, known for his skill with words, described it so well.

And of course, here in the darkness, she wanted to tell him the truth. How she was ruined. By whom, even. Not that it mattered. "A tale as old as time," she said simply. "Unsavory men have a devastating power over rebellious girls."

"Did you love him?"

The words stunned her into silence. There were so many things he could have said in response. She'd heard them all, or so she thought. But that question—so simple, so honest—no one had ever asked it of her.

And so she gave him her simplest, most honest answer. "I wanted to. Quite desperately."

Chapter 11

... Charming daughter or no, there is no doubt by this point that the reputation of Lady G— is unimpeachable. Are we to blame her for a peccadillo from so long ago? And one that has such vibrance and charm? There will always be room for the Lady on these pages. But will there be room for her in London's hearts?

... Lady M— appears positively bereft at social gatherings these days. Gone are her trio of lords, each showing interest in others. Perhaps the lady did not sell when she should? Earl H— is no doubt lining the coffers of a particular dowry even as we scribble ...

The gossip pages of *The News of London*,
April 30, 1833

He could have imagined her answering his question in any number of ways, from flat denial, to refusal to answer the question, to humor or evasion or a question of her own.

But he never would have imagined that she would tell him the truth.

Or that she might have loved the man who had ruined her.

Nor would he have imagined how much the information would bother him or how much he wished to wipe the memory of the man from her mind.

To replace him.

He resisted the thought. For a dozen years—longer—Duncan had sworn off women who requested intensity of any kind. He was opposed to anything that might end in a desire for something more than a fleeting fancy, than a mutual arrangement designed solely for the pleasure of both parties.

Commitment was not in the cards for Duncan West.

It could not be. Ever.

Because he would never saddle another person with his secrets, which loomed large and ever-threatening, always a heartbeat away from revelation and ruin. He would never leave another with the shadow of his past, with the punishment that would no doubt be his future.

It was the only noble thing he could ever do—staying himself from commitment.

Keeping himself from love.

And so, he should not care if Lady Georgiana Pearson loved the father of her daughter. It mattered not a bit to him, or to his future. The only way the man was in any way relevant to Duncan's life was if he were revealed—thus requiring column inches in Duncan's newspapers.

No, he should not care. And he did not.

Except he did. Ever so slightly.

"What happened to him?"

She did not pretend to misunderstand. "Nothing happened. He never intended to stay."

"Is he alive?"

She hesitated, and he watched her consider lying. "He is."

"You love him."

She took a deep breath and released it, as though the conversation had gone too far in a direction and she was not prepared to follow. Which, it occurred to him, was very likely the situation.

"Why don't you know how to dance?" she asked quietly, staring intently into the darkness.

The question and the way it twisted the conversation irritated him. "Why is it relevant?"

"The past is always relevant," she said simply before she faced him. Utterly calm. As though they discussed the weather. "I would like to teach you to dance."

The words were barely out when a boisterous group of revelers spilled onto the balcony, crossing paths with the group that had been there when he had found Georgiana. Making a quick, barely calculated decision, Duncan seized the opportunity for escape, clasping Georgiana's elbow and guiding her quickly and silently into the darkness at the edge of the space, where a set of stone steps led down into the gardens.

Within seconds, they had left the ball, without being seen.

He moved them around a corner of the great stone house, into the darkness, where anyone who saw them would have secrets of his own to hide.

Once there, in the shadows, she said, "How will we return?"

"We won't," he replied.

"We must. I've a cloak. And a chaperone. And a reputation to uphold. And you've promised to help do just that."

"I am taking you home."

"That isn't as easy as you would think."

"I've a carriage and I am familiar with the location of your brother's estate."

"I don't live there," she said, leaning up against the dark wall of the house, watching him in the darkness. "I live at the Angel."

"No," he said, "*Anna* lives at the Angel."

"She's not the only one."

The statement grated. "You mean Chase." She did not reply, and he added, "He lives at the Angel?"

"Most nights," she said, so simply that he had to bite his tongue to hold back his retort.

She clearly sensed his irritation. "Why does it make you so angry? My life?"

"Because this didn't have to be your life, nights spent on the floor of the casino. Carrying messages for Chase."

"To and from you," she pointed out.

Guilt flared. She was not wrong. "For what it's worth, I've an excellent reason for tonight's message. And I was not going to ask you to deliver it."

"What is it?"

He could not tell her that his sister was in danger. Could not bring her any closer to the knowledge that he and Tremley were more than passing acquaintances. If Chase knew how much the Tremley file was worth to him, he might hold it ransom. And Cynthia would be more and more in danger.

"It's not relevant to our discussion. My point is—"

"Your point is that you believe there was a life of tea and quadrilles waiting for me at the end of some path not chosen. Your point is that Chase has ruined me."

"As a matter of fact, it is."

She laughed at that. "Then you have forgotten what it is *Society* does to young women in my particular situation."

"You could have survived it," he said.

"No. I couldn't have." The words were so matter-of-fact, it was almost as though she weren't the victim of fate at all.

"You could have done this ages ago. Married."

She raised a brow. "I could have, but I would have hated it." She paused. "What would you say if I told you that this was my choice? That I wanted this life?"

"I wouldn't believe you. No one chooses exclusion. No one chooses ruination. You have fallen victim to a powerful man who has kept you in his pocket for too long, and now refuses to release you fully."

"You're wrong. I chose this life," she said, and he almost believed her. "Chase saved me."

Hatred flared at the words, the words of a woman in too deep. A woman who cared too much to see the truth. A woman who—

Christ. Was it possible that she loved him?

On the heels of that thought came another.

Was it possible that Chase was Caroline's father?

Anger flared, hot and devastating. He could ask her, but she'd never confess it if it were true. And it would explain a great deal—why she chose this life, why she lived at the Angel, why she protected Chase with all she had.

He didn't deserve it, her protection.

He deserved to stand in the sun and be judged like all the rest of them.

He swore, harsh and wicked in the darkness. "I want—" He stopped himself from completing the sentence.

She wasn't having that. "What do you want?"

It might have been the dark that made him finish the thought. Or it might have been the moment, earlier in the evening, when another man, who wielded his unwelcome power all too similarly to the one they discussed, had managed him. Whatever it was, he did finish the thought. "I want to tear him apart for the way he treats you."

She stilled. "Chase?"

"The very same."

"But you are . . . friends."

Everything inside him resisted the words. "We are nothing of the sort. We simply use each other to get what we want."

She was quiet for a long moment. "And what do you want?"

I want you.

He did not say it. While it was the most pressing answer to her question, it was not the one she sought. "I want to sell newspapers. What does Chase want?"

She hesitated. Then, "Why would I know that?"

"Because you know him better than anyone. You speak for him. You carry messages to him. You . . ." *You love him.* "Christ, you live with him."

"Anna lives with him," she repeated his words from minutes earlier.

He hated them. "She's not real."

"She's as real as any of us," she said, and he wished he could blame the alcohol for the statement. But he couldn't.

"How can you say that? You created her. When you live her, you do not live the rest of your life."

She met his gaze, all seriousness. "When I live her, I live all of my life. Without hesitation and with pleasure."

"It is not your pleasure," he retorted, her words infuriating him. It was Chase's pleasure. It was the pleasure of any number of men she'd been with since she began this charade.

She was a lady. The daughter of a duke. The sister of one. She was so much more than he was. So much more than he could ever have. And yet she sold herself short, accepting life under the thumb of a powerful coward.

"It is entirely my pleasure," she said, and the air changed between them, thickening with her words, nearly liquid with promise.

He let her lean in, enjoying the feel of her as she came closer. The heat of her, even as he resisted her lure. Even as his anger at her words threatened to overflow.

"I don't think you know pleasure," he said, knowing the words would rankle. Wishing them to.

Her eyes went wide, and she turned Anna, all seductress. "You think I do not understand it?"

He resisted the urge to pull her closer. "I think you are used to giving it. And I think it is time you see that when it comes time . . . when I am in control, I intend for you to do very little but receive it."

He watched the words run over her, the way her gaze widened and her lips parted on a breath she hadn't expected to require. He reacted to that expression with every fiber of his being. The honesty in it made him want to roar his desire. His power.

He did not give her time to reply, instead lifting a hand and running his fingers over the silken skin of her cheek. "Would you like that?" he whispered, "Would you like it if I took control of your pleasure? If I wrapped you in it? If I gave it to you over and over, until you could not bear it? Until you ached for my touch above all others?"

Her breath caught in her throat as he stroked the column of her neck, and he leaned in, slowly, pressing his lips once, twice to the soft, pale skin at the underside of her chin. "Tell me," he whispered there, and the sound of her exhalation nearly shattered his control.

"Tell you . . ." She hesitated, the wine and the sensation making it difficult for her to think. He cursed the wine, even as he waited for her to finish. She swallowed, and he felt the swell of it beneath his fingertips. She cleared her throat. Tried again. "Tell you what?"

"Would you like it?"

"I would," she answered, the words more breath than sound.

"What would you like?" Now he was teasing her. He knew she couldn't think, but the proof of it was making him feel more a man than he ever had before.

"I would like you to . . ." She hesitated.

He ran his teeth along the column of her neck, nipping at the soft skin of her shoulder. "To—?"

She sighed. "All of it. I would like it all."

He couldn't see the color of her eyes in the darkness, but he recognized their intensity. One of her hands came to his neck, fingers curving and sliding into his hair. She did not release his gaze, and for a long, breathless moment, he wondered if, perhaps, she would be in control after all. "Do it," she whispered, those gorgeous pink lips licking around the words. "Please."

"Do what?" They were close now, nearly kissing. He'd never wanted anything the way he wanted this woman.

"Do it all." Her fingers slid further, pulling him down to her. "Show me everything."

She leaned up. Or perhaps he leaned down. It did not matter, except for the fact that they were kissing, and she was in his arms, and he wanted nothing more than to explore every inch of her glorious, perfect body. Her arms were wrapped around his neck, and he was lifting her, turning her, pressing her against the side of the house, giving her everything for which she asked.

She sighed into his mouth and he caught the beautiful sound, pulling her against him. Her lips, soft and sweet and warm, parted in perfection, and he could not stop himself from claiming her with tongue and teeth, nipping along her full bottom lip before chasing the bite with a long, slow lick that made her groan with anticipation. Or perhaps it was he who groaned.

She had him on fire. He gathered her closer and deepened the kiss, changing the pressure. He delved deeper, stroked more firmly.

And she met him at every single stroke, finally using her own teeth to tease and tempt and punish, and he groaned, grasping one long thigh in his hand and lifting it, spreading her open and pressing into the soft core where he so desperately wanted to be. He rocked against her, giving both of them a small, unbearable taste of what they might have if it were a different night.

Of what they *would* have when it *was* a different night.

The thought tore him away from her, and he ached at the way she clung to him, as though she'd forgotten for a moment who she was and where they were and why they couldn't have each other . . . this . . . now.

He was the same way, leaning back in, taking her lips once more, firmly, thoroughly, without hesitation.

He released her thigh and her lips at the same time, pressing his forehead to hers as they both caught their breath. When he finally spoke, it was in a whisper only for her. "I will show you everything. But not tonight. You've had too much to drink for me to give you all I intend for you to take."

Her retort was instant. "I haven't had too much to drink."

She wanted him. He could feel it in the pulse beneath his fingertips, in the breath against his neck, in the fingers that clung to his coat. "Yes, you have."

"It doesn't matter."

He turned her so that she could see his face, handsome and serious. "It matters a great deal. You see, I intend for every bit of ecstasy, everything you've never felt before, everything you will ache to have again." He took a step toward her, his words wrapping around them both like sin. "I intend for it all to be because of me."

She opened her mouth to argue.

He stopped her before she could speak. "Me alone. Without question, Georgiana."

She closed her eyes at the name, capturing his hand with hers, tightly, as though she needed to steady herself. "You don't want Georgiana. You want Anna. She's the one who knows about passion."

"I know exactly who I want," he said, leaning forward, dipping his head to the place where her neck met her shoulder, where she smelled of vanilla and Georgiana. The scent was intoxicating and dangerous. And hers alone. He continued, letting his tongue lick along the spot. "I want Georgiana."

She turned to him and kissed him, as though the words were unexpected and desperately desired. He caught her against him and gave her a full, sweeping kiss before a thought whispered through him, and he pulled back, meeting her gaze.

"Caroline's father . . ."

She looked away, suddenly, remarkably looking like the girl she'd once been. "It's rather an inopportune time to discuss him, don't you think?"

"I don't, actually," he said. "Now is the perfect time to tell you that he was a fool."

"Why?" she asked.

It wasn't a search for a compliment. There was no artifice in the question. So there was no artifice in his answer. "Because if I had a chance to have you in my bed every night, I would take it. Without question."

He regretted the words almost immediately—the meaning in them. The power they gave her over him. But then she leaned into him, as though the words had pulled her to him. He caught her, the feel of her too welcome to resist.

When she spoke, she was all seductress. "You have a chance for it tonight, and you are not taking it."

The words had the desired effect, desire pooling deep in him. "That is because I am a gentleman."

Her lips made a perfect moue. "A pity. I was promised a scoundrel."

He kissed her once, quickly. "Tomorrow night, you get one." He spoke low and quiet at her lips before pulling away. Any more, and he would be desperate to have her. He had promised Temple he would take her home. "We must go."

"I don't wish to go," she said, and the honesty in the words was more tempting than he could have imagined. "I wish to stay here. With you."

"In the gardens of Beaufetheringstone House?"

"Yes," she said, quietly. "Anywhere that the light doesn't come through."

He paused. "You have a problem with light?"

"I have a problem with things that do not thrive in the dark. I am not comfortable with them."

He understood the words and the sentiment behind them, more than he was willing to admit. In fact, the way they resonated so unsettled him that he was suddenly quite desperate to get her home and away from him, before her liquid honesty inspired his own—drink or no. He took her hand. "We cannot stay here. I have things to do." She ignored him for a long moment, looking down at their hands, clasped together. Finally, he said, "Georgiana."

She looked up. "I wish we were not wearing gloves."

The thought of their hands, skin to skin, tempted him beyond reason. "I am very glad we are wearing them, or I might not be able to resist you."

She smiled. "You know just what to say to women. You might be a scoundrel after all."

He met her smile with his own. "I told you I was."

"Yes, but scoundrels are notorious liars. So I had no way of knowing if I should believe you."

"A great logical conundrum. If one tells the truth about being a scoundrel, is he scoundrel at all?"

"Perhaps a scoundrel with a gentlemanly core."

He leaned in and whispered, "Don't tell anyone. You shall ruin my reputation."

She laughed, and the sound gave him immense pleasure. He was sad when it was gone, stolen into the dark gardens on a breeze. After a long stretch of silence, she said, "You said you had a message for Chase."

Chase.

Duncan had avoided asking for Tremley's file for a plain, simple reason. It was stupidity on his part—she was bound to Chase in ways he did not understand and he could not stop— but it did not change the fact that he didn't want her near the founder of The Fallen Angel if she didn't need to be there.

He didn't want her near him if she *did* need to be there.

He'd get the file another way. Without using her. "It doesn't matter."

"I don't believe that," she said. "I saw your face when you sought me out. Tell me. I'll . . ." She hesitated, and he wondered what she meant to say. Before he could ask, she said, "I'll pass Chase your message. Give it to me."

He shook his head. "No. I don't want you involved in this."

"In what?"

In his mess.

In Tremley's threats.

It was bad enough that his sister was in danger, but he could protect Cynthia. He had less control over Georgiana. And he couldn't be certain that Chase would care for her if need be.

She had to remain clear of this.

He shook his head. "It's time you distance yourself from him."

"From Chase?" she asked. "If only it were as easily done as said."

He hated the words and the sadness in her small smile. "I shall help." He'd do whatever he could to get her away from Chase and his unfettered, unreasonable power over her.

She nodded. "Your papers will help. Anna will have to disappear once Georgiana is married."

He would help, papers be damned.

But she did not need to know that now.

𝒯he following morning, Georgiana sat at her enormous desk at The Fallen Angel, attempting to focus on the work of the casino, as Cross placed a parcel at the edge of her desk.

"From West," he said. "Delivered from his offices this morning."

She looked to the parcel, wondering for a fleeting moment if West had packed it himself. Before she could stop herself, she reached for the paper-wrapped parcel, her fingers toying with the string that kept its contents secret from prying eyes at his offices and hers. If he'd tied it himself, he'd had to have done it without gloves. She stroked down the ridge of one loop of the string. Just as she was without gloves now.

Just as she would be this evening, when he made good on his promise. And she made good on hers.

Realizing that she was being a cabbagehead, and that Cross was staring at her as though she'd grown a second head, made of cabbage, she snatched her fingers away. "Thank you," she said, affecting her greatest tone of dismissal.

She ignored the look of amusement on his handsome face. "A note arrived at the same time. For Anna."

He set the crisp ecru square on top of the parcel, and she resisted the urge to tear open the envelope, instead turning her face back to her work—a movement that both made her look exceedingly busy and hid her flaming cheeks from her business partner, who would no doubt tell all the others if he suspected her embarrassment. "Thank you."

He did not move.

She willed the blush away.

It did not work.

"Is there something else?"

He did not reply.

She had no choice. She looked up. He was trying not to laugh at her. She scowled. "I am not above turning you out on your ass."

His lips twitched. "You and which army?"

"Is there something else? Or are you simply being a pillock?"

Cross grinned. "The latter. I'm curious about that package. Temple says you're after him."

"Temple is married. Of course I'm not after him."

He laughed. "You think you're very clever."

"I am very clever."

"Temple says that you made a fool of yourself last night. When was the last time you drank champagne?"

"Last night," she said, crossing one buckskin-covered leg over the other and reaching for the package, pretending not to think on the evening that loomed ahead. Pretending not to seriously consider calling for a case of champagne to prepare for it.

She opened the package, knowing Cross would not leave until she'd done so.

He'd sent her the paper. If one could refer to Duncan West's gossip rag as "the paper."

The week's edition of *The Scandal Sheet* had arrived at The Fallen Angel two days before it would land on breakfast tables across London. Except it wasn't for her. It was a gift to the man known only as Chase.

No, not gift. Service. As requested.

"Scandal Becomes Salvation," the headline on the front page read, followed in smaller text with "Lady G— Rides Through *Ton*, Wins Aristocratic Hearts."

Cross laughed, craning his head to read the page. "Clever. I shall tell you—I know you did not like that cartoon, but the reference to Lady Godiva makes for excellent reading." He took the paper from the desk to read more carefully.

She pretended not to care, opening the note that accompanied Chase's package. "Lady Godiva was protesting outrageous taxation."

Cross looked up. "No one remembers that bit. They just remember the nudity."

"How is that to help me land a husband?"

He grew serious. "Trust me. Nudity helps."

"You used to be the one I liked best."

"I am still the one you like best." He leaned forward. "The important thing is when West makes an arrangement, he delivers. Look at the amount of attention he's devoted to you." He turned back to the page and read. "Lauding your grace and charm."

The lauding was not free, however. He'd sent Chase a note with the paper. A request for payment.

> *The girl receives her attention.*
> *You owe me the earl.*

The missive was written in thick black scrawl, so confident that there had been no need for Duncan to sign the note.

Her gaze flickered from the note to Tremley's file on the edge of her desk, waiting for delivery, to Cross, still reading, "He regales the reader with the number of titled men and women who have accepted Lady G— into their hearts and minds and world!" He looked up. "It's a pity it's not true."

"It does not need to be true. I am only interested in one suitor."

And she should thank her maker that Lord Langley was willing to at least consider her as an option. The lack of invitations and notes indicated that Georgiana remained too scandalous for the men of London.

"Langley." Cross did not hide his disdain for her plan.

"You take issue in Langley choosing me for his lady?"

"Not at all. Except he's not interested in choosing a lady."

She met his gaze. "We don't discuss his file. Ever. This

will be the last I say on the subject: His interests are not a concern, as I've no need of being courted."

"Then what's the hope for West?"

She wouldn't allow herself a hope for West. Nothing beyond their simple arrangement. Pleasure. Carefully. Until he made good on his promise and she was matched. "You cannot imagine that I'm angling for West's attention."

He leaned back in his chair. "I don't know what to imagine. But Temple seems to think—"

"Temple is addled from too many rounds in the ring."

Cross raised a brow, but did not reply.

She took a breath. Released it.

"West is—" She stopped, searching for something to say that would make sense of the moment. Of the way her entire, carefully constructed world seemed to come unraveled every time the man appeared. Of the fact that that his impact on her world did not make her wish he was far from her.

Of the fact that it somehow made her wish he was nearer.

There was an irony in that, she supposed, that he remained such a gentleman around her despite knowing her secrets. The evening before could have been full of scandal. Of more.

And he'd resisted her.

As though it had been the easiest thing in the world.

As though the kisses they'd shared hadn't moved him at all.

As though they hadn't been thoroughly earth-shattering.

She felt her cheeks warming again.

"West is complicated," she said.

"Well, then he's a terrible match for you, as you are so very simple." She smiled at the teasing in the words, grateful that Cross, somehow, blessedly, had not pushed her to elaborate. Instead, he brushed a speck from his trouser leg and said, "The men have not found anything on him."

A whisper of guilt came with the reminder of her earlier demands for information on Duncan. Before she'd met his sister. Before she'd propositioned him. Before she'd desired him quite so much. She pushed the unwelcome emotion aside.

She'd made the mistake of trusting another so long ago and been left destroyed. She would not make that mistake again.

She ignored the way her reply unsettled. "Tell them to keep looking."

He nodded, quiet for a long moment before he leaned forward. "Do you remember how you found me?"

"Of course." Neither of them would ever forget the night he'd been tossed out of another gaming hell, beaten black and blue for counting cards and running the tables one too many times. Georgiana had known the moment she'd heard the story that Cross was the fourth for which she'd been searching. They'd found him drunk and on the brink of destruction—at his own hand.

"You saved me that night."

"You would have saved yourself."

"No," Cross shook his head. "Without you, I would be dead or something far worse. Bourne and Temple would be dead in an alleyway in the East End. You saved us all in one way or another." He paused. "And we are not the only ones. Every person employed by The Fallen Angel. Most employed in our homes . . . they're all yours."

"Do not paint me a savior," she said. "The color does not suit."

"Nevertheless, it is what you are. Every one of us, saved by Chase." She did not reply, and he did not stop. "But what happens when it is Chase who needs saving?"

Her gaze snapped to his, the words coming quick and unbidden. "I don't."

He leaned back. Waited for a long moment. When she said nothing else, he said, "Perhaps not. But do not doubt that we will not stand idly by should hell freeze over."

He stood, brushing his hands down his trousers. "Pippa would like you to come to dinner next week." He paused. "You and Caroline."

She raised a brow. Cross's wife was the least likely person in London to invite someone to dinner. He smiled, seeming to understand her surprise, the love he had for his wife lightening his face, setting something off deep in Georgiana. "It's not a dinner party. It's dinner. And will likely end in all of us covered in dirt."

It was not a metaphor. The Countess Harlow was a renowned horticulturalist. Events at Harlow House often culminated in some kind of gardening. Caroline loved it.

Georgiana nodded. "With pleasure."

She returned her attention to the desk, her gaze falling to the second note, the one for Anna that tempted her from the edge of the desk. She wanted to open it quite desperately, but knew better than to do it with Cross in attendance.

He seemed to understand. "Don't hesitate on my account," he said, all amusement.

She scowled at him. "Why are you so interested?"

"I miss the days of clandestine messages ending in secret assignations."

The words grated. "It's not clandestine if it comes at eleven in the morning."

He smiled, and she marveled at the openness in the expression—something that was never there in the old, haunted Cross. "It's clandestine if it has to do with activities that are traditionally associated with eleven in the evening."

"It doesn't," she said, tearing open the envelope in a desperate attempt to prove him wrong.

There, in the same black script in which the note from Chase had been written, were three lines of text, again, unsigned.

> *My town house. 11 o'clock.*
> *Come well rested.*
> *And sober.*

The blush returned with a vengeance.

Cross laughed from his place by the door. "It doesn't, does it?"

He closed the door on her curse.

Alone once more, she let herself consider the words, the

square of rich paper that seemed far too luxurious for such a message. Or perhaps it was precisely as luxurious as it should be.

He seemed the kind of man who would not hesitate to be luxurious.

She lifted the paper to her nose, imagining she could smell him there, sandalwood and soap. Knowing she was being silly.

She tapped the paper to her lips, loving the way it brushed against them, soft and lush, like a kiss.

Like his kiss.

She dropped the note as though it was on fire. She could not allow him to consume her this way. Her proposition was not intended for him to reduce her to some quivering, ridiculous mass. It was not designed for him to consume her. Or control her.

It was designed for her to have a taste of the life she'd pretended to live all these years—the one she'd been accused of having—before she gave herself over to a new life that included marriage to a man with whom she would never have passion.

Passion.

It was not something that she lacked with West.

But she would be damned if she gave him all the control as well.

She reached for her pen.

I may be late.

He replied within the hour.

You won't be late.

Chapter 12

As with the Lady G— to whom she was compared in the now infamous cartoon that heralded her return, our Lady is wrapped in proud grace and effortless charm. We are not the only ones to notice, either, as Lord L— moves ever nearer at each event they attend.

... In other news, the Earl and Countess of H— may not have eschewed the scandal that brought them together after all. Rumors abound about a locked door at a recent exhibition at the Royal Horticultural Society ...

Pearls & Pelisses Ladies Magazine,
early-May 1833

She was early.

Two hours before Georgiana was to arrive at his town house, Duncan exited his offices, pausing on the steps to raise the collar of his coat to combat the cold. A bitter wind tore down Fleet Street, reminding everyone in London that, while the calendar might claim spring, English weather was beholden to no one.

He was not unhappy about the cold. It gave him reason to light a fire and close the curtains around his bed that night. To lay Georgiana Pearson back against a pile of furs and have his way with her, the rest of the world blocked from thought and view.

He went hard and heavy at the thought of her, the vision of her naked and open coming unbidden and thoroughly welcome. Indeed, he'd spent much of the last day in a similar condition, eager for her. Wanting her.

Ready to claim her.

He took a deep breath, willing away the heavy ache. He had two hours before she was with him. Longer if her smart reply to his note earlier in the day was any indication. She would be late, on principle. And she would punish them both with it.

He would punish her in return, he thought with a wicked grin. He'd drive her to the brink of thought and breath, until she could remember nothing but him and how desperately she wanted him.

And then he'd give her what she wanted. And reward them both for their mutual patience.

He bit back a groan at the thought, grateful that he'd decided to walk home—surely he could not remain in such a state after a half an hour in this cold. Though it did seem as though his body was willing to do its best to prove him wrong.

At the bottom of the stairs, he noticed the carriage.

It was thoroughly innocuous. Unnoticeable in the extreme. Black, with no markings and no lights despite it being half-nine, well into a late-March night. No outriders. Two black horses and a driver, high on the block, making a point of not looking.

And those things, combined, made Duncan approach the vehicle instead of walking away. The windows were black, not because of a lack of light inside. They were black because they had been painted so.

This was no ordinary carriage.

Anticipation flared, and the door opened to reveal a lushly appointed interior, dark red velour, golden candlelight, and tempting shadows. His gaze flickered to the black satin-clad hand that held the door open, and he stilled, transfixed by that hand. Wanting it on him. In any number of ways.

She spoke, the words coming from out of view, soft and full of promise.

"You are letting out the heat."

He lifted himself into the carriage, seating himself across from her as the door closed behind him, throwing them into quiet perfection. She was dressed as Anna, wearing a beautiful black gown, the skirts full and spread wide across her seat, the bodice tight and low, revealing a long, lush expanse of pretty, pale skin. A shadow slashed across her neck and one shoulder, hiding her face so thoroughly that he could not make out any of her features.

She had told him the previous night that she preferred the dark, and now he saw why. Here, she reigned. And damned if he did not want to get down on his knees and vow fealty.

"I was told not to be late."

He warmed at the words. At the battle in them. He had expected her to be late. He'd prepared for it, having received the contrary note earlier in the day. She'd made it clear by the missive that she was not interested in being controlled. That their time together would be equal, or nothing.

He'd read the damn thing a half dozen times, feeling as though he hadn't been so well matched in years. Possibly ever. He was reminded of it again now, as he stared into the darkness, the easy sway of the carriage beneath them.

He'd replied, wanting to win, and somehow not wanting that at all.

He'd expected her to be late, nonetheless.

She was not late, but he still had not won.

Indeed, she was early. So early that she'd come to his office to collect him. Yes, he could grow used to the way they matched. "You are ever a challenge, my lady."

A moment passed, and she shifted, the sound of silk

against silk like cannon fire in the dark carriage. The fall of her skirts brushed against his leg, and he remembered watching the way they clung to Langley on the ballroom floor.

Wondered at the ways they might cling to him.

Tonight.

Forever.

The word slid through him like opium smoke, curling and insidious. And unwanted. He pushed it aside as she replied, "I should not like to bore you, Mr. West."

There was absolutely nothing about this woman that could bore him. Indeed, he could spend a lifetime in this carriage, without the benefit of sight, and he would still find her fascinating.

He ached to touch her, and it occurred to him that he could do that. That she'd designed a scenario that would allow touching and more. Indeed, there was nothing stopping him. Not even her, if he had to wager.

But touching her would end the game they played, and he was not ready for that. He pressed himself back against the lush velour seat, resisting his baser urges. "Tell me," he said. "Now that you have me, what do you intend to do with me?"

She lifted a flat, wrapped package from the seat next to her. "I have a delivery for you."

He froze, suddenly irritated that Chase had infiltrated this quiet place, this evening, that promised so much. "I told you I did not want you involved in deliveries from Chase."

She set the package on her lap. "Are you saying you do not wish to receive it?"

"Of course I want it. I simply don't want it from you."

She fingered the strings of the parcel. "You don't have a choice."

"No, but you do." He heard the accusation in his voice. Disliked it.

She lifted Tremley's file and extended it toward him. "Take it," she said, the words firm and something more. Something sadder.

He narrowed his gaze. "Come into the light."

She took a deep breath, and for a moment, he thought she might not. For a moment, he thought that this whole night might end here, now. That she might stop the carriage and toss him out. That she might rescind her offer for a harmless affair.

Because suddenly, it did not seem very harmless at all.

She leaned forward, her beautiful face coming into view.

She wasn't wearing paint.

She might be dressed in Anna's frock and wearing Anna's wig, but she was Georgiana tonight. Come to him freely. For an evening of pleasure. A week of it. Two weeks. However long it took for her to secure her husband and her future.

A life away from this one, where she played messenger between London's two most powerful men.

She extended the file. "Take it, and return the evening to something more than business."

He looked at the parcel. Tremley's secrets, which he needed to protect his sister. To protect his life. Tremley's secrets, more valuable than anything else he owned, because they were the key to his future.

And yet a part of him wanted to toss the damn file out the window and tell the carriage to keep driving. To get her far from Chase. To get himself far from his truths, truths that seemed to haunt him more and more each day.

If not for his sister, would he do it?

He took the package. Placed it on his lap as she leaned back, returning to her shadows. "Something about it—about you being a part of it—makes the evening business whether we intend it or not."

And he hated that, even as he opened the parcel, eager to see what was inside. He extracted a pile of paper, written in Chase's familiar hand. Held the top sheet up to the small candle in its steel and glass compartment in the wall of the carriage.

Funds removed from the exchequer.

He turned a page.

Missives from a half-dozen high-ranking members of the Ottoman Empire.

Secret meetings.

Treason.

He closed the file, his heart pounding. It was proof. Undeniable, perfect proof. He returned the pages to the envelope in which they had come, considering the implications of their contents. The sheer value of this information was nearly incalculable. It would destroy Tremley. Wipe him from the earth.

And it would protect West without doubt.

He lifted the small scrap of paper that accompanied the package. Read the words there, in that bold, familiar scrawl.

> *I do not for a moment believe that your request was the result of a reporter's skill; you know something that you are not sharing.*
> *I do not like it when you do not share.*

Too goddamn bad.

West had no intention of sharing with Chase—either his connection with Tremley or his connection with Georgiana.

His gaze flickered to her. No. He would not share her. "You've done your job."

"Well, I hope," she said.

"Very well," he acknowledged. "This is more than what I imagined."

She smiled. "I am happy to hear it is worth your trouble."

There it was again, the implication that his assistance was purchased. And so it was. Even as he resisted the truth of it. He pushed the thought away. "And now we are here. Alone."

There was a smile in her voice when she said, "Are you suggesting that I've paid you for companionship?"

It sounded ridiculous. And yet, somehow, it didn't. Somehow, he felt manipulated, as though it had all been carefully planned.

"Tit for tat," he said, echoing so many of their conversations. Her words. His.

He could not see her face, but was keenly aware of the

fact that she could see him. The light in the carriage was designed to unbalance. To empower only one side—the side in the darkness. But he heard the emotion when she finally spoke. "It is not like that tonight."

"But other nights?" He hated the idea that this moment was a repeat of another. A dozen. A hundred.

Her hands spread wide across her skirts, silk rustling like nerves. "There are nights when the information is payment. And others when it is given freely."

"It is payment, though," he said. "It is payment for the articles in my papers. For every dance you've had with Langley. With others."

"Fortune hunters," she said.

"Every one," he agreed. "I never promised otherwise."

"You promised acceptance."

"And social acceptance you shall have. But a husband who is not a fortune hunter? You're not likely to find that. Not unless—" He stopped.

"Unless?"

He sighed, hating the deal they had. Hating the way it tempted him. Hating the way it whispered pretty possibilities in the darkness. "Not unless you are willing to show them the truth."

"What truth?" she said. "I'm an unwed mother. Daughter to a duke. Sister to one. Trained as an aristocrat. Bred for their world like a champion racehorse. My truth is public."

"No," he said. "It isn't near public."

She gave a little huff of humorless laughter. "You mean Anna? You think they would be more likely to have me if they knew that I spent my nights on the floor of a casino?"

"You are more than all that. More complicated."

He didn't know how or why, only that it was true.

He made her angry. He could hear it. "You don't know anything about me."

He wanted to reach for her. To pull her into the light. But he kept himself at a distance. "I know why you say you like the darkness."

"Why?" she asked, and the words sounded like she was no longer certain herself.

"It's easier to hide there," he replied.

"I don't hide," she insisted, and he wondered if she knew it was a lie.

"You hide as well as any of us."

"And what do you hide from? What are your truths?" It was a taunt as much as it was an admission. He wished he could see her eyes, which never seemed to hide as much as the rest of her.

Because she was not entirely this woman, queen of sin and night. She was not all the confidence she played at. She was not all the power in her poise. There was something else that made her human. That made her real.

That made her.

But they played this game nonetheless, and he did not dislike it.

He simply liked the glimpses of her truth more.

He set the parcel aside. Leaned forward. Down. Lifted one of her slippered feet from the floor of the carriage, up into his lap. He ran his fingers up over her ankle, enjoying the way the muscles tightened beneath his touch. He smiled. As still and calm as she pretended to be, her body did not lie to him.

He wrapped his hand around her ankle, slid the black slipper from her foot, revealing pretty black stockings. He traced his fingers along the bottom of her foot, loving the way she flexed against the touch. "Does that tickle?"

"Yes," she said, on a breath that tempted more than it should.

He continued his exploration, letting sliding fingertips along silk, over the top of her foot and along the ankle. Hinting at her calf before retracing his path. "Here is a truth; the first time I saw your slippers—outside the Worthington Ball—I wanted to do this."

"You did?"

There was surprise in her words. And desire.

"I did," he confessed. "I was drawn to your pretty silver

slippers, all innocence and beauty." He played at the ball of her foot with his thumbs, and she sighed at the sensation. "And then I was drawn to something entirely different— those stunning heeled slippers, all sin and sex."

"You followed me?"

"I did."

"I should be angry."

"But you aren't."

He slid his hand to her ankle again, and up her calf, loving the soft silk there, fingering the pretty white stitching on the stockings, wanting to lift her skirts and see her legs, long and clad in black. Wanting them open. Around his hips, his waist.

Wanting her.

"Are you?" he prompted.

She sighed. "No. I am not angry."

"You like that I know you. All of you. The two halves." His touch reached the back of her knee and the caress there seemed to unstick her.

She shifted, lifting the other leg, pressing her other foot against his chest, pushing him back. Staying his touch. "Tell me another."

"Another?" he asked.

"Another truth," she said.

He captured the foot at his chest, lifted it, pressed a hot kiss to the inside of her ankle, letting his tongue lave the soft fabric there until she sighed. "I want to take these stockings off you. I want your skin, softer than silk."

He nipped at her ankle, loving the gasp she let loose in the carriage, suddenly hot as the sun. "It is your turn."

She stilled. "For what?"

"Tell me your secrets."

She hesitated. "I don't know where to begin."

He knew that. She was filled with shadows, each one protecting some piece of her. Each one in need of light. "Begin with this," he said, sliding his hand up her calf to her knee, following it with a swirl of his fingertips. "Tell me how it makes you feel. Without artifice."

She laughed as the he tickled her. "It makes me feel—" When she stopped, he did, too, pulling his hand away from her. She stretched her leg after him, as though she could catch him. Return him. "It makes me feel young."

He did return to her then, surprised by the word. "What does that mean?"

She sighed in the darkness. "Don't stop."

He didn't, stroking again. And again. "What does it mean, Georgiana?"

"Just that—" She stopped. Her foot flexed against his chest, and he wished they were at his home. He needed more space. He needed to see her—touch her—at will. She took a breath. "It's been a long time . . . since . . ."

He knew the way the sentence ended. Since she'd been with another man. Since she'd been with anyone but Chase. He didn't want her to finish the thought. Didn't want the man's name here, in the darkness, with them.

But she finished it anyway. " . . . since I've felt this way."

And, like that, he was unlocked. There was something about this woman, about the way she spoke, the promises she made with simple, ordinary words, that made him thoroughly desperate for her. But when she confessed her feelings, with utter honesty, surprise and a touch of wonder in her beautiful voice, how was he to resist her?

How was he to ever give her back once he had a taste of her?

How was he to walk away, eventually?

Christ.

What kind of mess was he getting himself into?

He released her, setting her feet to the floor, and she resisted the loss of him just as his body resisted the loss of her.

"Wait," she said, leaning forward, her beautiful face coming into the light. "Don't stop."

"I have no intention of stopping," he promised her. Himself. "I just want to make a few things clear."

Her brow furrowed, "How much more clear must I be?

I propositioned you in Hyde Park. I met you outside your office dressed like a . . ." She hesitated. "Well, like the kind of woman who does those things."

It occurred to him that she often dressed in such a manner. "I don't care what you wear."

When she spoke, the words were dry as sand. "You certainly seemed to like the stockings."

The memory of black silk with silver piping took over, and what would have been a laugh became a growl. "I like the stockings very much."

She blushed, and he marveled at it. He leaned forward until he was inches away from her face. Her lips. "I wonder," he whispered, "Do other bits of you go red when you are embarrassed?"

The flush grew. "I don't know. I've never looked."

"Well, I am most certainly going to look."

"In the name of investigative journalism, no doubt."

He grinned. "I am the best newspaperman in London, love. I simply cannot leave the work at the office."

She matched his smile for a long moment, until the expression faded into seriousness. She looked down at her hands, clasped in the space between them. "You are making me like you," she said.

He watched her carefully. "You don't already like me?"

She spoke softly. "Of course I like you. But now—you're tempting me with things that I cannot have."

He knew immediately what she meant, and the words sent a wave of sadness through him. He was not the man for her. He could not give her a title. Could not give Caroline security. At best, he was born into mystery. Bred in the gutter.

And that was before she knew the truth.

Before she knew he was not what he seemed. He was nothing that he claimed to be. Before she knew that he had used and manipulated her to gain access to Tremley's secrets. Before she knew that he was a criminal. A thief.

Destined for prison or worse if he was found out.

When he was found out.

Because no matter how careful he was, no matter how well he threatened Tremley, as long as the earl drew breath, he was at risk.

And everyone he loved was at risk, as well.

So, even if she weren't on the hunt for a title, he could not be the man she wanted. And he certainly could not be the man she needed.

But he could be the man she had. Right now. For a brief, fleeting moment before they both had to return to reality.

He reached for her, lifting her off her seat, loving the little squeak she released as he pulled her into his lap to straddle him, silken skirts and petticoats cascading around them both. She rose above him, topping his long frame by several inches because of their position, and he adored it, the way she looked down at him, something like promise in her beautiful amber gaze.

"You can have it all tonight," he said, his voice harsh and graveled and unfamiliar to him. "Every bit of me. Everything you want."

She leaned back, the curve of her bottom pressing into his thighs, sending wicked, wonderful ideas through his filthy mind.

She began to roll her gloves down her arms. "I want to feel you."

Not ideas. Plans.

"I want to touch you," she added. One length of black silk was lost to the darkness of the other side of the carriage, and her hand was on his face, fingers tracing his cheek, his jaw, tilting his head up as she moved down, her lips skimming over the places where her touch had been. "I want to kiss you."

If she didn't kiss him, he was going to lose his mind.

She was seducing him with words and touch and scent, and he loved every goddamn bit of it. He wanted to pull her to him, to take her lips and remove the damn wig, to lift her skirts and make love to her until neither one of them could remember their names, let alone the ridiculous arrangement to which they'd agreed.

But he didn't move. He wouldn't. There was something about this woman who dealt in desire and sin and sex, something about the way she looked at him, the way she spoke, the way she touched, that made him wonder if she'd ever in her life taken her own pleasure.

And so he waited for her to do it. She would kiss him that night, or they would never kiss. This was her moment. Her pleasure. Her desire.

Once he got her into his house, it would be his turn to give her every inch of pleasure he could.

But now, it was her turn to take it.

She leaned in, and he thought she was going to kiss him. But at the very last moment she pulled back, making him think she'd devised some new and wonderful form of torture. He said her name, and it came like a curse in the darkness.

"Two weeks," she said.

"What?"

She smiled. "I do think you are addled, sir."

"This is what happens when you tease a man."

She ran her fingers into the hair at the nape of his neck, and every inch of him responded to the pretty sensation. "Two weeks. No more. Nothing that would get us into trouble. Two weeks and then we are through."

The fact that he'd thought nearly the same thing mere minutes ago did not stop him from being slightly irritated that she could think about terms for their arrangement.

He agreed, nonetheless. "Two weeks. Now kiss me, goddammit."

And, blessedly, she did.

She'd never kissed a man.

Oh, she'd been kissed, certainly. On multiple occasions, both wanted and unwanted. She'd been kissed by this man, and it had been magnificent. But she'd never once taken control of a moment such as this one, and kissed a man. Even with Jonathan, when youth and folly should have made her bold.

The heady pleasure of the experience was not something that she would ever forget. She adored it, the way he let her dominate, the way he leaned back against the seat, his hands at her hips only to steady her in case the carriage moved unexpectedly. The way he let her lead the caress, first with hands and then with lips.

And she adored the way he felt against her, hard and unyielding and so incredibly warm. He did not touch her, and she at once hated and loved the fact. She wanted the exploration. She wanted to tempt him. And touch him. And do her best to seduce him, for in all the years that she'd dressed as Anna, she'd never tried seduction.

Something that he seemed to do so effortlessly. Without even touching her.

She let her lips linger on his for a moment, getting her bearings before placing her hands on his shoulder and letting her tongue edge out to lick at him. He growled deep in his throat at the sensation, and she felt the rumble as much as she heard it. His lips parted, and she leaned in. Tested her power.

His grip on her hips tightened, and the kiss grew deeper, more intense. She turned her head, fitted herself more carefully to him. The growl turned into groan, and one of his hands finally, finally moved, coming up the side of her neck, cupping her jaw, holding her for his kiss. His tongue met hers, and she pulled back at the lovely sensation. For a moment, he seemed lost, and then he met her gaze and with complete control, reached up, pulled her back to him, and took the kiss for himself.

His hands were everywhere—sliding over skin and silk, up to her hair. She pulled away from the touch, "Wait," she gasped, grabbing his hands, pulling them away from her. "Not the wig. Not yet."

"I want it off. I want you," he confessed.

"And I want that, as well," she said. "But if anyone sees—"

It had to be Anna entering his house in the dead of night. Alone. Wearing black silk.

He groaned his agreement, placing his hands at her hips, instead, pulling at silk, shifting her, bringing them closer together. "There is far too much fabric in this dress," he growled as he pulled her down, lifting himself, fitting them together, hard and soft, rocking against her once, twice, before biting at her bottom lip and taking her mouth with lips and tongue.

It was her turn to groan at the onslaught of his kiss—and it was an onslaught, a carefully waged war of long, slow, drugging kisses, matched with movement and unspoken promises that made her hot and cold and desperate for him all at once.

She lifted her head, wanting to see him. To understand this moment, when they seemed the only two people in the world. His eyes opened at the loss of her. "I had not planned this," she whispered, her fingers running along the crests and valleys of his face.

"The carriage?" he asked.

"The pleasure," she said.

He paused, watching her carefully, and she nearly closed her eyes, afraid of what he might find. "That's interesting, as your pleasure is all I had planned."

He stroked down the sides of her body, sending ripples of that promised pleasure through her, from shoulders to hips and back up to the place where her bodice seemed too tight, desperate for loosening.

Desperate for his touch.

He gave it to her, running his thumbs over the tips of her breasts, hardened beneath the silk. She threw her head back at the sensation, and he leaned up to run his teeth along her bare collarbone. Following the sharp edge with the warm stroke of his tongue. "Stop," she whispered.

He did, instantly, pulling away from her. Surprise flared, his willingness to stop unexpected. He watched her. "Is something wrong?"

Yes.

But it wasn't what he thought.

It was all wrong—every bit of it—because it felt so damn right. Because it made her wonder, fleetingly, what she'd been missing all these years. *Whom* she'd been missing.

It made her question too much. Everything. She shook her head. "No," she lied. "Kiss me again."

But he could not, because the moment the words were out, the carriage slowed. He leaned into her, placing a long, lingering kiss at the edge of her dress, where she strained for breath. "Tell me we are at my home."

She laughed at the desperation in his voice, only because it was similar to her own. She moved off him, wishing she didn't have to. Wanting to stay there forever. "We are. I thought here, rather than the club."

He leaned over to help rearrange her skirts, and she loved the way his fingers lingered on the curve of her knee, the slope of her calf. "You thought well. I do not want us meeting at the club."

"Why not?" she asked as he lifted one foot and returned her slipper.

"I won't be seen with you there."

The words stung. "But you can sleep with me?"

He stilled, his gaze meeting hers, hot and full of promise. "First, you misunderstand. I don't want you there. I want you far from there. Far from scandal and sin and vice. I want to be the only scoundrel in your company.

"And second . . ." He lifted her other foot, stroking his fingers down the arch of it before placing it in her slipper. "I assure you, there won't be any sleeping."

The words sent a thread of pleasure through the core of her, as surely as if he'd lay her bare and whispered them against her skin.

He set her foot gently to the floor of the carriage, and she said, "Take me inside."

White teeth flashed. "With pleasure."

Chapter 13

. . . Truly, there are few stars in this Season's galaxy that shine even half as bright as our fair Lady G—. She grows ever more desired at public functions, and we have no doubt that the eligible bachelors of the *ton* desire her for functions that take place exclusively in chapels. As for Lord L—, however, as their company seems well-kept . . .

. . . In sad corners of ballrooms we have recently found poor, lost little lamb, Lady S—, once a welcome member of the Pitiless Pretties of the *ton*, now exiled for sins we cannot imagine. We have high hopes for her restoration, however, as she was seen dancing with the Marquess of E— . . .

The gossip pages of the *Weekly Courant*,
May 1, 1833

His house was massive, gilded and gorgeous, every inch of it appointed in the height of fashion. She stood in the main marble foyer, turning slowly, looking at the high ceilings and the wide, curving staircase that led to the upper floors of the house.

"This is beautiful," she said, turning to face him. "I've never seen a home so perfectly designed."

He leaned against a marble column nearby, arms crossed, gaze focused on her. "It keeps rain from our heads."

She laughed. "It does more than that."

"It's a house."

"Give me a tour."

He waved an arm to the doors on the far end of the foyer. "Receiving room, receiving room, breakfast room." And to the ones behind her. "Cynthia's morning room, another receiving room." He paused. "I don't entirely know why we need so many." He indicated a long hallway that led to the back of the house. "The kitchens and swimming pool are that way. The dining room and ballroom are one flight up." He returned his attention to her. "The bedchambers are lovely. They deserve personal inspection."

She laughed at his impatience. "Swimming pool?"

"Yes."

"You realize that a swimming pool is not precisely a common addition to a London town house."

"It's not precisely a common addition to London," he said, lifting one shoulder. "But I like being clean, so it makes for excellent sport."

"So do any number of men. They take baths."

He raised a brow. "I take baths, as well."

"I'd like to see it."

"You'd like to see me take a bath?" He looked positively thrilled by the idea.

She laughed. "No. I'd like to see your swimming pool."

He considered refusing—she could see it in his eyes. After all, a tour of his home was not part of their agreed agenda for the evening. But she stood firm, until he took her hand in his—warm and large and rough from years of work—and led her through the house, down the dark hallway and through the kitchens.

He came to a closed door, and set his hand to the handle, turning back to meet her gaze, he opened the door, and indicated that she should pass into the dimly lit room beyond.

She stepped inside, first noting the barely-there light that came from a half-dozen fireplaces on the far side of the room, and then noticing how very warm it was in the room.

"Stay here," he said softly at her ear, pushing past her. "I shall light the lamps."

She stood in the warm darkness, watching as he put a match to a lamp nearby, casting a small sphere of golden light in the massive room. The light was at the edge of the swimming pool, still and dark, and utterly compelling. She moved without even noticing, drawn to the mysterious water as Duncan followed the edge of the pool, lighting more lamps, until the room came into view.

It was magnificent.

The walls and floor of the room was tiled in the most beautiful blue and white mosaic, like sky and surf coming together. The lamps sat on beautifully wrought marble columns, each light made manifest as a golden orb of glass. She looked up to where the ceiling gave way to what must have been a hundred panels of glass, revealing the sky above London, darkness and stars.

She could look at that ceiling forever.

And that was without the swimming pool, reflecting the stars and lamps on the water, wine dark, like Odysseus's seas. She met Duncan's gaze where he stood several yards away, adjusting the brightness of one of the lamps. No, not Odysseus. He was Poseidon, god of this place, strong enough to bend water to his will.

"This is . . ." She paused, not knowing how to describe the room. The way it called to her. " . . . stunning."

He came toward her. "It is my vice."

"I thought your vice was the card tables."

He shook his head, reaching out for her, brushing one of her curls back from her face. "That's work. This is play."

Play.

The word curled around them, a promise in the darkness. She wondered at it, wondered how long it had been since she'd thought it. Since she'd had it.

Wondered if he would give it to her. She smiled up at him. "It seems like glorious play."

"Glorious play," he repeated the words, refusing to release her gaze. "It does seem like that."

She did not think the room could get warmer, but it did. "There are so many fireplaces."

He looked over his shoulder, toward the wall of hearths. "I like to swim year-round, and the water gets cold if not for the fires."

The whole room, the whole experience, it must have cost him a fortune—the heating, the lamps, the extravagance. The Angel prided itself on having a half-dozen expansive, utterly unnecessary rooms designed purely for members' whims, but there was nothing like this at the club.

There was nothing like this anywhere in London.

She looked to him. "Why?"

He looked away, to the water, black and tempting. "I told you. I like to swim."

He hadn't said that. He'd said he liked being clean. "There are other ways to swim."

"It is best at night," he said, ignoring the question. "When there is nothing but water and stars. Most of the time, I don't light the lamps."

"You feel your way," she said.

He ran his hand down her arm, taking her hand in his. "Feeling is underrated." He pulled her close and wrapped one arm around her waist. He kissed her, deep and lush, and she didn't know if it was the heat of the room or the caress that made her lose thought.

No, she knew. It was the caress.

He pulled back. "Do you know how?"

It took a moment for her to understand. "I do."

He watched her for a long moment, as though gauging the

response to his inevitable question. As though wondering if he should risk her saying no.

As though she would ever say no.

"Would you like to swim, my lady?"

The honorific swirled around her, soft and full of promise. How much did it tempt her? How much did it make her wish for a moment, for this night, that she was his lady?

More than it should.

"This evening is going quite differently than I expected," she said.

"And I." He kissed her, quick and rough. "Discard the damn wig."

Her hands were doing his bidding even as he moved away, to the wall of fireplaces, crouching down to stoke the flames of first one, and then the next. His instructions followed, she calculated that it would take him several minutes to set fires blazing in each of the six hearths, and so she sat, removing her shoes, her stockings, her drawers, setting each neatly to the side, until all that was left was the dress.

The dress she wore was designed for Anna, not Georgiana, and it did not require a maid for removing. It was structured with hidden catches and ties and an interior corset, all designed for ease of donning and doffing.

Though she wondered if the dressmaker who had performed this feat of fashionable engineering had ever imagined this particular moment, when the dress would find itself at the side of a swimming pool.

If all went well.

He turned from the last fire, facing her across the massive room, and she stood, watching as he returned to her, thoroughly focused on her, hunting her. She noticed his bare feet, and realized he'd taken a moment to remove his boots while he stoked the fire. He removed his jacket on the way, tossing it to the side, forgotten as he worked on his cravat, unraveling the long length of linen and letting it fall away. He did not take his gaze from her, and she did feel like prey.

No prey had ever wanted to be caught so well.

He reached her as he pulled his shirttails from his trousers, and she wondered at the comfort he had with the process. "Have you ever entertained here?" The question was out before she could stop it, and she wished to God she could have stopped it.

This night, it meant nothing. It was not forever. It was for now.

So she should not care if he had other women here. In this magnificent, extravagant, ridiculous room.

"I have not," he said, and the pleasure that came with the words—with the knowledge that he told the truth—was acute.

He removed his shirt then, pulling it over his head, revealing a long, sinewed torso, all curves and crevices. Her mouth went dry. No man outside of classical sculpture should look this way. No man outside of classical sculpture *did* look this way.

Poseidon flashed again, and she resisted the silly thought.

But she did not stop looking.

Until he reached for the falls of his trousers, his fingers working the buttons there, and she could not look any longer. Her gaze found his face, his gaze all knowing, as though he was in her head. As though he knew she had compared him to Poseidon in her thoughts.

He was an insufferable man.

"You are overdressed."

She willed the embarrassment away. She'd agreed to this moment, had she not? To this night? And she was Anna, was she not? Experienced in all things. In every way a woman should be.

It did not matter that the last was a slight fabrication.

Fine. A significant fabrication.

She had the dress to bear it out. And it was the clothes that made the man, was it not? In Duncan West's case, it seemed the clothes did him a disservice, but that was not the point.

She took a deep breath. Shored up her courage.

And dropped the dress, baring everything to him.

Later, when she was not so embarrassed, she would laugh

at the memory of his response—shocked to the core that she'd been able to undress without help and looking as though he'd received a very firm, very serious blow to the head.

But laughter was very far from her mind at the moment. Her mind was too occupied with embarrassment. And nervousness. And awareness of all the oddly shaped, strangely stretched bits that she usually kept under pretty, silk wraps. And the keen, unsettling combination of desire and terror.

So she did what any self-respecting nude woman would do in the same situation. She turned and dove into the dark pool.

She surfaced a handful of yards away from the edge, marveling at the temperature of the water, like a cool summer bath. She turned to face the spot where she'd entered, to find him there, watching her, hands at his hips.

Naked.

She tried not to look. She really did.

But it was rather difficult to miss.

She swam backward, grateful for the dim light. For the fact that he couldn't be certain that she was staring at him, long and hard and utterly unsettling.

"Is it comfortable?"

She swallowed. Brazened through even as she continued to put distance between them. "Quite."

"If you want to swim," he said, "you should do it now."

It was a strange thing to say, as it was a swimming pool, and she was already swimming. "Why?"

"Because once I get to you, swimming will be the last thing on your mind."

The words shot through her like lightning, enhanced by the feel of the water all over her body, on places that should not be bared to this glorious place. She waited for a moment, watching him, taking in the beauty of him, all muscle and bone. Perfection, wrought here, in this water.

Where he would have her.

The thought made her bold, and she stopped moving backward. "I find I've lost my taste for swimming."

He was beneath the water before she finished the sentence,

and her heart pounded as she waited for him to surface, the silence that fell after he dove making her fairly tremble with anticipation. She watched the ink black surface of the water, wondering where he would emerge.

And then she felt him, his fingers brushing against her stomach, followed by his palms, sliding to her sides. She gasped at the touch as he rose up, inches from her, Poseidon rising from the sea.

In her surprise, she set her hands to his shoulders, and he took the opportunity to pull her tight against him, his arms like steel around her waist, his legs tangling with hers. She felt him hot and hard against her stomach. "I am very grateful," he said at her ear, the words more breath than sound, sending a thrill of anticipation through her, "to whoever taught you to swim."

She did not have to think of an appropriate answer to the words, because he was already kissing her, lifting her effortlessly in the water, his hands spreading down to cup her rear, to pull her close, to match them in that dark, secret place where they were so evenly matched.

He groaned at the sensation, and she sighed her reply as he moved her to the edge of the pool. It was coming, she thought. She wanted it, quite desperately, and he was going to give it to her. It had been years since she'd been this close to another person, to a man. A lifetime.

At the edge of the pool, he spread her arms wide, laying her open palms against the beautiful mosaic tile, holding her up in the water. His face was cast in the orange light of the fires behind her, fires that seemed to burn hot as the sun as he slid his hands down the length of her arms, entangling his fingers with hers, kissing down the side of her neck and across the bare skin of her shoulders and chest

"You didn't give me a chance to look," he whispered there, just above the place where the water lapped against her, teasing the tips of her breasts, hard and aching for him. "You shocked the hell out of me and ran away."

"This does not feel like running," she said as he released

one of her hands and cupped a bare breast, lifting it above the waterline, running a thumb over the pebbled tip.

"No," he said, "but here we are again, in the darkness. And once again, I can't see you. I can't see these."

"Please." She sighed as his thumb worried her nipple. He was killing her.

"Please what?" he said, placing little chaste kisses around it.

"You know what," she said, and he laughed.

"I do. And I confess, I am grateful we are here, alone, because I'm finally going to taste you, and no one is going to stop me."

He lowered his mouth and took her, and she nearly came out of her skin at the sensation, at the way he licked and sucked and sent pleasure curling through her, pooling in a dozen places she had forgotten she had. She moved to clasp his head to her, and lost her balance in the water. He caught her without effort, but she returned her hand to the edge of the pool, not knowing what else to do. Not knowing what else to say, except "Dear God, don't stop."

And he didn't, worshipping first one breast and then the other, until she thought she might die here, drowned in this glorious place and in him. When he lifted his head after what seemed like at once an eternity and a heartbeat, she was sighing his name and eager for anything he wished to give her.

He took her lips, capturing her sighs, and pulled her close to him again, pressing all of him against all of her, so that there was no space for the water that lapped around them, in time to her writhing. When he ended the kiss, she pressed her hands to his shoulders, eager for something that would help her regain her power. Regain herself.

He gave her an infinitesimal amount of space, as though he understood what she wanted and understood, too, that she would hate it. Which she did. Because she simply wanted him again.

She took a breath. A second.

Cast about for something to say, something that would

distance him even as it kept him close. Settled on, "Why a swimming pool?"

He stilled, quickly recovering his surprise. "You don't want to know that," he said, the words graveled and dark and making her utterly wanton.

"I do."

He lifted a long, wet lock of hair from her shoulder, rolling it between his thumb and forefinger. "I was not a clean child."

She smiled, imagining him, a blond boy with mischief in his eyes and intelligence beyond his ears. "Few children are."

He did not return her smile. Did not meet her gaze. "I was not dirty from play." He spoke to her hair, his words lacking emotion. "I did a number of jobs. Bricklaying. Tarring roads. Clearing chimneys."

She went cold at that. None of the jobs was fit for children, but the chimneys—it was dangerous, brutal work, small boys sent up chimneys to clean them, the smaller the better. He would have been no more than three or four when he was a prime candidate for the torture. "Duncan," she whispered, but he did not acknowledge her.

"It wasn't so bad. It was only when it was hot, and the chimneys were too tight. There was another boy—my friend—" He trailed off, shaking his head as though exiling a memory. A thousand of them, she was certain, each more horrifying than the last. "I was lucky."

No child with that life was lucky. "Were you in London?" He must have been. In a workhouse, no doubt—forced to suffer at the hands of this great, burgeoning city.

He did not answer. "At any rate. I wasn't allowed to bathe afterwards, as I was destined to be dirty again the next day. The handful of times I was allowed to bathe, I was always last. The water was always cold. Never clean."

Tears came, hot and unbidden, and she was grateful for the fires at her back, for the way they hid her face from him.

She reached for him, wrapping one arm around his neck, threading her fingers through his beautiful blond hair, gleaming and soft and clean even now. "No longer," she whispered at his ear. "No longer," she repeated, wanting to wrap herself around him.

Wanting to protect him. The boy he was. The man he had become.

Dear God.

What she felt . . .

No. She refused to think it.

And she certainly would not admit it.

He caught her, and she noted the surprise on his face, as though he had just remembered that she was there. "No longer," he agreed. "Now I have a thousand square feet of clean water. Warm and wet and wonderful."

She wanted to ask more. To push him.

But she knew better than anyone that when Duncan West was through talking, he was through talking. So she found an alternative, kissing him, trailing her fingers over his shoulder and down his arm to where his strong hands held her open, pressed against him. She wanted to touch him, every inch of him. She wanted to touch some very specific inches of him. And she'd nearly shored up the courage to do it when he lifted her from the water, sitting her on the edge of the pool.

Water sluiced down her body, over its curves and valleys, and she resisted the position, on display above him. "Wait," she began, but he stopped her, pressing a lush kiss to one of her knees.

"But it is not the swimming pool I am interested in this evening," he whispered to the skin there, sliding his hand between her thighs, spreading her wide enough to press a kiss to the inside of her knee. "It is something else."

There was an urgency in his words, as though touching her, kissing her, making love to her could erase his past. The talk of it.

And perhaps it could. *Tonight.*

His fingers moved again, teased until she opened further, until there was room for him to kiss deeper along the edge of her thigh, his tongue swirling there, his knowing touch spreading fire. "Something else," he repeated, following a dark, wicked path up her leg, coaxing her open one devastating kiss at a time. "Something equally warm."

The words sent a shiver through Georgiana, and she closed her eyes against the image of him sinful and sweet between her thighs. "Something equally wonderful."

She was losing her balance, and she leaned back on her hands, not sure of what to do. Not sure she wanted this. And, at the same time, utterly certain she wanted this. Those wicked fingers moved again, but they did not have to push. She opened for him, granting him access even as he promised devastation.

He had told her he would be in control, and so he was.

She was wide open for him now, and his fingers played at the dark patch of hair that covered the most secret part of her. He looked up. "Are you equally as wet?"

The words thrummed through her, more devastating than the touch that matched them as he parted the delicate folds of her sex with infinite gentleness, dipping a single finger inside. They groaned together at the movement, at the sensation that rocketed through her. "More," he said, the word full of marvel as he stroked her in that dark, wonderful place. "I'm going to taste you here," he went on. "I'm going to taste you and touch you until you come and your screams fill this room, with only the water and the sky as witness."

The words weakened her even as they gave her strength, and he slid one hand up her torso to her chest, pressing her back against the warm tile, until she lay flat, her legs dangling over the edge of the pool.

"You're mine," he said, dark and full of sin. "My lady."

She ached at the honorific. At the truth in it. "I am," she whispered. Dear God, she was. She was his in every way he wanted her. In any way.

And then he was parting her folds, and his mouth was on the heart of her, and she did cry out at the immense, nearly unbearable pleasure of his tongue, stroking and swirling and doing all manner of terrible, glorious things. Her hands, which she hadn't known what to do with mere minutes earlier, found him, threading into his beautiful blond hair as he moved against her, tasting her wet heat with magnificent movements that threatened to rob her of breath and sanity.

She groaned at the immensity of the pleasure he gave her, lifting against him, boldly asking for more even as he gave it. She rocked against him, loving the feel of him, the sound of him, the way he held her open, wide, and growled "My lady," the words a lick of pleasure through her.

His lady.

His.

She would never feel anything like this. Never give herself in any way close to this ever again.

And then he was there, at the swollen, aching place where she wanted him most, circling and licking and sucking, sending pleasure rocketing through her until she could not bear it any longer, and her fingers clenched in his hair and she rocked against him. In response, he grasped her hips, holding her firm as she rode out her pleasure, calling his name in the darkness again and again and again until it was no longer his name, but a benediction.

And then she did scream, just as he promised, it was in view of none but the stars high above—beyond the glass ceiling that caught the sound and sent it echoing around them both, the only two people in all of London. In all the world.

He stayed with her as she returned to the moment, his lips soft and full at the curve of her thigh, his tongue tracing circles there, slow and languid, as though they could slow her rioting pulse.

She opened her eyes in the stunning room, made orange in the light of the fires behind her and within her, and realized that there was nothing ridiculous about this place—it suited him. A glorious temple to this man who wielded pleasure like power.

And perhaps it was power.

It was certainly more dangerous than anything she'd ever faced before now. He was too much. And not enough. She could never have him, and somehow, in this moment, she knew that she would never stop wanting him.

He would ruin her, as surely as she had been ruined the last time a man had touched her.

She stiffened at the thought, and he felt the change in her. Lifted his lips. "And there it is," he said, the words cooler than she would have expected. Cooler than she would have liked. "Memory returns."

She hated that he so easily understood her. She sat up, pulling her feet from the water, her knees to her chest. Wrapping her arms about her. "I don't know what you mean."

He raised a brow. "You know precisely what I mean. If you didn't, you would have reentered the pool instead of leaving it."

She smiled. "Would you not prefer a bed?"

"Don't," he said. "Don't bring her here. Not now."

"Who?"

"Anna. Don't offer me her false smile and her falser words. I'm not—"

When he did not finish, she asked, "You're not what?"

He swore, soft and furious, and swam backward, distancing himself from her. From the moment. "I'm not Chase. I don't want her. I want you."

"We are one and the same," she said.

"Don't insult me. Don't lie to me. Save your lies for your owner." He spat the word, and she heard the anger in it. The hurt.

When she had invented Chase years earlier, she'd never imagined she'd have to play such a delicate, difficult game as this one. She stood, following him down the pool, to the place where they'd entered. Where they'd begun this night. The place to which they could not return. He came out of the water, opened a nearby cabinet. Gave her a thick length of Egyptian cotton. She wrapped it about herself, searching for the right words.

Settling on, "Duncan, he doesn't own me."

She couldn't see his face any longer. He was the backlit one now, when every word she spoke was a lie. His words came from his great, looming shadow, inches from her, the frustration in his voice clear as crystal. "Of course he does.

You are at his whim. He gives you a package, you deliver it. He tells you to marry, you do so."

"It is not like that."

"It is precisely like that. He could have married you himself. He could have protected Caroline. He's the most powerful man in London. He could do any of those things. Instead, he foists you on Langley."

She should tell him the truth.

"There." He took her arms; his grasp warm and wonderful, and turned her into the light. "Just now. Tell me *that*. Tell me what you were thinking just then."

She knew the words were stupid. That they would wreck them both. But she said them anyway. "I was thinking that I should tell you the truth."

He stilled. "You should. Whatever it is—I can help you."

It seemed so simple to tell him the whole truth. That she was Chase. That she had protected that identity without hesitation for all these years because of Caroline. Because Caroline would need something more someday, some kind of perfect, pristine name that would help her have the life she wanted. The life she deserved.

It would be easy to tell him. He wielded power just as she did—he would see the threat her identity had to her life. To Caroline's. To the Angel. To her world. But he was too dangerous. He was the kind of person who threatened her with his very breath, not because he made his living on secrets, but because once he knew, he would hold Georgiana in his hands—her secrets, her name, her world, her heart.

It did not matter that he made her want to trust him.

It did not matter that he made her want to *love* him.

She had been betrayed by love—by its fleeting imperfection, by its lasting damage.

It was not to be trusted.

And the threat of it made him not to be trusted.

There was too much that hung in the balance, and Duncan West did not owe her enough to balance her secrets. He had too many of his own—too many that she did not know herself.

And this was their dance, secret for secret.

Tit for tat.

And so she did not tell him the truth. She chose to remind herself that more than security, honor, and respect, she needed someone who would not search for her secrets. She needed someone whom she would never trust.

Whom she would never love.

And if tonight taught her nothing else, it had taught her that she could love Duncan West. And love would only ever bring ruin.

"Goddammit, Georgiana, I wish you out from under his thumb."

She, who built an empire on lies, was coming to loathe the lies she was forced to tell to protect it. To protect herself. To protect the Angel.

To protect Caroline.

She shook her head. "I told you, my arrangement with Chase is . . . different now."

"And what of our arrangement? Yours and mine?"

Her gaze flickered to the pool. "Our arrangement is different as well."

"Different how?"

Different in that she had not expected to want him this much. She had not expected to care. "More complicated."

He laughed, the sound humorless. "Complicated is right." He walked away from her, and she watched him, unable to tear her gaze from the beauty of him, golden in the firelight, towel slung low over his hips.

Finally, he turned back, threading his fingers through his beautiful hair. "And if I paid for it? Your town house? Your life? Christ, tell me what the hell he has on you. I can fix it. I can make Caroline a darling of Society—I can give you the life you want."

It was the most tempting offer she'd ever heard. Better than tens of thousands of pounds on the roulette table. Better than a hundred thousand pounds against Temple in the ring. It was perfect. And she wanted nothing in her life more than to take it.

"Let me help you start a fresh life. Without him."

If she were another woman, a simpler one, she would let him do just that.

If she were merely Lady Georgiana Pearson, she would throw herself into his arms and let him care for her. Let him repair all the damage she'd done. She would take the help he promised and build a new life. As a new person.

Hell, she might even beg him to marry her, in the hopes that his partnership would allow her to live out the rest of their days in the happiness she'd been promised long ago.

But all the promises were fantasies. And she was not that woman.

She was Chase.

And this life, the life she'd built for herself, the choices she'd made, the path she'd taken . . . they did not lead to him. And she should disabuse both of them from any notion that they did.

She met his gaze. "You can't give me the title." He opened his mouth to reply. She stopped him. "The title, Duncan. It's the title that matters."

There was a moment when she saw everything in his gaze, all the truth and sadness and frustration that she felt, mirrored in his beautiful eyes. And then it was gone. Replaced with calm reserve.

"Then you are lucky, my lady, that Chase paid his fee. My papers are at your disposal. Your title you shall have."

She wanted to reach for him. To beg him to make good on their arrangement. She wanted her two weeks. Perhaps two weeks with him would be enough to survive a lifetime without him.

She couldn't stop herself from asking, "What of tonight?"

What of his touch? Of his promises?

What of his control?

It turned out he was in control after all.

"Get dressed," he said, ending the evening. She was dismissed. He was already turning away. Heading for the door. "Get dressed and get out."

Chapter 14

. . . The darling of this year's season continues to win her peers with honest charm and unimpeachable beauty. The Lady was spotted at Mme. H—'s modiste shop this week, purchasing gowns in proper, pale silk with perfect, high necks. She is modesty incarnate . . .

. . . With utter glee, we report that Lord and Lady N— are in town for the Season, an unexpected change for a couple who so rarely leave their house in the country. The lady has been spotted in several storefronts on Bond Street, allegedly purchasing clothing for newborns. Perhaps the winter will deliver Lord N— a long awaited son now that he's quite full of daughters?

The News of London, May 2, 1833

The next morning, Duncan handed his card to the butler at Tremley House at half-nine, only to be told that the earl was not in.

Unfortunately, the butler at Tremley House had not been

alerted that Duncan West was through with aristocrats turning him away.

"The earl is in," he said.

"I am sorry, sir," the butler said, attempting to close the door.

Duncan set his boot in the jamb, preventing his dismissal. "Strange, as you do not sound sorry at all." He set a hand to the door, pushing firmly. "I shall stand here all day. You see, I haven't a reputation to uphold."

The butler decided it was better to let Duncan in than to do battle in the doorway, where anyone wandering through Mayfair might see them. He opened the door.

Duncan raised a brow. "Smart man." The butler opened his mouth, no doubt to assure Duncan that the earl was not, in fact, in. "He's home and he'll see me." Duncan removed his coat and hat and thrust them into the servant's hands. "Will you fetch him? Or shall I find him myself?"

The servant disappeared, and Duncan waited in the great foyer of Tremley House, feeling not nearly as satisfied as he should.

He should be elated, finally, finally in possession of something that would free him from the yoke of Tremley's blackmail and threats. Today, finally, West would show his hand and win.

And now, after eighteen years of it, he would be able to stop running. Stop hiding.

He would be able to live a life. Mostly.

He should be celebrating his victory.

Instead, he was thinking of his defeat the night before. He was thinking of Georgiana, bared to him, cast in the golden glow of his fireplace, on the edge of his most prized possession—his most beloved location—in the wake of a pleasure that he had never known. He was thinking of the way she'd closed herself off, resisted his promises and his help even as she vied for his touch.

He was thinking of her rejection.

He'd never offered anyone what he'd offered her in that

dark room. He'd never offered his protection. His funds. His support. *Himself.*

He turned, stalking to the far end of the foyer. Christ. He'd told her his secrets. He'd never told anyone about his childhood. About his obsession with cleanliness. About his past.

When she'd asked where he'd been when he was a child, he'd nearly told her. He'd nearly revealed everything . . . in the hopes that his honesty would unlock her own. Would help her to trust him. To tell him the truth about herself. About her past. About her mistakes.

About Chase.

But he didn't. And thank God for that.

Because she didn't want his truths. She didn't want him.

I was thinking that I should tell you the truth

Her words from the prior evening rang through him as though she stood next to him. She should have told him the truth. He could have helped. But she hadn't. She'd rejected his assistance.

Rejected him.

Instead, she wanted what he could do for her. The papers. The gossip. The restored reputation and the title that would come with it.

And even as he thought the words, he knew she was right. Because his truths changed nothing. Even now, even as he prepared to face the man who had controlled him for years, as he prepared to free himself, West remained unmarriageable.

Even now, as he wielded power and fortune and might, he would never be more than the boy born into nothing, raised in nothing.

He would never be enough to raise her out of scandal. He had nothing to give her. No title. No name. No past.

No future.

He was a means to her end.

So why not take what she offered? Her premarital arrangement? Why not lay her bare and make love to her in a dozen places in a score of ways? She did not wish him to play her savior, fine. She did not wish to share her truths, fine. But she offered herself. Her pleasure. Their mutual pleasure.

Why not take the pleasure and leave everything else?

Because he'd never been good at leaving things behind.

"It's damn early," Tremley said from the first-floor landing, drawing Duncan's attention as he descended the stairs, his hair still damp from his morning ablutions. "I hope you've brought what I asked."

"I haven't," West said, putting Georgiana out of his mind, not wanting her here, in this place, sullied by this man and his sin. "I've brought something infinitely better."

"I'll be happy to judge that." Tremley paused at the bottom of the stairs, straightening his sleeves, and a memory flared.

West watched the careful play of fingers at the earl's cuffs, and finally said, "Your father used to do that."

Tremley stopped fidgeting.

West lifted his gaze. "Before anyone of import might see him, he would even his shirtsleeves."

Tremley raised a brow. "You remember my father's eccentricities?"

He remembered more than that. "I remember everything."

One side of the earl's mouth lifted. "I fairly quake in my boots." He sighed. "Come, West. What have you? It is early, and I have not yet had breakfast."

"You could invite me to eat."

"I could," the earl said. "But I think my family has fed you enough for a lifetime. Don't you?"

West's fists clenched, and he did his best to keep his anger at bay. This was his game. His win. He took a breath, rocked back on his heels. Affected the kind of boredom that came with power. That had always oozed from the Earl of Tremley. "Would you like to hear what I have learned?"

"I told you. I want Chase's identity. If it has nothing to do with him, I don't care to know it. Certainly not at this hour." He turned to a footman at the far end of the hallway and snapped his fingers. "Tea. Now."

The servant moved without hesitation, and West detested the way Tremley's sharp orders were delivered and obeyed . . . in the same manner his father's had been done. Without question. Out of fear of retaliation. Cruelty ran in the family, and young servants learned quickly to move fast enough to escape the notice of the Earls of Tremley.

He watched the young footman scurry away and turned to Tremley. "As a matter of fact, this does have something to do with Chase."

Tremley waited for Duncan to speak. When he did not, the earl said, "Christ, West. I haven't all day."

"Your study would be a better place for it."

For a moment, West thought he'd disagree. And, to be honest, he wanted to do it here, in near public, where the walls of this immense house, bought and paid for with treasonous funds, had ears. He wanted to reveal his knowledge— the contents of the supremely edifying file from Chase—in front of a half-dozen servants who wanted nothing more than the destruction of their unyielding, unpleasant master.

But revelation to the world was not the goal.

The goal was that of all discussions of information since the dawn of time. A trade. West's secrets for Tremley's. Freedom for them both. Revelation for neither.

He waited a heartbeat. Two. Five.

He had waited much, much longer.

The earl turned on his heel and led the way to his office, dark and enormous, filled with unused windows, heavy velvet curtains blocking the light and any prying eyes beyond.

Duncan was keenly aware of the pistol in his boot. He did not think he would need to use it, but he was comforted by its presence in the dark room. He sat in a wide leather chair by the fireplace, stretching his legs long across the floor of the space, crossing one ankle over the other, resting his elbows on the arms of the chair and tenting his fingers together above his chest.

"I did not say you could sit," Tremley said.

Duncan did not move from his position.

Tremley watched him for a long while. "You seem terribly

sure of yourself for someone who is a heartbeat from jail with a single word from me."

Duncan considered the wide ebony desk on the other side of the room. "That was your father's."

"What of it?"

Duncan lifted a shoulder. "I remember it. I remember thinking it was massive. That I'd never seen a desk as large. That he must have been very powerful indeed to require such an enormous piece of furniture."

He remembered other things, too. Remembered staring through a keyhole, knowing he shouldn't. Seeing his mother on that desk. Seeing the old earl take what he wanted. Give nothing.

Not love. Not money.

Not even help when they needed it most. When *she* needed it the most.

Tremley leaned against the desk, crossing his arms and blocking the memories. "And? Your point?"

"Only that it does not seem so large anymore." West shrugged one shoulder, knowing the movement would irritate Tremley.

You do that when you want someone to think that you aren't interested in what they are about to say.

Georgiana's instant understanding of his interview tactic had unsettled him when she'd noticed it. No one else ever had.

Tremley certainly did not. His gaze narrowed. "What do you have on him?"

"Chase?" West asked, pretending to brush a piece of lint from his trouser leg. "Nothing."

Tremley straightened. "Then you are wasting my time. Get out. Come back when you have something. Soon. Or I shall pay our Cynthia a visit."

West resisted the urge to lunge for the earl the moment the words were spoken, the possessive pronoun hanging in the air like an invective. Instead, he played his first card. "I don't have anything on Chase, but I do have something on you."

Tremley smiled, arrogant and unperturbed. "You do."

West matched the expression. "Tell me, do you think His Royal Highness would be interested in hearing that his closest advisor is skimming the exchequer?"

Something shifted in Tremley's eyes, the barest proof that West was right about the embezzlement. But what of the rest of the file—Lady Tremley's accusations? Her proof? Had she made worthy payment for membership at the Angel? "You haven't proof of anything close to that."

West's smile did not waver. "Not yet. But I do have proof that you took the money to pay for arms in Turkey." Tremley stilled, and West continued. "And I've proof that the Ottoman Empire is happily paying you to keep them well supplied with information."

Tremley shook his head. "There is no proof of that."

"No?"

The earl met his eyes. Lied. "There is no proof, because it's a false accusation. And I should have you run up on charges of slander."

"It's libel in the papers."

"You wouldn't dare cross me." West heard the edge of nervousness in the earl's voice. Uncertainty, for the first time in years. "You don't have proof."

West sighed. "Oh, Charles," he said, letting all his disdain show in the name he had not used since they were both children, when their power was far more imbalanced. When Charles was preceded by "Lord," and West had had no choice but to take the blows he struck. "Have you not learned that I am exceedingly good at my job? Of course there is proof. And of course I have it."

"Show it to me." Tremley was nervous.

West was growing more excited by the moment. It was true. This was it. He was going to gain his freedom. He cocked a brow. "I think it is time you offer me breakfast after all, don't you?"

Tremley was furious, darkness and shadows coming over his face as he placed his hands to the edge of the desk. "Your proof."

"Letters from Constantinople. From Sofia. From Athens."
The earl stilled. "I should kill you."

"And the threat of murder to top it all off." West laughed.
"You are a prince among men. No surprise why His Royal
Highness is so very beholden to you . . . But he won't be
for long, will he? Not after this is revealed." He paused. "I
wonder if you'll be hanged in public?"

Tremley's eyes had narrowed to slits. "If I hang, you hang
right alongside me."

"It's doubtful, that," West said. "You see, I haven't committed high treason. Oh, it's quiet, nearly undiscovered high
treason, but it is high treason nonetheless." West paused,
loving the look of vitriolic fear on Tremley's face. "Don't
worry, though. I shall be there when they hang you. You may
look into my eyes at the end. It would be the least I could do."

Tremley regained his confidence, clearly deciding that he
should soldier on. "If a breath of it gets out—I ruin you. I
shall tell everyone who will listen about your past. Coward.
Runaway. Thief."

"I've no doubt you would," West said. "But I am not here
to destroy you, however much I would like to do just that."

Tremley's gaze went curious. "What then?"

"I'm here to offer you a trade."

The earl immediately understood. "My secrets for yours."

"Precisely." The thrill of the win shot through him.

"Tit for tat."

He'd last heard the phrase on Georgiana's lips. He hated
hearing it on Tremley's. He inclined his head. "However you
would like to define it. I prefer to call it the end of your dominion over me."

Tremley looked at him with thorough vitriol. "I could kill
you now."

"You should have killed me years ago," West said. "Your
problem is that you enjoyed using me."

"No one would ever doubt my innocence if I did it," Tremley pointed out.

"Killing me would never free you from the fear of discovery. You see, I am not the only one who has the proof of your transgressions."

There was a long silence as the earl considered the possible identities of West's coconspirator, shock finally flashing when he realized the truth. "Chase?"

West did not reply.

Tremley swore harshly, then laughed, shrill and humorless, the sound unsettling. Duncan did his best to remain still, to affect a state of utter calm. "You think you've won," Tremley said. "And perhaps you would have if it were merely you and me in the game." He paused. "But you brought in a third player. And in doing so, you've lost everything to him."

The words sent a chill through Duncan, but he said, "I doubt that."

Tremley laughed again, the sound turning cold. Humorless. "You've made a terrible mistake getting into bed with Chase. Sharing information with him. You think he won't hesitate to destroy me if need be? Hell, if he has even an inkling to do so? When has Chase ever hesitated to end a man?" Duncan heard the truth in the words. Knew instantly what came next, but could not understand how he had not seen it before. "Our fates are intertwined now, by your design," Tremley said. "If Chase ruins me, I ruin you."

Christ.

"So you see, you may no longer have to worry about me," said the earl, "but now you must worry about Chase." He looked down at the floor, seeming suddenly much more comfortable with the events of the morning. "And he is not the kind of dog easily kept on a leash."

When he returned his gaze to Duncan, it was to issue a dark, cold-blooded order. "Now he is the enemy, Jamie. He is the one who must be silenced."

*H*ow had he not seen it?

He collected his coat and hat from the Tremley butler, and

headed for the door, prepared to exit the town house and head to his office to spend the day researching Chase.

How had he not seen it?

How had he been so very off his game that he had not recognized that the information Chase had offered him had the power to destroy even if Duncan himself never used it? Had he been blinded by power? By the heady promise of freedom?

He'd like to say yes. He'd like to say every moment—every step of this plan—had been in service to a vengeful, blinding god who wanted nothing more than for Duncan and Cynthia to be free of Tremley and his horrifying hold. Certainly, that would have been the reason a year ago. A month ago. A week ago.

But as a man who lived lies so well, he did not care much for lying to himself, and so he admitted, there, on one side of the great door of Tremley House, that he hadn't seen the logical flaw in his reasoning because of the woman who was so exquisitely tied to this particular exchange of information.

She was exquisitely tied to Chase, as well.

Chase, the puppet master, who set them all to dancing on his whim.

I do not like it when you do not share.

Even the words in the note, delivered with a parcel of information that Chase could never have imagined existed, made certain that West knew who was in control of their partnership. And now that Chase had the information on Tremley, it was only a matter of time before he either decided to use it or wondered why West wasn't using it.

And then he'd have to explain everything to this man shrouded in darkness and mystery, who was reviled and adored in equal measure. Sometimes by the same person. He thought of Georgiana again, knowing that her actions had, from the start, been the result of Chase's threats. Of Chase's power.

West left the house, the main door closing sharply behind him, loud enough for him to hear its meaning—*Do not return*.

Surely she reviled Chase more than she adored him.

Shouldn't she?

He thought of his mother, who had never found the strength to choose revulsion. Dear God. Was it possible that Georgiana was the same?

His mind reeled. Now, with Tremley's secrets known and his own valuable enough to threaten his future, West had no choice but to go after Chase. And if he did, the outcome was not debatable—he had to win without hesitation. Without any question.

And to do that, he had to go after the only thing Chase held dear.

His identity.

Tit for tat. Chase's name to protect his own.

To protect Cynthia.

To protect Georgiana.

But what then? Georgiana still wouldn't be his. She still couldn't be his. He couldn't marry her. Couldn't give her the life she deserved. The life she wanted.

It did not matter, he realized as he stood outside his enemy's home, all of Mayfair around him, as he'd still not be enough for her.

You can't give me the title.

He wondered how many times he'd hear those words before he forgot the sound of them on her lips. He couldn't give her a title. But he could get her free of Chase. And in doing so, free himself.

He caught a movement across the street—a man leaning against a tree, hands in his pockets, who should not have been worthy of notice, but whom West noticed nonetheless.

With the longtime training of a skilled reporter, West did not look, and yet saw everything. He saw how the man's collar was tipped up against the cold, as though he'd been standing there for a long while. He saw broad shoulders beneath beautiful clothing—broad enough to be built somewhere beyond butcher shops and boxing rings. This man was no common appearance. He was clearly trained for his size.

Duncan headed to his curricle, pretending not to notice

the brute. He could be there for any reason—Tremley had no doubt given spies enough reason to pay close attention.

But those spies did not travel in a carriage with blackened windows, altogether too like the one he'd ridden in the previous evening.

First, he thought it was she. That she'd followed him. And he struggled to decide if he was furious at or exhilarated by her presence. But as he moved closer to the conveyance, the guard came off the wall, making it clear that Duncan would have to fight for proximity, which, considering the activities of the previous evening and her obvious willingness to continue them, seemed off.

And then he realized that she wasn't there.

And that the carriage was not supposed to have been noticed.

He was being followed.

As though he was a child.

He moved more quickly, the guard moving to stand in front of West as his destination became clear and his temper became hot. He met the guard's gaze and spoke, without hesitation, all the anger and frustration of the morning roiling within him.

"I am certain you were told not to lay a hand on me."

"Don't know who you are, sir." The words were a long, low drawl.

West lifted his chin. "I wonder what it would take to restore your memory."

The thug smiled, a gap in the expression where one of his front teeth should have been. "I'd like to see you try, gent."

West threw a punch, but at the last second—while the bodyguard flinched and prepared to block the blow—he feinted, turning, instead, to the carriage and opening the door to peer inside.

Recognition dawned.

The Marquess of Bourne was inside the carriage.

He was being followed by The Fallen Angel.

Goddammit. He moved to lift himself into the coach, but

the pause as he recognized Bourne gave the man outside enough time to recover and catch West's coat sleeve, pulling him back.

He turned on the guard. And this time, his punch connected. Intentionally. The security detail at the Angel were not amateurs. The guard hit back, quick and economical, hard enough to sting. Before West could attack again, Bourne spoke.

"Enough. It's Mayfair in broad daylight." Bourne grabbed West's shoulder and stayed his blow. "Get in the damn carriage. You're shocking the ladies."

Sure enough, there were two young women across the street in their pretty outdoor finery, eyes wide, mouths agape at the utterly unprecedented scene. West removed his handkerchief, pressing it to his nose to discover that he was bleeding. The brute had excellent aim. The other man's eye was swelling shut, which gave West a modicum of pride. Removing his hat, West slapped the man on the back and turned him to face the ladies. "Good morning, ladies."

He was impressed that the women's eyes did not escape their sockets, particularly when his companion bowed and said, "Lovely mornin'."

"Christ," Bourne said from inside the carriage, and West returned his attention to the matter at hand. He released his opponent, and lifted himself into the carriage, placing himself across from the marquess, who opened his mouth to speak.

"No," West said, anger having turned to fury. "I don't give a damn why you are here. I don't give a damn what you want or what you think or what you have to say. I am through with the lot of you—managing me, following me, negotiating with me. Fucking manipulating me."

West registered the calm in Bourne's gaze, as though he were not surprised by the words. "If I did not wish for you to know you were being followed, I assure you, you would not know."

Duncan cut him a look. "No doubt you believe that."

"Tremley is a monster," Bourne said. "Whatever you plan to do with the information you have on him—whatever you've told him—he's a monster. And as a friend—"

West sliced a hand through the air. "Don't. Don't call yourself my friend. You and Temple and Cross and your fucking *owner* have called me a friend too many times meaning too little of it."

Bourne's brows lifted. "Our owner? I don't like the sound of that."

"Then perhaps you ought to release yourself from Chase's apron strings and make a name for yourself on your own."

Bourne whistled, long and low. "You are angry, aren't you."

"I'm merely disgusted by you people."

"We people?"

Bourne knew well enough to whom Duncan referred. "Aristocrats who think the world bends to their whim."

"Well, when you have the money and power we have, the world does bend to your whim," Bourne said. "But this isn't about us, is it?"

West narrowed his gaze. "You don't have a single idea what this is about."

"I do, though. I think it's about a woman."

A vision flashed, the woman to whom Bourne referred. Half sin, half salvation, equally as beholden to the men of The Fallen Angel. To their leader. So beholden to him that she did not have room for West.

Not that it mattered.

He met the marquess's gaze. "You deserve a thrashing."

"And you think you're the man to give it to me?"

He was. He was the only man in London who could give it to him. He was tired of being manipulated and used with complete disregard.

"I think I'm the man to end you all," he said, the words cold and dark and unsettling in the quiet.

End them and save her.

Bourne stilled. "That sounds like a threat."

"I don't make threats," Duncan took hold of the door handle and opened the door.

"Now I know it's about her."

Duncan turned back, resisting the urge to take out his anger on the marquess. To do to him what he wished to do to Chase—the mysterious, unknowable Chase.

Instead, he said, "It's not a threat. Tell that to Chase."

Chapter 15

. . . Our favorite Lady was seen eating lemon ice from Merkson's Sweets with Miss P— earlier this week. It seemed not to concern either flaxen-haired beauty that the weather was far too cold for lemon ice. It should be added that a source close to Merkson's reports that a certain Baroness will be stocking lemon ice at her next ball . . .

. . . London's finest casino continues to indebt gentlemen with little sense and less money, apparently. We have it on good authority that several aristocrats will be offering land in exchange for loans this spring, and we pity their poor, put upon wives . . .

The News of London, May 4, 1833

"Cross says that you've selected a husband."

Georgiana did not look up from her place by the fireplace in the owners' suite, where she pretended to be enthralled in a pile of documents requiring her attention. "I have."

"Are you planning to tell us who it is?"

In The Fallen Angel and the lower club the founders owned, seventeen members owed more than they could repay from their cash coffers, which meant that she and the other partners needed to decide what they were willing to accept in lieu of money. This was not a small project, nor was it to be taken lightly. But there was no possible way a woman could work with her business partners' wives collected about her.

She looked up to find all three seated nearby, in the chairs that usually housed their husbands.

Or, at least, the chairs that had housed their husbands before those husbands had gone soft. Now they housed a countess, a marquess, and a duchess and future duke—aged four months.

Lord deliver her from men's wives.

"Georgiana?"

She met Countess Harlow's serious gaze, wide and unblinking behind her spectacles. "I feel certain that you know the answer to that question, my lady."

"I don't," Pippa replied. "You see, I've heard two possible names offered."

"I heard Langley," Penelope, Lady Bourne piped up, reaching to take the infant from the arms of his mother. "Give me that sweet boy."

Mara, the Duchess of Lamont, relinquished her son without question. "I heard Langley at first, as well, but then Temple seemed to think there was another, more suitable possibility."

Not at all suitable.

"There is no such thing."

"Now that is interesting," said Pippa, pushing her glasses farther back on her nose. "I am not certain that I have ever seen a lady in trousers blush."

"You would think that embarrassment would not be so easy for someone of your experience," the marchioness added, her tone fit only for the child in her arms.

Georgiana was fairly certain that the sound that came from

Temple's son was best described as laughter. She considered tossing them all out of the room. "You know, before any of you turned up, this was called the owners' suite."

"We're virtually owners," Penelope pointed out.

"No, you are literally *wives* of owners," Georgiana retorted. "That is not the same thing at all."

Mara raised an auburn brow. "You are not entirely in a place to condescend about wives."

Her partners' wives were the worst women in London. Difficult in the extreme. Bourne, Cross, and Temple deserved them, no doubt, but what had Georgiana done to warrant their presence now, as she reconciled herself to the events of the past day? She wanted nothing more than to sit quietly and remind herself that it was her work and her daughter who were the most important things in her life, and everything else—every*one* else—could hang.

"I heard that West was in the running," Pippa said.

Starting first with her gossiping business partners and their nattering wives.

"*Duncan* West?" Penelope asked.

"The very same," Mara said.

"Oh," Penelope said happily to the boy in her arms. "We like him."

The boy cooed.

"He seems a very good man." Pippa said.

"I've always had a soft spot for him," Mara agreed. "And he seems to have a soft spot for women who are followed by trouble."

Something unpleasant flared at those words as she found she did not care for Duncan West having a soft spot for any women, particularly those who might decide they wished to be protected by him in perpetuity. "Which women?" Only after she'd lifted her head and spoke did she realize she was supposed to be pretending to work. She cleared her throat. Returned her attention to the file in her hand. "Not that I'm interested."

Silence fell in the wake of her statement, and she could

not resist looking up. Penelope, Pippa, and Mara were looking at each other, as though in a comedic play. Temple's son was blessedly asleep, or he would no doubt be watching her as well.

"What is it?" Georgiana asked. "I am not interested."

Pippa was the first to break the silence. "If you are not interested, then why ask?"

"I was being polite," Georgiana rushed to answer. "After all, the three of you are chattering like magpies in my space, I thought I might play hostess."

Penelope spoke then. "We thought you were working."

She lifted a file. "I am."

"Whose file is that?" Mara asked, as though it were perfectly normal for her to ask such a thing. And it might be.

But damned if Georgiana could remember whose file it was.

"She is blushing again," Pippa said, and when Georgiana turned a glare on the Countess Harlow, it was to find herself under a curious investigation, as though she were an insect under glass.

"There's nothing to be ashamed of, you know," Penelope said. "We've all found ourselves drawn to someone who seems entirely wrong for us."

"Cross wasn't wrong for me," Pippa said.

Penelope lifted a brow. "Oh? And the bit where you were engaged to another man?"

"And he was engaged to another woman?" Mara added.

Pippa smiled. "It only made the story more entertaining."

"The point is, Georgiana," Mara spoke this time, "you should not be ashamed of wanting West."

"I don't want West," she said, setting down her file and standing, the frustration of these women and their knowing gazes and their attempts at comforting words propelling her away from them, to the massive stained glass window that looked out on the casino floor.

"You don't want West," Mara repeated, flatly.

"No," she said. But of course she *did*. She wanted him a

great deal. But not in the way they meant. Not forever. She simply wanted him *for now*.

"Whyever not?" Penelope asked, and the other women chuckled.

She could not bring herself to confess that he did not seem to want her. After all, she'd very overtly offered herself to him the night before—and he'd refused her. Wrapping a towel around his handsome hips and stalking from the room that housed his swimming pool without looking back.

As though what had transpired between them meant nothing.

Georgiana leaned into the window, splaying her fingers wide and pressing her forehead to the cool, pale glass that made one of Lucifer's broken wings. The position gave the illusion of floating, of hovering high above the dimly lit pit floor, the tables empty and quiet now, untouched until the afternoon, when maids would lower the chandeliers and light the massive candelabras that kept the casino bright and welcoming in the darkness. Her gaze flickered from table to table—faro, *vingt-et-un*, roulette, hazard—every table hers, placed with care. Run with skill.

She was royalty of the London underground, vice and power and sin were her dominion, and yet a man, who made pretty offers and tempted her with lovely promises that he could never keep, had somehow flattened her.

After the long silence, Mara said, "You know, I never thought I could have love."

"Neither did I, though I wanted it quite desperately," Penelope added, standing and moving to the pram in the corner, where she settled the sleeping future duke into his pristine cocoon of blankets.

"I did not think it was real," Pippa said. "I could not see it, and therefore, I did not believe it."

Georgiana closed her eyes at the admissions. Wished the three women gone. Then said, "There are days when I find myself sympathizing with MacBeth."

"MacBeth," Pippa repeated, confused.

"I believe that Georgiana is suggesting that we are like witches," Penelope said dryly, turning from her place across the room.

"Secret, black, and midnight hags and all that?" Pippa asked.

"The very same."

"Well, that's mildly unkind."

Georgiana turned and asked, "Don't you have places to be?"

"As we are indolent aristocrats," Mara said, "no."

It wasn't true, of course. Mara ran a home for boys, and had raised thirty thousand pounds in close to a year to expand the home and send the boys to university. Pippa was a renowned horticulturalist, always speaking to some society of old men about her work with hybrid roses. And between raising a lovely little girl and preparing for a second child—who Bourne was certain was going to be a boy—Penelope was one of the most prominent, active members of the ladies' side of the club.

These were not idle women.

So why did they insist on hounding her?

"The point is, Georgiana—"

"Oh, there is a point?"

"There is a point. Namely, that you think you are somehow different from every woman who has ever come before you."

She was different.

"Even now, you think it. You think that because of this life you lead, because of your casino and your secret identity and the company you keep—"

"—present company excepted," Penelope interjected.

"Obviously," Mara agreed, turning back to Georgiana. "But because of the company you keep other than us, and the damn trousers you wear . . . you think you are different. You think you don't deserve what every other woman deserves. What every other woman seems to have. Even worse, you think that even if you did deserve it, you don't have the opportunity for it. Or maybe you think you don't want it."

"I don't." The words shocked everyone in the room, none more than Georgiana herself.

"Georgiana—" Mara was out of her chair, headed for her, when Georgiana held up a hand.

"No." Mara stopped, and Georgiana was grateful for it. "Even if I could have it. Even if there were someone willing to give it to me—someone to have me despite my being saddled with ruin, an unwed mother, a casino owner with three male business partners and a bevy of prostitutes at my beck and call—I don't want it."

"You don't want love?" Penelope sounded shocked.

Love. The thing that had seen her through the heights and depths of life. The threat of it had ruined her ten years ago, then the reality of it had made her strong and resolute when Caroline was born. And then, last night, it had lured her. "I do not. While it teases with its pretty words and prettier touches, love has already had a run at me, and I am too wrecked by it."

There was a pause, then Mara asked, "But if he would have you? If he would give it to you?"

He. Duncan West.

"He does not seem the kind of man who would ruin you," Penelope said.

"They never seem like the kind of men who would ruin you," Georgiana replied.

They had lied so much to each other. It was hard to imagine the truth between them. She shook her head, spoke the words that she thought whenever he was near, and she ached for his touch, and she wished for more than one night. One week. "It is too dangerous."

"For whom?"

An excellent question. "For both of us."

The door opened, revealing Bourne. He crossed the room, not even looking at Georgiana, focused only on his wife, beaming at him from her place by the pram. He smiled, pulling her into his arms. "Hello, Sixpence, I would have come more quickly, but they only just told me you were here."

Penelope smiled. "I came to see Stephen." She nodded at the pram. "Doesn't he look just like Temple?"

Bourne leaned over the sleeping child. "He does, indeed. Poor thing."

Mara laughed. "I shall tell him you said it."

He smiled. "I shall tell him first." He looked to Georgiana, his smile fading. "But first, I've something to tell you." He moved to sit in one of the large chairs, pulling Penelope down to his lap, placing a large hand over the place where his second child grew. "West went to Tremley today."

She did not hide her surprise. "Why?"

Bourne shook his head. "It is unclear. But it was early, and he was not entirely welcome." He paused. "And then he was somewhat irritated that we were following him."

Her eyes widened. "You were seen?"

"It was Mayfair at nine o'clock in the morning. It's not easy to hide."

She sighed. "What happened?"

"He hit Bruno." Bourne shrugged. "Bruno hit back, if that's any consolation."

It wasn't.

"But the point is, there's something there. He didn't just want Tremley for the papers. He wanted him for more. And you should also know that he is furious with us."

"With who?"

"With the Angel. And I think you're the one to talk him down, so—"

A sharp knock sounded, interrupting the words, heralding one of the handful of people who knew that the owners' suite existed. Pippa moved to the door, cracked it. Turned back. "I believe my line is, *Something wicked this way comes.*"

She opened the door wide to reveal Duncan West.

What in hell was he doing here?

Bourne was out of his chair instantly, setting Penelope on her feet as Georgiana headed for West, who was stepping over the threshold and into the room, his gaze taking in everything from the stained glass behind her to her aristocratic companions, finally settling on her. She saw irritation in his eyes when he looked at her, as though he had not been expecting her.

As though he had been expecting another.

But behind the irritation, somewhere in the depths of his beautiful brown eyes, she saw something else. Something akin to thrill. She knew it, because she felt it, too. Felt it, and feared it.

She stopped short. "Who let you in?"

He met her gaze, spoke. "I am a member of the club."

"Members are not allowed in this room," she said. "Members are not even allowed on this floor."

"Perhaps you ought to tell that to Bourne."

"I was going to say," Bourne said from the doorway, ignoring the look she sent in his direction, "that you should know I invited him up."

Anger flared, hot and unwelcome. She turned on her partner. "You had no right."

Bourne raised a supercilious brow. "I am an owner, too, am I not?"

Her gaze narrowed. "You violate our rules."

"Don't you mean *Chase's* rules?" Bourne said, and Georgiana wanted to slap his face for the sarcasm in the words. "I wouldn't worry. Chase seemed to forget those rules in certain cases."

She did not misunderstand. At one point or another all three of the women in the room had been invited to The Fallen Angel by Chase, without the permission of their husbands. She didn't care that Bourne was somehow viewing West's invitation as retribution, she was too busy being furious at him for ignoring the rules. For smugly disregarding their partnership.

For the way he seamlessly stripped her of power here—the only place where she had any power to begin with.

Before she could argue with him, West spoke. "Where is he?" West's words were clear and firm in the dimly lit room, as though he fully expected to be heard and responded to despite the fact that he did not belong here.

Despite the fact that she did not want him here.

"Where is who?" she replied.

"Chase."

He had not come to see her. Of course, she should have known it. She should not be surprised. But she was, nonetheless; after all, they had spent much of the prior evening together, and . . . shouldn't he wish to see her? Or was that mad?

Should she not wish him to wish to see her?

The thought ran through her head and disgusted her with its stupid, simpering simperingness. And then she was disgusted with the fact that she could not think of a better word than simperingness.

She did not wish him to want her. Everything was easier without that.

But there was something about the way he looked— thoroughly serious and thoroughly dismissive, as though she were nothing but a door-man to the room he wished to enter—that made her hate the fact that he was not here to see her.

Except, of course, he was.

He just didn't know it.

"He is not here." A lie, and somehow not one at all.

He took a step toward her. "I'm sick and tired of you protecting him. It's time he face me. Where is your master?"

The angry question hung in the air, seeming to reverberate off the stained glass. Georgiana opened her mouth to brazen it through when the Duchess of Lamont interjected, "Well. I think it's time for Stephen and me to find Temple."

The words unlocked the rest of the room. "Yes. We must be home as well," Penelope said as Mara pushed the pram to the door, more quickly than any young mother had in history, Georgiana imagined.

"We must?" Bourne asked, looking as though he weren't at all interested in leaving the drama unfolding before them.

"Yes," Penelope said firmly. "We *must*. We have things. To do."

Bourne smirked. "What kinds of things?"

His marchioness narrowed her gaze. "All kinds of things."

The smirk became a wicked smile. "May I choose the things that are done first?"

Penelope pointed to the door. "Out."

Bourne heeded her instructions, leaving Pippa only. The Countess Harlow had never been very good at perceiving social cues, so Georgiana hoped she might stay and protect her from this man, his questions, her answers, and her silly feelings about the whole thing.

Hope was a fleeting, horrible thing.

After a beat, Pippa seemed to realize she'd been left. "Oh," she said. "Yes. I should . . . go . . . as well. I have . . . well . . ." She pushed her glasses higher on her nose. "I have a child. Also . . . Cross." She nodded once and left the room.

West watched her go, his gaze lingering on the door for a long moment before he turned to Georgiana. "And then there were two."

Her stomach flipped at the words. "So it would seem."

He did not release her gaze, and she marveled at the way he seemed to see and ask and somehow *know* everything with a simple look. And then he said her name, soft and tempting in this room she loved so well. "Georgiana." He paused, and she wanted to go to him. Wanted to curl into him and tell him everything, because if she did not know better—she would think the word was spoken in understanding.

But she did know better. And if she did not understand, it was impossible that he did.

He asked the only question she could not answer. "Where is he?"

$\mathscr{S}$he was wearing trousers.

It was the first and only thought he had when he'd entered the room—his gaze flying past Countess Harlow, to the woman who had consumed his thoughts for what seemed like forever. She stood against the far wall of the room against an enormous stained glass mosaic, one he knew well. One he had seen a thousand times from its opposite side.

He'd always assumed there was a room here, on the far side of Lucifer's fall, but he'd never imagined this was how he would find it, with the beautiful Georgiana framed by the dark angel beyond. Wearing trousers.

It was the most sinful, spectacular thing he'd ever seen, and when she'd come toward him, an avenging queen, insisting that he was trespassing, he'd wanted to catch her in his arms, carry her to that glorious window, press her back against it, and show her all the ways he would like to trespass.

But then the frustration had taken over. She'd been protecting this place in spite of the fact that it was overrun with the wives of The Fallen Angel's owners and in spite of the fact that the Marquess of Bourne had paid him escort.

Which made him realize she wasn't protecting the place.

She was protecting the man, just as she had the night before.

He doesn't own me.

He heard her words again. The lie in them.

Because it was clear Chase owned her, just as he owned every bit of this club and all the men and women who frequented it. There was no freedom at The Fallen Angel. Everything—everyone—belonged to Chase.

And even now, as they stood alone in this dark room, with none but Lucifer to hear them—Georgiana protected the man who had ruined her life. Who continued to do so. And he was through with it. He wanted her out from under him. He wanted her far from this place and its sin and vice and history of taking lives for sport.

He wanted her safe, for God's sake. Her and Caroline.

He'd get her married. But not because Chase had asked.

Because she deserved a chance at happiness—she, more than anyone he'd ever known.

He only wished he could be the one to give it to her. But he couldn't, his secrets too legion, too dangerous. And so he would secure it for her in another way. He would face Chase. Free her, first. Protect himself, second.

Because somehow, in this strange play, she had become the most important.

His question hung between them. "Where is he?" And he willed her to tell him. To open the door and point in the direction of this mysterious man. To free herself along with the information.

She did not.

"He is not here," she said.

He bit back his disappointment. "Bourne told me I would find him here."

"Bourne does not know everything. I am the only one here."

"And so I find you, once again, protecting he who does not need it."

"He does—" she started, and he found he could not hear it any longer.

"Stop."

She did, blessedly.

He came toward her, closing the distance more quickly than he would have liked—the speed betraying the emotions he had promised himself he would no longer reveal to her. Not after last night. Not after she'd so thoroughly rejected him.

Not that he could have given her what she deserved.

He met her eyes, willing to give anything to see the truth in them. "Stop," he repeated, and this time, he was not certain if he meant the words for himself or for her. "Stop defending him. Stop lying for him. Christ, Georgiana, what does he have on you? What is this power he holds over you?"

She shook her head. "It's not like that."

"It is, though. You think I have lived an entire life and not learned to identify a woman in a man's thrall?" He hated the words as they came—the truths they betrayed in him. He lifted his hands, cupped her face in them, adoring the way her skin felt at his fingers, soft and terribly tempting. "Tell me. Is he the one? Did he ruin you all those years ago? Did he offer you pretty promises that you could not refuse and that he did not keep?"

Her brow furrowed. "What?"

"Is he Caroline's father?"

The furrow cleared and her eyes went wide. "Is Chase Caroline's father?"

"Say it," he said. "Tell me the truth, and I will take pleasure in destroying him. In avenging both your names."

She smiled, small and surprised. "You would do that?"

Of course he would. He would do anything for this woman, so perfect, so unmatched. How did she not see that? "With unbridled pleasure."

The smile grew sad. "He is not Caroline's father."

There was truth in the words, and he hated that. Hated that there was not another reason to loathe this man who dominated her as surely as he breathed. "Then why?"

She lifted one shoulder. Let it drop. "We are two halves of a coin."

The words were so simple, so honest, that they tore him asunder. *Two halves of a coin.* For a moment, he considered the implications of the words. The meaning of them. He wondered what it would be like to be so needed by her, so cared for by her, that he was the other half of her coin.

He pushed the thought from his head, liking it far too much.

He released her, moving back far enough to be out of her reach. He did not think he could bear her touch at this point.

"I am here to speak to him," he said. "It has been six years, and I've never asked to meet him. It is time."

She hesitated, and it seemed to him that she hovered on some kind of precipice in the moment—as though whatever decision she made would change her world. And perhaps it would.

If Chase gave him what he wanted, it would.

Chase's identity for her freedom. For his own.

"Why?" she asked. "Why now?" He did not reply, and she

pressed him again. "Six years and you've never cared to meet him. And now . . ."

She trailed off, and he filled the silence. "Things have changed."

Now his life was on the line. His life, and Cynthia's secrets.

But those reasons paled in comparison to the one that loomed so powerfully here and now. Chase was the key to Georgiana's freedom. And he found he would do anything for that.

"Take me to him," he said, and the words sounded more plea than demand.

When she nodded and headed for the door, he thought for a moment that she would toss him out. But then she opened it and stepped into the hallway beyond, turning back, silhouetted by the dim corridor, her face awash in color from the stained glass. "Come," she whispered.

He followed, realizing that he would follow her anywhere.

She led him through a maze of corridors, curving and turning in ways that made him feel as though they had doubled back more than once, finally reaching a massive painting, a dark oil featuring a man stripped of his clothes and belongings, lying dead at the feet of two glorious women as his killer crept from the frame. He looked to Georgiana.

"Charming," he said, referencing the gruesome, stunning piece.

She offered a small smile. "Themis and Nemesis."

"Justice and Vengeance."

"Two halves of a coin."

The words were an echo from moments earlier, her description of her relationship with Chase, and they stung. He looked carefully at the divine figures in the painting, one holding a candle, presumably to light the way to justice, the other holding a sword to exact vengeance on the thief. "Which are you?"

She smiled at the painting—the expression small and filled with something he could not quite understand—and placed her hand at the frame of the painting. "I cannot be both?"

She punctuated the question with a tug on the enormous artwork, which swung out on a hinge, revealing a great, yawning blackness. He bit back his surprise. He'd always imagined that there were secret passageways throughout The Fallen Angel—it was the only way to explain the ease with which the founders appeared and disappeared—but this was the first evidence he'd seen of them.

She waved him inside, and he did not hesitate, his heart and mind racing with the knowledge that he was closer to Chase than he'd ever been. With the knowledge that she trusted him enough to bring him to the owner of the casino.

With the knowledge that that trust was not easily given.

She stepped in with him and closed the portal behind her, and they were cloaked in darkness, a hairsbreadth from touching. He could have moved back, pressed himself against one of the walls and allowed her space, but he didn't wish to. He wished to revel in the heat of her. The smell of her. The temptation of her.

He would give anything to touch her.

Her breathing was shallow and quick, as though she could hear his thoughts. As though she was thinking the same ones.

She seemed to hover there in the darkness for a long moment before she turned away, the fabric of her breeches rustling, sending his thoughts to the place where the wool rubbed, where her long, beautiful legs met. He could not stop himself, reaching out his hand, capturing her arm, letting his touch slide to her fingers, interlacing them with his own.

"You risk a great deal by bringing me here."

Her fingers twitched in his grasp, and he wondered what they would feel like on him. The time in his swimming pool had been so fleeting, and her touch had been like a breath, there, then gone.

Gone because he'd pushed her away.

Gone because she belonged to another.

To the man he was about to meet.

He released her. "Lead on."

She hesitated, and for a moment he thought she might

speak, might tell him something in the darkness that she could not find words for in the light. But she was stronger than any woman he'd ever known . . . and her secrets were well-guarded.

She led him down the corridor, and he counted four doors before she paused in the dim glow of a candle near a dozen yards away, the shadows of the flickering flame playing across her face, hiding her truths from him. She reached for the silver chain that hung heavy beneath the linen shirt she wore tucked into those sinful breeches, and he watched as she extracted the pendant that lived there between her breasts, warm from her skin.

She threw a catch on the locket and extracted a key and set it in the lock, revealing her unrestricted access to these rooms. To the man inside them.

Jealousy flared, hot and angry.

She swore she did not belong to Chase and here she was, unlocking his rooms. Providing entry to them.

What else had she unlocked? Where else did she have entry?

The door unlocked, she replaced the key, her hand settling on the handle. Duncan could not bear the idea that she would bring him here, to this place. To this man. He reached to stop her from turning it, loving the softness of her skin as she stilled beneath his touch.

"Georgiana," he whispered, and she looked up at him, those amber eyes slaying him with their attention.

He didn't want her here. Not for this. He wanted her far from here. He wanted her safe and secure, somewhere across London. In his town house.

Forever.

Christ. The word came from nowhere and lingered, wrapping him in promises that could not be kept. In thoughts he was too intelligent to entertain. Even if he could give her everything for which she asked, his past was too dark and his future too threatened to give her everything she deserved.

So he did what he could, offering her freedom in this moment. "You don't have to come with me."

Her brow furrowed. "I don't understand."

"Let me face him on my own. He needn't know you led me here."

She exhaled, and the breath was heavy with emotion. "Duncan—"

"No. I can face him. Whoever he is. Whatever he is."

She smiled at that. "Whatever?"

"He's such a legend, I would not be surprised to discover that he is something beyond human." He paused. "I would not be surprised to find the Oracles themselves behind this door."

She chuckled. "Themis or Nemesis?"

He met her smile with his own. "I suppose I can rule them out."

Her brows rose. "Oh?"

He explained. "As they are female and I find it difficult to believe that there is another woman either on earth or in the pantheon with your strength."

Something lit in those beautiful amber eyes, but he did not have time to identify it. He wanted this moment done. For a heartbeat, he considered telling her the truth—that he did this for her even as he knew she would not accept his help.

But there would be plenty of time to explain—to fight for her—once Chase was beholden to him.

Once he had Chase, he had the keys to Georgiana's freedom. And if he could not guarantee his own, he would do everything he could to secure hers.

"Let me do this," he asked quietly, his hand still on hers, staying her movement. "Let me keep you from this, if from nothing else."

She looked up at him. "You care to protect me?"

He watched her for a long moment before he said, "In my experience, there are few things worth protecting. When a man finds one, he should do his best to keep it safe."

She opened her mouth, as if she had something to say, but seemed to think better of it, ultimately releasing the handle, pulling her hand from beneath his, making him wish they were somewhere else—anywhere else—alone, with an eternity to fill with nothing but touch.

His desire for her terrified as much as it threatened.

For Georgiana Pearson was the most dangerous woman he'd ever known.

He wondered what he would not do for this woman and her beautiful mind and her tempting body.

He turned away from her and opened the door with a quick, economical movement, stepping into the room.

He took in the space, registering two things instantly.

First, the room was enormous and nearly blinding in its brightness, heavy white curtains pulled back from floor-to-ceiling windows to let in the daylight. The room was decorated in crisp, clean white lines, carpet, settee, even the art white and welcoming. There was nothing dark about the space. Nothing that indicated its inhabitant owned a casino. Nothing that hinted at the sin and vice that reigned feet away from the office.

And second, Chase was not there.

Chapter 16

. . . Our Lady G— may be winning hearts and minds across the *ton*, but if there are any that remain closed to her, let her grace in the face of adversity prove her worth! Certainly, it has proven something to Lord L—, this author believes a match may soon be reported in these very pages!

. . . On to the Duke and Duchess of L—! The pair—still as striking together as they were nearly a decade ago when the Duke professed his love in public and the Duchess refused him—was espied on horseback one morning this week in Hyde Park. No doubt the pair thought it was early enough that a passionate kiss would not be seen, but we, too, are early risers . . .

The Scandal Sheet, May 5, 1833

She stepped into the room behind him, desperate to contain her nervousness.

There were a half-dozen people in the world who had been

inside this room, where she played the role of Chase, where she managed the work of The Fallen Angel, and where she ruled London's darkest corners.

And now she stood here, with a man desperate to know her secrets.

With a man to whom she might find herself confessing all if she was not careful.

She watched him take in her space, his brown eyes narrowing in the bright light as they settled on the large, comfortable chairs she'd had custom-built and upholstered in white velvet, on the plush white carpet that cushioned their feet, on the yards and yards of bookshelves that spanned the fourteen feet from floor to ceiling.

And then his gaze settled on her desk.

He moved toward the wide and wonderful centerpiece of the room, and she watched as his fingers traced its edge, wondering at the touch.

Envious.

She started at the thought. The man made her jealous of furniture.

She rushed to speak, to push back the inane idea and fill the silence. "It was made from wood salvaged from a shipwreck."

His fingers stilled on a dark knot in the wood. "Of course it was," he said, quietly.

She could not help herself. "What does that mean?"

He smiled, but the expression lacked humor. "He honors destruction in whatever way possible."

That wasn't what had drawn her to the desk at all. "I think it is more likely that Chase chose the piece because it is a resurrection from ruin."

He met her gaze. "As you are?"

Exactly as I am.

But she could not tell him that, so she looked away.

"You knew he would not be here," he said.

She considered lying, but could not do so. "I did."

He looked away, frustration and fury on his handsome

face. "Then why bring me here? To torture me? To show me my weakness?"

"Your weakness?" He was in no way weak. He was strength personified.

He came toward her. "To show me that even now, even as I stand ready to battle him, he is one ahead of me? To show me that he will always—" He stopped.

She prodded. "Will always what?"

He moved again, pushing her back, stalking her toward the door, which she suddenly regretted closing. "To show me that he will always come first with you, despite the fact that he treats you so poorly."

"He does not treat me poorly."

"Except he does. He does not believe in you. He does not see your worth. How very valuable you are. How very precious you are."

She stilled, and he saw the surprise in her eyes. "You think me precious?"

He met her gaze. Refused to let her look away. "I know you are."

The conversation was dangerous. It made her think of things that could never be. She shook her head, her heart pounding as she pressed against the door and his hands came to the oak surface on either side of her head. "He knows your secrets. And you know his. And you'll protect them forever, even as it destroys you."

He was so close, the words whispered at her ear, sending threat and thrill through her. "It won't destroy me."

"Of course it will," he said. "Your choices are ruining you. This place over freedom. Langley over love. Chase over—"

Me.

She heard the word even as he did not say it.

"I don't," she whispered, her hands coming to his chest, sliding up to the bare skin of his neck, to the strong line of his jaw. She might not be able to have it, but her choice was clear. "I don't."

He was so close, she thought she might die if he didn't

do something—if he didn't touch her. If he didn't kiss her. "What, then?" he asked.

"I told you," she said, aching for him, loving the warmth and the breath and the strength in him as she confessed, "I choose you."

"Not forever," he said.

Did he want her forever?

Was he offering it?

Did she want it?

Even if she did, he could not save Caroline.

She met his gaze, wishing she could hide from him in this too-light room. Wishing the truth weren't so clear. Wishing that he was less than what he was—handsome, noble, good. Wishing she did not want him so very much.

Wishing she could have him, nonetheless.

If only wishing made it so.

She shook her head. "Not forever."

He nodded. And she thought she saw something in his eyes, there and gone so quickly that she might not have recognized it if she did not feel it so keenly herself.

Regret.

She rushed to say more, knowing she merely made things worse. "If I could . . . if I were a different woman . . . if this were a different life—"

"If I were a different man," he offered, the words somehow both hot and cold.

"No," she said, wanting the truth here. Now. Where it had never been before. "I would never want you a different man."

His lips twisted in a humorless smile. "You should want that. Because as it is . . . as I am . . . We are impossible."

"If I did not need the title—"

He cut off her thought. "Where is he?"

She met his gaze. "Nowhere near here."

"When will he return?"

"Not today." She didn't want Chase to return. She wanted this moment, with Duncan, to last forever. Hang the rest of the world.

He slid the fingers of one hand into her hair. "Even if you did not need the title," he said. "I would not marry you."

The words were a blow—one she no doubt deserved. He was angry, furious that she'd brought him here, to Chase's office, but not to Chase. She understood pride well, and he was a man who had more of it than most. But still, the vow echoed through her, and she hated it. Hated that he could so easily resist her. Could so easily discount her.

Hated that he could hurt her so well.

That they could hurt each other.

She could not resist fighting back. "You lie."

He raised a brow and tilted her head back, leaving her lips open for him. "You lie more."

He kissed her then, his hand sliding down the wood to throw the lock as he lifted her high, pressing her into the door, letting her legs wrap high around his waist as he took everything she offered and left her desperate to give him more. To give him everything.

She gasped, her arms wrapping around his neck as he held her off the ground, as though she weighed nothing at all, as though she were a puppet on a string. And perhaps she was. Perhaps he was her puppet master. His hands were everywhere, at her bottom, in her hair, between them, palming her breasts as he pressed into her, promising ease to the parts of her that ached, desperate for him.

She'd never wanted anything the way she wanted this man.

She threaded her fingers through his hair, clenching tight in the blond curls as he released her mouth and slid his lips across her cheek and down her jaw to the lobe of her ear, soft and tremendously sensitive. She gasped, turning her head into the caress as he licked and bit there, at that place about which she'd never really thought.

Her knees went weak, and she was grateful for his firm grip, for the way he held her, strong and without hesitation, as though she weighed nothing at all. He palmed her backside, lifting her higher, pressing deeper, and whispered at her ear. "Here is something that is not a lie; I am going to make you scream your pleasure. You will beg for me to stop, and then, when I do, you will beg for me to start again. You won't know what to do with yourself when I am done with you, because you will not remember your body outside of the pleasure I intend to give you."

The words intended to shock her, and they did. She watched the promise on his lips and closed her eyes against the flood of anticipation they caused deep within her, unable to stop herself from moving against him, thoroughly wanton. She sighed at the feel of him there, between her legs, where she wanted him, repeating the motion, loving the way he pressed against her, bold and unyielding and without apology . . . and then loving the way he groaned his pleasure at the sensation even more.

He swore, the word dark and full of sin. "You know what you do to me, and you do not care."

She leaned forward and bit his lower lip, pulling him to her for another long, drugging kiss. When they parted, they were both panting their pleasure. She smiled. "I do not care in the slightest."

He lifted her, turned her, carried her across the room, setting her on the edge of the massive desk, running one hand up the outside of her thigh as he talked, the words sending heat and promise through her. "I adore these trousers," he confessed, his large hand exploring the muscles and bones of her leg, curving over her thigh to find the soft, untouched place inside, inching along the fabric there until she wished he would pull the damn things off her and do what his touch promised.

She placed her hands to the desk behind her and leaned back, watching him watch her, watching his touch wash over her. He spoke, his words following his caress. "I am viciously jealous of them, though."

She leaned back, and they both watched his fingers play along the inside seam of the leg. "Why?"

"They are able to touch you here," he said, the words lush and lovely, his fingers at the outside of her knee, teasing up the line of the breeches. "And here," he added, his touch at the inside of her thigh. "And . . ." He trailed off as he reached the place where her thighs met, and she shifted. He growled at the movement. "That's right," he whispered. "Spread yourself for me."

God forgive her, she did, parting her thighs, affording him access to the place they both wanted him most. He took what she offered, his strong hand cupping the most secret part of her, and she sighed her pleasure at the touch, even as she was desperate for more of him.

"You like that," he said, as though he were discussing a painting. A meal. A walk in the park.

"I do," she said, not taking her gaze from that hand, from the place where he held her, firm and with an unbearable promise. "God help me, I do."

"He won't help you," Duncan said, his other hand coming to the buttons on her linen shirt, releasing them one by one until she was looking down at the swell of her bare breasts. "This is the domain of another, far less perfect." He cursed again, the word reverberating through the room as he spread the two halves of her shirt and bared her to him. "You are the most beautiful thing I have ever seen."

She watched that hand, large and bronzed, slide across the skin of her stomach, a wicked promise. "Please," she said, desperate for him.

"Please what?" he asked.

"Don't make me beg."

He looked at her then, knowledge and understanding in those unbearably gorgeous eyes. "I fully intend to make you beg, love. I promised you pleasure of the highest order. I promised you that I would control our time together. And I promised you would enjoy it to distraction. And you want all that, don't you?"

She did not have the energy to lie. She nodded. "Yes."

He leaned forward then, rewarding her truth with a long, lingering suck at one nipple, until she cried out her pleasure and put her hands in his hair.

The moment she touched him, he stopped. "Put your hands on the desk."

She did what he asked without question.

He liked it. "Look at yourself," he commanded, letting one finger draw a wicked circle around the straining tip he had just anointed. She looked fully the wanton, Anna, in all her glory, and Georgiana took the moment to arch her back, presenting her bare breasts to him. Tempting him once more.

She was rewarded with another long caress, this time on the breast he had previously ignored. And then he lifted his head and said, "I want you to enjoy this."

She smiled. "I have no concerns that I shan't enjoy it."

He was utterly serious. "If I do anything you do not like, I want you to tell me."

"I shall."

"I shall know if you are lying."

She met his gaze. "I shan't lie. Not in this."

In all other things, but not here. Not with him.

She took a deep breath. "Shall we go to my bed?" It was a heartbeat away, behind a nearby door. Large and plush and made for him. She would be lying if she said she had not spent many a night in that very bed, thinking of this man, of this moment. Of the way he might touch her one day. Of the way he might *want* her one day.

And that day had come.

He shook his head, his fingers playing at the tip of her breast, sending a thrill through her. "I don't want you anywhere he's had you."

Chase.

She shook her head. "You don't have to worry."

She saw the storm cross his face at the words. She wished him to know the truth. "I have not . . . with anyone . . ."

He held up a hand, staying the words. "Don't."

He did not believe her. "Duncan—" she began, letting the words sound her urgency.

He did not let her finish, instead pulling her to the edge of the desk. "Here."

She looked down at the oak. "Here? On the desk?"

"On his desk."

She heard the slight emphasis on the pronoun, barely there. Barely noticeable if one did not expect it. She also heard the frustration in the words, instantly understanding its roots—he thought there was no place in the club where she and Chase hadn't done this.

And so he took ownership of this place, where he believed Chase was king.

He wanted her here.

And, God help her, she wanted him just as much.

More.

She nodded. "Here."

He watched her for a long moment, and she saw the myriad of emotions chase through him: anger, frustration, desire.

Pain.

She reached for him, wanting to stop it, but he resisted, pulling away from her touch, instead moving to lift one of her feet in his enormous hands. "I want you here," he said, gruffly, unlacing her boot. "I want you naked," he said, punctuating the slide of the boot from her foot as he set it on the arm of a chair perched nearby and set to work on the second. "And I want you mine."

Mine.

The word curled through her on a flood of desire, robbing her of breath. When had anyone ever wanted her like this? When had anyone ever honestly desired to claim her? Yes, men wanted her body when she dressed in her bold silks and satins and paraded through the casino as Anna, but this was different. He wanted *her*—Georgiana—in a way no one ever had. Not even the man she had given herself to all those years ago.

But the way he spoke that word—*Mine*—it was not a request. It was, instead, a gruff promise. A claiming. A possession.

And she found she wanted to be possessed.

Very much.

The thought was punctuated by the slide of her second boot, removed with a single, firm tug and tossed to the floor as Duncan returned his hands to her stockinged feet. He took her ankles in his hands, lifting her legs, parting them, stepping between them. She instinctively wrapped herself around him, pulling him closer until they met, hard and hot, where they each wanted the other. She threw her head back as he pressed into her, and he wrapped one strong arm around her waist, holding her weight, keeping her arched and open to him.

"Say it," he growled, meeting her eyes, his free hand coming up to palm one aching breast. "Say it, and I'll give you everything you want."

She did not have to ask what he meant. She knew. Knew, also, that it would not be a lie. Somehow in this mad world, in this mad time, she had come to adore this man. She had come to belong to him. And it was beautiful.

But it could never last.

But nothing beautiful lasted—was that not the lesson she had learned all those years ago, wrapped in warm arms and crisp hay? Love was fleeting and ephemeral, the desperate dream of a naïve, innocent girl.

And so she would give herself to this, and then walk away and live the life she intended.

But first, freedom.

First, him.

"I am yours," she confessed.

He rewarded her with a deep, wonderful growl and a long, devastating kiss that ended with him pulling her to the edge of the desk and setting his hands to the fall of her breeches, working at the buttons with intent skill, unfastening them one after the other until the trousers loosened and he slid them down her legs, taking her stockings with him.

"My lady," he said, Stepping back, watching her with vivid concentration. She could not meet his gaze, too keenly aware of what she must look like—shirt hanging open, loose around her shoulders, the last vestige of her clothing.

Too keenly aware of her past, of the lies she'd built around her about this act. Of the fact that she'd only ever done this once before.

"Look at me." The words were full of command, and she should have hated them, but she didn't. Her gaze snapped to his, recognizing the power in him.

Wanting it.

"My lady." He whispered, the words both prayer and promise.

"Open for me." The command stole her breath, and she hesitated, not knowing if she could. It was one thing to bare herself to him in the dark waters of his transcendent swimming pool, but another thing entirely to do it here, in broad daylight.

It had never been like this. The only time she had ever come close to this experience had been a decade earlier, with a man who had lied to her. Ruined her. Left her.

There had been nothing about those fleeting, life-altering moments in the hayloft at Leighton Manor that had come close to this moment with this man.

Nothing about that time that even approximated this. This was freedom—the last breath of her life before she committed to a new world as aristocratic wife, committed to nothing but her daughter's legacy.

And so why not enjoy it?

Why not welcome the moment and drink from its cup?

Lifted her chin, pressed her shoulders back, bold as brass. "Make me."

Something wicked flared in his beautiful brown eyes. "You think I cannot?"

"I think you wish me to do your work for you." She willed him forward. Willed him to touch her.

Instead, he took a step back and sat in a leather chair that stood by the desk, leaning back, deceptively relaxed. Nervousness flared deep in her, but she resisted it.

His gaze raked over her as he stretched out in the chair, his booted feet mere inches from her bare ones. "Open for me," he repeated.

She gave him a small smile. "It shan't be so easy."

He raised a brow. "No. It shan't." He lingered on her breasts, and her skin heated at the regard as he moved his gaze down, toward the place she wanted him quite desperately. He watched her until she thought she might die from his attention. Just when she was about to give in to him, he said, "You are going to open for me, and when you do, you will regret not doing so when I asked."

Her eyes widened. "Is that a threat?"

His lips curved in a slow, near-mercenary smile. "Not in the slightest." He lifted one hand and set it to his jaw, assessing her with a long, leisurely look, his index finger stroking over his lower lip in a gesture a lesser woman might deem pensive.

Georgiana was not a lesser woman. The movement of that finger was not pensive. It was predatory.

And every inch it moved on his lips seemed to light a fire in her.

"You will regret it, though," he went on, "as every moment you are not open to me is a moment I do not touch you. A moment you do not feel my hands, and my mouth, and my tongue."

The words sent a shock through her as she imagined all those things, a repeat of the night in his swimming pool. The glorious feel of him against her.

"A moment I do not stroke . . . or kiss . . . or lick."

She exhaled at the final word, at the way it seemed to deliver on its meaning, leaving a trail of fire straight through her to the place he asked for . . . to the place she wanted him.

He understood. "You enjoy it when I lick you, don't you, my lady?"

Good God. She was not a prude; she'd spent the last six years surrounded by gamers and prostitutes. She ran London's finest gaming hell, for heaven's sake. But all that seemed entirely ordinary and acceptable compared to this man, who had turned into sin incarnate the moment they'd touched.

It was broad daylight, and he spoke of licking as though it were the weather.

"Georgiana," he prompted, her name a slow promise. "Do you enjoy it?"

That finger on his lips was driving her mad. She pressed her thighs together, reminding herself of their game. "I seem to recall it being quite pleasant."

Something flared in his eyes. Humor. Understanding of the part she played. "Only pleasant?"

She smiled, small and soft. "As I remember."

"We have differing memories, then," he said, "As I remember your hands in my hair, your cries in the darkness, your legs wrapped around me like sin." His gaze fell to the apex of her thighs. "I remember the flood of you when you came, the way you arched toward the sky, everything forgotten except pleasure. Wrought by me. By my tongue in all the places you ached."

She forgot the game, her muscles going weak as he spoke.

"I remember the taste of you, sweet and sex . . . and the feel of you, like decadent silk, soft and wet . . . and mine."

That word again. His.

He was seducing her with nothing but words, promising her everything she'd ever wanted if only she gave in—if only she opened to him. She took a deep breath and matched him once more. "You speak of before," she said, unable to keep the breathlessness from her words. "But what good is that to me now? Here?"

His brows rose in surprise before he leaned forward, his words part danger and part play.

And all desire.

"Open for me and let's find out."

She giggled. The sound shocking them both with its honesty. She was almost embarrassed—would have been if he hadn't dropped his hand and leaned forward the instant the laugh escaped her lips. "You are the most beautiful thing I've ever seen." He reached for her, then, one large, warm hand curving around her knee, the touch erasing the game they played.

Her legs parted.

"So goddamn beautiful," he said, his gaze not leaving her face as he came off the chair, falling to his knees at the edge of the desk, between her thighs. "So goddamn perfect." He pressed a kiss to the inside of her knee, then her thigh. "So goddamn *honest*."

She stiffened at the last, even as his lips curved high at the crease of her thigh, where it met the part of her that ached for him. For this.

Honesty.

She hadn't been honest with him. There was nothing honest about this. Nothing honest about her. And he deserved better.

He sensed the change in her, lifting his lips, meeting her eyes across the long expanse of her torso. "Don't think it."

She knew he did not understand, but replied nonetheless, shaking her head. "I cannot help it."

He pressed a kiss to the soft hair above the most secret part of her, the caress long and lingering and somehow sweet. "Tell me," he said.

There were a dozen things she should tell him. A hundred she wished to tell him. But only one that found its way out. And it was perhaps the truest thing she'd ever said.

"I wish it could be like this. Forever."

*H*er words nearly killed him. The truth of them, the way they mirrored his own thoughts, here in this place that was not his. Was not hers. This place that would ruin them both without question.

He wanted it forever, too, but, it was impossible. His past, her future, neither was conducive to forever. Those outside forces that loomed, they were barriers to forever.

No, forever was for simpler people and simpler times.

He leaned forward on his knees, keenly aware of the position, of the way he worshipped her, as though she were a goddess and he were her sacrifice. He pressed a kiss to the pretty soft curls that hid her secrets. Her position—the trust in it—the pleasure in it—made him harder than he'd ever been in his life.

He wanted this woman.

He might not be able to have her forever, but he could have this moment, this memory . . . This could last. It could stay with him on dark nights.

And it could ruin her for every other man who came after him.

"I've never tasted anything like you," he whispered, letting his breath tease those curls as he parted her slowly, adoring the way she glistened, warm and pink for him. "Sweet and sinful and forbidden." He ran one finger down the wet slit gently, and she lifted her hips toward him. She was so tender, so ready for him. "Slick and wet and perfect."

He ran one finger down the center of her, listening to her breathing, to the way her breath hitched and rattled as he explored. "And you know it, don't you? You know your power."

She shook her head. "No."

He met her gaze, leaned in, let his tongue stroke once, long and lush along her. He reveled in the way she gasped, the way she closed her eyes against the pleasure. "No," he said. "Don't look away."

She opened her eyes, and he licked again, loving the way desire flooded her. "Tell me."

"It feels—"

He repeated the movement, lingering at the top of the caress, where she wanted him most, and she cried out. He spoke there. "Go on."

"Glorious."

"More."

He swirled his tongue over the little, straining bud, and she sighed. "Don't stop."

"I won't if you tell me."

"It feels like . . . I've never . . ." He sucked, loving the way she lost her words. "Oh, *God*."

He smiled, letting his tongue play at her. "Not God."

"Duncan." She sighed his name, and he thought he would die if he wasn't inside her soon.

"Tell me."

"It's beautiful." Her hands found his hair, her fingers pressing him toward her as her hips rocked against him. "You're perfect," she whispered, and he was shocked by the words. And then she said something thoroughly unexpected. "It feels like . . . love."

And there, in that moment, with the word hovering in the air, he realized that that was precisely what he meant for it to feel like.

He loved her.

The realization should have terrified him, but instead, it washed over him with the warm pleasure that came from truth, finally revealed. And at the far edge of that pleasure was the edge of something unpleasant. Devastation. Denial.

He ignored it, instead making love to her with slow, slick strokes. She moved against him, showing him what she liked, where she liked it, and he gave it to her without hesitation. She was manna, and he fed upon her, wanting to bring her pleasure only to give her pleasure. To give her the memory of this moment.

Of his love—a love that could not be.

Slow circles became fast, moving in time to her breath and her sighs and the feel of her fingers in his hair and the rise and fall of her glorious hips. And then she found her release, and he held her, stroking her, kissing her softly, guiding her through it, and back.

As her last, pleased sigh echoed around them, he rose from his knees, desperate for her, adoring the way her gaze tracked him, eyes wide, lips parted. He stripped out of his coat and cravat, watching her watch him, wanting her as she wanted him. He pulled his shirt over his head, lowering his arms and resisting the urge to preen as her attention fell to his chest, to his stomach.

She closed her mouth, and he saw her throat move as she swallowed.

He wanted to roar his pleasure at her obvious approval.

"Poseidon," she whispered.

He raised a brow in silent question, wondering if he would be able to wait for her answer before he took her in his arms and made her his. *Forever.*

He could ignore the word and its insidious whisper in the dark recesses of his mind, because she answered. "At your home, in your swimming pool . . ." She reached for him, her fingertips running along his shoulder, down the curve of his arm, where his muscles were taut with the effort it took not to claim her. "You were Poseidon in the water, so strong . . ." The fingers moved to the muscles of his abdomen. "So perfectly made . . ." trailing up through the hair there, "so handsome . . ." sliding over the skin of his chest until they found the flat disc of his nipple and he nearly groaned his pleasure. She leaned forward, pressing her lips to his chest in a lovely, lingering caress.

She pulled away and met his gaze. "God of the sea."

"And you, my siren," he said, reaching for her, letting his fingers slide into the soft hair at the nape of her neck, lifting her face to him.

"I hope not," she said, and he paused, waiting for her to explain. She smiled, and the expression was small and filled with sin. "Poseidon could resist the sirens."

He could not resist her. Not for all the world. He took her mouth in a deep, lingering kiss, even as her hands came to the fall of his trousers and he thought he might die from the wait as she worked at the buttons there. She fumbled with the fastenings and he moved to take over.

"No," she said, pulling back and meeting his gaze. "I want to do it."

He took a breath, steeled himself. "Do it, then."

And then there was a glorious release, and her hands were sliding into the placket of his trousers, finally, finally touching him. He swore, the word harsh and soft in the room as she freed him. He watched her, loving the way her gaze fell to him, the way her eyes widened and her lips parted, and he would have given his entire fortune to know what she thought of him. And then the tip of her pink tongue came out, sliding along her lower lip, and her hands moved, stroking, long and lush.

Once. Twice.

He placed his hand on hers, staying the movement. "Stop."

She froze, her gaze flying to his. "Am I . . ." She hesitated. Tried again. "Did I do something wrong?"

He stilled at the words, at the expression in her wide eyes— concern, apprehension. He narrowed his gaze on hers, hating the falseness. He loved her. And still she lied to him. "No. Don't play the innocent. I want the real you. Not the fantasy." He put his hands to her cheeks, turning her up to him. "I don't care about the past. Only about the present."

The future.

No. He could not care about that.

It was not for him.

Something flashed in those beautiful amber eyes. Something like frustration. She looked away, then down at where their hands were entwined, wrapped about him. "Show me," she whispered finally. "Show me what you like."

He leaned in, kissing her again, wanting to return them to the moment. He slid his lips to her ear. "I like it all, love. I like every bit of you on every bit of me. And I like your hands wrapped around me, tight and hot like a promise." Her breathing was fast at his ear, and he guided her hands on him. "I like your beautiful eyes on me. I like you watching me. I like you watching yourself touch me." He moved back enough to let her look down their bodies, at their hands, at the length of him, so close to her. So close to the place he wanted to be. "Shall I tell you what else I like?"

She stroked him several times before she answered, the whisper filled with desire. "Yes."

I love you.

No. It would only bring them both pain.

He reached for her, sliding one finger into her, slick from his mouth and her desire. "I like your pretty pink lips."

She laughed at the words, breathless. He slid one finger deep into her tight, dark channel, and the laugh became a gasp. He looked up at her. "And I would like very much to be inside you."

She met his eyes. "I want that, too."

He kissed her, then set his forehead to hers as she placed him where she wanted him, at the entrance to her, and he bit back a curse at the sensation, so hot and wet—for him. He eased into her, so tight, and she sucked in a breath. He met her eyes, registering the discomfort there. "Georgiana?" he asked, something unsettling him even as he thought he might die from the pleasure of her.

She shook her head. "It is fine."

Except it wasn't. She was in pain. He eased back.

She clamped her legs around his waist. "No. Please. Now."

If he didn't know better . . .

She pulled him closer, and he lost the thought until her breath hitched again. "Stop," he said. "Let me . . ."

He pulled back, then rocked in again, in short, gentle slides, each deeper than the last, until he was deep inside her, buried to the hilt. "Yes," she whispered as he bent and placed a long, lingering kiss to the place where her neck met her shoulder. "Yes."

He could not have said it better himself.

He pulled back, met her eyes. "Is it—?"

She leaned up and kissed him, letting her tongue slide between his lips in a stunning kiss. When it was through, she said, "It is magnificent." Then she pressed her hands to his chest, pushing him back enough to look down between them. "Look at us."

He did, following her gaze, and he felt himself grow even harder, deep inside her. She inhaled, then smiled. "You seem to be enjoying yourself, sir."

Christ. He loved her.

He wanted her. Playful. Brilliant. Beautiful. Sinful.

Forever.

He matched her smile with his own. "I can think of ways I would enjoy myself more."

She placed her hands at the curve of his buttocks and squeezed. He groaned. "Show me."

And he did.

He moved in deep, decadent strokes, and she matched him, lifting her long legs, his name on her lips like a mantra, first soft and barely there, and then a cry of pleasure, making him wish this moment would never end. He wrapped one arm around her waist, holding her close as he thrust, and her hands came to his shoulders, wrapping tightly around him as she cried out for him.

As though he would leave her.

As though it were possible for him to leave her.

He would never leave her.

She pulled back at the last moment, as he thrust fast and strong against her. She met his gaze. "Now," she said, the word full of desire and wonder, hinting at something he would be able to grasp if his head weren't so damn full of her. "Now."

Now, indeed.

She fell into pleasure, tight and perfect around him, with such power that he thought he might not survive it. She called his name as he thrust once, twice, hard and fast and glorious until his release raced toward him, and he pulled out of her, coming hard and fast and like nothing he'd ever experienced.

As one.

And he knew, instantly, that he had not ruined her for other men.

She had ruined him for other women. For life.

He pulled away, and she sighed a protest at his departure, making him ache for her once more. He wasn't ready to leave her, but he fastened his trousers loosely, and removed a handkerchief, lifting her in his arms and carrying her to one of the large chairs on the far side of the room before settling her into his lap and cleaning her.

"You didn't . . ." she trailed off.

"I didn't think you would want the risk." Not that he didn't secretly enjoy the idea—a collection of tiny blond children with their mother's pretty amber eyes. "You did not choose the last time. You should choose the next."

Tears sprang to her eyes, and he pulled her close, wanting to keep her safe now. *Forever*.

Christ. That word again.

She curled into him as he stroked his hands over her beautiful, soft skin, replaying the event in his mind as their breathing returned to normal, turning over her words, her movements, her sounds.

The moments of surprise. Of wonder. Of desire.

Of discomfort.

Realization dawned.

She lifted her head when his hands stilled on her. "What is it?"

He shook his head, not wanting to answer.

Not wanting it to be true.

She smiled, pressing a kiss to his jaw. "Tell me."

I have not . . . with anyone . . .

She'd said it. He simply hadn't believed her.

Who was she?

What game did she play?

What game did Chase play?

He met her eyes, noting the openness there, the honesty. So rare. Something must have shown in his own gaze, because hers went wary. "Duncan?"

He didn't want to say it, and yet, he could not stop himself. "You're not a whore."

Chapter 17

. . . It is a constant surprise to this publication that Lady G— was so easily dismissed for nearly a decade. What we would not offer for a peek into the lady's past! Alas, we shall have to settle for watching her bright future . . .

. . . Several critical votes are before the Houses of Parliament this week. The owner of this very paper is a vocal proponent of setting clear limits for child labor, and watches carefully as this great Nation's leaders decide the fate of her youngest citizens . . .

The News of London, May 9, 1833

She froze at the words.

Perhaps she could have brazened it through, if not for the way he'd made her feel, the way he'd slowly, effortlessly dismantled her guard, leaving it on the floor with her trousers and his cravat and all their inhibitions.

The way he'd somehow given her pleasure and peace

and the promise of more, even as she'd known all of it was fleeting.

Perhaps she could have lied, but how could she? How could she pretend to know the tricks and trade of London's finest lightskirt when he'd so thoroughly destroyed her with his kiss and touch and kindness?

She'd expected the kissing. The touching.

But the kindness had been too much. It had stripped her bare, leaving her with nothing to protect her from his careful observations and his probing questions.

For the first time in an age, she did not know what to say. She left his lap, standing, moving naked to the place where he'd divested her of her clothing and her lies. She lifted her shirt from where it had landed on the arm of a chair, and slid into it, pulling it closed around her as he spoke again. "You cannot hide from me. Not in this. You and Chase clearly have some kind of plan—something of which I am a part. Unwillingly." The words sent fear straight through her, as this brilliant man discovered one of her best-kept secrets and came closer to uncovering all the rest.

The irony, of course, was that most men would be thrilled to know that they had not just slept with a prostitute.

But there was nothing about Duncan West that was like other men.

And there was nothing about him that appeared pleased with the discovery.

He did not seem to care that she was virtually naked, or that she was emotionally bare, or that she was unsettled by his statement, or that she did not wish to discuss it. "When was the last time you slept with someone?"

She tried to hedge her way out of the conversation, leaning down, retrieving her trousers. "I sleep with Caroline quite often."

His gaze turned furious as he leaned forward and she tried her best to ignore the way his muscles shifted, rippling beneath his smooth skin. "Let me rephrase, I forget sometimes where you have chosen to make your life. When was the last time you fucked a man?"

The curse was a gift, reminding her that she was more than this moment, that she was queen of London's underworld, more powerful than he could imagine. More powerful than anyone could imagine.

Even he.

She should have been angry with him. Should have squared her shoulders, nakedness be damned, and told him precisely what he could do with his foul language. Should have stalked, bare and bold, to the wall and rung the bell to call security to this place, where he should not be.

Where she should not have brought him.

Where she would never forget him.

She looked away. The whole afternoon had gone pear-shaped, and instead, his anger made her want to tell him the truth. To mend the moment. To answer his questions and return to his arms and restore his faith. Not an hour earlier, he'd vowed to protect her.

How long had it been since someone had wished to do that?

"Look at me." It was not a request.

She looked at him, desperate to stay strong. "What we did . . . it wasn't . . ." She couldn't bring herself to say the word. "That."

He narrowed his gaze. "How would you know?"

He meant to hurt her, and he did, the question a blow. Not undeserved, but a blow nonetheless. She answered him, laying herself barer than she had ever imagined she could. "Because the last time I did this, it was." His brown eyes searched hers, and she let him see the truth. Finished her thought, the words quieter than she'd expected. "This wasn't the same. This was . . . more."

"Christ." He came to his feet.

She met his gaze. "It is something more."

"Is it?" he asked, the question filled with something like doubt. He ran his hands through his hair, frustrated. "You lied to me."

She had, but now she did not wish to, even though she'd

wrapped herself in lies. Wrapped them both in them. Even though her lies were layered in myriad ways, too many and too complex to tell him the truth. Too connected to too many others to find their way into the light of honesty.

"I want to tell you the truth," she confessed.

"Why don't you?" he asked. "Why don't you trust me? I would have—had I known that you—that Anna—that none of it was true, I would have—" He stopped. Regrouped. "I would have taken more care."

She'd never in her life felt more cared for than in the last hour, in his arms. And she wanted to give him something for it. Something that she'd never given another person. Her darkest secret, kept only in her deepest thoughts. "Caroline's father," she whispered. "He was the last."

He was silent for a long moment, before he asked, "When?"

He still did not understand. "Ten years ago."

He sucked in a breath, and she wondered at the sound, at the way he seemed pained by her truth. "The only time?"

He knew the answer to the question, but she replied nonetheless. "Until now."

His hands came to her face, lifting her chin, forcing her to look at him. "He was a fool."

"He was not. He was a boy who wanted a girl. But not forever." She smiled. "Not even a second time."

"Who was he?"

She blushed at the question, hating the answer. "He worked in the stables at my brother's country estate. He saddled my horse a few times, rode out with me on one occasion." She looked away, wrapping her arms tight around herself. "I was . . . bewitched by his smile. His flirt."

He nodded. "So you took a risk."

"Except it wasn't a risk. I thought I loved him. I'd spent my young, entitled life without a care in the world. I wanted for nothing. And, in the great error made by every entitled child since the beginning of time, I searched for the thing that I did not have instead of celebrating the things that I did."

"What was that?"

"Love," she said simply. "I did not have love. My mother was cold. My brother was distant. My father was dead. Caroline's father was warm, and near, and alive. And I thought he loved me. I thought he would marry me." She shrugged the memory away with a smile. "Foolish girl."

He was quiet for a long moment, his handsome brow furrowed. "What is his name?"

"Jonathan."

"That's not the part I want."

She shook her head. "It's the part I will give you. It does not matter who he is. He left, and Caroline was born, and that is that."

"He should pay for what he has done."

"How? By marrying me? By becoming Caroline's father in name as well as deed?"

"Hell, no."

Her brow furrowed. Everyone with whom she'd ever discussed Caroline's birth had agreed that if only she would name the man, all would be well. Her brother had threatened her with marriage, as had half a dozen women who lived with her in Yorkshire, after she'd birthed Caroline and raised her into childhood. "You don't think he should be forced to marry me?"

"I think he should be forced to hang by his thumbs from the nearest tree." Her eyes widened, and he continued. "I think he should be stripped bare and made to walk down Piccadilly. I think he should meet me in the ring in the heart of this place, so I can tear him apart for what he did to you."

She would be lying if she did not say she enjoyed the threats. "You would do that for me?"

"And more," he said, the words not boastful, but quick and honest. "I hate that you protect him."

"It is not protection," she said, trying to explain. "It is that I don't wish him relevance. I don't wish him the power men hold over women. I don't wish him to be a part of me. Of who I am. Of who Caroline is. Of who she might become."

"He is none of those things."

She watched him for a long moment, wanting to believe him. Knowing the truth. "Maybe not to me . . . but to them . . . to you . . . of course he is. And he will be, until there is another."

"A husband. With a title."

She did not reply. Did not have to.

"Tell me the rest."

She lifted one shoulder. Let it fall. "There is not much to say."

"You loved him."

"I thought I loved him," she corrected. And she'd believed it. But now . . .

Love. She turned the word over and over in her mind, considering its meaning, her experience with it. She had thought she had loved Jonathan. She'd been so sure of it. But now . . . here . . . with this man, she realized that what she had felt for Jonathan was minuscule. A thimbleful.

What she felt for Duncan West was the wide sea.

But she would not put a name to it. That way lay danger.

Because, for all her secrets, for all the lies—he had them, too.

She shook her head and looked down at her lap, where his long, bronzed arm crossed her pale legs. She placed her hand on that arm, playing with the golden hairs there. Repeated herself. "I thought I loved him."

"And?"

She smiled. "I told you, a tale as old as the hills."

"And after?"

"You know that, newspaperman."

"I know what they say. I wish to hear what *you* say."

"I went to Yorkshire. I ran away to Yorkshire."

"They say you ran with him."

She laughed, the sound humorless even to her ears. "He was long disappeared from my life by then. Gone before daybreak the morning after we—"

He inhaled his anger, and she stopped. "Go on," he urged.

"I took a mail coach. My maid's sister's aunt knew of a place in Yorkshire. Somewhere girls could go. To be safe."

He raised a brow. "A duke's sister, riding by mail."

"There was no other way. I would have been caught."

"Would that have been bad?"

"You did not know my brother then. When he discovered what had happened, he was furious. And not a little bit terrifying. My mother was filled with hate and disdain. We never spoke again."

He narrowed his gaze. "You were a child."

She shook her head. "Not once I had a child of my own."

"So, this place . . . it took you in."

She nodded. "Me, and Caroline." She thought back to Minerva House, to its welcome inhabitants and its lush lands. "It was beautiful. Peaceful and warm. Filled with acceptance. It was . . . home." She paused. "The last home I really had."

"You are lucky you had one at all."

She watched him carefully, sensing that there was more to the statement than it seemed, but before she could press him, he asked, "How long were you there?"

"Four years."

"And then?"

"And then my mother died." He tilted his head in question, and she explained, lost in the tale. "I came home, feeling that I should be in London to mourn her. I brought Caroline—ripped her from the safety of her home, where no one had ever judged her—I brought her to this horrible place. London in season. And one day, we took a walk down Bond Street, and I counted the stares."

There had been hundreds of them. Enough for hatred to begin to settle, hot and unyielding, in her breast.

He seemed to understand. "They did not accept you."

"Of course they didn't. I was ruined. Unwed. A mother of a daughter, who is nothing. If she'd been a boy . . ." she trailed off.

"If she'd been a boy, she could have made her way."

But she hadn't been. And that had turned the hatred into rage.

And then into a plan to hold dominion over them all.

"And then Chase found you."

Like that, they were returned to the present. To this place. To its secrets. To the lies she told.

She looked away. "On the contrary, I found Chase."

He shook his head. "I don't understand. Why masquerade as a whore? Anything could happen to you. Hell, Pottle nearly—" He did not finish the sentence, closing his eyes briefly. "What if I hadn't been there?"

She smiled. "Women in my position, we hold tremendous amounts of power. I chose to be here, in this place. I chose this path. I choose this world." She paused. "How many other women have the choice?"

"But you could have chosen anything. You could have been a governess."

"Who would have hired me for that?"

"A dressmaker."

"I cannot sew a straight line."

"You know what it is I am saying."

Of course she did. She'd heard it a dozen times from her brother. A hundred. And she'd told him just what she told Duncan. "None of those positions held the power of this one."

"Consort to a king."

King herself.

"I wanted power over all of them—every last one who stared down their nose at me. Every last one who judged me. Every last one who cast their stones. I wanted proof that they lived in glass houses."

"And Chase gave it to you. Chase and the others, all wanting to do the same. You became the fifth in their merry band."

Tell him.

There was no fifth. She was fourth.

She was first.

She could tell him. She could say the words. *I am Chase.*

Except she couldn't. She'd just told the story of her deepest betrayal, the one that had ruined her, threatened Caroline, and would ever be the reason for her secrets. If she told him the rest, if she laid herself at his feet, what then?

Would he protect her, even once he knew she was the man who used him? Who manipulated him?

Would he protect her club?

This life she had worked so hard to build?

Perhaps.

She might have done it, if he hadn't gone on. "And still, you protect him," he said, and she heard the bitterness in his voice. "Who is he to you? What is he to you? If not your master, your consort, your benefactor? Who the hell is he?"

There was something in the last, something that was not for her.

Something that was not curiosity.

Something like desire. Like desperation.

He wanted Chase's secret. Hers.

But if he had it, would he entrust her with his own?

She resisted the question, hating that even now, even here, after they had shared the powerful moment, they still dealt in information. Traded it.

He'd been with Tremley earlier in the day—taken the information she'd given him and done something unexpected with it. Something indefinable.

"Tell me who he is, Georgiana," he said, and she heard the plea in the words. What did he want with her? With Chase?

She met his gaze, on alert. "Why is it so important?"

He did not hesitate. "Because I have been nothing but his good soldier for years. And it is time."

"For what?" she asked. "To ruin him?"

"To protect myself from him."

She shook her head. "Chase will never hurt you."

"You don't know that," he said. "You are blind to his power. To the things he does to keep it." He waved a hand at the door. "Have you not witnessed it? The way he plays with lives? The way he bolsters the men belowstairs? The way he tempts them to wager until they've nothing left? Until all they have belongs to him?"

"It's not like that." It was never so cavalier. Never so unplanned.

"Of course it is. He deals in information. Secrets. Truths. Lies." He paused. "I deal in those things as well—which is why we make such a pair."

"Why not leave it at that?" She didn't want it to change. Everything else was shifting beneath her, around her. "You are well compensated. You have access to information throughout London. You ask, you receive. News. Gossip. Tremley's file."

He stilled. "What do you know?"

She narrowed her gaze on him. "What are you not telling me?"

He laughed at that. "The sheer sum of what you will not tell me, and you have the gall to ask for my secrets?"

She buttoned her shirt, protecting herself in more ways than one. "What is your relationship with Tremley?"

He met her gaze without hesitation. "What is your relationship with Chase?"

She was quiet for a long moment, considering the next. Considering the implications of her truth. Finally, she said, "I cannot tell you."

He nodded. "And so it is."

She stilled, watching him. He, too, had secrets. She'd known it, but she'd had no proof. But now, she did. And while the discovery should have made her immensely happy—as she was not the only one who spread lies between them— instead, it made her devastatingly sad.

Perhaps because his secrets would keep hers locked away.

Neither of them was honest.

There was no point in defining the way she felt for him.

And certainly no reason to define it as love.

Duncan West had saved her a great deal of heartache, she supposed, ignoring the tightness in her chest. She swallowed around the lump in her throat. "That is that, then?"

He stood, pulling on his own shirt and buttoning his trousers, which she realized he'd never fully removed. She supposed he had left them on in case Chase entered. In case he had been required to give pursuit. He wrapped his cravat carefully, watching her as he completed the economical movements from memory, without the aid of a mirror.

As she willed herself not to beg him to stay.

When he was finished, he lifted his coat off the floor and shrugged it on, not buttoning it.

Stay. She could say it. And what?

She looked away.

He pulled his cuffs to bare an even inch of crisp white linen at the edge of his sleeve. When he was through, he looked to her. "You choose him."

"It's not that easy."

"It's exactly that easy." He paused. "Tell me one thing. Do you want this? Do you want to be so thoroughly entwined with him?"

Not anymore.

Who had she become?

He saw the reply on her face, the frustration, the confusion, and he turned to steel, hiding all emotion from her. "Allow me to leave him a message, then. Tell him I am through being beholden to him. I am done. Today. He can find another to do his bidding." He unlocked the door. Opened it.

"Good-bye, Georgiana."

He left without looking back, closing the door behind him with a soft click.

She watched that door for a long moment, willing any number of things to happen. Willing him to return. Willing him to take her in his arms and tell her it was all a mistake. Willing him to tell her the truth. Willing him to kiss her until she no longer cared about this world, this life, this plan that had become so important.

Willing him to want her enough for all their secrets.

To love her enough.

Knowing that it was impossible.

She took a deep breath, and sat at her desk, extracting a piece of paper, considering the blank expanse for a long moment, thinking of all the things she could write. All the ways she could change their mutual course.

What if she told him everything? What if she put herself—her heart—in his hands? What if she gave herself to him?

What if she loved him?

Madness.

Love between them would never work. Even if they found space and time to trust each other, he was not an aristocrat. He could not give Caroline the future Georgiana planned.

There was only one way that would keep her secrets safe.

That would keep her heart safe.

She reached for a pen, dipping the nib in ink and writing two lines.

> *Your membership has been revoked.*
> *And you will stay away from our Anna.*

Our Anna.

The words were a joke at best, the last vestige of a girl's silly desire. She'd always secretly desired the possessive, wanted to be wanted.

And for longer than she would like to admit, she'd desired him.

She folded the paper once, twice, into a neat square, then sealed it with crimson wax, unlocking the heavy silver locket that hung at her breast and stamping it with an elaborate C before ringing for a messenger to fetch it for delivery.

It was for the best, she told herself, deliberately setting the missive aside and reaching for another file, one marked "Langley."

She had other plans for her life. For Caroline's.

And loving Duncan West was not in them.

Not even if she wanted it very much.

She returned to her work. To her world, empty of him.

*H*e left the club, furious, and headed to his offices, desperate for proof that he held some kind of power in this world that seemed to be spiraling out of his control.

Tremley, Chase, Georgiana—they all wished to own him. To wield him like a weapon—his newspapers, his network of information, his mind.

His heart.

Only one of them threatened his heart.

He corrected his earlier assessment of the situation. She did not wish to own his heart. On the contrary, she seemed not at all committed to the organ.

He pulled his greatcoat around him, lowering his hat and marching up Fleet Street as though the wind was a worthy foe. He kept his head down, trying his best to keep from seeing the world.

From letting it see him. His doubt, his frustration, his pain.

And it was pain—the sensation high in his chest. He'd thought their afternoon would change her mind. He'd thought it would win her heart.

What an idiotic fool he was.

She'd been with Chase for too long to turn her back on the man, and there was something powerful in her commitment to the owner of The Fallen Angel. Something made even more remarkable by the fact that it was not tied to the physical.

Memory came, dark and unbidden. Georgiana leaned back on the desk, her golden hair floating down behind her to brush the hard oak. Her breasts high for him. Her thighs parted. Her gaze on him.

She'd given herself over to him, physically, yes—to his kiss and touch—but more than that, she'd given herself to him in a myriad of other ways. She'd entrusted him with her pleasure, with her secrets.

Most of her secrets.

Except it was not hers, the one for which he asked. Chase's identity had nothing to do with her. And yet she remained beholden to the man, refusing to give up the only thing that could protect Duncan.

There was a nobility in her actions—a loyalty that he could not help but respect even as he hated it. Even as he envied it.

Even as he wanted it for himself.

Just as he wanted her.

Just as he loved her.

He looked up, mere yards from his offices, only to discover a pretty chestnut tied to a hitching post outside the entrance to the building. It was a familiar horse, but either because of the day or his frustration, he could not place it. He climbed the stone steps and let himself inside, nearly walking past the building's receiving room before realizing that there was a woman seated inside, reading the latest issue of *The Scandal Sheet.*

A young woman.

A *very* young woman.

He removed his hat and cleared his throat. "Miss Pearson."

Caroline put the paper down immediately and stood. "Mr. West."

He raised his brows in her direction. "May I help you?"

She smiled, and he marveled at the way the expression turned her into a younger version of her mother. "I came to see you."

"So I gathered." He supposed he should send a note to Georgiana, apprising her of her daughter's location, but instead he said, "I happen to be free for the next quarter of an hour. May I interest you in tea?"

"You have tea here?"

His lips twitched. "You seem surprised."

"I am. Tea seems so . . ." She paused. " . . . civilized."

"We even serve it in cups."

She seemed to consider that. "All right, then. Yes."

He led her into his office, indicating to Baker that they required food. "And speaking of civilized," he added as he waved the girl into a chair, "where is your chaperone?"

Caroline smiled. "I lost her."

He allowed his surprise to show. "You lost her."

She nodded. "We went for a ride. She did not keep up."

"Is it possible that she was not certain where you were going?"

The smile was back. "Anything is possible."

"And you simply turn up here?"

Caroline lifted one shoulder and let it drop. "We established that I read your newspapers; the address is right on the page." She paused, then added, "And I am not here to visit. I am here for business."

He tried not to smile. "I see."

Her brow furrowed in an expression that he'd seen a dozen times on her mother. "You think I jest."

"I apologize."

He was saved from saying more by the arrival of tea, along with scones and clotted cream and a pile of cakes that surprised even Duncan. But perhaps the most rewarding part of the tea service was the way that Caroline came to the edge of her seat, considering the sweets with wide eyes befitting her age. She was unsettlingly beyond her years most of the time—a younger, more forthright version of her mother—but right now, the nine-year-old wanted cake.

And that was something that Duncan could manage. "Help yourself," he said as Baker set a pile of letters on the desk and took his leave.

Caroline immediately went for a fondant-covered oval at the top of the pile and had it halfway to her mouth when she froze, looked at him, and said, "I am supposed to pour."

He waved her on. "I don't need tea."

She did not care for that answer. "No. I'm supposed to pour."

With great control, she set her cake on a plate and stood to lift the heavy teapot, pouring steaming liquid into one of the cups. When it was full, she said, "Milk? Sugar?"

He shook his head. "As it is." It was bad enough he was going to have to force down a cup of the stuff, but the girl seemed so proud of herself as she offered him the teacup, rattling in its saucer, that he did as any decent man would do, and drank the damn tea.

"Cake?" she asked, and he heard the yearning in her young voice.

"No, thank you. Please, sit."

She did. He did not miss the fact that she did not pour a cup for herself. "You don't want tea?"

Her mouth was full of sweets, so she shook her head, swallowing before saying, "I don't like it."

"You asked for it."

That shoulder lifted again. "You offered. It would have been rude to say no. That, and I hoped there would be cake."

It was precisely the kind of thing Georgiana would say. Mother and daughter might not have spent the lion's share of the years together, but there was no question that they were connected—clever, quick-witted, and with a smile that would win over an army.

She would no doubt be exceedingly dangerous when she came of age.

"What can I do for you, Miss Pearson?"

"I came to ask you to stop helping to get my mother married."

It appeared she was exceedingly dangerous *now*.

He resisted the urge to lean forward. "What makes you think I am doing that?"

"The columns," she said pointedly. "Today's was the best yet."

Of course it was. It was the one he'd written after the night in his swimming pool, when he'd hated and adored her all at once.

"It made her seem positively respectable," Caroline added.

He blinked. "She is respectable." He ignored the fact that he'd made love to the woman in question not an hour earlier.

She met his eyes, all seriousness. "You are aware that I am a bastard, are you not?"

Good Lord. The child was as brazen as her mother. She shouldn't even know the damn word.

But she reminded him too much of another girl, another time.

The same word, whispered as he walked past with his mother. His sister.

"I never want to hear you say that word again."

"Why not?" she asked. "It's what I am. Others use it."

"They won't once your mother and I are through with them."

"They will," she replied. "They just won't do it to my face."

She was too wise, this girl. Knew too much about the world. And he—who had only known her for a week—hated that she had no choice but to know it. That her life had always been embroiled in scandal and muck.

All that could be done was to give her a chance at propriety. Which was why Georgiana had come to him. Together, they could give Caroline that opportunity, just as he'd given it to Cynthia all those years ago.

And it was in that moment that he understood why Georgiana hid from him.

He didn't know how he hadn't seen it before—how he hadn't recognized the way she moved the pieces across the chessboard of Society. Hadn't he done the same? Hadn't he packed up his sister and run into the night, afraid of being caught, but even more terrified of leaving her there, in that place, with those people who judged her with every breath? Hadn't he built this life to keep Cynthia safe?

To keep their secrets?

And now, as he stared at Georgiana's daughter, he understood that she was doing what she could to save Caroline. This girl, with her smart mouth and her independent spirit and her winning smiles—Georgiana would do anything to save her. To give her the life Georgiana had not had. To keep her secrets.

And that meant keeping Chase's secrets, too.

How many times had he seen Chase destroy a man? How many times had a debt been collected to the demolition of a history, a life, a family?

How many times had West aided and abetted those destructions?

Granted, they had always been men who deserved the demolition, but that only made it more tempting to partner with him. It was easy to climb into bed with Chase. But virtually impossible to climb out.

There had been resignation in Georgiana's eyes earlier—when he'd left her—as though she had no choice but to play Chase's guardian.

To play his fool.

And now, staring at this girl, he understood why.

Chase held too much power over her.

Chase held too much power over every one of them.

No one had ever resisted his sway.

No one had ever been strong enough to do it.

Until now.

"I am not a fool," the child across the desk told him.

"I never said you were," he replied.

"I know the way of the world," she insisted, "and I see what my mother is doing. What she's asked you to do for her. But it isn't right."

He could have denied the charges, but this girl, who had spent her whole life in darkness, deserved light. "She wants to marry."

"She doesn't want to marry. Anyone can see that."

He changed tack. "Sometimes, you make choices to protect the ones you love. To keep them happy."

She narrowed her gaze on him, and he was instantly uncomfortable with the knowledge there. "Have you done that?"

He had built a life on it. "Yes."

She watched him for a long moment, as though she could see the truth in him. Finally she said, "Was it worth it?"

It had left him deep in debt to Tremley, a man who was willing to do anything to keep his power. It had built him a life of dependence on informants and scandalmongers. But it had also built his empire, established his power. Kept Cynthia safe.

And it would keep Georgiana and Caroline safe, as well.

Even if it would not make him worthy of them.

"I would do it again without question."

She thought on that. "What about keeping my mother happy?"

He would do that, too, if only she'd let him.

He smiled at the girl. "Your mother has made her goals clear."

"Me, in a house somewhere, preparing for Society events."

He nodded once. "Eventually. Until then, I think she'd just like you to be happy."

There was a long silence, until Caroline said, "Do you have children?"

"I do not," he replied. But as he looked at this girl, all strength and smarts, like her mother, he thought perhaps he might like one or two.

"It isn't only she who wants me happy," she said after a long pause. "I wish her happy, as well."

As did he. Quite desperately.

He stood, having every intention of coming around the desk to—he didn't know what—but he hoped it would be the right thing to comfort this girl who so clearly wanted to have some control over her life.

He stopped, however, when he saw the small ecru square on the desk, and recognized the seal there.

It was from Chase.

He was opening it before he could stop himself, reading the words written black and forceful across the paper.

Rage flared, hot and welcome, not because of the fact that he had lost his membership—there were a dozen other clubs that would have him—and not because of the insistence that he stay away from Georgiana.

The fury came with the single, possessive word that rippled through him like poison. *Our.*

Our Anna.

He wanted to roar his disagreement with the words. She was not Chase's. Not any longer. She was his. She, and the girl who sat across from him.

He would get them their new life.

He would keep them safe.

He might not know what was to come, but he knew this: Chase's power was at an end. Duncan wanted him weakened, never again dictating his actions, or Georgiana's, or Caroline's. Duncan would see them protected from Chase and his unmatched control. And he would see them blossom.

Even if they were not with him when they did.

"Let me take you home. Your companion will no doubt be terrified to have lost you." He came around the desk, noticing that she watched him carefully.

"What of my request?"

"I'm afraid that I already have an arrangement with your mother. She wants a marriage, and I have promised to help her."

"It is a bad idea."

He knew it. She would not be content with marriage. She would certainly not be content with Langley. And he wanted her content.

He wanted her blissful.

He could make her so.

Of course, he couldn't. Not really. Not with his past. Not with the future that loomed every time Tremley threatened.

"What is in the message?" Caroline asked.

He shook his head. "Nothing of import."

"I don't believe you," she replied, her gaze falling to his hand, where the paper was crushed in his fist.

He looked down at it, then said, "It is the next move in a game I've been playing for years."

Her gaze turned curious. "Are you losing?"

He shook his head, his next step resolved, for the woman he loved. "Not any longer."

Chapter 18

... It is the opinion of this publication that Lady G—
has been fully returned to society. At the S— Ball last
evening, the lady was given not a single respite from
the festivities. And she was seen dancing with Lord
L— on three separate occasions ...

... As this year's Season finds itself fully underway,
this author has discovered, without question, that it is
the ladies of London who rule ...

The gossip pages of *The Weekly Britannia*,
May 13, 1833

That night, Lady Tremley arrived at The Other Side battered and bruised and asking for Anna.

Georgiana—dressed as Anna—met the countess in one of the small rooms reserved for the female members of the club, where she pulled the door closed behind her and began immediately helping the lady dispense with her clothing. It was important that they quickly assess the damage the earl had done.

"I've summoned a doctor," she said quietly as she unlaced the bodice of Lady Tremley's dress. "And if you'll allow it, I'd like to send a man around to fetch your things from Tremley House."

"There is nothing there that I need," the lady said, sucking in a breath as her loosening corset returned feeling to bruises that might have best been left without it.

"I am sorry, Imogen," Georgiana said, guilt and anger making the words bitter on her tongue. She'd sent the woman home knowing that this might happen.

"Why?" The lady sucked in a breath as Georgiana ran fingers over her ribs. "You didn't do it."

"I invited you here. I should have stopped you from returning to him." She lifted her hand. "You've a broken rib. Perhaps more than one."

"You couldn't have stopped me," Lady Tremley said. "He is my husband. It is the proverbial bed in which I lie."

"You shan't go back to him." Georgiana would stand nude on St. James if it would help to stop the woman from returning to her demon of a husband.

"Not after this, no," the lady said, the words nasal and strained through a swelling nose and lip. "But I haven't any idea where I will go instead."

"I told you, there are rooms here. We can provide you sanctuary."

The lady smiled. "I cannot live in a casino in Mayfair."

Georgiana rather thought that a casino in Mayfair was far safer for the girls who lived and worked there than Tremley House was for its countess. Than dozens of aristocratic homes were for the women who lived in them. But she did not say so. Instead, she said, "I don't see why not."

The countess paused at the words, then allowed the wildness of the moment to wash over her. She chuckled, clearly not knowing how else to behave, before wincing in pain. "Life is mad sometimes, is it not?"

Georgiana nodded. "Life is mad all the time. Our task is to not let it make us mad in the process."

They were silent together for long minutes while Georgiana dipped a cloth in a basin of water and cleared the blood from Imogen's cheek and neck. Tremley had beaten his wife well. Guilt flared again as she rinsed the cloth and lifted it again to the woman's face. "We should not have involved you."

Imogen shook her head, reaching up to stay Georgiana's touch. When she spoke, she was as regal as any queen. "I shall only say this once: I was grateful for the invitation. It gave me a way to fight him. To punish him. I do not regret it."

"If he was a member, I . . ." Georgiana paused, remembering herself. Tried again. "If he was a member, Chase would ruin him."

Imogen nodded. "As he is not a member, you can imagine that he will do his best to bring down this place. He had me followed. He knew I was a member."

Georgiana met the woman's blue eyes. "He knew you had to give up information for membership."

"As I did not have anything of mine . . ." The countess looked away. Whispered, "I am weak. He told me he would stop if I confessed it."

"No." Georgiana came to her knees at the other woman's feet. "You are so very strong."

"I've put this place in danger. My husband is a powerful man. He knows what I gave you. What Chase has."

What Duncan had.

Duncan, who had been to Tremley House earlier that day. Who had met with Tremley at two balls, she'd noticed. Who had the information to destroy the man, and had not yet used it.

"You must warn Mr. Chase," Imogen said. "When my husb—" She stopped. Rethought. "When the earl arrives, he will do anything to demolish this place and anyone involved with the building of it. He will do whatever it takes to keep you quiet."

"You think you are our first member with a bastard of a husband? It will take more than that to destroy us," Georgiana said with more bluster than she felt. She dipped Imogen's hands in the warm water, hating the way the woman hissed her pain at the sensation. "He is not the first to threaten us, and he will not be the last."

"What did you do with the information?" the countess asked. "What will become of it? When will it be used against him?"

"Soon, I hope," Georgiana said. "If it does not appear in the *News of London* within the week, I shall release it myself."

Imogen froze at the words. "The *News of London*. West's newspaper."

Georgiana nodded. "We passed the information to Duncan West for release." The countess stood, wavering on her feet. Georgiana stood with her. "My lady, please, you should sit until the doctor arrives."

"Not West."

The words, filled with shock and something dangerously, disturbingly close to fear, struck deep. Georgiana shook her head. "My lady?"

"West has been in his pocket for years."

Georgiana froze. Hating the way the words struck. Hating the fact that she knew, without question, without hesitation, that the countess told the truth.

Bourne's report earlier in the day.

West at the Worthington Ball, at the Beaufetheringstone Ball, on the sidelines because he could not dance—speaking to the earl.

She should have known it. Should have seen it . . . that Tremley and West were partners in some strange, perverse play.

It could not be true.

Why not? It would not be the first time she'd thought she knew a man. It would not be the first time she thought she loved a man.

Except she did not think it this time.

She knew it.

And so the betrayal hurt infinitely more.

Memory flashed, the night he came to the club and revealed her as Anna. The threat she'd goaded him into issuing.

I shall tell the world your secrets.

She didn't want to believe he would do it, but suddenly, she did not know him.

Who was he?

She crossed her arms tight over her chest, resisting the urge to grab the lady by the shoulders. Resisting the pain that flared high and tight. "Do you have proof?"

Imogen laughed, the sound high-pitched and wild. "I don't need it. The earl has boasted about it for years. Since before our marriage. He tells anyone who will listen that West is his lapdog."

Georgiana pulled back from the word. *Lapdog.*

It did not sound like Duncan. She could not imagine him lying down for anyone, let alone such a monster as Tremley. Collusion with the earl would mean that Duncan knew everything—Tremley's treasonous activities, his penchant for hitting his wife, his black soul.

It did not seem right.

But here the countess sat, bloody and bruised, more than one part of her broken, Georgiana had no doubt, and she told the tale of Tremley and Duncan as cohorts.

She was transported to the night she'd met him as Georgiana, on the balcony, when he'd removed a feather from her hair and painted it down her arm, across the skin of her elbow, making her wish she was bare to the tickling touch. To him.

Wouldn't you rather know precisely with whom you are dealing?

The question had been so forthright, and she'd given herself over to it. To him. Telling herself that she knew fact and fiction, truth and lies.

She knew good men, and bad.

And then he'd come to her club. Followed her there.

On purpose? Dread came with the thought. Was it possible he'd followed her? Was it possible he'd known from the be-

ginning that she was two instead of one? That she was both
Anna and Georgiana?

Was it possible he'd always intended to use her to get whatever Chase might be able to find on Tremley? Was it possible
that he would use this woman? Collateral damage in whatever battles the earl fought?

Christ.

He'd kissed her. He'd touched her. He'd come a heartbeat
from promising her a future.

But he hadn't promised her any kind of future.

In fact, even as he'd lain her bare and made love to her,
he'd told her they had no future together. *As I am . . . we are
impossible.*

She went cold at the memory.

Christ. Who was he? How had he teased and tempted and
lied his way into her heart? She, who wielded such control
over the wide world . . . how had he come to control her so
well?

What is your relationship with Tremley?

What is your relationship with Chase?

Their secrets matched.

Something broke in her . . . something she had not realized
had ever been repaired from when she was a child. Something that was utterly, completely different from when she
was a child.

She had not loved Jonathan. She knew that now.

Because she knew, beyond question, that she loved Duncan
West. And that such love—powerful beyond reason—would
destroy her.

She met the countess's gaze. "I did this," she confessed. "I
brought you here and put you at risk." She shook her head.
"He—"

A knock sounded at the door and she was saved from fin-
ishing the thought aloud. But as she crossed the room, she
finished it a dozen times in her head.

He lied to me.

But why?

She turned back to the countess, standing, fists clenched, as though she might have to do battle. "It is the surgeon—nothing else."

Lady Tremley nodded once, and Georgiana opened the door to find Bruno, serious and sentinel. She tilted her head in question, and his gaze flickered over her shoulder, lingering on the countess behind. "Tremley is here," he said, quietly.

Georgiana met his gaze, all Chase. "As he is not a member, he is not our concern."

"He says he knows his wife is here, and he is willing to bring the royal guard with him the next time if we do not let him in now."

"Tell the others."

"He wants you."

She looked over her shoulder to ensure that the countess was far enough away not to overhear, then leaned toward the massive man. "Well, he can't very well have Chase."

Bruno shook his head. "You misunderstand. He wants Anna."

Fear shot through her at the words, strange and unfamiliar. "Anna," she replied.

"He says that you are the only person to whom he will speak."

"Well, then me he shall have," she said.

"You and a security detail," Bruno said, all protection.

She did not disagree with the plan. She turned back to the lady. "I have been summoned by your husband, it seems."

Imogen's eyes went wide. "You cannot face him. He will force you to tell him everything."

Georgiana smiled, hoping to give the countess hope. "I am not a woman who is easily forced."

"He is not a man who is easily defeated."

That much, she knew. But he was a man who understood power and sway. And she was not afraid to use it to do battle with him.

"All will be well," she assured the other woman, her gaze

sliding over cuts and bruises that no woman deserved, anger flaring deep within her. For Imogen. For Duncan.

For the truth.

The words whispered through her on a thread of faith—faith that he had not lied to her. Hope that he was what he seemed, and nothing less.

Was it possible for the man to be all he seemed?

Because he seemed a great deal.

She put the thoughts out of her mind as the surgeon arrived to assist Lady Tremley. Confident that the newest resident of The Fallen Angel was in capable hands, Georgiana navigated her way through a vast network of passageways and corridors to a small room on the men's side of the club, reserved for its worst offenders.

Among the staff, the room was called Prometheus, a reference to the overlarge oil painting within—Zeus in the form of an eagle, punishing Prometheus with slow, excruciating disembowelment for stealing fire from the gods. The painting was designed to intimidate and to terrify, and she had little doubt that it helped to ensure that when she entered the room, flanked by Bruno and Asriel, to face Lord Tremley, the earl's heart skipped a beat or two.

He stood at the far end of the windowless room, a wide oak table between them. Georgiana did not hesitate to begin the conversation. "May I help you?"

The earl smiled at her, and it occurred to her that at a different time, as a different woman, she might have found him attractive. He was empirically handsome, with dark hair and deep blue eyes and a line of straight white teeth that made her wonder if perhaps he'd been born with more than the usual amount.

But his eyes did not smile, and she had seen enough evil in the world to know that it lurked in him.

"I am here for my wife."

Her head tilted to one side with practiced innocence. "There are no women at the club, my lord. It is men only. In fact, I was rather surprised you would ask for me."

His gaze narrowed. "I hear you speak for Chase."

She played coy. "You flatter me. No one speaks for Chase."

He leaned forward, his hands forming fists on the oak table. "Then perhaps you can fetch him for me."

She met his eyes. "I am sorry, my lord. Chase is unavailable."

Something flashed in his gaze. "I grow tired of this conversation."

"I am sorry we have wasted your time." She smoothed her skirts and made to turn away. "One of these fine gentlemen will be happy to escort you out of the building."

"I would rather these . . ." He trailed off, his disdainful gaze flickering over first Asriel and then Bruno. "Well, I'm not about to call a pair of moors gentlemen." She stiffened at the disgust in his tone. "But why not have them leave altogether, and we can discuss my concerns with this establishment one-on-one."

"The gentlemen stay." The words brooked no refusal. "Though if you refer to them with disrespect again, I shall not."

"Let's dispense with the trivial, Anna," he said, as though they'd met a thousand times before. "I don't care what happens to the men. Or to you, for that matter. Or to my wife, whom I have no doubt is somewhere else in this massive building. Save her life, don't save her life. It does not matter to me. I am only sorry she ran before I could kill her."

"If we are dispensing with the trivial, my lord, I would be very careful about how you threaten the lady. Need I remind you what the Angel knows about you?" Georgiana wondered if London would miss the disgusting man if he were disappeared. "I should not have to tell you that we are more than willing to release it."

"I am well aware of what you have on me."

"To be clear, we are speaking of proof of your treason?" she asked, wanting to see him flinch. Enjoying it immensely when he did. When his perfect teeth clenched, she smiled. "It's widely known among the staff of the Angel. A lovely file, filled with a great deal of proof. You, sir, are a traitor to the crown."

He leaned back. "You have discovered my dark secret."

"I am certain there are darker ones."

The smile was back, cold and grotesque. "No doubt."

She released a sigh. "Lord Tremley, now it is you wasting our time. What precisely do you wish?"

He raised his brows. "I want Chase's identity."

She laughed. "I think it is amusing that you think I would ever dream of giving that to you."

He smirked. "Oh, I think you will give me precisely that for which I ask, because I am prepared to take from you something that you hold very dear."

"I cannot imagine what it is you think that might be."

He leaned in again. "I am told that you and Duncan West have an arrangement." She did nothing to acknowledge the words, her heart pounding at Tremley's mention of Duncan. Were they friends or foes?

"At first, I thought it was the way things are here at The Fallen Angel. He's handsome, rich, and powerful—a tremendous catch if you like the common man."

She narrowed her gaze on him. "These days, I prefer them to aristocrats."

He laughed, the sound cold and unsettling. "Clever girl. Smart mouth."

Her lips twisted in a smile. "My time, my lord. You consume it."

"But you'll want to hear this bit," he said casually, pulling out a chair and sitting, leaning back, enjoying holding court over them all. "At any rate, I thought you were simply a plaything for him. But then I spoke to him. And he seemed rather . . . committed to you. It was all very chivalrous."

She wanted to believe it. But there was a connection between these men—one she did not understand. One she did not trust.

Tremley went on. "Not being a member, how was I to know that you did not whore yourself out to the highest bidder?"

Bruno and Asriel stiffened behind her, but she did not look to them. "What are you trying to say?"

The earl waved a hand. "I hear that you and West have an arrangement. You were seen together here, apparently caught in a scandalous act by the Duke of Lamont. You were seen in an unmarked carriage at his office, and again at his home. I was told you appeared significantly more . . . used, shall we say? On the way out than on the way in."

Her heart began to pound.

"And he was quite put out when I referred to you by your profession instead of your name." He paused. "Though, to be honest, I'm not certain I've ever heard your name in full. You're usually simply referred to as Chase's whore. But now you're West's whore. So . . . there is that."

She'd heard the word a hundred times over the years, as she rollicked and reigned over the club floor. A thousand but now, here, tonight, it stung in ways she had never imagined it could.

Somehow, in all of this, she had become the mask. She'd become Anna. She would give herself to Langley for the most obvious of reasons. For the title. And she would resist giving herself to West, because he could not pay her price.

But it did not make her care for him less.

"I will ask you one more time. What is it you are attempting to say?"

"This is the bit where it would be better to speak without your sentry," he said. "Because it's the part where I convince you to betray your employer."

"As it will never happen, there is no need for them to leave."

His brows rose in surprise at the insolence in her tone. "You give me Chase's name and I will leave this place and never return. Consider it collateral against any . . . future engagement."

"We keep your secrets, you keep ours."

He grinned. "What they say is true, you are not just a pretty face."

She did not return the expression. "You, sadly, appear to

only have a pretty face, Lord Tremley. You see, the arrangement you suggest only works if both parties have information the other wants protected." She leaned forward and spoke to him as though he was a child. "We have your secrets. You don't have ours."

"No, but I have West's."

She stilled. "Mr. West is no longer a member. We have no need for his secrets."

"Nonsense," he said. "I am not a member, and you took information on me. Besides, even if Chase does not want these secrets, you will. They are legion."

She met his gaze. "I do not believe you."

If West's secrets were big enough to be worth a trade for Chase's identity, she would know them already. He would have told her, wouldn't he?

As she had told her secrets?

She met Tremley's gaze, saw the humor there, as though he read her thoughts. "There is *my* proof," he crowed. "You care for him. You care for him, and he hasn't told you, has he?" His tone turned falsely sympathetic. "Poor girl."

She feigned disinterest, ignoring his words. "If he had secrets worth knowing, the club would know them."

He met her gaze. "Shall I tell you? Would you like to know who your love is? Really?"

She ignored the questions, the way they baited her.

The way they made her want to scream, *Yes.*

He leaned forward and whispered, "I shall give you a hint. He's a criminal."

Her gaze flew to his. "We are all criminals in one way or another."

He smiled. "Yes, but you have no illusions about me." He stood. "I think you should ask him yourself. Ask him about Suffolk. Ask him about the grey stallion. Ask him about the girl he kidnapped." He paused. "Ask him his real name. Ask him about the boy from whom he stole it."

Her heart pounded at the words, as she struggled to believe them. As she struggled not to believe them. As she fought the twin emotions of feeling that she was betraying Duncan by even listening to the earl, and feeling as though Duncan had betrayed her bitterly by not telling her his truths before he tempted her into his arms and his life and his damn swimming pool.

Before he made her love him.

Who was he?

"Get out," she said to the earl, low and quiet and full of threat.

"You think I won't hurt him? You think I wouldn't wreck him? He means nothing to me . . . but he seems to mean quite a bit to you. Are you sure you want me to leave? Without giving me what I ask?"

"I am sure that I do not wish to breathe your air ever again."

He smirked. "Shouldn't you end that sentence with 'my lord'? You really are too comfortable with your betters, aren't you?"

She looked to Asriel. "Get him out. He is no longer welcome here."

"I shall give you three days," the earl said. "Three days to confirm that everything I have said is true."

She shook her head, turning away. She did not need three days. She knew it was true.

She did not even know his real name.

She knew about secrets. Had built a life on them.

Who was he? Why hadn't he told her?

Why didn't he trust her?

What is your relationship with Tremley?

What is your relationship with Chase?

The irony of her questions was not lost on her. They held too many secrets between them.

It was best, likely. Honesty made one dream.

"Anna." She turned back to look at the earl from the open doorway as he repeated, "Three days to decide where your loyalty lies . . . with Chase, or with West."

Chapter 19

    . . . Lady G— was a vision in white at the R— Ball, it makes one wonder: If she is so beautiful at a workaday event, how will she stun at an event devoted entirely to her? It will be a lucky man who gets the closest look . . .

    . . . Known as perhaps the Rogue Extraordinaire of Society's rakes, Lord B— appears to be at risk of losing his rakish title. He was spotted climbing the steps to the home he now shares with his Lady and their three children, arms loaded with parcels and packages and something that looked suspiciously like a Christmas pudding—in April! . . .

Pearls & Pelisses Ladies Magazine, late-May 1833

Duncan stood in the dark gardens of Ralston House, the annual Ralston Ball beautiful and raucous behind him, waiting for Georgiana to appear.

He wanted to see her. Quite desperately.

He had meant to find her the previous day, after he'd resolved to get her out from under Chase's thumb, but it wasn't easy to find a woman who played two vastly different, secret roles in Society. Lady Georgiana had not been at Leighton House when West had seen Caroline home, and West no longer had access to The Fallen Angel to search for Anna, as his membership had been rescinded.

So, he'd spent the evening making arrangements for his return salvo in his war with Chase, a war that would decide any number of futures—Georgiana's, Caroline's, his sister's, his own.

But he was no fool, and if all went well, his carefully laid plans would deliver him and Cynthia safety, and Georgiana and Caroline everything they wished. She would keep her secrets and get her husband. She would get the life she desired.

She'd danced every dance tonight, been partnered by some of the best and brightest in Britain. War heroes, earls, a duke known for his impressive work in the House of Lords. Every one would be a good match.

His papers—and he—had secured her a future. Secured her daughter a future. Georgiana would marry well—someone with a clean history, an unsullied title.

Perhaps even someone she could love.

He hated the bitterness that rose in him at the thought, the desperate desire to stop her from being with another. From loving anyone but him.

But he could not give her what she wished—even if he had a title . . . he could not promise her a future. Not one without fear.

And he would not wish that on this woman whom he loved so much.

If all went well, she would be returned to Society without a care in the world, without the shadows of her past looming, without the threat of a future without security. If his plan worked, she would be married within two weeks.

Two weeks.

The words echoed through him, the little agreement they'd

made what felt like a lifetime ago. They were intelligent people. They should have known that their lives were too complicated for even two weeks of simplicity. Not that he would ever dream of calling their time together simple.

She was the most complex woman he'd ever known.

And he adored her for it.

And tonight, he would show her that, one last time—stealing one final moment with her to help her find happiness, whatever that might be.

But first, he would tell her his truths.

He heard her before he saw her—the rustling of her skirts like cannonfire in the darkness as she approached. He turned toward her, loving the way she was silhouetted by the ballroom behind. The light cast a pale golden glow over her white gown, cut dangerously, decadently low, revealing the swell of her breasts, and making him want to steal her away from this place, forever.

She stopped several feet from him, and he hated the distance between them. He stepped toward her, hoping to close it, but she stepped back. She lifted a gloved hand and brandished a small ecru square. "You left me yesterday," she said, and the pout in her voice made him want her even more. "You cannot simply decide to summon me out of a ballroom into a dark garden."

He watched her carefully. "It seems to have worked."

She scowled. "It shouldn't have. I shouldn't be here. Our arrangement was supposed to bolster my reputation. This threatens to do the opposite."

"I would never allow that."

She met his gaze. "I wish I could believe that."

He stilled, not liking the words. "What does that mean?"

She sighed. Looked away, then back. "You left me," she said, the words small and soft and devastating. "You walked away."

He shook his head. "I didn't understand why you wouldn't tell me the truth." He thought she laughed at that, but he couldn't be sure—the gardens were too dark and he could not see her eyes. "And then I realized that you cannot trust me blindly. That you have been devastated before. You keep your secrets to keep her safe. You keep his secrets to keep her safe." He paused. "I won't ask you for them anymore."

She came to him then, stepping forward, and he was overcome by the nearness of her . . . the smell of her . . . vanilla and cream. He wanted to pull her toward him and make her his here, in the darkness. For what might be the last time.

He wanted his two weeks.

He wanted his lifetime.

But he could not have those things, so instead, he would settle on this night.

"Why don't you know how to dance?" she asked.

The question came from nowhere, and it shocked the hell out of him. He would have expected a question—something about his own secrets. His own past. Something about Tremley. About Cynthia. But he had not expected such a simple query. Such an all-encompassing one.

He should have, of course.

He should have expected her to ask the most important question first.

Of course, he answered it, his discomfort with the subject matter—with all the bits and pieces of his life that somehow were connected to it—making him more hesitant than usual. He started simply. "No one ever taught me to dance."

She shook her head. "Everyone learns to dance. Even if you never learn the quadrille or the waltz or any of the dances they dance in there"—she waved at the house—"someone dances with you."

He thought back. Tried again. "My mother danced with my father."

She did not speak, letting him tell his story. Letting him find his way. It was a memory long forgotten, dredged from some dark corner where he'd sent it to die. "My father died when I was four, so it is a surprise I even remember it." He paused. "Perhaps I don't remember it. Perhaps it's a dream, not a memory."

"Tell me," she said.

"We lived in a cottage on a large estate as tenant farmers. My father was large and ruddy-cheeked. He used to lift me in the air as though I were featherlight." He paused. "I suppose I was to him." He shook his head. "I remember him by the fire in the cottage, twirling my mother around and around." He looked to her. "It wasn't dancing."

She watched him carefully. "Were they happy?"

He struggled to remember their faces, but he could remember the smiles. The laughter. "In that moment, I think they were."

She nodded, reaching out for him, sliding her hand into his. "Then it was dancing."

He clasped her fingers tightly. "Not like the dancing you do."

"Nothing like the dancing we do. Our dancing is for show. For circumstance. A way to show our plumage and hopefully find favor." She stepped closer, near enough that if he lowered his chin, he might graze her forehead with his kiss. He resisted the urge. "Your dancing was for fun."

"I wish I could dance," he whispered, as she looked up to him. "I would dance with you."

"Where?"

"Wherever you wish."

"By the fire in your home?" The whisper nearly slew him with memory and want.

"In another place. Another time. If we were other people."

She smiled, sadness in the expression, and slid her left hand up to his shoulder, placing her right hand in his. "What about here? Now?" He wished they weren't wearing gloves. He wished he could feel her touch as well as her heat. He wished a great many things as they moved, slowly, circling in slow time to the music spilling into the darkness.

After long moments, he pressed his lips to her curls and spoke. "I've watched you dance a dozen times . . . and I've been jealous of every single one of your partners."

"I am sorry," she said.

"I have stood at the edge of the ballroom, watching you, Poseidon watching Amphitrite."

She pulled back to look at him, tilting her head in question. He smiled. "I, too, know about Poseidon."

"More than I do, apparently."

He returned his attention to their movements. "Amphitrite was a sea nymph, one of fifty, the opposite of the sirens . . . the saviors of the sea." They turned, and her face was cast in the glow of the ballroom. She was watching him, "On a night in late summer, the nymphs gather on the island of Naxos and danced in the surf. Poseidon watched."

Humor flooded her gaze. "I imagine he did."

He grinned. "Can you blame him?"

"Go on," she urged.

"He ignored all the Nereids, save one."

"Amphitrite."

"Is this my story or yours?" he teased.

"Oh, excuse me, sir," she replied.

"He wanted her desperately. Came out of the sea, nude, and claimed her for himself. Vowed to love her with the passion of the surf, with the depth of the ocean, with the roar of the waves."

She was not laughing anymore, and neither was he. Suddenly, the story seemed incredibly serious. "What happened?"

"She ran from him," he said, the words soft and serious, punctuated by his kiss on her brow. "She ran to the farthest edge of the sea."

She was silent for a long moment. "She was terrified of his power."

"He wanted to share it with her. He followed, desperate for her, aching for her, refusing to rest until he found her. She was all he wanted. He was desperate to worship her, to marry her. To make her goddess of the sea."

She was breathing heavily now, as was he, lost in the tale. "When he could not find her, he became lost, refusing to rule the sea without her by his side. He neglected his duties. The seas rose up, and storms devastated the islands of the Aegean Sea, and he could not bring himself to care.

"When Amphitrite realized what Poseidon had offered her, what she had refused, how he had searched, she wept for him. For the love he had for her. For his passion and desire. For what she had lost." There were tears in Georgiana's eyes now, the story taking on a new meaning. New power. "Her tears were so many that she wept herself into the ocean. She became the sea itself."

"Lost to him, forever," she said softly.

He shook his head. "No. With him, forever. His strong, tempestuous partner. His equal in every way. Without her, there is no him."

The music in the ballroom stopped. He pulled back from her. "You run from me."

"I don't," she said, and they both knew it was a lie. She pulled away, took several steps back, putting space between them. She tried again. "Yes. I do."

"Why?"

She took a breath. Released it. "I run from you," she said, sadness in her tone, "because if I didn't, I would run to you. And that can never happen."

He kissed her then, because he did not know what else to do, savoring her taste, beauty and life and scandal and sadness. It was the sadness that stopped him. That had him pulling back, waiting for her to speak.

"Who is Tremley to you?"

She surprised him with her directness. Of course, he should not have been surprised by her. She was not one to shy away from difficult conversation. "He came to me last night."

He went cold at the words. Cold, and furious. "Why?"

"He nearly killed his wife. She fled to the club, searching for sanctuary."

"Christ," he said, falling back a few steps. "I did that."

She met his gaze, anger and betrayal showing. "We. We did it."

"Is she—"

"She will heal," Georgiana said. "She will heal and she will triumph. We will find her a place to live out from under his thumb."

The words made him weak—weaker than he'd ever in his life felt. Weaker than when he did Tremley's bidding. "By we, you mean you and Chase."

"Among others."

"I want him dead," West said, the words coming out ragged with frustration and guilt over what he'd done to Tremley's innocent wife. And for what? "I want him ruined forever."

"Why not do it?" she asked, the words high-pitched with confusion. "You have the means to do it. To destroy him. I gave them to you. Who is he to you? What hold does he have over you?" She paused. Collected herself. "Tell me. We can fix it."

She meant it. He could not stop the laugh that came at the ridiculous pronouncement, as though she had any control over Tremley, Or Chase. "There is only one way to fix it," he said. "A secret is only a secret before a second person knows it."

"And Tremley knows yours."

If only it were that simple. "This story is not as good as Poseidon and Amphitrite."

"I shall be the judge of that," she said.

He couldn't stand still as they talked, not for this. Not as he revealed his past sins for the only time. So he turned and walked, and she followed, keeping pace, but seeming to know—as she always seemed to know him—that he could not bear her touch. Not now.

He did not want the reminder of what he might have had, if not for this.

Finally, he confessed. "Tremley has known my secrets for all our lives."

She'd known there was a connection, of course, but not what it was. It had never occurred to her that he and the earl might have been so connected for so long.

She watched him carefully, working to keep the shock from her face. Working to keep herself from asking the myriad questions immediately on the tip of her tongue.

"My father died when I was no more than four." He looked away, into the darkness, and she watched him in profile as he spoke, loving the strength in his face. The emotion there. "And my mother, saddled with a child and no knowledge of how to live on the land, was offered a place in the main house."

"Tremley's house," Georgiana said.

He nodded. "She went from farmer's wife to washwoman. From sleeping in her own house to sleeping in a room with six other women, her child in her bed." He looked up at the trees rustling in the spring breeze. "And she never once complained."

"Of course she didn't." Georgiana could not stop herself from speaking. "She did it for you. For you and your sister."

He ignored the words. Pressed on. "The estate was horrifying. The former earl, if you can imagine it, was worse than the current one. Servants were beaten. Women were assaulted. Children were pressed into service too harsh for their age." He looked into the darkness. "My mother and I were lucky."

Georgiana had not even heard the story, and she knew there was nothing lucky about it. She wanted to touch him, to give him comfort, but she knew better. She let him speak. "He took an interest in her."

She'd known the words were coming, but she hated them all the same.

"He offered her a trade—her body for my safety." Her brow furrowed at the words, and he noticed. "Or, rather, not my safety. My presence. If she did not give him what he wished, he would send me away. To a workhouse."

Georgiana thought of her own child, of her own past. Of the threats she'd faced—never so cruel. Never so damning. Even when ruined, she'd still had the luck of the aristocracy. Not so this woman. This boy. "Why?" she asked, "Why torture her?"

He met her gaze. "Power." He paused and collected his thoughts. Went on. "I was allowed to stay, but made to work—I've told you this bit." She reached for him then, unable to stop herself. Unable to resist comforting the boy he'd once been. He pulled away from her touch. "No. I won't be able to tell it all if you . . ." He hesitated, then said, "Once, I resisted the work. He punished her."

"Duncan," she whispered.

"I could not stop him."

She shook her head. "Of course you couldn't. You were a boy."

His gaze snapped to hers. "I am not a boy any longer. And I could not stop him from hurting his wife."

"You cannot compare the two."

"Of course I can. Charles—the young earl—he was as bad as his father. Worse. He was desperate for approval, and he took pleasure in the power that came with being the future earl. He learned to throw a remarkable punch." His fingers came to his jaw, as if the words brought back the blows. "He did terrible things to the servants' children. I stopped him more times than I could count. And then . . ." He trailed off, lost in thought for a long moment before he looked back to her. "The countess never goes back," he vowed. "I'll pay for her to go anywhere in Christendom. Anywhere she chooses."

She nodded. "Yes."

"I mean it," he said, and she recognized the fury in his gaze.

"I know."

He took a long breath, released it on a wicked curse. "When I was ten, my mother became pregnant."

She'd done the math already. She'd known Cynthia was not his full sister. Now, she finished the calculation. Her eyes went wide. It was his turn to nod. "You see how it fits together."

"Tremley."

He dipped his head. "She is his half sister."

"Christ," she whispered. "Does she know?"

He ignored the question. "The earl pushed my mother to be rid of her, first when she began to increase and then again when Cynthia was born. He threatened to take her away. To give her to some well-meaning family somewhere on the estate. My mother refused to allow it."

"I am not surprised," Georgiana said. "No woman would be willing to let you go."

He looked to her. "I imagine you would have done the same."

She lifted her chin. "With my dying breath."

He put his hand to her face, cupping her cheek in its warmth. "Caroline is lucky to have you."

"I am lucky to have her," she said. "Just as your mother was lucky to have you both."

"There should have been three of us," he said. "The third was stillborn. A brother."

"Duncan," she said, putting her hand to his on her cheek, her eyes filling with tears for him. For what he had seen.

"I was fifteen. Cynthia was five." He paused. "And my mother . . . she died as well."

She'd known it was coming, but the words still tore at her.

"He killed my mother," he said.

She nodded, tears spilling down her cheeks for the loss of the woman she would never know. For the loss of the boy she would never know. For Duncan. She filled in the rest. "You ran."

"I stole a horse." *A grey stallion.* "It was worth five times what I was worth. More."

It was worth nothing compared to him. "And you took Cynthia."

"Kidnapped her. If the earl ever wanted her . . . if he ever found us . . . I would hang." He looked toward the ballroom. "But what could I do? How could I leave her?"

"You couldn't," she said. "You did the right thing. Where did you go?"

"We were lucky . . . we found an innkeeper and his wife. They took us in, fed us. Helped us. Never once asked about the horse. He had a brother in London who owned a pub. We went to him. I sold the horse, planning to pay the pub owner to take care of Cynthia while I enlisted in the army." He stopped. "I would never have seen her again."

There was fear in the words, as he was lost to their memory. She spoke. "But you did. You see her every day."

He returned to the present. "The night I returned, money in my pocket, ready to change our lives, there was a man in the pub. He owned a newspaper. Offered me a job running ink and paper at the press."

"And so you became Duncan West, newspaperman."

He smiled. "A few steps in between—a careful investment in a new printing press—the retirement of a man who saw something in me that I did not know was there—but, yes. I started *The Scandal Sheet—*"

"My favorite publication."

He had the grace to look chagrined. "I apologized for the cartoon."

"I was happy that you felt you owed me a penance."

The laughter in his eyes disappeared at the reminder of their deal—of his promise to help her marry. She hated herself for bringing it up.

"Once I was Duncan West"—he looked back to the ball—"I suppose I should have expected Tremley to find me once he inherited the title and took his place in Parliament. But once he did, he owned me."

She understood, immediately. "He holds your secrets. And they are more valuable to him in private, where he can use you for news, than in public, where you end up in prison."

"Horse stealing is a hanging offense," he reminded her, all macabre. "As is fraud."

Her brow knit. "Fraud."

"Duncan West does not exist." He looked down at his feet, and she saw a glimpse of the bruised boy he'd once been. "There was another boy who saw us leaving," he said, the words soft and full of memory. "He tried to follow.

"But he was younger, and he wasn't strong enough, and I

already had Cynthia. I made him take his own horse." Dread pooled in Georgiana's stomach. "It was dark, and his horse balked at a jump. He was thrown. Died." He shook his head. "I left him. I got him killed, and I left him."

She placed her hand to his face. "You hadn't a choice."

He still did not look at her. "His name was Duncan."

She closed her eyes at the words. At the trust he must have for her in order to confess it.

A trust she had not shown him.

"What was yours?"

"James," he said. "Jamie. Croft."

She pulled his face down to hers, letting their foreheads touch. "Jamie," she whispered.

He shook his head. "Gone now. Forever."

That word, promise and weapon at once.

"And Cynthia?" she asked.

A cloud crossed over his face. "Cynthia does not remember anything before the innkeeper and his wife. She doesn't remember our mother. She thinks we shared a father. Thinks his name was West." He shook his head. "I didn't want her to know the truth."

"That her father was a monster? Of course you didn't."

He met her eyes. "I took her from that life. She had no choice."

"You did what was best."

"She is half aristocrat."

"And all West." She refused to let him be ashamed of it. "You chose that for yourself?"

"I chose it for her," he said, and she understood that more than he could ever know. "When we left Tremley Manor, it was dusk. We rode toward the sunset."

"West."

She lifted herself onto her toes and kissed him, long and slow and deep, as though they had all the time in the world. As though their secrets weren't thundering toward them at breakneck speed.

His hands were at her jaw, cradling her with such care, that she thought she might weep—if she did not want him so very much. She sighed into his mouth as he kissed her again and again, pulling her tight against him, fitting them together in a way that made her wish they were somewhere else. Somewhere indoors. Somewhere with a bed.

He pulled back finally, and said, "So, you see, I keep Tremley's secrets for Cynthia. But now that they are with Chase . . ."

Of course, now that Chase knew Tremley's secrets, Duncan and Cynthia were under threat. And there it was, the reason he had pressed her for Chase's identity. The reason he had threatened her.

And now Georgiana knew Duncan's secrets, she would do anything to protect them. To protect him.

Tremley had asked her to choose—Chase or West. And there was no question anymore.

She might not be able to have him with her forever, but she could ensure that his forever was happy, and long, and without fear.

He was so noble. There was so much about this man that she adored. He was deeply, undeniably worthy of this world. Of life. Of love. She came up on her toes and pressed her forehead to his. "What if we married?"

It was not meant in seriousness. It was a strange dream in this quiet moment. And still, he felt he should answer her honestly. He shook his head. "I cannot marry you."

The words shocked her. "What?"

He saw immediately what he had done. "I cannot—I would never saddle you with my secrets. If my past were revealed, my wife would be destroyed. My family. I would absolutely go to prison. And I would likely hang. And you would suffer with me. And Caroline."

"If we keep Tremley quiet."

He shook his head. "As long as Tremley lives, my secrets live with him." He paused. "And besides, I can't give you the title."

"Hang the title."

He smiled, and there was sadness in the expression. "You don't mean it."

She didn't. This whole life—everything she had ever done for the last decade—had been for Caroline.

"I wish . . ."

She trailed off as his arms came around her. "Tell me."

"I wish we were other people," she said, quietly. "I wish we were simple, and all we cared about was food on our table and roofs over our heads."

"And love," he added.

She did not hesitate. "And love," she agreed.

"If we were other people," he asked, "would you marry me?"

It was her turn to look to the sky, to imagine that instead of here—in Mayfair, by the light of a glittering ballroom, wearing a gown worth more than most people made in a year—she was in the country, children pulling on her apron strings as she pointed out the constellations.

And how magnificent that would be. "I would."

"If we were other people," he said, pleasure in his tone as his fingers stroked over her face, "I would ask you."

She nodded. "But we aren't."

"Shh," he hushed her. "Don't take it away. Not yet." He turned her in the darkness, until her face was in the light. "Tell me."

She shook her head, sadness coming quickly, on a wave of tears. "I shouldn't," she said. "It is not a good idea."

"I have made a life on bad ideas," he said. "Tell me." He kissed her, quick and lovely. "Tell me you love me."

The tears spilled over, but she could not look away from him. She could not tell him that she loved him, because she might not be able to walk away from him then. And if she could not walk away from him, all of this—this entire mess into which she had dragged him—would be for naught.

"Tell me, Georgiana," he whispered, sipping the tears from her cheeks. "Do you love me?"

If she told him she loved him, she knew without question that he would never allow her to do what must be done.

And so, instead of answering his question, she answered Tremley's question from the night before. She reached up, slid her fingers into her love's hair, and pulled him down to her, grazing her lips against his once, twice, before saying, "I choose you. Always."

She chose West. Here and now.

He kissed her, deep and long and wonderful, rewarding the words even though they weren't precisely what he wished for. When he pulled back, he said, "I choose you as well, my lady. Forever."

She adored this man, in all the dark corners that she'd thought she'd locked away forever.

Forever.

It was a long time . . . and belonged to him.

She would give it to him. "I can repair this," she said.

He grew curious. "Repair what?"

He began to walk again, edging them through the garden gate to the mews at the side of the massive house, where a crush of carriages waited for their owners to call for them.

"All of it," she said, her fingers trailing over the great black wheels of a coach, then along the silky flank of one of its horses. "I can convince Tremley never to betray your information."

"How?"

"With Chase." For the first time since they had met as Georgiana and West, she did not feel guilty referring to Chase as other. Not now, not as she was willing to sacrifice the false identity to save Duncan.

He stopped, turned to her. "I don't want you anywhere near this, Georgiana. Isn't it time you leave him? Isn't it time you begin your life without him?"

She shook her head. "Duncan, you don't understand—"

He took her arms in his grip. "No, you don't understand. I've taken care of it."

Everything inside her stilled. "What do you mean?" Was he planning to confess? "Duncan, you must not—"

"I have taken care of it," he repeated. "But listen to me. Chase is dangerous. He has the power to bring us all down if he wishes. This entire mess exists because Tremley does not trust Chase not to release the information on his treason.

"I don't know what it is that keeps you so beholden to him—I swore I would not ask ever again. But I do know that it is time for you to sever whatever ties you have to this massive, mythical man." His words grew more impassioned and his anger began to show. "It is time for you to leave him. To leave that place. To end this part of your life."

"I know."

His hands cradled her face once more, tilting her up to meet his. "Christ, if you don't do it for yourself, or for Caroline . . . do it for me."

She was doing it for him. "I will."

"Do this one thing for me," he begged. "End it with him . . . whatever it is. Stay away from the club."

"I will." Two more days, and she would never look back at it.

"Do this, and I will never ask you for another thing again."

She wanted him to ask. She wanted to be his partner in this. His Amphitrite. "Duncan . . ." she trailed off, not knowing what to say. Hating fate and fortune, and wishing she were someone, anyone else. Wishing she were a woman who could fall into Duncan West's arms and spend the rest of her life there.

"Promise me," he whispered, his lips on hers, neither of them caring that they were in full view of half of London's coachmen. "Promise me you won't let him win in this."

She returned the kiss. "I promise." It was the closest that she would ever come to telling him she loved him. "I promise," she repeated, and it was truth. Chase would not win this.

They walked to the next carriage in the line, and he opened

the door. She peered in. There were newspapers scattered across the floor. Her heart began to pound. It was his carriage. Was he taking her to his home? Abducting her away from this place? From all the things that kept them chained to this world?

He handed her up into the carriage. "And promise me something else . . ."

"Anything."

The wide world.

His hand slid down her leg, sliding under the skirts of her dress, his fingers caressing the skin of her ankle.

"Stay out of the club tomorrow."

He closed the door and banged on the side of the carriage, signaling to the driver. "Take the lady to Leighton House," she heard him say as the conveyance lurched into motion. She instantly understood what had happened—he didn't want her sleeping at the club, so he was sending her to her brother's house in his own carriage.

She should have been annoyed, but she could not quite muster the energy. She was using too much of it to love him.

She settled back into the soft seat of his carriage, considering all the things she had to do prior to her deadline with Tremley tomorrow—most importantly, telling the other partners that Chase was about to be revealed.

How many times had she shaken her head at the actions of men in love?

They were nothing in comparison to the actions of a woman in love.

A light from a streetlamp outside shone bright in the window, illuminating the newspaper on the seat next to her.

She stilled, sure she had misread.

She lifted the paper, not believing it at first, turning the page to the street, waiting for a light to confirm the words. And then the date. The paper she held in her hand would release the next day, ironically, on the same date that Tremley's offer expired.

There, across the entirety of the page, was a single head-line:

Reward for the Identity of The Fallen Angel's Owner

And beneath:

£5,000 for proof of the identity of the elusive Chase

Chapter 20

Editors of this prestigious paper have had enough of the monopoly of power that exists in London's darkest corners. We encourage our readers to do what they can to ensure that the country have only one monarch, and one who reigns in public . . .

—*The News of London*, May 17, 1833

The Fallen Angel was under siege.

As it was only half-eleven in the morning, the casino floor was dark, but there was nothing quiet about the space, filled with echoing shouts from outside the steel doors of the casino, loud banging on the doors of the building, and the constant din of men outside, filling St. James Street in the hopes of getting their chance for five thousand pounds.

Inside, Temple and Cross sat at a roulette table, waiting for a member of the security team to appear with news.

Bourne arrived first. "What in hell is happening?" he called, pushing through the inner door to the casino from the entrance hall, barred with double locks and a door-man twice the size of a normal person.

Cross looked to Bourne. "You look as though you've been through a war."

"Have you seen how many people there are out there?

They're desperate for entry. Do they simply think we're going to announce Chase's identity? Simply because West has lost his mind?" He looked down at the sleeve of his coat and swore roundly. "Look what the bastards did to me! They tore my cuff."

"You are like a woman when it comes to clothes," Temple said. "If I were you, I would be more concerned about arm tearing. As in limb from limb."

Bourne scowled at Temple. "I was concerned about that. Now that the immediate threat is gone, I'm irritated about my cuff. I'll ask again; what in hell is going on?"

Temple and Cross looked at each other, then at Bourne. "Chase is in love," Cross said, simply.

Bourne blinked once. "Honestly?"

"Besotted," Temple said. The word was punctuated by a crash high above, where a well-aimed rock broke a small window and rained glass down onto the casino floor.

They watched the fall of glass for a long moment, before Bourne turned back to his partners. "With West?"

Cross nodded. "The very same."

Bourne thought for a moment. "Is it me? Or does it seem fitting that Chase's love story is the one that nearly destroys the casino?"

"It's going to do more than *nearly* destroy it, if West doesn't call off his dogs."

Bourne nodded. "I assume you've—"

"Of course," Temple said. "First thing. The moment we saw the paper."

"And she doesn't know."

"Definitely not," Cross said. "Did she ever give us the courtesy of letting us know that she was going to meddle in our affairs?"

"She did not," Bourne said with a sigh as he sat. "So we are waiting, then?"

Temple waved to a seat nearby. "We are waiting."

Bourne nodded. They were quiet for a long moment, all watching Cross spin the wheel again and again. Finally, Bourne said, "It's less fun when there's no ball."

"It isn't that much fun when there is a ball."

"I wonder why Chase loves it so much," Temple said.

"Because roulette is the only game of chance that is entirely random," Cross said. "You cannot force a win. And so, it is even ground."

"Pure chance," Bourne said.

"No calculated risk," Cross agreed.

There was heavy banging on the door, long and loud and with little threat of giving up. When it stopped, and a door opened, the security team no doubt using all their might to keep the crowds at bay.

Bourne laughed, and the others looked to him, confusion on their faces. He shook his head. "I am simply imagining all those starchy nobs from White's and Brooks's, turning down St. James's, unsuspecting."

Cross laughed, too. "Oh, they shall be furious with us. As though they didn't loathe us before."

"Hang them," Temple said, his lips curving into a grin. "Never let it be said that The Fallen Angel doesn't bring entertainment to the neighborhood."

The statement had them all laughing, each louder than the other. They almost did not notice that Bruno had appeared at the edge of the room. "He is here," the enormous guard announced.

"I can see myself in," Duncan said, pushing past the massive man and onto the darkened floor.

The founders stood as one, straightening sleeves—except Bourne, who simply swore again over the condition of his sleeve—each intimidating in his own right, but together, a trio of power more intimidating than most men would be willing to face.

Duncan approached without hesitation.

Bruno watched his back. "Even though I think we should leave him to the crowds."

"We might well do that," Temple said.

"Give it time," Cross added.

"What the hell is this?" Duncan asked, brandishing a small

square of paper. "You think insulting me is the way to convince me to rescind the reward?"

Bourne plucked the missive out of his hand and opened it. Read aloud. " 'You are an idiot, wandering blind in the woods.' " He nodded, looking to Temple. "There's a poetry to that."

Temple looked rather proud of himself. "Thank you. I thought so."

Duncan snatched the paper out of Bourne's hands in exasperation. "Insulting me and then summoning me to your side hasn't put me in a generous frame of mind. What in hell do you want?"

"You know," Bourne said, "I once heard you described as a genius." He looked to Cross. "Except, for a genius, he is something of a lummox."

"Well, to be fair, he's in a situation where intelligence does rather go out the window," Cross said. "I have a theory that women actually siphon off our cleverness during the courting phase, and keep it for themselves. Which is why they always seem to see the endgame before we do."

Temple nodded, as though the earl had said something tremendously sage.

"That is a very good theory," Bourne said.

"You're all fucking mad," Duncan said, brandishing the note. "I did not come for your insane ideas. I came because you promised me Chase. And looking at the three of you, you lied."

"Excuse me," Temple said, affront in the tone.

"We did not lie." Cross replied.

"Well then?" Duncan asked.

"The reward was a very good move," Temple said. "It certainly got our attention."

"Did it get Chase's?"

"I imagine it did, yes," said Bourne.

"Then why am I talking to you three instead of him?"

Cross leaned back against the roulette table, folding long arms over his chest. He lifted his chin in the direction of the door at the far end of the room, beneath the enormous stained glass window. Duncan's gaze fell to the exit, and he realized that he had never in all his years of membership seen that door unguarded.

He looked back to the owners.

"Go ahead, then," Cross said. "Talk to Chase."

His brow furrowed. "Is it a trap?"

"Not in the way you think," Temple said, ominously.

He turned away. "You waste my time."

"It's not a trap," Cross said. "You'll survive it."

He looked from one founder to the next. "How do I know to trust you?"

Bourne shrugged one shoulder. "She loves you. We would not hurt you, even if we wanted to." The words were punctuated by a cacophony of shouting from the street outside—the sounds matching the beating of his heart.

She loves you.

"You have all mistreated her. Abysmally," Duncan said. "Letting her live this life."

Temple smiled at that. "That you think we ever *let* them do anything is a testament to your senselessness." He lifted his chin to the door. "Chase's office is through that door."

Duncan's gaze lingered on the door in question. If it was a trap, so be it. He had brought them to this moment, forcing their hand. He'd offered the reward, sending half of London to their doorstep to smoke out the elusive owner of the casino.

He would face this head-on.

He crossed the room, opened the door to reveal a long staircase, ascending into darkness. Looking back, he saw the three men who were the public face of the casino, standing shoulder to shoulder, watching him. As he closed the door behind him, blocking them out, it occurred to him that their fourth was missing—the woman who reigned over this floor. Their partner in this impressive place.

The thought echoed through him. She was their fourth.

She was their fourth.

He climbed the stairs, moving more and more quickly as

his mind turned the events of the past six years over and over again . . . all the references to Chase, all the missives carried on his behalf by the beautiful, brilliant Anna, a Society cast-out hidden in plain sight. She knew so much about the place, about its members.

She was their fourth.

The door at the top of the stairs opened onto a familiar corridor, the wall opposite him boasting an enormous oil painting he'd seen before. Themis and Nemesis. Justice and Vengeance.

Who are you? he'd asked when they'd stood here before.

I cannot be both? she'd replied.

She was both.

He nearly ripped the painting from the wall as he opened the entrance to the secret passageway. To Chase's office.

He counted the doors, stopping at the fourth. Grasping the handle. Knowing that whatever—whoever—was behind this door would change his life. Forever. He took a single, stabilizing breath, and opened the door.

He was right.

She was behind her desk, head bowed, writing, a stack of cards next to her on the great expanse of oak. Memory flashed—days earlier. She, on the edge of that desk in this white room. His hands and mouth and body on hers.

He'd rushed, thinking they were in Chase's offices.

Thinking they would be caught.

Thinking she belonged to another.

Wanting her for his.

He was consumed by anger and fascination, disbelief and respect.

She did not look up from her writing as she heard the door open, instead waving a hand in the direction of the stack of letters at her elbow. "These are ready to go," she said. "Is Bourne here yet?"

He closed the door, locking it in a single motion.

She looked up at the sound of key in lock, her gaze finding his, shock in her eyes as she shot out of her chair.

She was wearing trousers again.

"Duncan," she said.

"Bourne is here," he said.

Her brow furrowed, and it took her a moment to understand what exactly he meant by the words. "I—" She stopped. "Oh."

"Tell me," he said, and it occurred to him that the night prior, he'd spoken the same words to her, hoping she would finally tell him that she loved him.

Now he would simply settle for the truth.

When she did not reply, he repeated himself. "Tell me." The words came out harsh, nearly broken. When she shook her head, he repeated himself, the words coming on a near-shout, "Tell me!"

There were tears in her eyes, in those beautiful amber eyes that he had marveled at so many times. He wondered what the tears were for—if they were because he'd discovered her secrets, or if they were because she realized that a betrayal of this size would be impossible to forgive.

That a secret of this magnitude changed everything.

She opened her mouth. Closed it.

"Duncan," she whispered. "I was not ready for you to know."

"Know what?" he asked. And he commanded her a final time. "Tell me. Say it. For once in our lives, tell me the truth."

She nodded, and he watched her throat work as she searched for the words. Not many words. Three of them. Utterly simple and somehow tremendously complicated.

Finally, she met his gaze, unwavering. And spoke.

"I am Chase."

*H*e was quiet for so long, she thought he might never speak.

A dozen possibilities rioted through her, every one a question. But when he did speak, it was not a question, but a statement, filled with disbelief and awe and something else that she hesitated to name. "I was so damn jealous of him."

She did not know what to say when he ran a hand through his hair and continued, "I thought he owned you. I couldn't understand why you were so committed to him. Why you protected him so well. I couldn't understand why you fell into my arms even as you chose him, time and time again."

"I didn't choose him," she said.

He met her eyes. "You chose this place."

"No," she said, wanting him to understand. Wanting him to see. "I chose safety. Security."

"I could have given that to you," he said, the words coming out like rolling thunder. "Christ, Georgiana, I wanted to give it to you. All you had to do was trust me."

"Why would I do that?" she asked, suddenly desperate for him to understand. She came out from behind the desk. "I've spent my life around dangerous men . . . and you might well have been the most dangerous one of all."

"Me?" he asked, the word incredulous. "From the moment we met, I offered you help."

"No," she said. "You offered Georgiana help, but once you discovered her connection to the Angel, once you discovered that I was also Anna, you offered me a trade."

He stilled.

She knew she should not punish him for it—knew she had done far worse—but she could not stop herself. Feeling defensive, she said, "Tit for tat, Duncan. And a threat to reveal my secrets." She shook her head. "I was party to the deal, no doubt. But do not for a moment think I have not learned in all my years as Chase that business is not friendship. And that trust is not a part of business."

"This hasn't been business for a long time," he said.

She knew that, of course. Knew, too, that this might be the only time she was ever able to tell the truth.

And she wanted it to be him who heard it.

She leaned against the desk, placing her palms flat to the top of it. "I wanted to be something more than what they made me." She paused, trying to find the words to explain. "Do you recall the house in Yorkshire?" He nodded. "There were so many of us there . . . so many of us who had run. Who had found the strength to defy expectations." She shook her head. "I was the weakest by far, and I could afford to be. When I left—when I returned home—I saw the way the world looked at me. At us. And I hated them for it. I wanted to do something tremendously powerful . . . something that would hold them under my thumb, these people who talked propriety and lived sin and vice when they closed their doors.

"At first, it was for revenge. I wanted to punish anyone who crossed me. Who dared insult Caroline. I wanted to murder gossip and kill *ton*. A casino was the ideal place for all of that. Decadence, sin, vice—they make for excellent partners in vengeance."

He smiled. "And then you realized you weren't God."

She raised her brows. "No, then I realized I did not wish to be God. I wished to be something very different. I wished to reign over them. I wished them to be in debt to me, with secrets and money and whatever else they wanted to put on the table."

"And Chase was born."

"My brother put up the money for the club, helped me choose my partners." She smiled. "Bourne and Temple came first, and I'll never forget the look in their eyes when my security guards tossed them into my carriage, and I introduced myself." She paused. "Bourne called me any number of names before he settled down and realized that what I offered was really quite magnificent."

"Ownership in a men's club."

She shook her head. "Resurrection from the gutter. He'd lost everything. Temple, too. I could give them a chance to rebuild. I did not need the money . . . I needed the titles. The faces. The skills they brought to the table."

He nodded. "Where did the name Chase come from?"

She grinned. "Bourne gave it to me. I was leading London on a merry chase, he used to say. It stuck.

"We opened the casino with my brother's help and his connections. Within months, people were clamoring for memberships. And for the first few years, I did not care what they thought of Georgiana. *I* barely even thought of Georgiana. I was Chase, and I was Anna, and I was free . . . and it was glorious." She looked away. "Until it wasn't."

"Until Caroline was old enough to notice their censure."

"Until Caroline was old enough to become the object of it."

"And then it became about her."

She met his gaze, saw the understanding in it. He had faced a similar battle, knowing that he must protect his sister from the world. "I didn't steal a horse, Duncan. I stole a world."

"And we believed you," he said.

"It wasn't as difficult as it would seem," she said. "People believe what they are told, mostly. Once we decided that Chase would never be seen, it was easy to convince the world that he was more powerful than any of them. His mystery became his power. My power."

"You're wrong." He was close to her, close enough to touch, but she resisted the urge as he continued, "I have known you as Georgiana and as Anna. And I have felt the full heat of your power. I have railed at it and basked in its glow. And there is nothing about that power that is Chase." His hand came up, cupped the nape of her neck, and she caught her breath at the touch. "It is all yours." She looked up at him as he added, "And she will know it."

Tears came at the words, unbidden and unwelcome. How did he know that was her worry? In the dark of night? How did he know that she was terrified that Caroline would one day look at her and hate her for the choices she'd made?

She looked away, trying to hide from him.

"Don't," he said, forcing her to return her gaze to his. "Don't hide from me. You pushed me away at every turn. You used Chase as a shield."

"No—" she began, but he cut her off, anger and sorrow in his eyes.

"Yes. You were afraid of me. But why? Were you afraid

of what I might do? Of what I might tell the world? Did you actually think I might betray you?"

Her brow furrowed. "I did not know . . . the only other man I had ever given myself to . . ."

He went on. "You weren't afraid of me. And you weren't afraid of repercussions from Chase . . . we know that now," he offered the words, with dry humor. "You were afraid of what I make you feel."

Truth.

She met his gaze. "Of course I was." Her honesty took them both by surprise, but it was time to be honest, was it not? "I was on my own. I had to fight for myself. For Caroline." She paused. "*Am* on my own. *Must* fight for her. I must use every weapon in my arsenal to secure her future. That meant Chase . . . which was easy. And you . . ." She hesitated. "But that is the bit that became more difficult."

"You disinvited me to the club," he said.

"I apologize. You are welcome to be a member again." *For as long as the club exists.*

"I don't care about the damn club. I care about you sending me away."

"I couldn't have you close," she said, setting the truth free. "I couldn't have you near without wishing you near forever."

That word again, insidious and tempting.

He swore, and pulled her close, wrapping his arms around her like steel, making her wish that this was all there was. That there was no Chase, no Anna, no Tremley beating down the door with his deadlines and his secrets. No Fallen Angel.

Because she did not wish to use him. Not anymore. She did not wish for him to be anywhere near the falseness that was her future. Did not wish for him to have any more reasons to think ill of her.

He misunderstood. "Christ . . . Georgiana," he spoke to the top of her head, his arms around her like steel, strong and welcome. "The paper. The reward."

She turned her face into his chest, reveling in the scent of him. "Chase is done for."

He had been since the moment Tremley had made his offer—her secrets for Duncan's. It was an offer she would never refuse. A trade she would gladly make. Chase and Anna would disappear from the world, and they would be replaced by Duncan's safety.

If only it would be enough.

He swore softly. "I did it. I ruined him." He paused. "You. I ruined all you worked for."

She would have ruined it herself—still planned to—but that was the final secret she could not reveal to him. Instead, she smiled. "He had to be done, eventually. I could not continue here and preach propriety for Caroline. I thought I could . . . but now, I see the ridiculousness in that plan."

"I will find a way to keep you safe. To keep Chase safe. I'll rescind the reward."

She put her hands to his lips, silencing him, running her fingers over his cheekbones, down the long line of his jaw. "All this time . . . from the beginning, you have told me to trust you."

"I have," he said. "And now, you must believe that I will find a way—"

She stopped him. "It's your turn, Duncan. It's time for you to trust me."

His gaze narrowed. "What does that mean?"

She leaned up to kiss him. "Exactly what I say."

"I do trust you." He took the kiss, returned it. "What are you planning?"

"That's not trusting me."

He started to reply. Stopped. "I don't want to do this anymore. I don't want to talk." He lifted her in his arms, her legs wrapping about his waist. "I just want to love you. All of you. Once, before it's over."

Before it's over.

The words crashed around her as she took his face in her hands, and returned the kiss he settled on her lips, deep and longing. She didn't like the finality in them. The sense that everything important was ending tonight.

Not sense. Truth.

Tonight would end the myth of Chase. It would end the fabrication of Anna.

And it would leave Georgiana alone once more, to face Society and its wolves.

To create a new future.

But she did not want the future. She wanted the present. This moment.

This man.

"I wish . . ." his words were low and dark in her ear, and she met his gaze.

"What?" She moved against him, rocked into him sending pleasure through her and, she hoped, through him.

It worked. He smiled, his eyes closing. "It sounds mad, but I wish we'd done this in a bed. Like ordinary people."

"There is a bed."

He tilted his head, looking pleased as punch. "There is?"

She nodded. "There is."

He set her on her feet and she guided him into her apartments through several doors and into the room where she slept most evenings. He paused in the doorway, looking at the bed, upholstered and curtained in white. He shook his head. "All this time, London has wagered and sinned and bathed themselves in vice . . . and you have reigned from this white bed—fit for a pristine princess."

She smiled. "Pristine no more."

He turned his hot gaze on her. "No more."

And then she was in his arms, and he was lifting her, carrying her, setting loose an ache deep in her. She—who'd spent the last six years giving the men and women of London everything they desired, who considered herself an expert in want—she'd never wanted anything more than this man.

Than this moment.

He stood her next to the bed and slowly undressed them both, boots and breeches and shirts, shucking his own and then hers, kissing the bare skin he revealed in long, lingering licks until she thought she might die from the pleasure of him.

Until she thought she might from her desire for him.

He laid her down, naked, back against the cool sheets, and climbed over her, pressing his face to the soft skin of her belly, breathing deep, pressing his open mouth to the swell there, to the faded marks that told the tale that he alone knew.

"I love you," he whispered, soft and privately, to the skin there, so easy that she thought perhaps he hadn't said the words at all.

She gasped as his mouth moved, finding the tip of one breast, and then the other, his hands cupping her, lifting, caressing, ensuring that she would never forget this moment, the way he touched her. The way he loved her. She held him, fingers in his soft golden hair as he whispered to the skin between her breasts, "I love you."

He repeated the words like a benediction as he licked and sucked and worshipped until her breath was coming in short, nearly unbearable pants, and he lifted himself over her, covering her with his body, hard and warm and perfect in every way.

He looked into her eyes. Spoke. "I love you."

And she loved him back, desperately, reaching up, pulling him down for another kiss, into which she poured everything she had ever felt for this brilliant, magnificent man.

He slid into her slow and true, as though they had done this a thousand times, as though they belonged to each other, as though he owned her and she owned him. And he did own her, she realized. He always would.

His movements were deep and thorough, long, lush strokes that had her craning for him. For more of his touch. For more of his love. He seemed to know it, leaning down, repeating his vow again and again at her ear. She did not know if it was the words or the movement, but soon she was begging for release that only he could provide. He stilled, rising up over her, eyes closed in pleasure and pain and she knew he steeled himself to leave her, refusing to release inside her. Refusing to risk her.

"Duncan." He opened his eyes, stealing her breath with the emotion in them. "Don't leave me," she whispered. "Not this time."

He watched her for a long moment, as if searching for the truth in her words. She shook her head. "Not this time," she said, tears welling as she was struck by the keen knowledge that this was the last time they would ever do this.

He took her mouth in a scorching kiss, deeper and more passionate than anything they had shared before, and he reached between them, setting his thumb to her, stroking over and over until she was crying out her release. Only then did he move, thrusting deep, spilling inside her, and she was lost to herself, to the world.

He came down over her and she wrapped herself around him, cradling him as the tears spilled over, and she wept. She wept for the beauty of this moment, the two of them against the world, she wept for herself, for the sacrifice that had set her on this path . . . the one she had vowed to make, somehow infinitely more devastating now that she understood what it was she gave up.

Love.

When he woke, she was gone.

He should have expected it, but it still rankled, the fact that she had left him here, in the heart of her casino, as she went to fight God knew what battle on her own.

I was on my own. I had to fight for myself. For Caroline.

No longer.

Did she not understand that he was her champion? That he would fight her battles? That he would do anything he could to save her and this place she loved?

He might not be able to have her forever, but he could give her this.

And it would be enough.

Christ. He had to rescind the reward. The Pandora's box he had opened would ruin her and the club if he did not close it. He stood, pulling on his clothes quickly, wasting no time in returning to the main room of the offices.

It was empty now, and he approached the desk in awe and

admiration. He thought of the first time she stood in this room, a girl of, what, twenty? Taken down by Society for a moment of risk. For a single mistake.

And she'd built an empire from here. From behind this desk.

And he'd thought he was the hardest-working man in London.

His fingers grazed the blotter, the silver pen that lay there, haphazardly, as though she'd dropped it in a rush to finish some other work. He smiled at the idea—his industrious love.

They made a perfect match.

He ignored the thread of sadness that coursed through him at the thought. At the way he ached for it to be true. For it to be their future. But his secrets were legion, and he would never saddle her with them. With the threat of his discovery. Of his punishment.

Of scandal, once more.

He looked away, his gaze falling to a small stack of letters on the edge of the desk—there were maybe ten there, a final, forgotten stack of what had been dozens of identical squares covering the surface of the desk when he'd entered the room.

He lifted the messages, knowing he shouldn't. Knowing it was not his business, but somehow unable to stop himself. Each one was addressed in the strong, black hand that he had come to know as Chase's.

Not Chase's. Georgiana's.

The letters were made out to members of the club—men he'd seen on the floor dozens of times. There was nothing about the names that linked them—some old, some young, some wealthy, some less so, a duke, two barons, three men in trade.

He lifted one addressed to Baron Pottle.

He slid a finger beneath the seal and opened the note—dread pooling deep within him—to reveal one line.

Tonight, the Angel falls.

Chapter 21

$\mathcal{H}$e'd never seen the floor of the Angel so full of people.

Of course, he'd never seen the floor of the Angel on a day such as this. All of London had turned up for what they were claiming would be the last night of The Fallen Angel. The rumors and gossip swirled as hundreds of members arrived, brandishing the same square note, penned in Georgiana's hand.

"What does it mean?" a young man whispered to his cronies, collected around a faro table.

"I don't know," came the reply. "But what I do know is that a night like this at the Angel is better than twenty in ballrooms across Britain."

That much was true. The room fairly teemed with members, a wide, rippling mass of black coats and deep voices, peppered with several dozen women wearing brightly colored silks—the ladies of The Fallen Angel had been allowed onto the floor tonight, masked and myriad.

What was she planning?

He'd been looking for Georgiana since he'd arrived, having lost her and all the owners of the casino earlier in the day. When he had left her rooms and headed to the floor of the hell, the place had been quiet—if one did not consider the banging on the doors, the shouting, and the near riot in the street.

He'd thought to destroy Chase and set Georgiana free.

And, instead, he'd destroyed all that she'd worked for.

"Good play with the reward, West." A man Duncan did not recognize approached from a nearby table, clapping a hand on his shoulder. "It's time we scare the bastard out of his hole—after all, he's been fleecing us for years! I'm surprised they're still letting you in!"

Another approached. "But you are willing to put five thousand quid on it? You'll get hundreds of people tossing false names at you."

He already had them—speculation had begun arriving at his offices, theories based on everyone from His Royal Highness to the son of a Temple Bar fishmonger. "I shall know the truth when I see it," he said, disengaging from the conversation.

Of course, he had not known the truth when he'd seen it. In the hours since her revelation, he'd found a dozen ways he should have known that she was more than she seemed. That she was stronger, smarter, more powerful than the men who gamed at these tables each night.

But he had misjudged her, just as the rest of London had.

At the far end of the room, he saw Viscount Langley at a hazard table, throwing the dice with gusto. If the cheers that rose around him were to be believed, Langley was on a roll. He was moving before he had time to think better of it.

Making his way across the floor toward the viscount, Duncan thought back to that first night, on the balcony with Georgiana, when she'd named Langley her choice of suitor.

He remained a good choice.

Unmarked. Noble. He would care for her.

Or West would make certain he suffered abominably.

Langley tossed the dice. Won again. Frustration settled heavy in Duncan's chest. Why did this man win, where Duncan would no doubt lose?

He watched the viscount for long minutes, until he lost, and the dice were relinquished to a croupier. Duncan resisted the pleasure that came at the groans. "Langley," he said, and the viscount turned toward him, curiosity made even greater by the fact that they'd never spoken.

He pulled the viscount aside. "My lord, I am Duncan West."

Langley nodded. "I recognize you. I confess, I am rather a supporter—you have won my vote for a number of bills that we'll be looking at this season."

Duncan was set back by the compliment. "Thank you." He'd support the marriage, but did he have to like the man?

He took a breath, released it, and the viscount tilted his head, leaning in, "Sir, are you unwell?"

Yes.

He would be unwell forever once she became the Viscountess Langley, but he had promised her this moment. This win.

Tit for tat.

"You are courting Lady Georgiana," he said.

Surprised, Langley looked away and then back, and West saw the guilt in his eyes. He did not like the pause—the meaning in it, as though Langley was not, in fact, courting Georgiana.

Except he did like it.

He liked it a great deal.

"Are you not?"

Langley hesitated. "Is this for publication? I have seen how keen your newspapers have been for Lady Georgiana's return to Society."

"It is not for publication, but I hope my newspapers have made a positive impression."

The viscount smiled. "My mother is certainly invested in the lady."

Success, he supposed.

"I imagine some would call my interactions with the lady courtship," Langley replied, finally, and Duncan heard the edge of doubt in the words.

Duncan wanted to roar his disapproval. Did the man not see what he had been offered? "Are you mad? She is a tre-

mendous catch. Beyond measure. Any man would be proud
to call her his. She could have a king if she wished it."

What had begun as surprise on Langley's face was soon
transformed into careful curiosity, making Duncan feel like
a proper ass when he was finished.

The viscount did not hesitate in his reply, keen understanding in his tone. "It strikes me that it is not a king who wishes
for her. Quite the opposite."

Duncan's gaze narrowed at the suggestion. At the truth in
it. "You overstep yourself."

"Likely, but I know what it is to want something you cannot
have. I see now why you have taken such a keen interest in
the lady." Langley paused and said, "If I could trade my title
for your freedom, I would."

Duncan was suddenly deeply uncomfortable with the conversation. "That is where you are wrong. There is no freedom
in being untitled. Indeed, if anything, there is less of it."

The title brought security. Safety.

He, instead, lived in constant fear of discovery.

And that fear would ever shadow his future.

He met the viscount's gaze. "You are her choice."

Langley smiled. "If that is true—and I am not certain it
is—I would be honored to have the lady to wife."

"And you will care for her."

One of the viscount's brows rose. "If you do not, yes."

The insolence from the titled pup made Duncan want to
upend the hazard table from whence he'd come. He could
not care for her. He would not saddle her with his life. With
his secrets.

And she did not wish them.

What if we married?

For however long he lived, he would remember that question, spoken softly in his arms—the little possibility that
came on a silly dream. When he breathed his last, in prison
or at the end of a rope, that question would be his last thought.

It did not matter that she hadn't meant it. Not the way he
wished.

She wished the title. She wished safety and comfort and propriety for her daughter. And he knew better than any how important those were. How much she would give up for them.

And he would give them to her.

The viscount punctuated the thought. "You should be the one to care for her."

"I will be," he said. "This is how I will do it."

Langley considered him for a long moment before nodding once. "Then if she will have me, I will have her."

Duncan hated the way the words rioted through him, the visceral fury that came with them. The way he wanted to rail against God and the world that this was his fate—to love a woman he could not have.

But instead of that, he said, "If there is ever anything I can do for you, my lord, my papers are at your disposal."

Langley rocked back on his heels. "I may come and see you sooner than you think."

The viscount turned away, and Duncan was left alone at the edge of the casino floor, watching the crowds, waiting for her.

"I see your membership has been reinstated," the Marquess of Bourne said at his elbow. "So you can see the fruits of your very idiotic labor?"

Duncan winced at the words, but did not resist them. He'd put a price on Chase's head, and by extension, on this place and all her owners. Instead, he asked, "What is she planning?"

"All I know is that she's about to make a damn mistake. But no one tells Chase how to live."

"What mistake?" Duncan asked, not taking his gaze from the crowd. Desperate to find her. To stop her from doing whatever it was she was going to do. He'd made the mess of posting a reward for Chase's identity—it should be he who cleared it up.

"She wouldn't tell us anything else. Only that it was her decision to make—which is debatable at best—and some idiocy about us all having families now, and plenty of money, and the club having run its course."

Dread pooled deep within. "She's giving up the club?" *But why?*

"In Chase's fashion, she's thought it all through," Bourne said, exasperation in his tone, as though this were the whim of a silly girl and not the destruction of years of her work and dreams.

Duncan swore roundly.

"I couldn't agree more."

He couldn't allow it. He could save her in another way. He searched for her again. "Where is she?"

"Knowing Chase, she's going to make an entrance." Bourne paused. "It goes without saying that if she is hurt in any way . . . if Caroline is marked in any way by this night . . ."

Duncan met the marquess's eyes. "I would expect repercussions."

"Repercussions," Bourne scoffed. "We will disappear you, and you will never be found."

"I assume you were sent with precisely that message?"

"That, and one other," Bourne said. "You should not let her go."

His went cold at the words, then hot. "I don't follow."

Bourne smirked, but did not take his gaze from the crowds. "You're the smartest man I know, West. You follow perfectly well."

You should not let her go.

As if he had a choice.

The crowd grew more and more raucous—drink flowed freely throughout the casino, and every table on the floor was filled with gamers basking in the glow of chance. The place was alive with sound, the calls of the croupiers, the cheers of the audience at hazard, the groans of those at roulette. He imagined he could hear the rasp of the cards at *vingt-et-un* as they slid over the baize, each sound more lush and magnificent than it had ever been—because he now knew it was her doing . . . her creation.

"I will say this for her, though," Bourne said, watching the floor, considering the sheer number of gamers before them.

"If we close our doors for good tonight, it will be with a bigger take than we've ever had."

"I have to stop her."

Bourne raised a brow. "I confess, I had hoped you would consider doing so. I've a family to feed."

The Marquess of Bourne had enough money and land to feed all the families in Britain, but Duncan had other things to do than joust with the man. "Where would she be?"

Bourne looked up, to the stained glass, where Lucifer tumbled to the casino floor. "If I had to guess . . ."

Duncan was on his way, pushing through the crowds, weaving between tables, headed for the heavily guarded door at the far end of the room. He was nearly there when he heard his name, behind him, in a voice that at The Fallen Angel was equally familiar and foreign.

After all, the Earl of Tremley was not a member.

Duncan said as much, and Tremley smiled, coming closer. "I was invited tonight. By your Anna. I was told she was pretty, but once one meets her—she is—glorious."

The words sent fury through Duncan, who could not bear the thought of Georgiana and Tremley breathing the same air, let alone being in the same room. "What have you done?"

"Nothing that you didn't do yourself," Lord Tremley sneered. "Indeed, you painted with a rather broad brush— five thousand pounds for Chase's identity? You think he will simply lay back and let the hordes come to find him? I got it done."

He froze. "Got what done?"

"Your girl. We made a trade. It was really quite sweet."

No.

Duncan knew what was to come before Tremley revealed it. "She did it for you, the poor creature. Thinking that if she revealed Chase's secrets, she would save you." He looked to West. "We both know that's not true."

She was doing it to save him.

She'd said as much, hadn't she?

Tremley had given her a choice: her club or him.

I choose you.

She'd made the choice without hesitation.

It is time for you to trust me.

He could not let her ruin her life. Could not let her give up this world that she had worked so hard to build. Something danced at the edge of his thoughts—something that did not sit well. Her plan—if it was to be a public reveal—would not help Tremley. If the whole world had Chase's identity, Tremley was still beholden to the Angel, which held his secrets.

But now, he knew how to make Georgiana dance.

And Tremley would do it. Forever. He would hold Georgiana and this place in his sway with the same simple threat he'd held over Duncan for a lifetime.

And Duncan had had enough.

He'd spent years waiting for Tremley to report his crimes, to send him to prison, to string him up. He'd spent years amassing fortune and favor to ensure that, should it ever happen, someone somewhere would care for Cynthia. He'd groveled and scraped and done Tremley's bidding.

But he was done.

He opened his mouth to tell the earl just that when a cacophony of shouts came from across the room, where Georgiana stood, dressed head to toe in scarlet, atop a hazard field. Behind her, Lucifer fell.

She was going to do it.

"Gentlemen! Gentlemen!" she called out, moving her arms to indicate that they should settle. "And ladies." She looked to a small band of masked women at the edge of the room.

A man on the floor by the table reached for her slipper. West was already in motion, heading to destroy the vermin, when she stepped on the blackguard's wrist, eliciting a sharp cry. "Oh," she said, all smiles. "Do excuse me, Lord Densmore. I did not know your hand was so near to my foot."

He stopped, a roomful of masculine laughter crashing around him as she continued, "We are all so happy that you have joined us for what will be a supremely edifying evening."

Shit.

She was going to do it.

He was moving toward her, but the crowd was thick and would not budge. This was, after all, the strange occurrence for which they'd been waiting.

"As you know, our dear friend Duncan West has put out a reward for Chase's identity . . ."

West froze as her words were met with a chorus of boos and hisses and hear-hears. Several men nearby clapped him on the back. "She's after you, West," one man whispered.

"And we have no doubt that very soon, one of you enterprising gentlemen will discover the truth about the founder of the Angel." She paused. "Five thousand pounds is, after all, a great deal of money to a motley group that loses blunt so well."

More laughter, but Duncan ignored it, desperate to get to her. To stop her, however he could.

"But we believe in fairness here! Or, at least, we believe that money should be flowing into our pockets, instead of out! And so it is time for a confession . . ." She paused for dramatic effect, and he realized he would not reach her in time.

She spread her arms wide. "I am Chase!"

It hadn't occurred to him that they wouldn't believe her, but as the laughter that came with the pronouncement rippled over them, he realized how he could save her, and the club, and how he could set them all free.

How many times had she told him?

People believe what they wish to believe.

And not one of the men in attendance wanted to believe that Chase was a woman.

He took to the nearest faro table, pulling himself up, standing to face her. "I shan't pay until you provide proof, Anna," he said, injecting his tone with relaxed teasing. He looked out across the room. "Would anyone else like to make an announcement? I'll repeat myself, here in this glorious place Chase built. Five thousand pounds for his identity. I'll pay this very night."

He stopped, and prayed that one of her business partners was smart enough to see what he was doing.

Cross stood first, climbing high on a roulette table. "I don't suppose you'll believe that I am Chase, will you, West?"

Duncan shook his head. "I will not."

"Nor I?" Temple was on a *vingt-et-un* table at the other end of the room. He reached down and pulled his wife up onto the table with him. "Perhaps the duchess?"

Her Grace called out, "I am Chase!"

And the room laughed.

One by one, men and women beholden to Georgiana claimed Chase for themselves from around the room. The club's security detail, the pit boss, Bourne, croupiers, the women who worked the floor of the Angel. Two footmen. The club's French chef somehow heard the commotion, came in from the kitchen, climbed up on a roulette table and proclaimed herself, "La Chasse."

And then others got in on the fun—men who had never met her, never come close to her. They simply wanted the laugh that came when someone proclaimed, "I am Chase."

Each time it was offered to the room—a bold, firm "I am Chase"—the gamers on the floor laughed, and Chase became myth. Legend.

For certainly there was no single Chase, not if all these people admitted to being the man behind the stained glass window, watching from his domain high above their world.

Duncan looked to Georgiana, standing, incredulous, on her table, watching her world stand for her. Without hesitation.

She met his gaze, and he saw the tears glistening in those eyes. He wanted to climb over the tables to get to her, to tell her how much she was loved. To tell her how remarkable she was.

"No!" The Earl of Tremley howled from his place on the floor of the casino, and Duncan turned to find the man clamoring to get to him. "It's not true!" Tremley cried, high-pitched and nasal as he climbed up onto another table, facing him. "You only play at this game with your whore to keep your own history secret!"

Silence fell at the anger in the earl's tone.

Duncan's heart began to pound as Tremley turned to the

room. "Ask yourselves, who is this man who runs your newspapers? Where did he come from? How did he rise?"

Duncan looked to Georgiana, taking in her wide, frightened gaze, knowing that this was the end—that Tremley would reveal everything, and with that, he would lose everything.

And strangely, as he waited for the axe to fall, the only thing he cared was that Georgiana was safe.

Tremley asked one final question. "What is his name?"

There was silence as Tremley's words echoed through the room.

Duncan was holding Georgiana's gaze, ready for what came next, so he saw it when she replied, her red lips curving into a bold smile that did not reach her eyes.

Her eyes were too full of fear.

"Don't tell us his name is Chase, my lord."

And with that single, well-placed sentence, she set the casino to laughing, his beautiful, brilliant love. She saved him. Just as he had saved her, in front of the wide world, where none but the two of them could see it.

At the laughter, Tremley went mad, reaching into his coat to remove a pistol, turning it on West. "I am through with you."

The laughter in the casino died the moment Tremley extracted his pistol, quickly replaced by shock.

Georgiana could think only of Duncan.

She had not just saved him in one way to lose him in another. She looked across the room at Bourne and Temple, both of whom were headed for the place where Tremley stood, but they were too far and the club was too full. They'd never get to him in time.

Duncan raised his hands into the air. "My lord," he said. "You do not want to do this."

Tremley laughed, "There are few things in the world I

want to do more than this. How dare you think you can use my sins against me? Does it not occur to you who I am?"

"I know who you are," Duncan said. "Many people do. Everyone here. And if you kill me, they will know it."

"But they won't care."

"I think they will," she announced, impressed that she was able to keep the fear from her tone. Terrified that he would shoot.

Terrified that she would lose Duncan before she had a chance to tell him how much she loved him. Terrified of life without him.

Tremley turned the weapon on her, and she'd never in her life been more grateful than when Duncan was no longer in harm's way. "They certainly won't care if I kill *you*."

"No!" Duncan's shout came loud and clear and full of fury, and from the corner of her eye, Georgiana saw him running for the earl, leaping from table to table.

Georgiana focused on the pistol, wondering if Tremley had the courage to pull the trigger. Wondering who would care for Caroline if she were killed.

Wondering who would love Duncan if she were killed.

Wishing she'd had the courage to tell him she loved him. Just once.

"Tell me, my lord," a strong, clear voice rang out next to Georgiana, and she turned to see a masked woman, standing on a table behind Duncan. "Who will care if *I* kill *you*, you treasonous bastard?"

It was Lady Tremley.

Georgiana placed the voice a split-second before Duncan leapt to tackle Tremley to the ground, and a gunshot sounded in the massive room.

Tremley and Duncan fell from the tables, and Georgiana was instantly in motion, heading for them, her heart in her throat, before they hit the ground.

The crowd went wild, screaming and scattering, nearly trampling each other in their rush to get away from the weapon and the scene of the murder. Georgiana couldn't find

Duncan—between the smoke from the pistol's report, and the crush of people, she could not see him..

She flew over the tables, staying on high ground, leaping from roulette to faro to *vingt-et-un* to hazard, crossing the casino floor to where he had been moments earlier.

Praying that he was safe.

When she found him, he was on the floor, on his back, eyes closed. She leapt down beside him, crying his name. "No . . ." she whispered, putting her hands to his chest, unbuttoning his coat. "No no no no." The word became her chant as she slid her hands into his jacket, throwing the lapels back, searching his chest for blood or a wound. Or anything.

He captured her hand in his. "Stop."

Her breath caught. "You're alive."

He opened his eyes. "I am."

She burst into tears.

"Oh, love," he said, sitting up and pulling her into his arms. "No. Don't cry." He pressed a kiss to her temple. "Christ," he whispered to the hair there. "You were magnificent. You saved me, you gorgeous, perfect girl."

"I thought you were dead," she said.

He shook his head. "I am not." He looked past her, finding Tremley's motionless body on the floor nearby. "The lady is an excellent shot."

Tremley was dead.

Duncan straightened his coat, feeling in his pockets for brief moments before he turned back around to look at the floor.

"What is it?" she asked.

He leaned over, lifted something from the carpet nearby. "In your desperation to touch me, you nearly lost my most prized possession." He straightened, brandishing a feather.

Her feather.

Plucked from her coif on the first night they'd met as Georgiana and West, at the Worthington Ball.

The tears came again as she watched him slip the feather into his coat pocket, against his heart. He reached for her, brushing the tears from her cheeks. "Don't cry, darling. I am well. Sound. Here."

But for how long?

"I thought he was going to kill you," she said, hating the way the words shook from her, the way her body had gone cold and shaking in the wake of his near loss. "I thought I would lose you."

"He didn't kill me," he promised. "And you'll never lose me. You've ruined me for all others. Forever."

She loved him. She should tell him so.

But he was pointing to Lady Tremley. "*She* did kill *him*, however. Perhaps we ought to do something to keep her from the end of a rope?"

Yes. That was something she could do.

Anna stood, and the entire room went silent, every person assembled stunned by the events of the evening—none more so than Lady Tremley, who seemed thoroughly shocked by the fact that she'd murdered her husband.

And it was murder; Lord Tremley grew cold even as the owners of The Fallen Angel looked to each other. Something had to be done, for if there was ever a man who deserved killing—this was he.

Georgiana surveyed the room in the silence, finally deciding to take control, returning to the tabletop, taking her spot on the roulette field. "I shouldn't have to remind any of you that every one of you has a secret kept in our confidence."

Temple understood immediately what she was saying, pulling himself back up to stand on a table. "If a breath of what happened here tonight—"

Bourne rose, too. "Not that anything has happened here tonight—"

"Nothing besides obvious self-defense," Georgiana said.

"And, of course, saving two perfectly innocent people from their own demise," Duncan pointed out, joining her.

Cross spoke from his place on the floor. "But if something had happened, and information left this room, every one of your secrets—"

"To a man," Georgiana said.

Duncan climbed up beside her. "—will be printed in my papers."

There was a beat as the words sank in around the room, silence fell as the membership of The Fallen Angel remembered why they came to this place, where their dues were paid in secrets.

For the tables.

The gaming began almost immediately.

Georgiana and Duncan climbed down from their perches, easing to the side of the room, where he stopped and smiled down at her, and she, up at him.

Tremley was dead. And Duncan was alive.

Alive and free. No more fear for his future.

The threats had perished with the man who delivered them.

He leaned down to whisper in her ear. "We are a tremendous team, love."

It was the truth.

They were a perfect match.

She took a deep breath, terror still shaking the air in her lungs. "I thought he would kill you," she repeated. "And I would not have had the chance to tell you that—"

Something flashed in his gaze. Something like pleasure, chased quickly away by regret. By loss. "Don't," he whispered, pressing his lips to her temple. "Don't tell me you love me. I'm not sure if I will be able to bear it when you leave."

When she left.

It would come, and all that had happened today to Anna and Chase . . . it would not affect Georgiana. Tomorrow, she would still require propriety.

Tomorrow, she would still need to think of Caroline.

The title. The respectability. Chase and Anna and West had been saved . . . but Georgiana was still a scandal.

She ignored the ache in her chest that came with the knowledge that he was right. That none of it mattered.

Tonight, everything had changed. And somehow, nothing had.

Chapter 22

Two mornings later, Georgiana awoke in her bed at her brother's home, to the smell of flowers and the face of her daughter.

And to a deep, abiding sadness, which had come the moment Duncan West had left The Fallen Angel two evenings prior, and hadn't left.

Didn't show signs of leaving.

"Something has happened," Caroline said from the side of the bed. "And I think you ought to know about it."

A thousand things had happened. Her club had been saved. Her identity had been protected along with her secrets. A traitor had been killed, his wife saved—already on her way to Yorkshire, to make a new life for herself.

And Georgiana had learned to love, before she'd had no choice but to turn her back on it.

But she did not think Caroline meant any of those things.

Georgiana sat up in her bed, moving to make room for Caroline, who refused to climb in, which was rare. "What has happened?" She reached out to touch the pink rose haphazardly placed in her daughter's hair. "Where did that come from?"

Caroline's green eyes were wide with excitement as she touched the rosebud as well. "You've flowers. A great deal of them." She lifted Georgiana's hand. "Come. You must see."

Georgiana dressed for expedience rather than impression, pulling on her most comfortable breeches, a half corset, and a fine linen shirt before Caroline led her downstairs to the dining room, where a dozen bouquets waited for her.

Two dozen. More.

Roses and peonies and tulips and hyacinth—arrangements in a tremendous variety of sizes and shapes and colors. Her breath caught, and for a moment, she thought they might be from Duncan.

But then her gaze settled on the white roses, arranged in the shape of a horse. She raised her brow. "Did something else happen?"

Caroline smiled, looking very much like the cat that got the cream. "There is another cartoon." She lifted the paper from beside Georgiana's breakfast plate. "It's a good one, this time."

Dread coursed through Georgiana. She doubted very much any cartoon was "a good one."

She was wrong.

There, on the front page of the *News of London*, was a cartoon at once familiar and thoroughly unfamiliar. A woman sat high atop a horse, dressed in beautiful attire, a dress worthy of a queen, her long hair streaming out behind her. Riding a half length behind, a smiling girl, dressed in her own finery, sat on her own steed.

But where the last cartoon had featured Georgiana and Caroline suffering the disdain of family and peers, this one was different. In this picture, they were surrounded by men and women on their knees, paying fealty, as though they were queens themselves.

The caption read: "The Fine Ladies on their White Horses: Winning the Hearts of London."

Most of those presented as subjects were men, some in uniform, some in formal wear. Georgiana's attention fell to one of the men in the foreground. If she did not recognize him from his straight nose and his blond hair, she would have recognized him by the feather that protruded from his coat pocket.

The feather he'd plucked from her hair.

The feather he'd rescued after he was nearly killed at The Fallen Angel.

It was a very good cartoon.

"I think it's us," Caroline said, pride and pleasure in her young voice.

"I think you are right."

"Though I am not certain why I'm carrying a cat."

Tears threatened as Georgiana thought back on the day they'd walked in Hyde Park. The day she'd told Duncan that she wanted Caroline to have a normal life. "Because girls have cats."

Caroline blinked. "All right. Well, I also think this is why the horse with white roses arrived. Though it does seem to be a little much."

Georgiana chuckled, tears welling. "I think you might be right." She seemed unable to keep the wretched things from spilling over.

"It's a beautiful cartoon, don't you think?" Caroline looked to her. Noticed. "Mother?"

Georgiana brushed the tears from her cheeks, trying to laugh them away. "It's silly," she said, taking a deep breath. "But it's very kind of Mr. West."

Caroline's gaze narrowed thoughtfully. "You think it came from Mr. West?"

She knew it. But instead she said, "It is his newspaper." Georgiana looked down at her daughter, whose rose was toppling out of her hair. She leaned down and pressed a kiss to the top of her head, reminding herself that this was what she lived for. This girl. Her future. "Shall we see who sent them?"

Caroline collected all the messages that had come with the cards as Georgiana ran her fingers over the cartoon once more, tracing the edge of Duncan's shoulder, the line of his sleeve. He'd put himself into the cartoon.

Even as he gave her up, as he gave her everything she'd thought she wanted from the beginning, he honored her with his love.

Except, now, she did not want any of this.

Caroline returned with the messages, and they began to sift through the cards, each sender more eligible than the last. War heroes. Aristocrats. Gentlemen.

Not one of them a newspaperman.

She grew more and more frantic as she got closer to the end of the pile, hoping that one of the bouquets was from him. Hoping that he had not forsaken her. Knowing that he had.

Do not tell me you love me. I am not sure I could bear it when you leave.

She should have told him. From the beginning. From the first moment that she loved him. She should have told him the truth. That she loved him. That if she could choose her life, her future, her world . . . it would be with him in it.

There was a knock at the door to the room, and her brother's butler entered. "My lady?" The words came with slight censure as they always did. Her brother's starchy butler did not care for her choice of trousers over skirts when she was at home. But truthfully, no one ever came to see her.

She turned toward the man, hope flaring. Perhaps there was another message from him? "Yes?"

"You have a visitor."

He had come.

She was up and out of the room, desperate for him, sailing into the foyer to meet the man who stood there, hat in hand, waiting. She stopped.

It was not Duncan.

Viscount Langley turned to face her, surprise in his eyes.

"Oh," she said.

"Indeed," he said, all affability.

The butler cleared his throat. "Traditionally, one waits for the guest to be seen to a receiving room."

She looked to the servant. "I shall receive the viscount here."

The butler was disgruntled, but left silently. She returned her attention to Langley. "My lord," she said, dropping a little curtsy.

He watched, fascinated. "You know," he said, "I've never seen a woman curtsy in trousers. It looks somewhat ridiculous."

She ran her palms over her thighs, and offered him a little smile. "They are more comfortable. I was not expecting . . ."

"If I may suggest." He raised the newspaper in his hand. "You should expect. You are the talk of the *ton*. I imagine I am the first of many callers."

She met his eyes. "I am not certain I wish to be anything to the *ton*."

"You are too late. We have, of course, claimed you for our own after two weeks of utter adoration in our news."

She paused. Then, "Huzzah? I suppose?"

"Huzzah indeed." He laughed. "We have never stood on ceremony."

She shook her head. "No, my lord."

He smiled. Leaned in. "Then, as that is true and you are wearing breeches, I think we can dispense with the formalities."

She smiled. "I would like that."

"I came to ask you to marry me."

Her face fell. She didn't mean it to, but she couldn't help herself. It was, of course, what she had wanted from the beginning. He'd been carefully selected for his perfect balance of need and propriety.

But she suddenly wanted much, much more than those things in a marriage. She wanted partnership and trust and commitment. And love.

And desire.

She wanted Duncan.

"I see that you are not elated," the viscount said.

"It's not that," she said, tears welling again before she could stop them.

She dashed them away. What in hell had happened to her in the last forty-eight hours?

He smiled. "Ah, well, I was told that some women cry at their proposals. But usually that is out of happiness, isn't it?

As I am neither a woman nor an expert in marriage proposals . . ." He trailed off.

She laughed at that, brushing away her tears. "I assure you, my lord, I am not an expert in marriage proposals, either. Which is why we are in this mess to begin with, remember."

They stood in silence for a long moment before he spread his arms to indicate the marble floor. "Shall I get down on one knee, then?"

She shook her head. "Oh, I wish you wouldn't." She paused. "I am sorry. I am making a hash out of this."

"You know, I don't think you are," he said, softly, coming toward her. "I think you simply don't care for mine to be the marriage proposal you receive today."

"That's not true," she lied, imagining him another taller, blonder, more perfect man.

"I think it is. In fact, I think you wish I were another man. Entirely different. Untitled. Brilliant." Her gaze snapped to his. *How did he know?* He rocked back on his heels. "What I cannot understand is why you would settle for me when you could have him."

She knew what to say to that. She *was* making a hash out of it. Indeed. "Marrying you would not be 'settling,' my lord."

He smiled. "Of course it would be. I am not Duncan West."

Lying or feigning ignorance would not do. Not for this man who deserved her respect. "How did you know?"

"We are members of the same club. He came to me. Told me to marry you." She looked away, but could not have stopped listening if she tried. "Lauded me with your qualities. Promised me I would be supremely lucky to have you. And I was convinced. After all, we both know that our marriage would be for convenience. Better marriages have been forged on less." She returned her attention to him. "And then the strangest thing happened."

"What was that?" she said, hanging on his words, wanting desperately to hear them.

"I saw how much you loved him."

Warning flared. "I don't know what you mean."

He smiled. "Do not worry. We all have secrets. And considering who you are when you are not here wearing trousers, you know mine well."

There was a time when she would have used them. When she would have threatened him and manipulated him until she got what she wanted. But Chase was no longer so ruthless. Indeed, now, Georgiana simply ached for him when he added, "And I know the particular sadness of knowing, in your heart, that you will never have what you most desperately want."

The tears came again.

"What do you want, my lady?" he asked.

"It is not important," she replied, the words barely a whisper.

"That is the bit I do not understand," he said. "Why do you deny yourself happiness?"

"It is not explicit," she said, trying to explain. "I do not deny myself. I simply do what must be done to ensure that my daughter is never denied it. To give her the opportunity to have whatever she wants."

Understanding dawned on Langley's perfect face, but before he could reply, someone else did. "Then why not ask me what it is I want?"

Georgiana spun around to face Caroline, standing in the doorway to the dining room, all seriousness. "Go on," her daughter said, "ask me."

She began, "Caroline . . ."

The girl stepped out of the room, toward her. "My whole life, you have made decisions for me."

"Your whole life," Georgiana pointed out, "totals nine years."

Caroline's brow knit. "Nine years and one-quarter," she corrected before going on. "You sent me to live in Yorkshire, brought me to live here, in London. You have hired the best governesses, saddled me with chaperones." She paused. "You've bought me fine clothes and even finer books. But you have never once asked me what I would like."

Georgiana nodded, remembering her own youth, always

coddled, given everything she could ever want, but never a choice. And so, when she'd finally had a choice, she'd leapt into it without thinking. "What would you like?"

"Well," the girl said, coming closer. "As I would like to marry for love when I am old enough for it, I should like you to do the same." She turned to Langley. "No offense, my lord, I am certain that you are quite nice."

He inclined his head with a smile. "None taken."

Caroline returned her attention to Georgiana. "My whole life, you have shown me that we cannot let Society dictate our lives. That we cannot allow others to set us on our path. You chose a different path for us. You brought us here, despite knowing that it would be a challenge. That they would laugh at us. That they would reject us."

She shook her head. "What am I to think if you marry someone whom you do not love? For a title and propriety that I may not want? I am surrounded by women who have carved their own path, and you think it is a good idea to put me on this one?"

Georgiana spoke then. "I think this is the easy path, love. I want it to be easy for you."

Caroline rolled her eyes. "Forgive me, Mother, but doesn't that sound terribly boring?"

Langley laughed at that, apologizing when they looked to him. "I am sorry," he said, "but she is right. It does sound terribly boring."

God knew it did.

And yet, "But if you fall in love—if you want an aristocrat—you will want the respectability that comes with a title."

"And if I fall in love with an aristocrat, will he not give me the title I require?" It was an excellent point, made in perfect simplicity by a nine-year-old girl.

Georgiana met her daughter's serious green gaze. "Where did you come from?"

Caroline smiled. "From you." She lifted the stack of cards that had come with the morning's flowers. "Do you want to marry any of these men?"

Georgiana shook her head. "I do not."

Caroline nodded in Langley's direction. "Do you want to marry him? Apologies, my lord."

He waved the words away. "I am quite enjoying myself." He turned to Georgiana. "*Do* you wish to marry me?"

Georgiana laughed. "I do not. I am sorry, my lord."

He shrugged. "I do not take it personally. I do not entirely wish to marry you, either."

"Mother," Caroline asked quietly. "Is there someone you do wish to marry?"

There was, of course. There was a man in a house halfway across London, whom she wished quite desperately to marry. Whom she loved beyond measure.

She thought of the cartoon, of Duncan down on his knees, her feather in his pocket. Her breath caught in her throat. "Yes," she admitted, softly. "I would very much like to marry someone else."

"And will he make you happy?"

Georgiana nodded. "I believe he will. Quite desperately."

Caroline smiled. "Don't you think you should set an example for your daughter, then? And take your happiness?"

Georgiana thought that was a very good idea.

It seemed that nine-year-olds knew quite a bit, after all.

*H*e had swum an ocean in this pool since he'd left her.

Every time he had thought to go to her, to snatch her from her bed and carry her off into the night, to keep her locked up until she realized that her plan was idiocy, to make love to her until she realized that he was the man she should marry and hang propriety and scandal and the damn aristocracy, he went for a swim.

But where there had been deep solace and tremendous pleasure in this place before he had met Georgiana, now there was none. Now, every inch of this pool reminded him of her, standing tall and proud and beautiful in this room. As walked through the room, he saw her standing by the fire; as he touched the edges of the pool to mark his laps, he saw her legs, dangling in the water; as he wrapped himself in a towel and made for his bedchamber, he felt her pretty, soft skin, warm and willing; as he looked up at the sky through the hundreds of panes of glass, he saw her smile.

And everywhere, he felt the loss of her.

He touched the edge of the pool, turned. Swam another length.

For two days, he'd been swimming, hoping to exhaust himself, to put her out of his mind, stopping only to eat and sleep, and barely that, because when he closed his eyes, he saw her. Only her.

Ever her.

Christ.

He had stopped himself from going to her a dozen times, not knowing what he would say. He'd crafted his little speech a hundred times, designed with pretty words to convince her that she was wrong. That he was the right choice, and hang the rest of the world.

And he had regretted his decision a thousand times to stop her from telling her she loved him. He should have let her say the words.

He might have found peace in them.

Might have.

But it was more likely he would have played them over and over until he hated them.

So perhaps it was best.

He cut through the water, his shoulders aching from the movement. Eyes closed, he reached for the wall at the end of his lap, grabbing it from memory as he let himself glide to the end of the swim. It was enough for now, he hoped, throwing his head back, letting water stream down his face and hair one last time before he exited the pool.

He opened his eyes, his gaze landing on a pair of brown boots a foot away. He looked up, his heart knocking in his chest.

Georgiana.

She stared down at him, all seriousness. "May I tell you now?"

"How did you get here?"

"Langley drove me," she said before repeating, "May I tell you now?"

"Tell me what?"

She sank to her knees, then to her hands, bringing herself closer to him. "May I tell you that I love you?"

He reached for her, cupping the back of her neck and pulling her close. "You may not," he said, his heart threatening to beat from his chest. "Not unless you mean to say it every day. Forever."

She smiled. "That will depend upon you."

He looked into her eyes, trying to read her meaning. Trying not to hope that she said what he thought she was saying. "Georgiana . . ." he whispered, loving the way her name curved over his lips and tongue.

"I cannot say it every day if we are apart, you see." Her voice cracked, and he was desperate to hold her. "So if you'll have me—"

"No."

He hoisted himself out of the pool, effectively cutting off her words. She gasped as water sluiced off him, and flooded the tile work at the edge of the pool, dampening her trousers and no doubt ruining her boots.

He was on his knees next to her, turning her to face him. "You are stealing my part." He took her hands in his. "Tell me again."

She met his gaze, and he lost his breath at the truth in her beautiful amber eyes. "I love you."

"Untitled scoundrel that I am?"

"Rake. Rogue. Whatever you like."

"I like you."

She smiled. "I hope that's not all."

"You know it isn't," he whispered, pulling her close. "You know I love you. The first moment I laid eyes on you, you stood in the darkness and defended yourself and those you love, and I have adored you since then. I have wanted to be counted among their ranks."

Her hands were on his cheeks, cupping her face. "I love you."

"Say it again," he said, kissing her deep—long and slow until they were both gasping for breath.

"I can't say it if you are kissing me," she protested.

"Then save it," he said, his lips once again on hers. "Tell me when I am through." He kissed her again and again, the caresses deep and drugging, and every time he lifted his lips from hers, she whispered, "I love you."

Over and over, the words echoed around him, warming him, until he finally, finally pulled away and said, "It's always been you." He put his forehead to hers. "Marry me. Choose me."

"I will," she promised. "I do."

"When?"

"Now. Tomorrow. Next week. Forever."

He stood then, lifting her high in his arms. "Forever," he said. "I choose forever."

And forever it was.

Epilogue

One Year Later
The Fallen Angel

Georgiana stood inside the owner's suite of The Fallen Angel, watching the floor far below. The casino teemed with gamers, and her gaze fell to the roulette wheel at the center of the room, spinning in a whirr of red and black. A half-dozen men leaned in as the wheel slowed.

"Red," she whispered.

Red it was, and even better, a man at the table threw up his hands in glee. He had won. And winning at the roulette wheel was a triumph.

Chance was a remarkable thing.

She had built this empire upon it—upon luck and fate, fortune and destiny. She'd learned remarkable lessons about lies and truths, about revenge. About scandal. But she still grew breathless when the roulette wheel spun.

The door to the suite opened, and she knew without looking who had entered, the way the air shifted, the way her breath quickened. Duncan's arms were around her, warm and strong, and he followed her gaze to the floor. "A dozen games on the floor of your hell," he whispered at her ear. "And you always choose roulette. Why?"

"It is the only game that is truly left to the fates," she said. "It is the only game that cannot be calculated. Its reward is risk as much as anything else." She turned in his arms, reaching up to clasp her hands behind his neck. "It is like life—we spin the wheel and . . ."

He kissed her, long and deep, his hands coming to her waist, pulling her tight against him.

When he released her, she sighed. "And sometimes we are well rewarded."

His hands slid to the heavy swell of her stomach, where his child grew. "Sometimes we are," he agreed. "Though I will tell you that I often worry that my luck has been too good— that I am due to run out."

"You have lived enough bad luck for a lifetime. I don't intend for you ever to run out."

He raised a brow. "And you have the power to deliver an edict to the fates?"

She grinned. "On days when you do not have luck, you must rely on something else."

He kissed her again, then turned her to the window once more. They watched for long moments as cards turned and dice flew and men played their games before she stretched, trying to ease the kink in her back. "You promised me you would sleep more," he said, his hands coming to the small of her back, pressing, soothing the ache that seemed to live there now that she neared the end of her term. "You are not supposed to be here."

She looked up at him, surprise on her face. "You cannot imagine that I would miss the game," she said. "It might well be my last. The baby shall be here too soon."

"Not soon enough," he said. "I never allowed myself to wish for children; there were too many ways I could ruin their lives."

"Once he is here, you will wish him gone again," she

teased, turning back to the casino floor. "He shall scream and squawk."

"Once she is here, I will wish her near me all the time," he vowed. "Alongside her mother and her sister."

She smiled. "Your passel of adoring admirers."

"I can think of worse things," he said, wrapping her in his arms and letting her lean into him. His hand slid down her stomach to her thigh, fingers gathering her skirts, pulling them up until she was bare to the knee.

"I have always adored you in trousers, love, but skirts must be the best thing about your pregnancy." His fingers grazed the skin of her thigh, and she parted for him, letting his touch creep higher until he reached the place where she was suddenly ready for him.

"We cannot." She sighed, leaning into him, letting him hold her safe. "They are coming."

He sighed his disappointment. "You could be coming as well, you know."

She laughed as the door to the suite opened again, and he dropped her skirts, pressing a hot kiss to the side of her neck. Taking her earlobe between his teeth, he promised her, "To-night."

She turned to face her partners, a blush high on her cheeks.

Bourne seated his wife at the card table, before raising a knowing brow in Georgiana's direction. As he headed to the sideboard to pour himself a scotch, he said, "Good evening, Mrs. West."

She warmed at the name just as she always did—she could have kept the "Lady" into which she was born. It was her due as the daughter of a duke, but she did not want it. Every time someone referred to her as Mrs. West, she was reminded of the man she married. Of the life they had made together— three, soon to become four.

Georgiana and Duncan West ruled London's ballrooms with their combined power—the newspaper magnate and his glittering, clever bride. Still a scandal, but one worth having at a dinner table—and the aristocracy did enjoy that.

And when they were not dining at tables across Britain, she continued to run the club as Chase. Anna, on the other hand, had taken her leave soon after Duncan and Georgiana were married, after a particularly dangerous evening that ended in a surgeon having to be called after Duncan attacked a member who was altogether too friendly with Anna.

It was best, because the two of them struggled to keep their hands from each other, and it would have been only a matter of time before someone connected the spots between West's two loves.

Pippa and Cross took their own seats at the table, Cross extracting his deck of cards and setting them in front of him as Pippa craned around to see Georgiana. She blinked. "You grow bigger by the minute," she said.

"Pippa!" Lady Bourne said. "You are gorgeous, Georgiana."

"I did not say she was not gorgeous," Pippa said to her sister before returning her attention to Georgiana. "I simply said you were growing. I think it might be twins."

"What do you know about twins?" The Duchess of Lamont entered, trailed by Temple, who was discussing a file with Asriel.

"I've delivered several sets of multiples," Pippa asserted.

"Really?" Duncan asked, pulling out a chair and helping Georgiana into it. "That is good to know, in case we require your assistance."

"You did not ask her if they were human multiples," Cross said.

"I've done it with dogs many times," Pippa defended herself. "And I've had two human children, you might recall, husband."

"Yes, but not twins. And thank God for that."

"Agreed," said Bourne, now father to three. "Twins is just bad luck."

Duncan was turning pale. "Can we stop discussing twins?"

"It won't be twins," Temple said, coming around the table to hand the file he'd been looking at to Georgiana.

"It might be," she teased. "Pippa says I'm enormous."

"I certainly didn't say enormous!"

Georgiana opened the file and considered its contents. She looked up at Temple, "Poor girl," she said, "Let her out of the box."

"Who?" Duncan asked.

"Lady Mary Ashehollow."

There was a collective sound of understanding around the table, but Duncan was the only one to comment. "You've decided to end your revenge play?"

"She made me angry."

He raised a brow. "She is a child."

"She is in her third season, so she's not quite that. But yes," Georgiana said. "And if it is any consolation, she's going into the betting book as one of the prime ladies of the season. Will that do, husband?"

"Quite well." He leaned over to give her a long, lingering kiss.

Cross spoke up. "As we are on the subject of the betting book, I believe you owe me one hundred pounds, Chase."

"For what?" Duncan asked, all curiosity.

"For taking a foolish bet a year ago," Cross said.

"Cross thought you and Chase would marry," Temple explained. "Chase . . ."

"Didn't," Bourne said.

"Michael!" Penelope scolded. "That's not very kind."

"It's true."

"How would you like them to tell the truth about our courtship?" Penelope asked.

Remembering, no doubt, that the Marquess and Marchioness of Bourne were married after a late-night abduction in the country, Bourne had the grace to stop talking.

Duncan looked to Georgiana, a smile on his handsome face. "It sounds like you lost a bet, my lady."

As it had for a year, the honorific sent a flood of heat through her. "It does not feel much like losing."

He grinned. "It doesn't, does it?"

"Well, since we are talking about Chase's potential husbands, now is as good a time as any to discuss Langley, who has asked us to join him in making an investment," Temple added.

The table groaned.

"This man. Chase, you must stop giving him our money," Bourne said.

"He's a terrible record with investments, and we keep helping him," Cross pointed out.

"I am sorry—I did not know the two of you were so close to the workhouse," Georgiana said.

"He is a good man," Duncan interjected. "He practically delivered me my beautiful wife."

"Only because he did not want her himself," Temple teased, and all the scoundrels laughed.

"I refuse to be insulted," she said. "And Duncan likes the sound of this one."

He nodded. "Something called a photographic negative."

"It sounds like something from a novel," Bourne said. "Like flying machines and horseless carriages."

"I don't think those things sound so implausible," Pippa said.

Bourne looked to her. "That's because you think implausibility is a challenge."

She looked to Cross with a smile. "I suppose I do."

The earl leaned in and kissed his wife soundly. "It is a large part of your charm."

"Shall we play?" Georgiana asked, leaning forward and reaching for the cards.

What had once been a game only for the owners had become a standing weekly faro game for the eight of them.

Temple sat with a sigh. "I don't know why I play. I never win anymore. It all went to hell when we let the wives in." He looked to Duncan. "Apologies, mate."

Duncan smiled. "I am happy to be a wife if you don't mind my fleecing you each week."

Mara put her hand to her husband's cheek. "Poor Temple," she said. "Would you like to play something else?"

He met her gaze, all seriousness. "Yes, but you won't want to play it in front of everyone else."

Another round of groans went up as the duchess leaned in to kiss her duke.

Georgiana sat back. "Perhaps we should not play."

Bourne looked up from where he was pouring scotch. "Because Temple wants to take his wife to bed?"

She smiled. "No . . ." She looked to her husband. "Because I believe we are about to discover if it is twins after all."

Far below, through the famed stained glass window, the roulette wheel spun and the dice rolled and the cards flew, and that night became legendary—the night fortune smiled on the members of The Fallen Angel.

Just as it smiled on its founder, and her love.

Acknowledgments

As this series comes to a close, I realize that a powerful village has helped to raise my Scoundrels. On the heels of that realization comes another, far more unsettling one—that I will never be able to thank you all enough.

As with all my books, this one could not have been written without the patience and faith of my literary Sherpa, Carrie Feron, the hard work of Nicole Fischer and Chelsey Emmelhainz, and the tremendous support of Liate Stehlik, Pam Spengler-Jaffee, Jessie Edwards, Caroline Perny, Shawn Nicholls, Tom Egner, Gail Dubov, Carla Parker, Brian Grogan, Tobly McSmith, Eleanor Mikucki, and the rest of the unparalleled Avon Books team.

Thank you to Carrie Ryan, Lily Everett, Sophie Jordan, Morgan Baden, Sara Lyle, Melissa Walker, and Linda Frances Lee, for your insight, support and brilliance as I wrote Chase's story, and to Rex and the staff at Krupa Grocery for cheerleading and caffeine.

My father told me the story of skull drinking in Castel Teodorico when I was much younger than Caroline, and I was thrilled to be able to finally put it into a book. I am deeply grateful for his never once thinking, *Perhaps she is too young for this.* Thanks to David and Valerie Mortensen for the trip to Hearst Castle that inspired Duncan West and his magnificent swimming pool, and for raising a son who is all gentleman and no scoundrel.

To my wonderful readers, thank you for taking this journey with Bourne, Cross, Temple, and Chase, for loving them as much as I do, and for the endless encouragement online and by mail. To every single reader who gasped when you discovered that Chase was a woman, and took a chance on her story nonetheless, you will never know how much your faith meant to me.

And finally, to the woman who accosted me in a bathroom in Texas in early 2012 and announced, "I think Chase is a woman!," I'm very sorry I lied to you.

Do you love historical fiction?

Want the chance to hear news about your favourite authors (and the chance to win free books)?

Mary Balogh

Charlotte Betts

Jessica Blair

Frances Brody

Gaelen Foley

Elizabeth Hoyt

Eloisa James

Lisa Kleypas

Stephanie Laurens

Claire Lorrimer

Sarah MacLean

Amanda Quick

Julia Quinn

Then visit the Piatkus website and blog
www.piatkus.co.uk | www.piatkusbooks.net

And follow us on Facebook and Twitter
www.facebook.com/piatkusfiction | www.twitter.com/piatkusbooks

piatkus